Rampant

Saskia Walker

Spice

Recycling programs
for this product may
not exist in your area.

RAMPANT

ISBN-13: 978-0-373-60542-2

For questions and comments about the quality of this book please contact us at Customer_eCare@Harlequin.ca.

Printed in U.S.A.

For my wonderful agent, Roberta Brown.

For my exceptionally talented editor, Susan Swinwood.

For my rock, the man who supports me
every step of the way, Mark Walker.

Prologue

THE UNMISTAKABLE SOUND OF A WOMAN BEING pleasured echoed through the woods above the village of Carbrey. The sound was deeply sensual, and powerful—as if she dared anyone to defy her needs. The witch master watched over her with a sense of satisfaction, breathing in the sexual power that filled the atmosphere. The woman was his willing acolyte, and he nodded at the other members of the coven who circled nearby, eager for a taste of her.

Midsummer moonlight filtered through the trees, lighting the spot where she lay naked on the woodland floor. Her knees were pulled up, legs open. With one hand she stroked herself. With the other she beckoned to the tall young man who stood between her feet, inviting him to come closer.

"Take me," she urged.

"I'm ready," he replied. Stripped to the waist, his finely-muscled body was taut with restrained lust, the muscles on his back flexing as he grappled for the belt on his jeans, undoing it even as he dropped to his knees between her legs. He looked down at her writhing body with undisguised hunger. The coven master circled them, watching with pride.

Her ecstatic moans grew louder when her lover locked his hands around her hips, holding her steady while he buried his face in her pussy, sucking on her clit before he ran his tongue deeper, lapping at her eagerly.

Satisfaction flowed in the coven master's veins as he anticipated all that would be made possible here. The sexual power that would manifest through their union would be his. The two powerful witches bucking together on the forest floor would open a channel through which he would commune with the Hidden World.

The female acolyte's pale body glowed in the semi-darkness as she arched with pleasure. Juices glistened on her thighs; her breasts were tilted up, the nipples peaked and hard. Her chestnut-colored hair spilled across the ground, tangled here and there with leaves and earth. She looked over her lover's shoulder and flashed her eyes at the master. Recognizing what she was showing him, he smiled. She had access to strong magic and he had done the right thing choosing her from his coven for this task. She was powerful, an intelligent young witch coming into her mature period. The sexual ecstasy she radiated created an arc of energy that glowed in the atmosphere around them, heating the earth below the spot where she lay, breaching the boundary between this world and the spirit world.

"I feel her, I feel her spirit close by," she cried, her back arching again.

The coven master felt destiny closing. Both power and lust were potent in his blood. Between them, they could achieve this task, this thing that had called to him all these years—the resurrection of the soul of Annabel McGraw.

All had been properly prepared. Five small fires had been lit in a circle, and the acrid smoke from their sacrifice drifted between them, a numinous web that united them in purpose. A silver salver had been placed on the ground nearby. Some of Annabel's relics had been arranged on it— items the coven master had retrieved from her home after her death—a lock of her hair, a pendant she wore, fabric from her clothing. They were ready to commune with her spirit, to begin the awakening.

The master chanted the ancient words of occult ritual, while his male acolyte drove the length of his shaft inside the woman. Her cry was exquisite. Their sexual energy fuelled the ritual and the master watched them drive and thrust, anticipating joining them in their frenzied love-making when the time was right.

Lifting his hands he breathed deeply and began to speak, his voice ringing out across space, time and worlds. "Lord of all that is powerful and mysterious, hear my call. Help us in our task, for we seek to rouse the spirit of your most worthy of female acolytes. Give us the means to resurrect the soul known as Annabel McGraw, who was taken from her coven nearly three centuries ago."

For several long moments the grunts of the rutting couple on the woodland floor were all that filled the silence, and then the wind lifted. An ethereal mist moved though the trees.

The coven master chanted louder. "We beseech you to enable her to unite with us, her true brethren."

The mist that wisped around them was heavy with female allure, as if Annabel's spirit had stepped out of the trees when she heard his call. The master's head lifted, hope filling him. *Annabel, my Annabel.* So many years he had been alone, so many years that he had dreamed of his lost lover. Soon she would be with him again.

The mist whirled in on itself over the spot where the couple mated, and the master's loins instinctively flooded with desire, his erection throbbing. He thrust his hands into the mist, desperate to capture it. Power surged through his hands and into his body.

"Grant us the power to give Annabel new life—she who could capture souls in a glance, enslaving them to her. She whose magic was destined to be the most powerful witchcraft in all of Scotland!"

As he spoke, he unzipped his fly and grasped his cock in his fist, stroking it, his lust increasing. "She who hovers betwixt your world and ours, walking through *Her Haven* in ghostly form, waiting for this moment. She who will make our coven whole and invincible."

He stroked the length of his shaft, anointing it with the fluid that oozed at his cock's head. The power in the atmosphere intensified, the spirits of the forest emerging from the trees, awakened as they were by the ritual. Sprites and nymphs, the ethereal woodland dwellers of the Hidden World, darted hither and yon, magnifying the psychic energy on the atmosphere, playing with it as they looped around the unfolding ritual.

The witch on the forest floor was lost in her climax, her head rolling from side to side, her eyes glazed.

"She awakens from her slumbers," her young lover blurted, his back glistening with sweat. "I feel her, too. Join us, feel her essence rise from the earth."

Dropping to his knees, the master mounted the man's back. Working his palm over the engorged head of his cock, he drove it inside the kneeling man's anus.

The young male was close to climax at this point, and his buttocks worked the master's shaft as he bucked and ground into the female.

The clutch of his anus was so tight and hot that the master grunted, and then drove deeper, feeding on their fire and the vital energy that came from beyond.

The master cursed in awe when he saw the image of Annabel McGraw reflected in the salver that lay on the ground, her black hair shimmering. Her image was alight with dark, unruly fire, and she had one hand outstretched from her untimely grave.

His heart raced, for the power that was within his grasp held a dark thrill. His body shuddered, his balls lifting, his cock jerking. Even as the image of Annabel blurred and faded in his moment of release, he knew what they needed: a host.

A host who was not of the brethren.

1

AROUSAL. ZOË FELT IT AS SOON AS HER CAR approached the village of Carbrey. Her thighs instinctively pressed together, her hands moving on the surface of the steering wheel. It was almost as if a warm, lingering touch had moved over her entire body. The sensation was pleasant, and it caused a sensuous shiver to pass through her, but it was so odd that she had to glance into the backseat to reassure herself that there was no one in the car with her. She wondered if she'd driven into a humid weather trough. It *was* particularly hot, even for late August, but this was different. This felt as if the warmth were all around her—and inside her, too.

It was like, what? Being turned on?

Surely not?

"Too weird," she said aloud, her hands tightening on the steering wheel. She glanced at her reflection in the mirror. Running one hand around the back of her neck, she tried to concentrate. The long drive from London to the east coast of Scotland had got to her, that's what it was. She'd stopped overnight in York the night before, but had covered the rest of the journey in one lap. A coffee stop after Edinburgh might have been a good idea. Reaching for the air-conditioning, she flicked it up a notch.

Ahead, an old-fashioned black-on-white signpost pointed the way to the village. She was almost there. She'd memorized the directions, and she knew the right-hand fork led to the coast road, the left led down the cliff side and into Carbrey, the harbor village where she'd rented a cottage. She took the left fork and then pulled her car up onto the grass verge. Still she felt it, like warm breath moving over her skin, as if she weren't alone.

"I need fresh air," she murmured.

Just beyond the spot where she had parked was a heavily wooded area, and she got out of the car to take a better look. Stretching, she leaned up against the side of the car. The sun felt good on her back and she only vaguely registered the occasional passing car as she stared over at the tall trees that stood so close together against the cliff side, like sentries.

It would feel good to go in there, into the mysterious enclave of the forest, to walk barefoot in the moss and rest her body up against the large tree trunks. It wasn't something she'd normally think about, but she found the idea oddly compelling and she stared into the verdant gloom between the trees, imagining what it might feel like, what the scent of the forest would do to her. As she thought about it, she could almost feel the mossy ground beneath her feet and the brush of the leaves against her hands as she wended her way through the woods.

"Car trouble?"

The voice was close by and Zoë's heart leapt in her chest, her pulse erratic as she turned in the direction of the man who had spoken. She hadn't even heard the motor-cycle approach. It purred softly, all shiny black metal and chrome. The rider switched off the engine and took off his helmet. Pale blond hair spilled to his shoulders. Gray-green eyes scrutinized her.

"No," she managed to reply, "I was just admiring the view." She gestured in the general direction of the forest, unable to drag her attention away from him.

Built tall and distinctive-looking, he demanded her attention even more than the pretty countryside. He had a defined jaw and cheekbones, and the most sensuous mouth she'd ever seen. Taking a deep breath, she smiled.

"I saw you pull up as I came along the coast road. Thought you might have lost your way." He spoke with a rich Scottish accent, and one corner of his mouth lifted as he contemplated her. "Maybe I can help."

There was something that he could help her with, and that thing came to mind in blazing 3D graphics. An image of him climbing over her, thrusting inside her, flashed through her mind. *Where did that come from?*

She stared, rudely, but she couldn't help it. She wanted to drag him over her and demand contact. A chuckle escaped her lips. He was very attractive; her reaction was to be expected. Broad shoulders outlined in a leather jacket and faded blue jeans outlined strong muscular thighs to perfection. Her gaze was instinctively drawn to the bulge at his groin, and she caught her bottom lip between her teeth, her face heating before she managed to drag her attention away.

He kicked down the bike stand and climbed off it, peering at her with those intense gray-green eyes, the sort of eyes you didn't forget in a hurry. "Sure you're okay? You look kind of startled. Is that my fault?"

He gave her a slow once-over, his gaze lingering around her bare midriff, then he locked eyes with her, the question hanging in the air between them. She felt that weird feeling again, as if something had wrapped itself around her, sinuous, and oddly seductive. *Why the hell am I thinking about sex?*

Too long since I had it, maybe.

The sun shone bright behind his head and for a moment she felt dizzy and disoriented, gazing up at him.

Answer him.

She shielded her eyes. "I'm fine, thank you. I'm just about to set off."

He loomed closer, blocking out the sun, his face in shadow. "Stay very still," he instructed.

Her breath caught in her throat when he reached over with one leather-gloved hand and lifted her hair from where it clung to her neck. Something moved against her skin and she jumped.

"Still as you can," he whispered, and she felt his breath against her face. His proximity made her feel deliciously unsteady, her state of arousal increasing by the moment. As he bent over her neck, she was glad of the car at her back, holding her up.

Tension ratcheted inside her and she was about to question him when his free hand swooped in and closed over her skin. Sensation ran the length of her neck and then shot deep inside her when he ran his thumb against her skin, soothingly, before moving his closed fist away.

Opening his hand, he revealed his catch.

A large, spindly black spider sat in the palm of his leather-gloved hand, still as a statue.

"Oh, bloody hell." She shivered.

"He won't hurt you. It's a forest spider. He's wandered

in the heat and found somewhere appealing to hide. He likes you." He smiled, and rested his hand on the roof of the car, setting the spider free.

She jerked away from the car and found herself pressed up against him, one hand on his leather jacket. The spider scurried quickly across the roof of the car and away over the other side, as if headed back to the woods. Realizing that she was now pinned up against him, she glanced up at him.

He put his hand flat on the car roof, trapping her, a gleam in his eyes as he considered her. "You're safe now."

He didn't move.

For some reason she didn't feel safe, but she liked it. Looking at his mouth, just inches from hers, she wanted contact. His jacket beneath her hand felt solid and warm from the sun. She could smell the leather, leather and his cologne, something akin to the forest. Images of raunchy sex filled her mind, assailing her senses. Scottish biker on the side of the road—she wanted to be rolling on the grass with him, to have his powerful male body between her thighs, thrusting and grinding. Her legs felt weak when the idea of it forced its way to the front of her mind, and her pussy throbbed with longing. She squeezed her thighs together, trying to maintain some sense of decorum, hard though it was. "Thank you. I do appreciate you checking on me."

"No problem. I'll see you later." He stroked her hair as if tidying it for her, before returning to his bike.

She made herself look away, but stole another glance as he mounted the bike, her body growing hotter by the moment as he settled onto the machine, legs wrapped around the engine. He pulled on his helmet, revved the engine, and gave her one last wave with a leather-gloved hand.

He'd said, "see you later," she thought, as she returned the wave. Zoë was born and bred in London and it wasn't something she'd expect a stranger to say. This was a small village, though. That's why he'd said that, she reasoned, getting a good look at his physique as he sped off.

Leanly muscled back inside black leather. Fit rear end outlined in denim. Her fingers itched to touch him, to discover how that body might feel under her hands.

I want to sit on him, to ride him until I come.

Cupping her hand briefly over her fly, she ached to touch herself. What was the matter with her? She didn't normally look at men this way. Well, not quite so blatantly, at any rate.

When her mobile phone bleeped into life she leapt into the car seat and picked it up, glad of the distraction, fanning her face with her free hand as she glanced at the screen. It was her sister. "Hey, Gina."

"Are you there yet? I'm dying to know what it's like."

"Not quite there yet, but soon. The landscape is stunning. You were right, it's a great spot."

"Are you okay? You sound kind of fazed."

"I'm fine." She reached into her bag for her electronic organizer, bringing up the calendar to see if she could be premenstrual. There had to be a logical explanation for her being so bloody horny. That might be it. Her natural instinct was to check all possibilities, as if she were checking last-minute flights for her boss. The practical approach was second nature to her.

Her calendar flashed into action. Nope. It wasn't that. She would have known. She was a well-organized personal assistant in London, and she had to be on top of everything. Never distracted, never disorganized. If it wasn't that making her hot and horny, it had to be a freak weather condition, because of the village's positioning on the coastline.

"What was that?" Gina asked, when the organizer beeped.

"Just checking my calendar."

Gina groaned. "Zoë, leave your London attitude behind, for God's sake. You're on holiday, relax."

"I am. I'm fine. I just got hot all of a sudden and I wondered if I was premenstrual."

Gina sighed, heavily. "Good grief, woman."

"I'll be fine when I have a shower and a nap. I'm literally just outside the village. I'll call you back as soon as I get the keys to the cottage. Deal?"

Reluctantly, Gina agreed. "You better ring back soon. I'll be hanging by the phone waiting to hear all about it."

Zoë smiled as she put her phone away, feeling a tad more levelheaded. She wondered what the biker's name was. The accent had suggested that he was local, although she was no expert on Scottish accents. This was her first visit.

There was something about him, something compelling.

Her mother used to talk about people having auras. Zoë thought it was nonsense, but for some reason it came to mind now. The biker had an aura. That, and sheer animal magnetism. His hair was so unusual, white-blond and heavy. If he were in bed with a woman, would it brush over the woman's body, heightening her pleasure? The thought made her want to find out. With those stark cheekbones and unusual eyes, he had a hellish sexy look.

She couldn't help wishing she really had broken down and needed his assistance for a bit longer. She reached over to turn the radio up. The raunchy rock music she'd had on at a low level in the background had hardly touched her consciousness on the entire drive up here, and yet now it made her hum along. She signaled, checked the rearview mirror, and pulled back onto the road.

Winding down the steep cliff side into the village, she turned a corner, and there it was. Pretty, pastel-colored cottages lined up either side of a meandering road that led down to the harbor. "I made it."

Carbrey was a small fishing village. There were other villages nearby but the nearest large town was some twenty miles along the coast. Zoë had come for the sea views and the coastal paths, and the place was postcard perfect. She had a stack of books in her suitcase and her walking gear. That was all she needed, although a bit more time around that sexy biker might make it a holiday to remember, she mused.

The locals watched her car go by with undisguised curiosity. Several of the children waved, making her smile as she waved back. Passing by a pretty pub called the Silver Birch, a tiny school, and a chapel interspersed with quaint houses, she drew to a halt at the crossroads at the bottom of the hill. A marina provided safe harbor for around forty small boats that were bobbing merrily on the incoming tide. It was gloriously sunny but windy down here, the sky a blaze of blue, the fast-moving clouds barely blocking out the sunlight as they sped across it. A handful of tourists drifted about the harbor area, three teenagers eating ice cream, a young family posing for photographs by the boats. It was almost the end of the season and Zoë imagined it was much busier in the middle of the summer.

On her right a corner shop with a post office sign marked the place where she had to pick up the keys. To the left, Shore Lane ran down to the very edge of the water. The last few houses existed on a limited lifespan as the sea ate away at the land. That was a big selling point about the fisherman's cottage she'd rented. It was a beautiful little place, over three hundred years old, but in a decade or so the sea would erode another few feet of the coast and the cottages out on Shore Lane wouldn't be habitable.

She turned left, figuring she'd park up and walk back to the post office for the keys. In the distance she could make out a small island where a lighthouse stood. The sun gleamed on the water. Driving slowly along the narrow street, she marveled at how close the water came to the houses. On her right-hand side, a large workshop took the last bit of land, backing onto the marina, before it dropped away completely into the sea, right behind the wall at the edge of the lane. A sign read Logan's Boat Yard. As she drove by, a tall young man appeared from inside the boat workshop to watch.

He leaned against the upturned helm of a boat, staring blatantly at her. Something about the way he watched her compelled her to slow down and open her window to ask for directions. She didn't need directions. Zoë knew she was on the right track. A top-notch London PA always had her map memorized.

"Hello, am I in the right place for the cottage called Her Haven?" She blushed as she said the name of the cottage. She thought it was a silly coincidence, but her sister had found the place and insisted it would be the perfect spot for Zoë to take a break. Gina said it was meant for her, since she hadn't had a proper holiday in three years.

The young man smiled and sauntered over to the car, like a languorous young lion staking her out. Again she felt that strange feeling pass over her, as if someone was there in the car with her, turning up her internal thermometer and nudging her every time a sexy hunk of man passed by. Ridiculous though it was, she wondered if being away from home for the first time in ages had given her an over-exaggerated sense of self-awareness. Either that or the holiday spirit had infected her already. She'd read about women who had flings while they were away from home. Would the opportunity come her way?

She certainly wouldn't reject it, if it did. Her job kept her far too busy. She stifled a smile as a confessional magazine headline she'd read flitted through her mind: "My holiday fling with a lusty local hunk."

Would she have her own holiday confessional? Maybe.

The man bent down and leaned into her window, suddenly inside her personal space, a lazy smile on his face as he looked her over and then glanced around the interior of the car. "You're in the right place."

His brogue was heavier than the biker's had been. He had inquisitive blue eyes and thick brown hair. She estimated he was in his early twenties. Well built, under the loose T-shirt and combat pants he wore.

"Second house from the end of the row." He pointed farther along the narrow street, without breaking eye contact with her. "I'm Crawford Logan," he added, reaching one large hand into the car.

She rested her hand in his, taking a sharp breath when he squeezed it firmly with his boat builder's grip.

"Zoë Daniels," she replied, marveling at how quickly they had exchanged names. Living in London was so different, she supposed. In a small village like this they'd be interested in the tourists that came and went. "I've rented Her Haven for a few days."

That's pretty obvious, she realized, after she said it. Throw a girl out of her regular routine and this is what happens, one minute clinging to a biker on the side of the road, the next playing ditzy and wide-eyed for the local boat builder. It was no bad thing, though. She wanted to loosen up. She needed it.

Crawford seemed to let go of her hand reluctantly. She liked that. When he stood up, he saluted her and she drove on.

She parked the car outside the second cottage from the end of the row and got out, stretching as she did so. Over the door, a carved sign bore the words *Her Haven*. The front of the cottage suggested cozy and inviting interiors; white-washed walls, a heavy studded oak door to keep out any stormy weather in the winter. Picturesque windows with lacy curtains shaded the interior.

The house next door stood on the end of the row and didn't look quite so cared for. It was at the mercy of the elements, being right on the end. Over the door the word *Cornerstone* had been etched into the plaster.

She locked her car and walked back along the road, waving at Crawford, who still stood by, watching her with a half smile. She could feel his suggestive stare as she passed by, as if he was assessing her, intimately.

It had been too long since she'd been away from home, Gina was right. Gina was the one who'd insisted Zoë take a vacation, her first proper break since their mother's death three years before. Sure, she'd thrown herself into her work after that. She was good at her job and it made her feel needed, made her feel productive and useful. Why not? But she felt different here and now, out of her efficient business suit and heels. She felt more conscious of everything, and that made the old adrenaline pump. As she walked along the street she nodded at the passersby who smiled cautiously as they checked her out.

The village had a wistful, eerie quality about it, she thought, as if somehow captured in a bygone era. The staggered houses were built around the harbor and looked as if they were huddled together for security against the elements. It was unusual, and very appealing.

The post office looked like something out of the 1950s, and when she pushed the door open a bell tinkled overhead.

"Well, hello, you must be Zoë Daniels."

Zoë stared at the woman speaking to her from behind the counter. "How did you know who I was?"

"You're dot on time to pick up the keys to the cottage, and I know pretty much everyone who stops by here, apart from the day trippers." She looked Zoë up and down with a curiously satisfied expression on her face. "And you don't look like you're on a day trip, sweetheart."

There was a certain intimacy in the woman's voice that struck Zoë as odd. She had a confident, knowing look about her. Her chestnut hair was swept up and back in a ponytail, her eyes so dark brown they were almost black, her smile knowing, as if it held a secret. Her accent was less strong than the boat builder's, local, but as if she'd traveled. The woman's ears were heavily pierced and adorned with ornate silver rings. She was dressed in a Hard Rock Café T-shirt and jeans, not what you might expect from a postmistress, but Zoë supposed the normal rules didn't apply out here.

"I'm Elspeth McGraw, I'm the caretaker for the cottage. It's been in my family for years, but I live up at the top of the hill now. Let me get your keys." The woman couldn't seem to stop smiling to herself, as if secretly amused. Perhaps she was amused at the idea of a woman going on holiday alone. Zoë supposed it was fairly unusual.

While her hostess hunted behind the counter for the keys, Zoë scanned the place. Besides the post office counter, the shop sold newspapers, magazines, postcards, cold drinks, sweet treats and snacks. A massive ice cream cabinet on one side of the room looked as if it had been there for years. Behind the counter itself, she noticed an engraved panel on the wall. She scanned it quickly but then looked back, instead of moving on. Three symbols were carved on what appeared to be driftwood, nailed above the doorway that led through to the back of the shop, a doorway covered over by a long black velvet curtain. The symbols looked vaguely familiar.

Her mother had owned similar things, Zoë realized. That's why. She'd had the same sort of designs on jewelry, candles and ornaments. She'd been a spiritual sort—called herself a pagan and was into all sorts of heebie-jeebie nonsense. Not that it had done her much good. She'd been crushed to death in her Mini Cooper when an articulated lorry jackknifed in her path. Zoë, as a result, had a much more down-to-earth attitude and quickly dismissed anything she considered mumbo-jumbo.

An odd smell wafted through the shop. Incense, probably. She caught sight of herself in a mirror. Her layered black hair was a mess. Her eyes looked startled, the pupils dilated, and her natural color looked higher than usual. "I'm a mess," she whispered under her breath.

Elspeth turned back to her, a bunch of keys dangling from one finger. "You look absolutely perfect to me, sweetheart."

Strolling out from behind the counter, she leaned her back up against it, elbows resting on the surface, breasts pushing out from her torso. It was a cheeky, confident pose, and when she proceeded to stare at Zoë from top to toe, slowly, she smiled and licked her lips. "It's going to be a lot of fun, having you around."

Her eyes were bright, as if she had some secret that she was nurturing.

Zoë felt that odd feeling again—as if a presence sidled alongside her—and it made her skin tingle with awareness. It also made her feel slightly out of control, as if she couldn't trust herself to respond appropriately. *I'm horny, that's what it is. Horny as hell.*

This time she couldn't ignore the curious mixture of re-actions she experienced. She was partly afraid of something she couldn't quite rationalize, and partly seduced by it—and she didn't understand why on earth she was feeling either.

Fazed, she gathered herself to leave. That's when the door opened and the postmistress cursed aloud at the man who walked in.

2

GRAYSON MURDOCH PARKED HIS MOTOR-
cycle, pulled off his helmet and looked over at the smart
Audi cabriolet parked outside Her Haven. The woman
he'd seen at the fork in the road was coming here? He gave
a wry smile. That would explain the restless anticipation
amongst certain Carbrey locals. Every time a visitor came
to stay at the house their interest stirred. For most of them
it was idle curiosity about the visitor's reactions to the
ghostly presence that resided in the cottage. It was a long-
running sideshow for the locals. Amongst a select few,
however, there was more to it.

He was one of those select few.

He'd stopped off at the farm shop on the other side of
the village to pick up provisions. As a consequence, she'd
made it here ahead of him. He'd wondered where she was
headed, but he'd been distracted by her leaning up against
her car, looking longingly into the forest like a wood
nymph who thought she might have found home. Wistful,
that's how she'd appeared, and that keyed into something

buried deep inside of him. In her it was a simple thing—
a sense of loneliness, perhaps—for him it was somewhat
more complicated, but it attracted him to her nonetheless.
When he'd approached, she roused more than his aesthetic
appreciation. There was a burgeoning sensuality about her
that demanded his attention.

Glancing along the road toward the post office he caught
sight of her as she went inside. Crawford Logan was watching. He turned away and disappeared into his workshop
when Grayson eyeballed him. Dismounting, he pushed the
bike close against the wall of the Cornerstone cottage and
strode in her footsteps, covering the ground fast.

Elspeth's eyes narrowed and she cursed him when he
entered the shop, seemingly unable to hold back her annoyance that he'd walked in on them. The smell of ashes
was high in the air. Grayson's eyebrows lifted. She'd been
performing a ritual in the middle of the day?

The visitor looked from one of them to the other, clearly
startled by Elspeth's reaction.

"Ah, Zoë, here's your chance to meet your neighbor,"
Elspeth said, quickly recovering from her initial response to
his arrival. "The proverbial nosy neighbor, in fact." Sarcasm
rang in her voice. "Professor Murdoch is writing a book
about us."

"Not quite," he corrected, for the visitor's benefit. The
woman—Zoë—looked at him with interest, her eyes sparkling. "I teach at the University in Edinburgh. I'm here doing
research on local folklore. Grayson Murdoch, at your service."
He reached out and took her hand, squeezing it firmly.

"Folklore?" Her eyebrows lifted, and he recognized from
her expression that she was a skeptic. That would soon
change. If she was staying at Her Haven she would soon
learn that the supernatural was all too real.

"Yes, the area is rife with the paranormal. I'm on sabbatical from my university post, researching for a book about historic local witches."

"Witches," the visitor repeated, with a chuckle.

Elspeth looked pleased that the visitor was so dismissive, but she kept her attention on Grayson. He raised his eyebrows at her, unfazed by her attitude. Being blasé wouldn't cover her back when the time came, he reflected with no small amount of irony. "I thought you might be pleased about the attention a book would bring Carbrey, Elspeth. You'll sell more…postcards, after all."

She narrowed her eyes at him. She didn't like that. Unlike most practitioners of the craft who were content to practice their magic while maintaining a normal life, Elspeth treated her normal life as a nuisance.

"Professor Murdoch here actually bought Cornerstone." Elspeth interjected. "He paid good money for that house that's dangling into the sea, the very last house on the row. Death row, the villagers call it." She emphasized the word *death* and shot him a warning glance, her dark eyes swirling with evil intent.

Grayson gave a soft laugh. Elspeth still wasn't quite sure what he was about, and Grayson liked it that way. Besides, she was pretty powerless without her coven and her master.

The visitor, however, looked perturbed by Elspeth's comments, and who could blame her. "Death row?" she repeated. "How long have the houses got, before they become uninhabitable?"

"Long enough, with any luck," he replied, then gave her a friendly smile, trying to put her at her ease. He sensed Elspeth had already got to her and didn't want to unsettle her any more.

"What can I do for you, Professor Murdoch?" Elspeth

demanded, her annoyance visible. "I'm trying to give our guest a quick rundown on the local facilities."

He grinned. He had no intention of leaving the shop until the visitor did. "I'll take a first-class stamp, please, Miss McGraw."

Elspeth put down the keys she held in her hand, pulled open the drawer in the counter and slapped a single stamp onto the countertop.

He handed over the coins.

"I've left you a welcome package." Elspeth spoke again to the visitor. "Milk, coffee, some fresh bread. There's butter, bacon and eggs in the fridge, all local produce."

"Thank you, that's very kind."

Grayson took the chance to observe the visitor, Zoë. That rising sensuality he'd witnessed when he first met her was close to the surface and had an almost magnetic effect on him. *Why?* She was pretty, but it was something else, a lush, womanly quality that made him hanker for a taste of her. He wanted to see her on her back and watch her face while he made her come.

She had a subtle way about her that he liked. Blushed easily. Late twenties, and seemed to be traveling alone—a vulnerable target. No wedding ring, he'd checked that up at the lay-by. Independent woman? The car she drove suggested something a bit more high-powered than the way she was currently dressed, in a casual T-shirt and low-slung jeans. She was out of her usual circumstances, no surprise there, and it could partly account for the slight hesitation.

"You might like to try the local restaurant, the Tide Inn, if you don't feel like cooking," Elspeth continued. "It's at the opposite end of the bay to the cottage, on the cliff top. You can't miss it."

"That does sound good, I'll try it." Zoë looked his way, a smile lingering in her expression.

"The chef is excellent," Elspeth added. "People travel all the way out from Edinburgh to eat here. In fact, being from London yourself, you've probably heard of him, Cain Davot."

"The name does sound familiar."

Elspeth shot Grayson another glance. "Was there something else?"

"No. I intend to walk our visitor to her cottage." He faced Elspeth off with a smile.

The visitor blushed, obviously pleased with his comment about escorting her. She lifted the key from the counter where Elspeth had left it, and made a move to follow him out.

Grayson tensed his shoulders to combat the rush of hatred Elspeth sent his way as they exited.

"Was that a squabble?" the visitor asked, when the door jangled shut behind them.

He couldn't withhold a laugh. "Not quite. Let's just say she hasn't warmed to me since I first came here."

"The nature of doing research on the locals, perhaps?"

"You're probably right," Grayson replied, noticing the intelligent, humorous glow in her eyes. *Interesting,* he thought to himself.

As soon as they'd gone, Elspeth picked up her phone and punched in the speed dial number for Cain Davot. When his recorded message kicked in, she remembered he'd gone to Edinburgh that afternoon. She walked over to the door as she listened to his seductive tones on the recorded message, and flicked the sign on the door from "open" to "closed." She peered through the window to see if she could catch sight of Crawford. He was already on his way over. She smiled. He was a loyal and instinctive friend. They had known each other since childhood and she could always rely on him to be by her side when she needed him.

After the tone, she left her message.

"Cain, Elspeth here. The new tenant has arrived for Her Haven. You won't believe it, she's the perfect host. Hurry back. I suggested she visit the restaurant. I'm going to put a binding spell on her so that she can't wander far from Carbrey, and then I'll continue the rousing rituals."

She flipped the phone shut, and smirked at Crawford as he entered the shop. "Lock the door behind you."

Crawford did as he was told. "What do you think? Is she the one?"

Elspeth stepped closer to him and ran one finger down the length of his breastbone through his shirt, smiling. "Our time has come, Crawford. I've left a message for Cain. Come on." Her hand closed on his belt buckle, which she tugged suggestively. "It's time to push on with the rituals, now that we're sure. And the quicker we get on with this, the less chance there is of that bastard Murdoch sticking his nose in and scaring her off."

3

ZOË WATCHED AS GRAYSON SLID HER SUITCASE into the hallway, constantly aware of how close he was, and how good it would feel to be even closer. The biker jacket he wore was open now. The skintight black T-shirt underneath made her want to run her hand inside, to measure his body by touching it and having it respond. The idea of it made her shiver.

He noticed, pausing a moment, and then glanced around the interior of the cottage as he chatted on. He seemed keen to prove he was more charming and friendly than the postmistress wanted her to believe. But he'd already shown her that when he stopped to check on her at the top of the hill.

"As I said, I'm just next door. Feel free to give me a shout if you need anything. I'm pleased to help out. A bang on the wall should do it."

She watched him push his loose hair back as he spoke. It was so pale blond, and fell well below his chin, as if his scholarly life left him little time for the luxury of haircuts.

The blond hair, combined with the chiseled jaw and cheek-bones and fit physique, gave him the look of a Viking. To top it all, she was having a really hard time not letting her gaze drop below his shoulder level. A man that sexy, dressed in leather and denim, created an automatic compulsion to look lower, and she didn't want to embarrass herself. Or him. Not that he looked like the sort of man who was easily embarrassed. There was an aura of strength about him, and even though she still felt rather unnerved by her reactions, she couldn't help admiring him.

"Thanks," she responded. "I'll keep that in mind." She didn't want him to go just yet. "You aren't from around here, are you?" His accent was less strong than the locals, but with the occasional lilt.

"Well spotted. My dad was English. I grew up in Edin-burgh. My mother's side of the family is from this area, though." He looked a bit awkward as he explained his background, and then gave her that sexy, lopsided smile again.

"It was the family connection to the area that got me into folklore." He leaned one elbow up against the door frame while he spoke, flexing his torso in a very unselfconscious way.

Once again she was sorely tempted to run her hand down his side, to feel the hard muscle of his flank, to draw him closer against her. It was almost as if someone was egging her on to do so, a naughty girlfriend who was by her side and who'd had one too many drinks.

He glanced down, and she saw a lean, ginger tomcat had wound its way around his legs.

"Oh, you have a friend." The cat was rubbing up against him just the way she'd felt like doing a moment before.

"Hey, Cat." He ducked down and swooped the cat into

one arm. "He adopted me when I bought the house. He was a stray living off fish scraps, but he lives with me now. I'm going to have to take him with me when I go."

"He looks as if he'd be happy with the arrangement." The cat rubbed his head against that lean jaw, and Zoë noticed the slight stubble there. That had to feel good. "So, that's one local inhabitant who approves of the nosy professor and his research?"

"Yes." He smiled knowingly, amused at her comment. "The locals are friendly, kind people, for the most part. Don't be put off by the odd one or two."

It sounded like a subtle warning, but the whole of the conversation he'd had with Elspeth in the shop seemed to have a double-edged nature to it. Barbed, even.

"What do you call the cat?"

"Oh, just Cat," he replied. "He's my lucky charm."

She was about to comment when her phone bleeped at her from her bag on the hall floor. "I'm sorry, I better get that. It'll be my sister, she worries about me." She rolled her eyes.

"That's good," he replied, quite seriously, then he nodded and left her to it, the cat perched precariously on his shoulder as he went, looking back at her, blinking.

"Hi, Gina," she breathed into the phone when she eventually pulled it free from her bag.

"Well—you sound better. Have you had that shower?"

Zoë shut the front door. "No, not yet. I just got into the house. I've been meeting the neighbors."

"Anyone interesting?"

"Maybe."

"Ooh, tell me more, I'll pull up a chair."

Zoë gave a mock groan. Her sister was constantly trying to find her a boyfriend. Over the last couple of years she'd had to endure several painful dinners where Gina's husband, James, had brought along a work buddy for her. "Don't bother, nothing to tell."

"At least you're out meeting people, got you away from your stuffy office for a while."

Zoë felt a pang for her stuffy office. "I wonder how they'll cope without me."

Gina sighed. "You are replaceable, Zoë. I know you don't like to think that, but you are. The temp will do just fine."

It was hard to face up to, but Gina was probably right. Zoë liked feeling needed in her job, though. She liked the feeling of rightness and order it gave to her world. Just thinking about it made her want to run back to it, but she knew she needed to break away, even if only for a little while.

"I've got a question for you," she said, changing the subject. "Does a chef called Cain Davot sound familiar? He's got a restaurant up here. The name rang a bell but I couldn't place him."

"Hell, yes. I wondered what had happened to him. He had a TV show a few years back, very popular. There was some sort of a scandal in the papers and he disappeared from the scene. I'll see if I can remember. Are you going to check him out?"

"Check the food out, maybe, after I chill for a bit."

"Good. So what's the cottage like?"

"I'll walk you through it," she said, glancing up the staircase. She knew this is what Gina was after, because it was Gina who had found the cottage on an Internet site. She wanted to know her choice was a success.

"A live tour. I love it, go ahead."

"Okay, on the ground floor there's the hall and a

doorway into a big kitchen–diner." She walked through the doorway into the ground floor room. "Oh, you'd love it. There's a workstation in the center, with copper pots and pans hanging over it on a rack, very oldie worldie. And it's got a huge range, authentic looking, as well as a regular stove."

Zoë glanced at the pretty bowed window with its lace curtains, and the solid oak dining table and chairs against the back wall. "If I lived here I'd be in this room all the time."

"Now I'm jealous," Gina replied.

"Stairs." Zoë jogged up them. The staircase turned a corner onto a small landing, and she poked her head into the bathroom. "There are two rooms on the next floor. Nice bathroom, very compact but it has a shower, hurray!" She turned to the other doorway. "Bed looks inviting, lots of cottage-style pillows, thick quilt."

"You'll need a rest after the drive."

"Maybe," she replied, walking over to the window. "It's weird, because the house is very close to the water and the tide is coming in. It looks as if the water is going to come right up to the door." She glanced back over her shoulder. "It's carpeted, but it's got sloping floors, they're all over the place, makes you feel drunk." Walking back onto the landing, she took the second staircase, which wound up into the attic.

"Oh, yes, this is amazing. The attic's been converted into a sitting room, and it's got everything I need, fireplace, TV, long comfy sofa, books, magazines, reading chairs and two great big windows that look right out across the sea."

"I wish I was there with you now."

Zoë walked closer to the window and leaned up against the frame. She felt unbalanced, and she looked at the floor, wondering if it was uneven like the bedroom, but it looked as if it was a more recent addition. Even so, she felt as if she was slipping, or there was something rising around her. Her skin prickled with awareness, her palms growing damp.

"Tell me about the view," Gina urged, "then I'll let you go for that shower."

Zoë looked out along the bay, trying to ignore the strange feeling surrounding her. "The tide is coming in, and there are two small boats out there. It looks very pretty." As she spoke, warmth flowed through her body again, like a sirocco of sensation moving in and around her. She blinked and the room seemed to shift. She grasped the window frame, her chest tight.

"She used to stand here," she said, the words coming out of nowhere. "Looking out at the fishermen hauling in their catch. She watched their muscled arms work while she decided which of them she would win away from his wife that night."

Her eyes flashed shut.

Laughter rang through her mind and she felt wind in her face, as if she were out on the marina.

Which man shall I have tonight, which one will it be?

"What did you say?" Gina's voice reached her.

It hauled her back and she jolted away from the window, snatching her hand from the frame as if it was on fire. What *was* she saying? The words had just come out of nowhere, and it felt as if she was no longer alone in the house.

Turning on her heel, she looked around, her free hand at her throat. She glanced into the corners of the room, and then watched the staircase. She couldn't see anything moving. All was silent, but there was definitely a different feeling in the room since she had come up here. Something like she'd had as she drove into the village, but much more intense.

"Zoë?" Gina sounded concerned, her voice rising. "You still there?"

"Yeah, yeah. I'm fine." She gave a nervous laugh, wafting her T-shirt to let the air under it. "I guess I was thinking about who had lived here before."

"You definitely need to get some rest." Concern was evident in her sister's voice.

"Gina, I'm a grown woman, you don't have to fret. I'll be fine, I'll speak to you later in the week." She spoke with more confidence than she actually felt, but she didn't want her sister to worry.

When she switched off the phone she took a deep breath and steeled herself to go back down the stairs. All was quiet, and yet she couldn't shake the curious feeling that someone else was in the house with her.

"You're the only one in the house. You're just tired, silly woman," she told herself, as she went into the bathroom and flicked on the shower. "Have a shower, take a nap, you'll be fine."

Now why wasn't she convinced?

Cain Davot darted across the busy Edinburgh street while he listened to the message Elspeth had left him on his phone. When he reached his Aston Martin, he folded the phone into his pocket with a smile on his face.

At last. They'd tried a couple of women visiting Carbrey before, unsuccessfully. This one was about the right age, and Elspeth had hunted down a photo of her online that gave him much hope. As he slid into the soft, cream leather interior he turned the key in the ignition—and nudged the volume of the stereo up, filling the car with Wagner.

His most cherished lover would soon be back by his side, how magnificent. How defiant. Necromancy was considered forbidden by lesser witches than he. He scorned them, although dabbling in the art had earned him the name "Warlock" on occasion—a term bestowed on outcasts from the brethren. That tag had been a nuisance at times. No matter, he'd found a malleable coven in the very village where he'd been born, over two centuries before, and he'd bent them to his ways.

Elspeth would, at this very moment, be using another of the songbirds he'd obtained for this stage of the rousing rituals. The spell would distill the essence of the bird's final flight—each flap of the sacrificial bird's wings captured to assist Annabel's flight from the grave into this world.

They would need to keep up the pace with the ritualistic magic, be ready, and watch the woman as well. He channeled his thoughts toward the coven's lair while he drove, eminently ready for this. The need to make this happen had been growing inside him for decades. It was a worthy challenge for his skills, and with Annabel at his side he would finally be happy. She was the most powerful she-witch ever to have trodden Scottish soil. Once united, they would be invincible, and then he could turn back the clock that numbered his years in this world. His time was short, and he was not done yet.

He licked his lips with anticipation. Flexing his hands against the smooth leather steering wheel, the jet stone on his ring gleamed, catching his eye. It was incandescent with stygian power, just as he himself would also be, and soon.

Zoë rolled restlessly under the sheet, too unsettled to nap, too aroused. Even the shower and the cool cotton against her naked skin hadn't quelled the anxious feeling in her body. She'd pulled the curtains, hoping for an hour's sleep, but the late afternoon light seeped through the ochre-colored linen, giving the room an ethereal glow.

She could hear the gentle lapping of the incoming tide. The water sounded so close, but then again it was. The sea wall was a mere twelve feet from the front door. Shore Lane itself was a narrow boundary. That had been part of the appeal of the cottage. Or so she thought. The tension of the journey had done this to her, had to be. She lay still for several moments, willing the taut, anxious feeling in her body to go. It didn't.

Her skin prickled with awareness and her hands roamed her body, restless. Her nipples were hard with arousal, the fold beneath her breasts damp. Between her thighs, the nagging desire had grown to fever pitch. She cupped her hands over her pubis, squeezing the plump, aroused flesh until her whole body shuddered with need. Her head rolled against the pillow, her eyes closing as one finger slid easily into the damp niche of her sex. Her clit was swollen. She'd never felt it like this before, as if her sexual desire had multiplied since she'd taken the sea air.

"What's happening to me?" she whispered, desperate and confused. As she stroked herself her hips rolled back and forth, seeking relief from the pressure of her hand. It wasn't enough, she wanted to fuck hard, she wanted to lose herself and come over and again, screaming like a banshee. She moved her fingers faster, harder, but still she couldn't reach release, because something in her was resisting it.

Then the image of Grayson Murdoch came into her mind, and heat flared into her face. She rolled over, laying facedown on the bed, her body bucking and her breasts aching with sensation as they crushed against the surface of the bed. Attaching her actions to a man—a man so close by—was taking her closer. Heat and pleasure rolled through her, and her body grew taut. She pictured him over her, just as she had the moment she'd first seen him. She pictured his fit body working its way between her thighs, his cock filling her.

Oh, yes. Her finger thrust deeper, and she added another, her body tightening rhythmically on them as her core spasmed with release. She shuddered and moaned aloud, slick, liquid heat spilling onto her fingers as she came.

For several long moments she lay there, panting, then she sat up, throwing her hair back and lifting it from her neck, where it clung to her skin. The light coming through the curtains was fading. It was almost evening. She reached for the bedside lamp and switched it on, glancing immediately toward the landing. She'd been everywhere, into every cupboard and wardrobe; she was definitely alone, and yet…

Hugging her arms around herself, she stepped over to the window and peeped out through the curtains. Twilight. A lone heron stood on the rocks in the incoming tide. It was time to get ready to go out and eat.

She headed for the bathroom to splash her face with water. Closing the door behind her, she leaned against it. The towel hanging at her back felt good against her skin. Every inch of her body was thrumming with expectation. A shiver ran through her, but she wasn't cold. Her eyes closed.

She became aware of the sound of water running somewhere nearby. She'd heard the sound of the sea in the bedroom, but this was something else. A shower. She opened her eyes, looking at the reflection of herself in the wall-length mirror. The remaining light coming through the window was fast disappearing, and she was left in gloomy darkness. She could still see a slight glimmer, a reflection of herself in the mirror.

Grayson Murdoch's house is on the other side of that wall. The knowledge struck her oddly, and her curiosity grew, her heart beating faster. Transfixed, she listened to the sound of the shower beyond, her eyes fixed on the mirror. As she stared, the glimmering image of her reflection twisted, disappeared, and reformed into something altogether different.

What the hell?

It was Grayson Murdoch that she saw reflected there now. She was hallucinating, had to be, and yet she stared, mesmerized. She could see him in the mirror, through it, through the wall. He was in the shower, naked and soaping himself. Instinctively, she wedged herself back into the corner of the room, breathless and disbelieving.

His body was exquisite, highlighted by shadow and light as he moved within a cubicle that was lit from somewhere above it. She looked at the taut muscles of his buttocks and thighs as he moved, and tilted her head back, breathless, the heat between her thighs building, demanding her hand move there to provide relief.

Oh, how she longed to be in there with him. His damp hair clung to his head and neck as he turned under the running water. When he moved and faced her fully, the look of his muscled chest and torso called to her. The water ran over the contours, and lower, to where he was soaping his cock at the juncture of his powerful legs. His fist moved in sure, swift strokes on the long, hard shaft of his erection, his balls high against the underside of his fist.

He was masturbating in the shower, and she could see him! Her sex clenched, and her eyes flickered shut, her body going hot and cold all over, her breasts tightening.

"Oh, please," she murmured, sliding down against the wall, until she was sitting on the floor, her legs splayed, her hand buried in her pussy as she rubbed herself again, hips rolling back and forth, fingers slurping in her sticky, damp groove.

Carried forward on a wave of sheer lust, her mind struggled to make sense of it. Grayson was facing her, masturbating, while she did the same, pleasure rolling through her, building to a crescendo of sensation that finally left her weak and shuddering.

I want him to see me, too. The thought of him watching her while she did this made her crazy, pushing her over the edge and into a blistering orgasm.

Panting as she surfaced, she watched as Grayson's face contorted. He'd cupped his balls with one hand; the other still pumped the shaft of his erection. A jet of semen spurted up into the air, and then the image faded away into darkness.

Once again she saw only a glimmer of her own reflection. She sat there, trying to make sense of it. Then, staggering to her feet, she reached for the light. She barely recognized herself in the mirror.

She looked powerfully sexual, a woman on fire. Did she always look like that after orgasm? She didn't know, she realized, but she felt empowered, and she was glad of it.

There was silence at the wall to the next-door house. Stepping closer, she couldn't see through the wall at any point, either through the mirror or alongside it.

Either she had imagined the whole thing or…?

She stared at her reflection, her forehead furrowing. "I imagined the whole thing," she said, with a distinct waver in her voice.

4

CAIN DAVOT'S GOURMET RESTAURANT HAD A relaxed ambience and although it was a Monday evening, nearly half of the tables were occupied when Zoë arrived. She was glad she'd put on a classy dress, because it was an up-market kind of a place.

The Tide Inn. She turned the name around her mind while she enjoyed her meal. As well as the tides of the sea, and a reference to belonging to a place, it made her think of sex and bondage. Perhaps that was the intention. Or maybe there was something about Carbrey, she mused. She hadn't been able to get sex off her mind since she got here.

The food and wine were good, and she felt much more together after eating. Being around people helped, although she kept wondering what sexual position they favored, and made guesses at it to keep herself entertained. Later on, a tall man in a suit and open-necked shirt moved amongst the diners, pausing to chat, shaking hands with the men, kissing the women. Cain Davot, had to be.

Hooded blue eyes and the kind of looks that hinted at

a rogue gypsy heritage made him an attractive, self-assured individual. She could see how he'd got his own TV show. He oozed charisma, the sort of man who knew he could have any woman he wanted. Pausing to run his hand through his thick dark hair, pushing it back over his head, he glanced her way, and gave her a nod and a smile.

She returned the smile and sipped her wine, watching him some more. He looked as if he liked having sex every which way, she thought, picturing him naked, a woman riding his pole-like cock while he reclined on a sofa.

As he mingled, he seemed to be aware of everyone in the room. Zoë knew he would get to her eventually. She was looking forward to it. It would be something to tell Gina. Gina watched all the cooking shows on TV and would enjoy hearing about him.

When he finally came over it was at the point when the staff were lowering the lights and the other occupants were leaving. She'd also been about to pay and leave, having finished up a delectable dessert of toasted pineapple slivers served with rum-laced ice cream. She had her purse out on the table and was busy looking for her credit card.

"Welcome to Carbrey." He held two brandy glasses in one hand. The other carried an antique-looking bottle with a wax seal running the length of its neck.

She abandoned her purse and smiled. "Thank you. You are the owner, I presume?"

"I am indeed. Cain Davot." He set the glasses and the bottle on the table, and then took her hand, brushing his lips over the back of it, making the surface of her skin prickle. With one finger, he tickled her palm from beneath.

Automatically, she smiled.

He slid into the seat opposite her as he continued to speak. "And you are the current resident at Her Haven."

"News travels fast. Yes, I am. Zoë Daniels."

"It's a small village, and Elspeth is a friend of mine."

She nodded. Immediately, the image she'd had of the woman riding him became that of the postmistress, and she was going at it like the jockey who was about to pass the post and win the Derby. Zoë blinked, and then laced her fingers together, trying to push thoughts of sex out of her head. Not only were they constant, they were becoming increasingly naughty.

He sloshed a generous serving of brandy into each of the glasses and placed one closer to her.

"Thank you." The aroma of the brandy reached her, heady and delicious. The writing on the label looked French. "Elspeth mentioned that the house has been in her family for generations," she added, making conversation.

Cain picked up his glass, his eyelids lowering as he inhaled the scent of the brandy. "Some three hundred years, and it's said to harbor the ghosts of previous occupants, if you believe in such things." His focus sharpened as he waited for her reaction.

It seemed necessary to respond. "What previous occupants?"

His eyes narrowed. "You're a believer?"

"No. Just interested in history." She lifted the brandy glass, taking a sip. It was potent stuff, and she savored the heat of it in her mouth before swallowing.

"Ah. Well, it has plenty of that, as does the whole region." His attention was on her throat; as if he was observing the way she drank the brandy. "It's a magical part of Scotland," he continued. "Tell me, do you believe in magic?"

"No," she responded, with a soft laugh. Questions instantly arose in her mind, questions about everything she had experienced since she got here, but she pushed them away. She'd been tired, that was all. Her imagination had run away with her, had to be.

He seemed pleased with that, his smile growing. "A blank slate, my favorite kind."

Zoë put down her glass. His remark was rather condescending, but there was something else about it, something she couldn't quite put her finger on. It was smug. She gave him a chastising glance.

Cain responded with a soft laugh and opened his hands. "I meant in respect of Carbrey and all it has to offer. Forgive me. I enjoy introducing newcomers to the area, that's all."

"I see." Something about him made her wary, even if she was picturing him having sex with her, right at that moment. "Are you local?"

"Yes and no. My family line is from this area, but I moved away. I studied with restaurateurs all over the world and I lost contact with the place for a long while." He became thoughtful. "Then one day I had a yen to come home." He shrugged.

Zoë took another sip of the brandy. She'd already had wine with her meal, but it was too good. Glancing around, she noticed that almost everyone was gone. A lone waiter was folding tablecloths. "It must be quite something to be connected to a village with so much heritage."

"Oh, yes, so much to explore and enjoy." He smiled, as if to himself. "Come," he said, standing, taking her hand. He gestured at the large glass doors that lined one wall. "Let me show you what I mean."

Curious, she picked up her purse and went along with him. He led her through the doors and onto a wide, tiled terrace that stood at the very edge of the cliff overlooking the sea. The sound of waves crashing against the cliff wall reached them from below. The area was closed in by wrought-iron banisters and there were matching ironwork tables and chairs arranged in groups across the terrace. On the left she noticed that steps ran down the outside of the restaurant to join up with the road to the village. Cain took her over to the wrought-iron railing and made an expansive gesture with his hand over the bay and the sky. "Just look at the view."

He stood close behind her and she felt a little uneasy. Then he lifted her hair from the back of her neck and began to massage her shoulders as he spoke, as if they were old friends, or lovers, even. Instinctively she went to pull away, but his hands held her. His fingers were quick and deft, moving into the knots of muscle at the base of her neck, releasing the tension that had built there during the long drive from London.

Any anxiety she might have felt over his intimacy quickly ebbed away from her under his ministrations. Resistance was gone. In its place she felt something like a lazy trance taking hold of her.

He was right, she noticed, the view of the bay and the harbor was mesmerizing from up here. It appeared so much more dramatic than when she had admired it during her walk up to the restaurant. She could see right along the bay, from up here on the cliff top. The village with lights dotted here and there in cottage windows, the main street running out to Shore Lane where the lights grew dim and dropped away into the sea. The occasional light out along the marina united the land and the sea. She breathed in the air. It had to be past ten o'clock, but it was still comfortably warm enough to be out here in just a slip of a dress.

"The coastline can be welcoming or desolate, depending on the time of year," Cain continued, "but it's always beautiful. It's a place that demands you live up to it. I wasn't prepared for that, when I was younger. As I got older it called to me again. I wanted the challenge of drawing people here."

He was very good with his hands, she silently mused, as they moved across her shoulders, massaging all the while. What with that, the good food, wine and the brandy, she felt more relaxed than she had in ages. "You seem to be doing well, plenty of customers."

"Oh, yes."

She sensed it wasn't customers he wanted to talk about, and she was right.

"The village itself is steeped in history," he continued. "Some of the most powerful witches of all time have practiced their magic in these parts."

Witches? What was it with everyone and this talk of witches? "There you go talking about magic again," she responded, lazily amused by his remark. Maybe it was getting close to Halloween and they were just getting into the spirit of it.

"You'll feel it soon enough." He bent close to her neck and she felt his mouth whisper across her skin, a ghostly touch that made static cling to her skin.

"Just look at the stars," he whispered close against her ear. "See how bright they are…now that you are here."

Now that I am here? What did that mean?

The question flitted through her mind and then slipped away, because the stars did seem brighter, and closer, and as she stared at them the sound of the waves lapping against the rocks below grew louder. Her senses were fogged, but her skin raced with excitement, her breath coming ever faster.

His hands moved to her shoulders. "See how they grow even brighter just because you are looking at them."

It was true. Here and there across the night sky the light and color intensified, then exploded, like fireworks. As she watched, the color filled her mind. She felt him close against her back, and he was solid and warm, and he had an erection. It made her whimper aloud.

Her head dropped back, her eyelids instinctively lowering. She heard her purse drop to the ground, but barely cared. Grappling for the railing, her pulse grew erratic. The pit of her belly throbbed with heat, her pussy growing heavy with arousal. It swamped her. Her body felt as if it were somewhere between fluid and electricity. The pressure of his cock through their clothes was too good. It made her want to pull up her dress, drop forward over the railing, and have him enter her from behind. Her body swished and swayed of its own accord, her hips rocking against him.

Cain's voice still reached her, and then she thought she heard female laughter echoing in the distance. *Maybe I'm drunk,* she thought, *and one of the staff has seen me out here with him, cavorting in the dark.* The thought wisped away before it took hold. She was adrift, and as her eyes closed again she felt as if she were floating on a tide of unfamiliar but pleasurable sensations.

Her perception wavered, then altered. When her senses sharpened she found herself kneeling on a bed covered in red and black satin sheets. Cain was still behind her and she knew she was naked and that he was thrusting into her pussy from behind. But what harnessed Zoë's attention most of all was the fact she was kneeling over another woman, a naked woman, a woman whose hands were tied to the iron struts of the bed with a length of rope.

It was Elspeth, the postmistress.

Elspeth's head rolled against her taut, bound arms and

her hair spilled down toward her breasts. The lines of her body were smooth, soft and lean, and as she undulated against her restraints, Zoë's body resonated with an echo of movement and need. Elspeth widened her kohl-lined eyes at Zoë. Ruby lipstick was smudged on her lips and Zoë knew that she'd done that. She'd been kissing that mouth when Cain first thrust inside her. She didn't quite remember it, but the knowledge was there in her mind.

Cain's hands locked on her hips, holding her steady, which was just as well. Elspeth's legs were wide-open, her breasts lolling indolently to the sides. Her left nipple was pierced with the same kind of ring that she had in her ears, and Zoë could smell her female scent in the air. It made her writhe and dip, seeking out the source.

"Come on, you know you want to," Elspeth whispered.

She did, she wanted to run her tongue into the glistening slit of Elspeth's pussy. It was shaved bare, and her clit was large and swollen, the folds that framed it slick with juice.

Intoxicated, Zoë dipped her head down and rested a kiss on the bump of Elspeth's clit. The soft flesh gave way around it, focusing her mouth on the jutting head of her clit. It made Zoë desperate and she shoved her hips back, her core clenching on the hard cock thrusting inside of her.

Elspeth's body rose and fell and Zoë circled her clit with her tongue, everything else shifting in and out of focus when she tasted the nub and felt its resistance against her tongue. She sank her tongue down between the swollen folds of her pussy, tasting the silky nectar of the bound woman, her tongue moving easily into the entrance of Elspeth's sex.

Elspeth responded by thrashing and moaning, and Zoë liked that. She thrust her tongue again, reveling in the woman's receptive flesh.

Am I really doing this? she wondered.

Somewhere the faint sounds of music filtered through a wall. Elspeth growled, and behind her, Cain's erection seemed to be everywhere, like several cocks rubbing against her, inside and out. Was it just him, or were there other men? Against her breasts and between her pussy lips she felt them—one buried inside her sex, another pushing at her anus, opening her up, making her gasp and shudder, crazy for release.

Then, without warning, Zoë only saw dark shadows skittering away, and waves crashing on the cliff below.

She was gripping hard on to the railing of the terrace, bent right over it at the waist, her eyes focused below where the waves crashed violently onto the rocks at the base of the cliff. *It's not real.*

She struggled to gather herself. The hem of her dress flapped against the backs of her thighs. She hadn't been naked at all. *Did I imagine it?*

The atmosphere had shifted again and she gasped for breath, struggling to regain her equilibrium. Off to her left she heard a sound, and then another. She struggled to identify what it was. What the bloody hell had happened to her?

The sound—it was somebody clapping, slowly. Her head jerked around and she tried to focus. As she did, she saw her neighbor, Grayson Murdoch. He was just a few feet away, observing her. She felt dizzy, and a little nauseous, like a bout of travel sickness.

Cain had stepped away. With immense effort she managed to straighten up, noticing as she did that Grayson was entirely dressed in black, his long blond hair flying loose out to one side in the blustery wind that had whipped up around them.

"Very impressive," Grayson said, looking out at the sky. "Do you put on the show for all the visitors, or only the attractive female variety?"

His eyes flashed silver in the moonlight, and Zoë blinked. Glancing at Cain, she saw he had a smug smile on his face, as if he was amused that her neighbor had entered onto his territory.

They were like two tomcats stalking one another. It made her want to roll on the ground and expose her femininity to them, to find out which one would win in a squall. The idea flitted through her mind and made her core tighten with anticipation. Weird. It was so unlike anything she would normally think that she struggled to figure out if she were awake or asleep. She tried to step away from the railing and as she did her heels shifted under her. She kept a hold of it by two fingers until she felt steady. The wind was much higher than it had been and she felt so lightheaded that she wondered if she might be blown away.

Her purse was at her feet, and she leaned down to swipe it up, still holding the railing for support. The cliff seemed treacherous and she wanted to step away.

"I think I've had too much to drink," she said, trying to convince herself.

Grayson lifted his eyebrows at her, but he was smiling. "Have you been feeding her your fancy wine, Davot?"

There was an accusation in his tone. It leveled Zoë somewhat. Was he insinuating something? That bottle with the wax seal, she'd never seen anything like it before. Maybe it was particularly potent stuff.

She glanced at Cain.

"Don't be ridiculous," Cain said. "Watch your mouth, Murdoch." He'd adopted a nonchalant stance, but his expression gave away his annoyance.

They were enemies and they wanted to punch each other's lights out, that much was obvious to Zoë, even if everything else confused her all to hell. She wavered. Damn. She didn't want to look so ditzy, not to either of them.

Grayson smiled at her then, making an intimate connection. She was glad of it. It made her stand up straight and push her shoulders back.

He sauntered over. "Allow me to assist."

He lifted her easily into his arms, and she grabbed him around the neck, clinging to what felt strong and sure. He held her tight against him, and she laughed softly and glanced up at him. His eyes twinkled at her, and she felt something flutter open inside her. "Thank you," she whispered.

He turned and strode off, shouting something back over his shoulder to Davot as he went. Zoë didn't catch what it was. "But I haven't paid yet," she said, vaguely, remembering—then the shape of Grayson's shoulders under her hands and the look in his eyes made her forget that particular issue altogether.

She had the feeling she would be embarrassed about this in the morning, but right now—hell, no! The wild alley cat had swiped her right from under the nose of the other, and she tightened her grip on him, secretly thrilled.

Cain Davot snorted derisively.

"Amateur," he snarled under his breath. A woman like that, a city girl, would react badly to Neanderthal behavior, he was sure of it. He moved into the shadows so that he could observe them unseen as they flitted down the steps and away from the restaurant. Once they were on the road, Murdoch paused and set her down on her feet. She wavered unsteadily and held on to him for a moment and they exchanged a few words before she stepped away. Murdoch kept one hand on her for a few moments and then nodded in the direction of Shore Lane.

For a brief moment Davot entertained the idea of luring her back by means of magic. He'd been making progress. Once he'd unleashed a sensory spell around her she opened to the sexual suggestions he planted in her mind. That boded well. He couldn't, however, afford to freak her out. That's the only reason he'd let Murdoch take the upper hand.

Murdoch was nothing but a minor irritation, an upstart—a lone he-witch who knew enough bits of magic to be a nuisance, no more. The stranger said he was in Carbrey to do research, but was there more to it? Cain had him followed back to Edinburgh, where he worked at the university. He'd also sent out his most trusted people to find out what they could. The villagers along the coast knew of Murdoch, but wouldn't say more. As a consequence he'd tried a boundary spell around his patch, to keep Murdoch out. It hadn't worked. Cain had met his type before: tenacious, self-righteous, but a lone witch was ultimately useless in the face of a strong coven with a focused cause. Tomorrow he'd send his people in. Tomorrow they would ease the host away from Grayson Murdoch.

Reaching into his pocket he flipped open his phone, preparing to summon his coven. As he did, the woman, Zoë, glanced back over her shoulder in the direction of the restaurant. Murdoch said something, and she nodded. A moment later, she started walking toward the village with Murdoch alongside her. Davot shrugged.

There was still plenty of time to lure Zoë and prepare

her for the exact moment when she would be needed. He'd get what he wanted in the end, of that he was certain. Besides, if Murdoch did get in his way, he'd simply conjure him an instant and unsavory death.

5

SHORE LANE WAS DARK AND FILLED WITH mystery, and yet it was Shore Lane that called to Zoë. She was thinking clearly again, and she knew what she wanted. Grayson was at her side and he held her attention now. The sky above still glittered with incandescent stars, but she was barely aware of all that anymore. Desire ran back and forth between them as they walked, and she was ready for more.

They'd passed the post office and the streetlights grew dimmer, as if out here where the houses were destined to slip away into the sea, mystery prevailed. When they were almost at Her Haven, she paused. He turned, walked back to her and looked at her with a curious smile, as if he wasn't surprised by her actions.

Lifting her chin, she studied him, her pulse kicking up a notch as she did so. There was something contained about him, something invincible. It was incredibly attractive. She looked him in the eye. "What was all that about, back there?"

"Power." He said the one word simply.

His answer made her chuckle. "I thought as much." There it was, that mischievous echo inside her. Earlier it had made her feel dizzy and strangely out of control. But not so much, now. Not here in the dark on Shore Lane.

I can have him. I'm a woman and I can have this man.

Accepting that knowledge brought an unexpected jolt for Zoë, and yet the knowledge took root and became sure and solid inside her, driving her on to take action. She was aroused. She needed fulfillment. He was an attractive man, and she wanted him. Gone was the resistance she might have felt about getting it on with a man she'd only met that day. Something else had taken its place—something that had wrapped itself around her and melted into her very core, making her vital and alive.

"I appreciate you walking me back. Please, come inside." She opened her purse and found the key. When the door clicked open she sensed he was close at her back and she knew he'd follow. Stepping inside, she touched her hand along the wall, looking for the light switch.

A moment later, she heard him closing the door, and then came the slow, solid sound of the bolt sliding home. With it, a ragged sensation ran up her spine, as if something had shifted between them, some balance of power. Tension emanated from the place where he stood.

Her hand found the switch. The light flickered on but was nigh on useless, casting only a small pool of amber light in the gloom. Beyond it, moonlight funneled onto the stairs from a window on the landing above.

Grayson stayed in the darkness by the doorway, but she knew he was watching her as she walked toward the stairs and turned to face him. It struck her then that he always had a purposeful stance about him, and ever since she arrived in the village—hell, even before she had arrived—

he'd been there. He'd sparred with the postmistress, and then he'd turned up and competed with Cain Davot over her. While that had its own appeal, she couldn't help wondering why.

Maybe he just wants to fuck, like I do.

It was a blunt, wry realization, something she knew for a fact she'd never consciously thought before, and it embarrassed her, but she couldn't deny it. It made her curious, though, and she had to ask. "You always seem to be around when I might need help."

He stepped out of the darkness by the doorway and closed the space between them inside a heartbeat, making her breath catch in her throat. Lifting her chin with one finger, he looked deep into her eyes. "Is there something specific you need my help with, Zoë?"

His eyes flashed in the gloom.

She swallowed. His touch had started a riot amongst her nerve endings, and her sex clenched, needy and urgent. A moment before, she'd felt reasoned, back when she'd been focused on getting him inside the house. Now, his very proximity was washing that away.

"Your company," she mustered. "I've been hearing some strange stories about this house."

It was partly the truth.

Mostly she wanted to have sex.

"It has quite the history, that's for sure." He was watching her closely, unsurprised, fascinated even. "And something about the place leaves an imprint on visitors."

"Is that part of your study?" Even as she said the words, the urge to chuckle rose up inside her.

Of course it is. He can't wait to get inside and check the place out. The thought came out of nowhere, and she wondered how she knew that.

"I'd appreciate a chance to inspect the house…and its current occupant." One corner of his mouth lifted, humor and desire lighting his expression. His hand moved, sliding briefly down her throat and around one shoulder.

"The house, and me?"

"Mostly you." His breath was warm on her face, and her head dropped back to take his kiss. His mouth was firm and persuasive, and when she melted and moved against him, it became more provocative. Exploring her, he kissed her mouth until her body arched against his, and then he demanded more by thrusting his tongue between her parting lips, slowly moving in and out. The action was rhythmic and slow and filled with erotic promise. And then his hand was under her skirt. He broke the kiss and looked down at her while he closed his hand over her pussy through the thin lace of her knickers, and squeezed.

A soft moan escaped her. She couldn't help it.

He gave a dark chuckle, glancing down at her nipples where they were hard under the sheer fabric of her dress. "The heat coming off of you is fascinating." His expression grew serious. "Because it's not just in here…"

Again he squeezed her pussy, making her whimper and shuffle her feet in response, darts of sensation assailing her groin.

"It's all around you. It's so big it's filling this house, and I want to know why."

Gulping in air, she steadied herself. The logical part of her mind—the organized London PA—wanted to find a reason for this. "I saw you earlier," she admitted. "I saw you in the shower, it made me really horny."

He cocked his head a moment, and she thought he might laugh at her, but he didn't. "Oh, you did, did you? That intrigues me even more."

He reached down and lifted her dress, pulling it up over her head and off. She wasn't wearing a bra and she instinctively wrapped her arms around herself, but her own touch only maddened her skin.

Dropping the dress to the floor, he walked her back until the stairs were at the back of her heels. "Sit down right there," he said. "Let me look at you."

Oh, but that did bad things to her. She dropped down to sit on the stairs, her hands clutching the edge of the step either side of her. Her breasts ached for his hands. He stared down at her, making her even more restless.

"Open your legs." When he gestured for her to do as he asked, her entire skin burned. But she wanted to, and she planted her hands on her knees, pivoted on her heels, and swung her legs apart.

He stared down at her for what seemed an interminably long time and she squirmed her bottom around on the step, her hips rolling, her sex clamoring for him. Everything about him was hard and strong and somehow otherworldly. The hall light was now behind him, casting an eerie glow around his blond hair, but she wasn't afraid. Instead, she wanted to haul him over her and lose herself in him.

Eventually, he pulled his T-shirt over his head, and when she saw his toned torso she pushed her knickers down with trembling fingers, desperate to have them off, desperate to have him over her. Then he moved into the moonlight and it made her stomach flip, because it caught his eyes and they flashed silver, just as they had out there on the cliff.

She watched as he unzipped his fly and his cock bounced free, long and hard and thick. In the pit of her belly, she ached for it. Reaching into his pocket, he pulled out a condom packet.

She looked up, met his gaze. "Do you think we can make it to the bed?"

He tore the condom wrapper open before he responded. "No."

She caught her bottom lip and watched as he rolled the condom on, resting back, ready for him. The edge of the steps was hard and unrelenting against her shoulder blades, and she knew from the look in his eyes that he would be just the same way. He bent over her, stroking his fingers over her slick folds, thrusting one hard digit inside her.

Moaning aloud, her head rolled against the stair. "Please…"

Dropping to the floor, he knelt on one knee, and lifted one of her legs over his shoulder, draping it there, the action pinning her to the spot with her sex splayed wide open. The head of his cock nudged into her, stretching her open, readying her. Then he gave her the rest, an inch at a time. A garbled sound escaped her open mouth.

With one hand he cupped her head, his cock sliding fully home. "Your beautiful cunt is on fire."

She managed to groan as he moved his hands under her bottom, pulling back and then moving deeper still, filling her to capacity.

"Oh, God," she cried, her spine straightening.

She tried to move but couldn't. He was so deeply embedded it made her feel raw and edgy, as if it was too much—and then his thumb brushed back and forth over her clit and she cried out with joy. Her sex squeezed tight around his erection.

"I'm going to come," she blurted, wrapping her hands tight around his neck. Fluid ran down her slit and between her buttocks.

His eyes flashed and a smile passed over his face while

he worked the length of his cock in and out of her, that thumb on her clit making her experience acute, making every part of her full and richly pleasured.

He's a good lover, this man.

The thought echoed through her mind as her sex went into spasm, and she clutched at his hair with feverish hands. Still he rode her, the muscles in his neck cording, his shoulders gleaming in the moonlight. When he bent over her the curtain of his hair brushed over the bare skin of her breasts and shoulders, sensitizing her to the max. Flooded with pleasure, her body grew more supple by the moment. She locked her legs around him, her fingers digging deep into the stair carpet, loving how outrageously decadent she felt, doing it with this Viking of a man on the stairs of her rental cottage.

He watched her all the while, his eyes seeming to change color in the odd light of the stairwell. When her chin lowered and she broke eye contact, he kissed her, urging her to look up and meet his gaze again. When she did, he stroked one large palm around her throat and then moved it up and down in a figure of eight, fisting his hand gently against her breastbone each time, as if he were trying to capture something. The action seemed to make her core lift and swell, as if the very quick of her was responding to him.

"Oh, oh, oh," she cried. She was on fire. A second rolling orgasm hit her, winding her. Her juices ran down the crease in her bottom. She gasped for air, her senses reeling.

"On your knees," he urged, a moment later, pulling out. "You'll be more stable."

She wanted to, but right then she didn't seem to be in control of her legs. "I don't know if I—"

"I'm not done with this yet."

There didn't seem to be any arguing with that.

She wavered unsteadily, her hands grasping for the higher steps. He lifted her by the hips, positioning her. The carpet felt hard under her knees, but when he lunged back inside her slick sex, centering her, she vibrated with sensation, hot, rhythmic tides of pleasure washing through her entire nether region. "Oh, oh, oh…it's so good."

Arching her back, she spread her hands on the stairs above, pushed her bottom out to him.

Breathing hard, his hands manipulated her buttocks while he drove his shaft in and out of her, over and over. He seemed to be all around her, hot and strong and fierce. Then he meshed his long strong fingers with hers where they clutched on the steps above, and she felt his breath hot against her hair and he kissed the side of her face.

"Hold tight," he breathed, and his cock grew longer still, pressing hard against her cervix and jerking repeatedly.

The sensation was so intense it was closely bound up with pain, and she heard a sound that she didn't recognize as her own. The cry was wild and animalistic, and it sounded like victory.

But he held her, and she felt safe. She was vaguely aware of being lifted and turned, and then she felt him taking her strappy sandals off—a tender gesture after the determined actions that had gone before—before he lifted her into his arms and carried her up the stairs.

The bed was soft against her back and she lay back on it gratefully. Her awareness faltered, and she heard herself chuckle but wasn't sure why. She felt strangely trancelike, as if her mind was captured somewhere between the reality of this moment and a dreamlike state. Tired, that was why she felt herself adrift. Her eyes closed, and with great effort she opened them again. She saw the biker-prof standing there looking down at her, watching her closely.

He makes magic here tonight. The strange thought echoed around her mind even as she drifted off. *Can you feel it? Can you sense the power rising in the atmosphere?*

Her eyelids lowered, and she struggled to open them again.

The room was darker.

A breeze blew through her mind. On it, she could smell wood smoke. It was enticing, and somehow seductive, and it lured her into its spell…

The moon is full and heavy and it races across the fields, stirring the creatures from their burrows, beckoning to those of us who seek its thrall. My heart beats fast, for I crave the ritual that is to come.

The scent of the forest is high in the air, for the nearby brook flows fast with spring rain. New life is all around, from the sprouting undergrowth to the lambs in the fields beyond. I push my cloak back over my shoulders and lift my skirts free of the hawthorns and brambles, tracing the familiar path through the forest to our special place.

I am late, and the coven is already in the midst of their revelry. I see flames flickering between the dense trees as I approach. The fires are lit in the clearing and the smell of the kill is high on the air. I need not hurry, even though I am eager for the power I sense carried on the air, for I know the master will wait for me.

Two of the younger women look sullen as I approach, annoyed that I have arrived. Old man Cawley sits on the ground, playing the demon dance upon his flute. His eyes are bright and a flagon of ale is propped at his side. Beside him a young lad beats a drum, entranced by his own rhythm.

Three of the coven roll together on the ground nearby, all hands and tongues, their clothing undone, their faces flushed with lust and wine.

Ewan Findlay, our coven master, chants over the sacrifices laid out at his feet. Oh, but he is strong, and so wickedly handsome. My body quickens at the very sight of him. His dark hair falls long and unruly over his shoulders, his shirt is loose over his breeches, and his buckled shoes glisten in the firelight. He stands over the animals he's slaughtered on this full moon's eve, his hands raised to harvest their life-force and their souls. A skinned rabbit, the entrails of the deer he hunted this morn. On his back he wears the deer skin, fresh from the kill, an unholy cloak. It stains his shirt here and there with blood. The woman he chooses this eve will also be marked with that blood, painted with the ancient sign while he rides her.

And now he stares down into the fire, his dark eyes reflecting the flames. A smile plays around his mouth, and a determined set to his jaw makes my chest swell with anticipation. I am here for him, and I eagerly follow his footsteps into the forbidden. It arouses me, the power and the magic that is ours when Ewan communes with the dark forces of the Hidden World.

To his right flank a furrow has been dug into the earth. There the younger men will spill their seed before dawn, joining with the earth and the Hidden World. Ecstasy will unite the coven this eve, and one shall be chosen as Ewan's woman. He will declare her his divining rod, the witch he chooses to channel his magic.

Eight of us here hope to be chosen. Deep within I nurse the knowledge that it will be me, I am his chosen, and I will have him as I can have any man here in Carbrey. As we celebrate the surging brook and the rising crops he will declare me his consort, daubing my body with sacrificial blood and bedding with me under the full moon, closing the circle between him and I.

As I glance his way his gaze lifts to meet mine, and I know he has waited for me to arrive. Lust burns bright in his eyes and mine own surely reflect it. My cunny is warm and sticky as a honey pot, ready for him.

I drop my cloak to the ground, undoing the laces at my breasts, baring them. Pulling on my stiff teats with my fingers I step into the circle, ready for everything this night will bring.

6

GRAYSON STOOD BY THE WINDOW IN HER BED-room, watching over Zoë while she slept. When he glanced out along the bay toward Cain Davot's citadel, his thoughts clouded. Cain was bad news, really bad news.

Grayson had first come to Carbrey to investigate the rising number of sightings of the ghost in Her Haven, and when he arrived, he found Cain Davot in the village. Cain was a he-witch with a black heart. The stains on his soul and his hunger for power were obvious, and Cain brought dark ways into what had been a relatively happy community. Along this coast the practitioners of witchcraft nurtured and explored their magic as they went about their everyday lives and jobs. Unobtrusive for the most part, they were in league with the natural, elemental world, as well as the manmade world they were part of. Not so Cain Davot. He was the sort of witch that drew bad attention to them all, always greedy for power.

Earlier, Cain had cast a sensory spell over Zoë. Was it purely for entertainment, or was there another reason? Determined to find out, Grayson vowed to stay close and watch over the visitor while she was here.

He closed the curtains, and lay down alongside her.

At first Zoë's sleep seemed restless and troubled, and when he put his hand to her forehead he found her skin was overly warm to the touch, as if there was a fever in her blood. Concerned for her welfare, he studied her as she slept. She was quickly becoming part of the magic here in Carbrey. That was obvious. When she moved restlessly he noticed that her nipples were hard. Occasionally her thighs would squeeze together and she'd pull her knees higher against her, as if she were having erotic dreams.

She was an attractive woman, and she looked as if she were built for a sensual life, despite the smart car and the city attitude. After a while, the flickering of her eyelids and her rapid breathing slowed down, and she fell into a deeper, more restful sleep.

He pulled the quilt over her, reassured. Then he turned his attention to their surroundings, sprawling on the bed as he observed the phenomenon. The house was filled with psychic energy. It glowed and rumbled up from the staircase like a purring cat, wisps of it darting about like ethereal creatures freed from confinement. It was visually entertaining, but not that unusual in a house with a history like this.

He craved a tumbler of the old malt whisky he had next door, and perhaps a good Cuban cigar from the box his aunt had given him for his pondering moments. That's what he was doing now, pondering.

For some reason the ghostly occupant of Her Haven was no longer fragments of memory captured in time, echoing through the building. She had accumulated enough energy to manifest her presence and fill the house with sensuality and mischief. She had identified with Zoë. Why?

He'd been able to harness the spirit while they were down there on the stairs, turning it around inside of himself so that he could examine its nature. Fascinating it was, too. His interest was academic, that was no lie. But there was more to it. He sensed trouble. The spirit in this house was associated with a dark history.

Whenever he'd come to visit the area he'd been drawn to the cottage, partly because he'd heard Annabel McGraw's story, read all the accounts, and each time he visited the area her presence would be more powerful. In the beginning it was only a suggestion of a presence, mostly built around her legend. Not anymore. He'd wanted to taste her essence in order to know it better, and that he'd surely done. Annabel McGraw was causing havoc even from her grave, and he was going to find out why.

Meanwhile, Cain Davot was meddling in the occult, forbidden black magic, Grayson felt sure of it. That was not only dangerous, it would bring ill repute to the brethren. He sighed. It ran deep in him, the need to know the people of Carbrey and the neighboring town of Abernathy were safe from those who practiced the dark arts. His mother had been from Abernathy, and he owed it to the members of his family who still lived there to investigate.

He brooded on the situation until Zoë stirred in her sleep, drawing his attention back. Then there was desire. He was a man after all—in part, at least—and he knew when a woman wanted him.

Looking at the soft, sleeping woman next to him he wondered briefly if he should have handled it differently, denied the thrall. But he hadn't wanted to. As soon as he'd accepted Zoë's invitation, he'd had to stay focused, in order that it shouldn't consume him, too. Concerned, he hoped Zoë didn't think him too cold and distant. He'd tried to walk the line, to keep her safe and make her experience pleasurable, while examining the supernatural forces manifest in the house.

One thing was for sure—he needed her. He had to stay close to her while she was here. She had been chosen, by someone—or something—and he wanted to find out why. Reaching out, he stroked a stray hair from her face. She sighed and snuggled deeper into the pillows.

He stared at her, admiring her, wanting her again. As sure as the dawn would rise, she would think more independently in the light of day, when the spirits of the night whispered away taking their mischief with them. He sensed she wasn't the sort of woman who came on to men like that. How would she react to him in the morning? Time would tell.

At the other end of the bay all was dark in the Tide Inn. Above it, however, in the penthouse apartment that was built on top of the restaurant high on the cliff, the lights burned still. Cain Davot leaned back in the ornate Baroque-styled sofa in his extensive living room, and watched the woman who was stripping in front of him, while he tried to be patient.

The woman, Isla, had come to them from some city gutter, much as Annabel McGraw had been drawn to Carbrey three centuries before, a fallen woman with no family to speak of. A witch looking for brethren who she could learn from, a coven she could call her own.

Understandably, he couldn't get Annabel out of his mind tonight. He was so close to making it happen that he had to pace himself. He'd become obsessed with her these last few decades. He didn't choose to fight it, not anymore. He'd sought a she-witch such as her across the centuries and the entire globe, a woman that he could forge a powerful bond with. No one came close. He'd always loved her, always regretted her demise. The only answer was to bring her back while he still had time. He'd lived long on borrowed time, but his years were numbered. It had to be soon. *Be patient. It will be yours, all of it.*

After Zoë had left, he'd gathered his people around him, pouring expensive wine down their throats and encouraging them to explore their darkest desires, assuring them that the sexual energy they released would help their cause. It was an entertaining sight, watching them debauch themselves at his behest. Elspeth had run with his suggestion to invoke power, letting her dominant side surface. When it came to sex, she was a particularly gleeful pursuant of debauched behavior. That's why he liked her. No sense of shame whatsoever, just the pursuit of the eternal high.

When he'd met Elspeth he'd seen a lot of potential in her. She claimed to be related to Annabel, but that had nothing to do with it. Cain didn't believe it for a moment. Annabel had no family aside from a crone of a mother who had rejected her before she'd reached full maturity. But Elspeth did believe it, because she wanted it to be true. That's how greedy for the connection Elspeth was, for the notoriety and for the power it might lead to. Her name, however, was a mere coincidence. But Elspeth was far too focused on the gruesome delights of bringing someone back from the dead to consider the implications, to think about what might happen after the event. If they succeeded in their plan to reincarnate Annabel, Annabel would quickly usurp Elspeth as the dominant female in the coven.

He studied her as she strutted around his apartment in high heels and a tight, bloodred dress that barely covered her shapely derriere. She had one of his waiters, Warren Kirby, naked and bound with rope around the wrists, hanging from a beam at the far end of the room. She flicked a birch riding crop at his tensed buttocks, laughing with delight when he moaned pathetically and his engorged cock bounced against his belly.

The image of restraint versus power suited the rather decadent, sumptuous surroundings he had created for himself here at the head of the cliff overlooking the bay. He'd furnished it with treasure and wealth that he had gained on his travels around the globe. Through Europe he'd meandered, to Asia and beyond, to the New World. He'd never been able to forget Carbrey. The place where he had grown up called to him. He'd come home a stronger, more powerful witch, one who was able to build an empire that breached the gap between the Netherworld and the here and now.

Crawford was busy performing cunnilingus on one of the women. Daphne, a busty thirty-eight-year-old widow, was quite the vindictive shrew, and no one dared ask how her husband died. It certainly wasn't from natural causes. Daphne sat on a high-backed dining chair with her dress pulled up around her hips. She wasn't wearing any knickers and her pussy was almost completely shaven, bar a small dark line that seemed to function as an arrow directing wandering men into her hotspot. Crawford was kneeling between her legs, his hands wrapped around her thighs, his determination to bring her to climax visible as he went down on her. She cooed and gurgled, her hands alternately stroking her breasts and Crawford's tousled hair.

Cain glanced back at Warren, who was currently being teased mercilessly by their postmistress. She had his balls grasped in one hand while she moved her riding crop up and down his flank, occasionally flicking it. There was a lattice of fine red lines on his stocky body, a signature he would wear with pride.

"Cain…?" Isla flipped her bleach-blond hair back, hands on hips, her mouth pursed rather petulantly as she tried to get his attention.

She was vain and had a jealous streak, this one, making her less willing to share than the rest. Many years before he'd had those fatal flaws himself. He'd have to watch her, quell those traits.

Nevertheless, the sight of her opulent breasts spilling out of the shallow bra she wore was pleasing. Her underwear was all black, stark against her pale white skin. She licked her lips, happy that she'd drawn his attention back, and nodded down at his hips, where his erection tested the stitching on his expensive Armani pants.

"Let me see you, Cain, you know how much I love your cock." She fluttered her eyelashes as she reached around and undid her bra.

He couldn't help wishing she didn't sound quite so uncouth. He was willing to bet that woman from London, Zoë, wouldn't say something like that. Or would she? It would be quite a turn-on hearing it come out of her more refined mouth. He lifted his brandy goblet and enjoyed another mouthful of the aged cognac while he pictured it.

Isla paused before lowering her bra, as if she needed to know he was looking at her. He gestured with the glass, sighing inwardly. She peeled away the bra, her hips rolling from side to side as she held the bra loosely in place. She turned her back on him and cast it aside in slow practiced movements, dropping it to the floor before she glanced back over her shoulder, eyebrow raised as she looked pointedly at his groin.

He opened his legs, beckoning her closer. Maybe she

would take his mind off Annabel and the London woman; he needed help with that. Possession was no easy trick. It required refined, escalating magic ritual, and patience.

"I can make you come. You want me to, don't you?" It was Isla again, and she had dropped to her knees. She reached for his fly. Her smile grew when she pulled the zipper down and his cock stood up from his trousers, totemlike, in front of her. Squeezing his balls with one hand, she stroked his length with the other, licking her lips. He watched as her plum-painted lips stretched around his cock-head, her tongue instantly at the underside, stroking back and forth. His spine straightened and he eased his hips forward, watching as she took a good length into her mouth. She lifted away, fluttered her lashes and then took him in again, pumping him with her mouth. Now this was a skill Isla didn't need any help with, unlike her magic.

Resting his head back against the velvet cushions on the sofa he pictured Annabel kneeling between his legs, instead of Isla. Isla took his smile as a sign of encouragement and took him deeper. The pulse in his groin thudded, pressure building.

Annabel would be there soon, instead of this sorry bitch. His eyelids lowered, his balls high and tense. If it was Annabel, he'd have to possess her. He'd flip her onto her back, and bury his cock deep inside her.

The mouth on his cock lifted away. "You're thinking about someone else, aren't you?"

Cain's eyes flashed open. "Of course I am, you silly bitch. Now finish the job."

There was a petulant expression on her face, and her hand at the base of his cock tightened, stemming his seed. "It's that bloody Annabel, you're obsessed with her."

Anger flared in him. "Don't you dare speak her name in that tone."

Isla glared at him. It wasn't what she wanted to hear. "Bastard," she muttered, snatching her hand away.

The atmosphere in the room grew tense, the rest of the coven quieting as they observed the exchange. The urge to climax had gone, but he refused to suffer her insolence. Grabbing her wrist, he twisted it.

Her body buckled under her and she shrieked.

Cain rose to his feet, doing up his fly as he did so, and then kicked her flat to the ground. When she tried to get up, he put his boot over her forearm, pinning her to the floor.

"Cain, no!" It was Elspeth, but when he caught sight of the dismay in her expression it only urged him on. They needed to know that he would never, ever accept disobedience or insolent words from a member of his coven. Never had, never would. He'd brought them jobs, money and knowledge of magic far beyond what they already had. He expected unconditional loyalty in return.

Isla writhed on the floor beneath him. "I'm sorry, I didn't mean anything by it. Please don't, Cain. You're hurting me."

When she tried to pull her arm free, he pressed harder, trapping it while it twisted.

"Please, no!" Her eyes were wide, pupils dilated.

Her body stilled. She'd finally realized how serious he was. He put his weight through his boot and rocked, rocked until he heard the sound of bone breaking and her screams filled the room.

7

THE PILLOWS WERE SOFT AND WARM, AND ZOË nestled deeper, her consciousness stirring even while her body remained languid with sleep. Her hand moved between her thighs, where she felt pleasured and sensitive. Her breasts were tingling beneath the weight of the quilt, and she felt deliciously comfortable. Rolling onto her back, she stroked her hand over her breasts, squeezing rhythmically. An ache, like an aftershock, shot through her on each clutch of her hand.

It was the sound of gulls outside the window that forced her to surface. As she reached full consciousness, her hands stilled on her breasts. Strange bacchanalian dreams from the night before flitted through her thoughts—a wild party in the night, in the woods. It had seemed so real. She sensed the woods in her dream were the ones on the hill above Carbrey, the place that she had been drawn to on her way into the village.

I'm in Scotland. Her eyes opened and she took a deep breath. The tang of the sea was on the breeze coming in through the open window. She glanced around the room. Her suitcase sat on the floor, half unpacked, clothes spilling out of it in a heap of a mess. That wasn't like her, and she groaned at the sight of it. But she hadn't been away from home in ages, and the last time she did go away it had been with her mom, to a crummy caravan in Somerset. Zoë had always been the organized one, back then. She had to be. Being a "free spirit" meant her mother didn't bother with regular stuff like housekeeping. She was always too busy messing with tarot cards and other such nonsense.

Zoë glared at the clothes spilling out of the case. "Please tell me I'm not turning into my mother as I get older," she muttered to herself.

Groaning, she put her hand over her face. She recalled that she'd made an attempt to unpack before she left for dinner the previous evening, and then everything had… well, got away from her.

That's when it all came rushing back. Like a film flickering on the screen, images of what had gone on the night before flashed through her mind. Dinner at the Tide Inn, and that strange encounter with Cain Davot.

Grayson. Had she really done that down there on the stairs with him?

Sitting up, she peered out onto the landing, as if that would somehow answer her questions. Then her hand instinctively moved across the mattress beside her. The dent his body had made in the bed was there, but he wasn't. The dent was proof enough. She ran her hand back and forth over the place where he had been lying close alongside her, while she thought back over the raunchy sex they'd enjoyed.

Her pussy grew heavy and hot and she took a deep breath.

When had he left? That part was all a bit vague and dreamlike. She climbed out of the bed and walked to the window, peeping through the curtains at the sky. It was clear and blue, and the waves inside the bay were gently cresting in the breeze. It was going to be a beautiful day, and she was here to enjoy it—whatever it brought her way. Glancing back at the dent in the bed, she smiled to herself and headed for the bathroom.

It was when she stepped out of the shower that the smell of food cooking wafted up the steps to her. At first she thought she was imagining it. Was he still here? Clutching her towel around her, she pushed back her hair with damp hands and peered at herself in the mirror. Not too bad, considering. A little wild-eyed, perhaps. It really did smell like toast. Cocking her head, she listened. There were indeed noises emanating from downstairs. Her pulse raced as it fell into place. The biker prof was still here, and—by the sounds of it—he was making breakfast.

"Well, hello." Her voice ran over him, soft and seductive.

Grayson turned and when he caught sight of her standing in the kitchen doorway, he wondered if he should have put more than his jeans on. She was staring at him, wide-eyed, her lips softly parted. Perhaps a barefoot, bare-chested man wasn't what she wanted to find in her kitchen, the morning after.

Her hair was damp and loose, and the shirt she'd put on was clinging to her as if she hadn't dried herself properly. It clung to her breasts provocatively, drawing his attention. She was wearing low-slung jeans, and the shirt was open at the base, revealing a glimpse of her midriff. It seemed like an invitation to run the back of his hand over the soft, womanly curve of her bared abdomen.

"Hey, gorgeous," he said, and when she smiled his way, he wanted to take her back upstairs. That smile, and her aura—what a combination. The sexy morning-after look in her eyes told him she was thinking about what they did last night, and the added psychic aura that had attached itself to her glowed and vibrated with intense sexual energy. It suited her, too. She was a lush, sensual woman to begin with, and now her sexual aura was visible on the outside.

It was the house that had brought that to the surface in her, and the whole room was filled with energy and promise. He'd never seen anything quite like it, and it made him want to get physical with her, so that they could enjoy it all, together.

Grabbing the linen tea towel he'd flung over his shoulder, he dried his hands on it then cast it aside. "The house let me know you were awake, so I took the liberty of making some breakfast."

She lifted an eyebrow. "The house?"

"Creaky floorboards." He gestured upstairs.

"Ah." She looked amused by the explanation, but still she stayed close to the doorway, eyeing him across the kitchen, her hands pushed into the pockets of her jeans.

Did he make her feel awkward?

He closed the space between them, lifted her chin with one finger and kissed her mouth in greeting. She responded, her hands stroking his upper arms, circling his biceps. When her lips parted and her body arched against his, her breasts squashed against his chest. His cock hardened. He held her arms and pressed her back against the door frame. Kissing her more deeply, he almost forgot that he had planned to talk to her, to get her onboard with his plans. That goal faded for a moment because all he wanted to do was lift her and open her legs around his hips so that he could have her up against the wall, right there and then.

Something that sounded like a whimper escaped her and he pulled back. She looked up at him with rounded eyes, her pupils dilated, her luscious lips swollen and damp.

He brushed his thumb over her lower lip. "Would you like me to leave?"

It was the last thing he wanted to say. He simply *had* to be around her in order to find out what was going on here. She was a crucial part of something he needed to understand. However, his father had drummed good manners into him. That meant that he didn't want her to feel awkward, even if it put their connection at risk. It had to be her decision to keep him around, just as it had had to be her invitation through the door, the night before. Once she'd done that, he could take charge. Gentleman's rules, after all.

"Oh, no, please don't go." She smiled, her expression softening, the hesitancy he'd sensed in her evaporating. "I'm just not used to this." She gestured at the table, where he'd laid two places with cutlery, mugs, a jug of milk and a pot of tea.

"You don't eat breakfast?"

"That's not what I meant, and you know it." Her eyelids lowered as she said that.

"I hope you're hungry."

She nodded, and took a seat. "My sister found this place, but she didn't tell me it came with a sexy man included."

"It does if you want it to," he responded. "One-time offer though, just for you."

This might not be as hard as he thought. Of course, he still had to explain to her why he wanted to hang around. He turned his attention to the range. Once he'd served up the griddled bacon and softly scrambled eggs, he carried the plates over to the table. She was pouring the tea. There was a smile playing around her mouth. The domesticated picture amused her. He wasn't used to it either, but he didn't want her to know that, not right now. He caught the bread just as it popped out of the toaster, set it on a plate, and put it on the table.

She had her hands wrapped around the mug of tea and was sipping from it as she watched him. "Mmm, this looks so good. Thank you for going to so much trouble. Was all of this left by the owner, Elspeth?"

"No, I ran next door for the marmalade and the tea."

"I'll have to return the favor while I'm here."

"Sounds good to me." He grabbed the salt and pepper pot from the side of the range and put them on the table. Everything was to hand, so he took his seat opposite her.

"Being in Carbrey must be very different to life in Edinburgh," she said.

"Yes, it is. When I'm there my life is ruled by the academic timetable and my commitments at the university. I work at a different pace here. I was brought up in the capital and it's the place I know best, but my mother came from this part of the world. I learn about her whenever I'm here. It makes my work all the more rewarding."

It was why he had applied for the research project in the first place, but he didn't need to explain that. Nevertheless, when he saw the question in her eyes, he felt the need to explain a bit more. "I didn't know my mother. My dad raised me."

She looked at him, thoughtfully. "Well, that's something we have in common. I never knew my dad. It was my mother who brought us up."

"Coincidence. You have a sister, I recall?"

"Yes." She seemed pleased that he remembered. "It's more unusual," she added, "for a single parent to be the dad."

"Yes, indeed. My dad didn't agree with the way she lived her life, so—with her blessing—he brought me up alone."

"That must have been tough on you."

He hadn't meant to say so much about himself, and he certainly didn't want her to guess he was torn between a culture that espoused witchcraft, and one that dismissed it. But it was no bad thing that they had shared this much. He wanted to gain her trust, he needed to.

"Can you feel it?" He gestured with his hand, glancing around the walls. "House feels different—" he looked back at her "—since last night."

She buttered a piece of toast while she considered his comment. "I don't understand."

"There's a spirit residing in this house, and it's getting a bit lively—" he paused to smile "—since you arrived."

She didn't return his smile, opting to munch on her toast instead.

"Perhaps you've felt something," he added, trying to draw her out.

Eventually, she shrugged. "The house is new to me. I'm afraid logic prevails when it comes to talk of spirits and whatnot."

Fair enough. He needed to explain a bit more, give her a context. "The spirit here has responded to you being in the house. It manifests much more powerfully now because it thrives on sexual energy. I was able to center it last night."

She shook her head, and chuckled. "I'm sorry, I know this is your field, but it's all a bit out there for me. I don't believe in ghosts."

Grayson was pretty sure she'd be convinced by the "out there" ghost soon enough, if last night was anything to go by. That kind of power would multiply and grow more tangible, the longer she was around.

She lifted an eyebrow. "Are you seriously trying to tell me that there is a ghost in this house, and that it liked the fact we were doing the wild thing on the stairs?"

"Yes." Grayson would much rather she would have been intrigued, as most of his students were. But she had come into this blind. "Just because you don't believe in it, doesn't mean it doesn't exist." She looked thoughtful but didn't respond, so he continued. "You've never thought about ghosts?"

"I don't believe in them."

He sensed that she was pulling away from him, which was the last thing he wanted. He reached out and stroked her hand where it rested on the table. She responded, taking a quick intake of breath, her gaze shifting to meet his. The connection between them was so strong it surprised him.

She smiled. Better.

Maybe he needed to try a different approach and drip feed her information, keep it light. "If I told you that ninety percent of this village believes this house is haunted by a woman called Annabel McGraw, you'd have to take their opinion into account, wouldn't you? I mean, if you were a gambling person."

"I'm not a gambling person." She flashed her eyes at him, amused.

"I would have guessed that. Tell me, what's your everyday life like?"

"Oh, well, I have a busy routine. I work in London as a PA for a prestigious law company. I supervise several junior staff. It's chaotic and I love it. People rely on me to be well-organized and I have to be there for them, whatever they need." Her eyes twinkled. "A sense of humor helps."

"Interesting. I wish I could have you as my research assistant."

She threw him a sexy look, but he meant it. She had a good head on her shoulders, she was a conduit for supernatural power—whether she recognized it or not—and she was a damn sexy woman to be around. He'd be mad not to want her. His comment seemed to have got them back on level ground. "I didn't mean to get heavy about this. This is my job, consider that."

She observed him as she picked up a piece of bacon with her fingers and nibbled on it. He wondered if she knew how sensual she was, and what it did to him. He doubted it.

She shrugged. "I understand that, but what has it to do with me, other than that you want to check out the house while you are in here." She shot him another look.

There was accusation, but also a lingering sense of wonder there. What was she thinking about? Last night? He was. In fact it kept running over in his mind, because he wanted to do it again. "I did want to see the house. It's quite fascinating, but that wasn't the only reason why."

She was looking at his chest again, and he wondered if she'd even heard him. "Maybe I should go put a shirt on."

"It's what's coming out of your mouth that's unsettling me, not what you're wearing." Amusement rang in her tone. "Or not wearing." Her gaze lifted to his. Despite the sarcastic retort, he could see the sexual interest in her eyes. Her pupils were dilated, her movements slow and sultry as she lifted her cup to her lips.

He reached for her free hand and kissed her fingertips. "Run with me on this, humor me a little."

"Okay then, I'll humor you, but only because you make such good…breakfast."

She was teasing him. Well, that was something. At least she hadn't thrown him out. "The spirit that abides in this house was a very—" he chose his words carefully "—mischievous person, when she was alive. A naughty lady, shall we say."

"A woman of the night?"

She was getting a wee bit interested now. "No, not quite. I think that if we knew her, we'd consider her a sensualist, or a femme fatale, if you like."

"Ah, a seductress." She glanced around the kitchen and there was tentative curiosity in her expression.

"Exactly. Research shows that sometimes the mood of a person can abide within their home, especially if the spirit resides there."

"When you say 'the spirit resides there' are you avoiding using the 'ghost' word?" She'd adopted a slightly bemused expression, which tickled him no end. At least he had her attention, which was a step in the right direction. And just looking at her made him think about how she'd been last night, her receptive nature. Not just Annabel, no.

"Not necessarily. The spirit can reside in the form of psychic energy and not make a ghostly appearance. From what I can tell about Her Haven, the spirit was dormant until very recently. The visitors talked about the atmosphere changing."

He didn't want to mention sightings. He was pretty sure Annabel had already identified with Zoë, but whether she would appear to her was another thing altogether, and that depended on how Annabel wanted to play it, and why she was identifying with Zoë at all. He knew he couldn't go into too much detail too soon, or Zoë would run. He didn't want that, all he really wanted right then was to take her back to bed, and not for sleep.

"My proposition to you is that the house and the spirit in it encouraged mischief between us last night, and thrived on it."

Shaking her head, she pulled the marmalade pot closer and slapped some of it on a piece of toast. "You know, I've heard some far-fetched excuses from men when they decide it was a one-night stand and they regretted it." She paused, and color hit her cheekbones. "But this one takes the trophy."

Grayson had the feeling he was handling this badly.

"It's not an excuse for last night, that's not what I'm trying to say at all." At this point, he began to think that Annabel was much more likely to convince her than he was, with mere words alone. The residual psychic phenomenon was still manifest in the atmosphere, even though it wasn't visible to the naked eye. Soon enough, she would grow aware of it.

But he was trying to forewarn her.

"If you regretted what you did last night," she said, "just say so. We're both grown-ups here."

"I don't regret it at all, that's not what I'm saying."

"But you are trying to tell me that you only shagged me because some ghost made you do it?"

Now it was him that was frowning. Why couldn't Annabel have picked a more receptive person to channel through? "No, if anything I am suggesting that you were more willing to shag me because of the sense of mischief here."

Her eyes rounded.

Oh, boy, he was explaining this badly.

"So you don't think I am capable of wanting a man all

by myself, without some interference from…beyond?" She waved her hand at the walls.

He took a deep breath. She hardly knew him. He needed to gain her trust. "That's not what I'm saying, quite the opposite." He pushed his fingers through his hair, took another swig of tea. This was hard. Was it because he sensed her denial was deep-rooted or because he was physically distracted by her that he was messing up? "You're a very attractive, sensual woman. I wanted you, that was nothing to do with the house or the spirit."

She gave him a wary glance, then lifted her fork and ate a little scrambled egg.

"What I'm suggesting is that the spirit in the house tuned in to the attraction between us. The atmosphere has changed in here because of the psychic energy our…relationship has released."

She put the fork down and stared at him as if she couldn't quite believe it. She clearly thought he was insane. Why wasn't he explaining this better? Granted, he was used to talking to believers, or to receptive students and people in the field. Perhaps it was because he was crap at communicating with women. His only attempt at a long-term setup had exposed that. Fenella Warbuoys, a fellow academic, had told him he was a real hotshot when it came to all the touchy-feely stuff and the sex, but he didn't have the first clue how to communicate with a woman. That was some put-down, especially from a stern mathematician who dealt with cold, hard algorithms all day. He hadn't retaliated. If he had, he might not have been carrying her accusation this long. Whatever, it meant he never tried for more than fast, no-strings sex with the women he met.

And now a lot depended on him communicating successfully with Zoë here. Great. Just great. Keep it light, he told himself. She was here for a holiday. He had to make it sound interesting.

"Zoë, I enjoyed last night. You did, too. I know you did. If you're interested in a little more sexual experimentation, it would be fun to see what happened."

Looking at her, waiting for her response, he had the feeling that his suggestion was ill fated.

He was right.

"Oh…my…God." She stared at him, horror-struck, her eyebrows lifted. "First of all you seduce me in order to get in here." She waved her piece of toast around the room. A dollop of marmalade slid off the toast and splatted on her chest. She was too wound up to notice, and it was headed for her cleavage. "To do your so-called research," she continued, "and now you expect me to be your assistant on this wild goose chase?"

Yup, he'd hit the last nail in the coffin.

He stood up and reached for the tea towel that he'd abandoned earlier. Dropping to his knees beside her, he dabbed carefully at her chest.

"Marmalade," he explained when she pulled away, looking at him as if he were certifiable. He lifted most of it off with the tea towel. "It fell." There was still a sticky residue clinging to her, and now he was getting hard because he was two inches from her cleavage and he had one hand on her thigh, and all he could think about was pulling her legs apart and hauling her close against his cock.

Her nipples were as hard as pebbles. He could see them through her shirt. Cupping her left breast in one hand, he went in for the rest of the marmalade with his tongue, licking the sticky smear off her, repeating the action when he felt the tension in her body ease and she undulated against him, her hands shifting to hold his head close against her cleavage.

She moaned softly.

He kept licking her there, his thumb roving back and forth over her nipple. The marmalade was all gone, but that wasn't stopping him. He wanted to stay there, to sink into her soft feminine body and make it his again.

"Exactly how much marmalade did I drop down there," she murmured, "the whole jar?"

Mercifully, the tension between them had begun to dissolve. He could hear the amusement in her voice. Then he noticed that her hips were rocking against the hard wood kitchen chair and he wanted to be under her.

He took his chair and then pulled her from her seat and into his lap, wrapping her legs around his hips, positioning her over his cock. She held him, rocking against him, purring audibly as her fly rolled over his. The muted friction was good, but his cock throbbed for more, to be inside her, to have her sitting in this position, totally naked.

"I didn't realize you liked marmalade that much," she whispered, and gave a soft laugh, before resting a kiss on his forehead.

"You have such fabulous breasts." His words were muffled, as he planted one last kiss on the plump, soft curve that he could just about reach inside her shirt. Then he lifted his head—with reluctance—and looked at her. Humor had chased away most of the unease in her expression.

She sighed. "Grayson, I did enjoy last night. It's just that I don't believe in all this stuff." She stroked his head tenderly.

The physical pull between them was undeniable, but she needed time. "I can't force you to believe it. I'm sorry. I should have kept my thoughts to myself."

She was deeply in denial, even for a skeptic. Most skeptics

would laugh it off at this point. Not Zoë. There was more to this. He wanted her to be curious, needed her to be so, because for some reason Annabel was engaging with Zoë more than she had with any of the recent visitors. It was significant.

When she looked at him he saw that there was hurt in her eyes. "If people communicated from the afterlife I might believe it, but they don't." Her eyes shone with withheld tears.

This was making her unhappy, and he was adding to that by quizzing her. Damn it. He'd handled it so badly he'd gone and upset her. He rested another kiss against her throat, squeezing her breasts gently between his hands, wishing that he'd stayed in bed with her that morning and made love to her again, instead of trying to get serious about the situation so soon. Regret filled him. He'd handled this badly. "It's my job," he added, absentmindedly.

"I understand that." She looked at him as if she was about to say something else, reaching out to stroke him with both hands, when there was a loud knock at the door.

Clambering off his lap, she frowned. "Who on earth can that be?"

Grayson stood up and went to the window, lifting the lace curtains to get a look. It was Warren Kirby, one of Davot's people. He dropped the curtain, annoyed. "It's one of the waiters from the Tide Inn."

"Oh, right. It'll be about my bill." She straightened her shirt, her expression regretful.

"I'll get dressed," he said, and went upstairs before she opened the front door, taking them two a time.

The bedroom was practically humming with energy. He shrugged on his shirt, and glanced ruefully at the bed. Hell and damnation. If only he could open her mind to this so that she could see and feel it, and the doubts would be gone. What was even more annoying was that the psychic activity was at such a level he knew there had to be some external catalyst involved. This wasn't just about Annabel McGraw; something else was playing into this. This was beyond his interest in research.

Frustration hit him.

How the hell was he supposed to protect Zoë and the rest of the village, when she was being so stubborn? It took all his willpower to resist the urge to linger in the bedroom, to force her to stand there with him, where the atmosphere was still high with the vivid, rich energy that was associated with the ancient craft of sexmagic.

When he went back downstairs she was holding a phone in her hand. She was frowning. "It must have fallen out of my bag last night. Looks as if I've missed a call."

He wanted to tell her that she would have more to worry about than missed calls if she didn't listen to him. He pressed his lips together determinedly, close to saying the wrong thing again. Frustration was making him surly. He knew he couldn't force her to believe, time would do that for him. And he was a teacher, like his father before him. You couldn't pressurize knowledge into someone, that wasn't the way.

She looked up from the phone and folded her arms loosely as if she was guarding herself.

"I'll get out from under your feet," he muttered, and then kissed her forehead briefly before striding to the front door.

He so didn't want to leave her. With his hand on the door handle, he looked back at her. Her pretty mouth was pursed in contemplation and she was watching him with a rather wary look in her eyes.

If only they hadn't been interrupted. "Zoë, I want you to know that I'll be here for you, when you need me—and you *will* need me." As he stepped outside and shut the door behind him, he knew that his remark sounded intimidating. That couldn't be helped.

8

"BLOODY CHEEK," ZOË MUTTERED TO HERSELF as she stomped up the stairs. It was blatantly obvious that he'd only slept with her to get inside the house for the sake of his precious research. And now he expected her to hang around and assist him. Typical man—he wanted everything on his terms. Like she was going to take in that stupid nonsense about ghosts and spirits. He'd even tried licking marmalade off her chest to get her to soften up and fall into line.

No way. How stupid did he think she was?

Glaring at the unmade bed where he'd spent the night next to her, she shoved her phone in her pocket and took a shoulder bag out of her half-unpacked suitcase. She threw in a few things she'd brought to take on a day out, a book, a sweater, and some sunglasses. Then she sat down at the small dresser, brushed and clipped up her hair, still muttering to herself, and still annoyed.

The ridiculous thing was that she did want to hang out with him, in fact she couldn't think of anything more appealing. Shame he'd gone about it such an odd way, with all that spooky nonsense, putting his damned research first.

The fact she could see the disappointment in her own expression didn't help. Determined not to let him get to her, she rooted around in her makeup purse for a daytime lip gloss. She'd get out, go shopping and see some sights, forget all about him.

That's not going to be easy.

A great big sigh escaped her, and she paused. She peered at the reflection of the room in the mirror. Could it be true? Had other people really seen a ghost here? She couldn't deny that she'd felt as if someone else was in the house with her, the day before. And it wasn't exactly feeling "empty" in here right now. That was just being alone in the new place you are unfamiliar with, she was sure of it. Or was she?

She found the lip gloss she'd been looking for and bent closer to the mirror as she dipped her little finger into the pot and ran it over her lips. Other people had seen it—her—or so Grayson had said. There had been something, and there had been that weird business about thinking she could see him in the shower, when she clearly must have imagined it. Staring at the mirror, her gaze flitted around the reflection of the room as she screwed the lid on to the gloss. She noticed that she could see the landing from here, reflected in a full-length mirror that was beside the bed.

As she watched, something moved across her vision.

She dropped the lip gloss.

Turning around sharply, she looked first at the landing, then at the long mirror, and then back at the dresser, trying to work out what had caught her attention. Nothing.

"You imagined it," she murmured, trying to convince herself. But the atmosphere in the room had changed and it felt even less "empty" than it had felt before. In fact it was feeling distinctly "full." Zoë swallowed. There was somebody, or something, here in the room with her. An uncomfortable ball of tension gathered in her chest.

When she forced herself to look into the mirror on the dresser, her breath caught in her throat. There it was again. A shadowy figure reflected in the long mirror behind her. Zoë stared at it. It shimmered, fading in and out. Slowly, she turned around and looked at the full-length mirror. Nothing. When she looked back at the mirror on the dresser, she saw it again, and this time the image was stronger.

It was a woman, a woman in a low-cut, old-fashioned gown, with long black hair falling loose over her shoulders. Zoë swallowed, hard, forcing herself to breathe. It couldn't be real, and yet it seemed so very real.

The woman's skin was so pale it was translucent, but her eyes were strong and burning with vitality as she peered across the room. With a feeling of dread, Zoë realized the woman was staring directly her way, and she had tilted her head, as if she was having a good look. Zoë could actually feel the weight of her assessment, and it made a shiver run up her ramrod-straight back. Inwardly she recoiled. She pressed closer against the dresser, unable to move otherwise.

Why? What do you want from me?

The ghostly figure reached out one hand as if to touch her, and then she smiled to herself, faded, and was gone.

The room instantly began to feel less oppressive, but Zoë continued to stare at the now-empty reflection of the long mirror for a long moment, to be sure, before she pushed back the stool she was sitting on, and rose.

"He made this happen," she said aloud, asserting her

presence in the now empty-feeling room. "He put the suggestion in my mind and now I am seeing things."

Got to get out of the house, clear my head.

She snatched up her bag and cardigan from the bed, and walked down the stairs as slowly as she could—which wasn't very slowly at all—then grabbed her car keys from the hook by the door with fumbling fingers and bolted out of the house.

Outside, the sun glinted off the sea and the fresh salty air hit her. She breathed deeply, her intake faltering, and then headed for her car at a trot.

Ramming the keys in the ignition, she screeched away from the parking spot. Out of the corner of her eye she saw a blur of blue jeans and Aran sweater. It was the boat builder, Crawford, and he was standing by with one hand lifted in greeting. She'd shot past before she had a chance to fully register his attempt at communication. At the post office she turned the car up the hill, wended her way through the village and was soon at the junction to the main road, the place where she had first met Grayson the day before. Her attention lingered on the spot at the side of the road, above the forest. It was where he had first touched her.

The irony of it was *he* wanted a ghost, and now she bloody well *had* a ghost. Sighing, she wondered what it would have been like to spend the day with him, helping him with his research. She didn't even know what it would involve, but it would have meant being with him. It didn't matter, she decided. It wasn't going to happen. Signaling, she pulled the car onto the road to Dundee.

The road ran parallel to the coastline and was high on the cliff, making it feel as if the road was on top of the world. This is what she came for, the countryside. She glanced in the rearview mirror. Carbrey was fading away behind her. And yet it wasn't…

It felt as if part of her was still there, tugging her back. What was going on back there, now that she was gone?

"Nothing is going on, silly woman," she told herself with steely determination, focusing on the rolling road. She put her foot down, annoyed. Every time she sped up, a hankering feeling built inside her, as if she should be back there in the village. Her mind wandered. What would have happened with Grayson, had she stayed? Like a naughty little devil prodding her, her imagination made lewd suggestions about the possibilities.

She was halfway to Dundee when her phone bleeped into life on the passenger seat. She pulled up on the green verge at the side of the road and rooted about in her bag until she found it.

It was Gina. "Zoë, I've been trying to get hold of you. Are you okay?"

"I'm fine. I left my phone at the restaurant where I ate last night and I only just got it back. Stop worrying about me, for goodness sake."

"You always have your phone with you. You're good with stuff like that."

Zoë pursed her lips. In ordinary circumstances she was good with stuff like that. She was not in ordinary circumstances. "I thought you weren't going to call me until later in the week? I'm on vacation, remember?"

"I know, but it kept bugging me what had happened to that Cain Davot, the chef. So I searched for him on Google and as soon as I saw the headlines, the whole sordid story came back to me."

Sordid? Given her current state of mind, Zoë wasn't sure she wanted to hear this. "What did?"

"He had this swish restaurant in the west end of London and a TV series. He planned a chain of restaurants on the back of that. Then he was involved in a scandal that hit the press. A young woman died in his home under suspicious circumstances." Gina emphasized *suspicious,* and then rushed on. "The woman's death was eventually written off as suicide, and Cain moved away from London shortly after, shutting down the restaurant and scrapping the business plan. The newspaper reports, however, said that the young woman had been dabbling in black magic. There were weird symbols on the floor around the place they found her, and…dead birds."

There it was again. Magic. *Black* magic, no less.

Zoë's fingers latched over her seat belt, pulling it free of her chest.

"She was only nineteen. She'd been thrown out by her parents the month before because of her interest in the occult," Gina continued, "and they suggested that Cain had something to do with it, like it sounded as if maybe he was into the occult, too."

On top of everything that had gone on—the weird things she had been experiencing and Grayson's suggestions about ghosts in the house and other such nonsensical stuff—Zoë didn't feel able to give a balanced response. She held back a moment, determined not to let hearsay and spooky nonsense get the better of her good judgment—harder though that seemed to be with each passing moment. She forced a dismissive laugh. "Oh, come on, you know what the papers are like."

"Well, yeah, but there might be some truth in it, and it all sounds dodgy. Did you meet him?"

Zoë could hear the morbid curiosity in Gina's voice. Gina was more like their mother than she was, less grounded, more into the dramatic stuff. Gina was the one who followed celebrity scandals and speculated on philosophical subjects, whereas she preferred to be practical.

"I did meet him, yes, and he's not what you'd call an average bloke, for sure, but I'm not about to let the tabloid press color my perception. Never have, never will." She rolled her eyes and rested her head back against the car seat, loosening her grip on the seat belt.

"Yes, I thought you'd say that. So, what's he like?"

"A charmer, I suppose that's what you'd call him. Suave, handsome. He greeted all the restaurant customers personally, but I didn't talk to him for long." She tried not to think about the weird stuff that had taken place on the terrace. It was hard not to, after what Gina had just said.

"I wonder where he went, in between times," Gina responded. "Mom watched his TV show, did you know that?"

Silence ensued, and Zoë had to force herself to break it. "No, I didn't."

Gina kept trying to do this, kept trying to make their mother's death seem normal. How could it ever be normal?

Gina sighed. "Talking about it will help, you know that. You're still keeping it all inside."

"You don't half pick your times to give me a pep talk. I'm out for a drive in the beautiful countryside, trying to chill." She glanced out of the window, noticing how the hill rose and rolled away into the horizon beyond the hedge she'd parked beside. "I'm on my way to Dundee and you want to lecture me on dealing with grief, again."

She shook her head. The irony was that their mother would have loved all this nonsense about witchcraft and houses being possessed by mischievous spirits. Despite everything, despite all the strange stuff that was going on and her current confusion, it made her smile.

"I'm just trying to encourage you to open up a bit more."

You wouldn't be saying that, if you'd seen me with Grayson on the stairs last night. "Gina, believe me, I'm opening up like you wouldn't believe."

"I'm glad to hear it," Gina said, sounding unconvinced. "Just promise me you'll avoid that Cain Davot."

"Don't worry. He's not the only man here."

She'd said it as a cover-up, but Gina pounced. "Oh, so there *is* a man. What's his name?"

She sighed. "His name is Grayson Murdoch." She hadn't meant to mention Grayson, but he was on her mind. They'd parted on bad terms and she was beginning to regret that. However, if it got Gina to lighten up and stop worrying, it would be worth it.

"Mr. Grayson Murdoch, eh?"

"Professor Murdoch. He's doing research in the area."

"Professor, how lovely. You know, a professor sounds much more your cup of tea than a restaurateur with a dodgy reputation and a police investigation in his near past."

The memory of Cain touching her made Zoë's skin crawl. "Gina, it's not obligatory to consider every man I meet as possible boyfriend material." Zoë couldn't help wondering how long it would be before Gina would be doing an Internet search on Grayson to find out all about him. Still, that was no bad thing. She'd be back on the phone if she found out he had any skeletons in the cupboard. The irony made her give a wry laugh.

"Well, you sound happy, so I'm happy. Promise you'll call if you need anything."

"Deal." After she put the phone away, she stared out at the hedgerow. It was still there, that hankering need to turn back to Carbrey, that tugging sensation inside. It was hypnotic, as if she were under some sort of…spell. As soon as the thought occurred to her, she shivered and pushed it away.

She could be back there with Grayson, though. She sighed, remembering the night before, and how he'd looked over breakfast. What a sight that was, a gorgeous hunk who even made breakfast for her. And he had to go and spoil it all. She'd got so annoyed. What she really wanted to do was tell him to stop talking bullshit and make love to her again.

"Maybe I should have," she said with a soft chuckle, and turned the key in the ignition. Whatever his motivations were, he'd been a hell of a good lover. A clever woman would have humored him. It was a thought. She had to get away, if only for couple of hours. Grayson would be there when she got back. He'd promised he would be. Anticipation built as she thought about what that might mean.

As she covered the last few miles of her drive she could barely focus on anything else but going back to Carbrey. She'd focused the need on Grayson and she wasn't even thinking about the apparition she'd seen. She was thinking about rolling on a bed with his cock buried inside her. It was only her stubborn streak that fought the urge to turn the car around. Her body was aching to do so, her mind constantly filling with images of the men she'd met since she'd arrived in Carbrey. On a bed, on a floor, in the long grass. Hot, sexy images of Grayson interspersed with images of Cain pouring her a brandy then touching her body, manipulating her flesh until she was weak with pleasure while she thought lewd thoughts about him and the postmistress.

Retail therapy might help take her mind off it, she decided, as she drove in to the city of Dundee, something normal to ground her. She found a multistory car park and walked determinedly toward the shopping district. But the shops failed to lure her inside. Instead she felt Carbrey, beckoning her back.

She grabbed a coffee and a warm muffin from a street vendor, intending to sit in the city square and study the Gothic revival architecture and then go into the museum, but she ate it as she wandered, unable to rest for even a moment. Her libido was still simmering away expectantly, her thoughts in Carbrey.

To add to her confusion, she felt as if she wasn't alone. As she considered that, she realized that she hadn't felt alone since she'd arrived in Carbrey. Surely, away from the place, she should feel alone now? Restless—her mind a maze of questions—she covered the city center streets quickly, weaving back and forth, constantly looking over her shoulder. There was someone else here, someone who was following her.

It's a lover.

The thought darted through her mind, unsettling her even more. She paused by a crowd gathered to listen to a street musician and wrapped her hand around the back of her neck as she glanced back over her shoulder. The street was crowded, but she saw no one she knew. There was a presence, nonetheless. A man. Her restless libido clicked up a notch.

Why do I think it's a man? Because I'm horny?

Turning on her heel she walked quickly on, until the shops petered out, and stepped into a gloomy alleyway. She stood with her back against the wall, breathing rapidly as she waited. A moment later, a figure appeared at the end of the alleyway, and it was a man.

Her heart skipped a beat, and then raced on.

The man went to walk past, and then paused and looked in at her, before following her down into the shadows.

Pressed back against the wall, she craned her neck, trying to see his face. He stood in darkness, and the light was behind him in the tall, narrow corridor between the buildings. Then he closed the gap between them in slow, sure, lazy strides.

"You," she whispered, intrigued.

It was Crawford, the boat builder. He'd pursued her here, must have done. His eyes gleamed as he looked at her.

"You followed me."

He moved straight in against her, hands flat against the wall on either side of her head, caging her in. His eyes glowed strangely. He shrugged and gave her a lazy smile, a self-assured bloke who didn't have to explain himself to the world. "Can't help being curious."

The way he had contained her in the cage of his arms made her pulse race. She eyed the column of his neck, imagining what it would feel like beneath her mouth.

"Why did you leave?" he asked. "Are you running away?"

"No." She shook her head, denying it. His question had touched a nerve. Was she running away? From Grayson? The ghost? "I'm just doing tourist stuff."

"I wouldn't want you to go, not yet." His glance lowered to her cleavage.

He looked so cocksure and interested. She had to fist her hands to stop from reaching out and pulling his hips against hers.

He moved closer, breathing in the scent of her hair. "We haven't even got to know each other yet."

Her eyelids lowered. His presence was sweet medicine after the disagreement with Grayson earlier.

"You're so different today," he commented, almost to himself. Then he ran his hands around her hair, as if smoothing it, but without actually touching it. A knowing smile took up residence on his face. "Must be the sea air," he added, "you're glowing."

It was hard to muster a response with him looking at her the way he was. "Must be."

"When I saw you yesterday, you caught my attention. I'd like to get to know you better, if you're up for it?" He moved his fingers over her neck and up, teasing over her earlobe, toying with her earring.

"Yes, I'd like that."

"Good." He trailed his hand down to her torso, cheekily brushing the tip of her breast through her shirt as he did so.

He barely touched her, and yet her skin hummed beneath the thin barrier of her clothing. It was the most tantalizing contact, and it tugged on something deep inside her. Then he circled his fingers in the air right above her breast, above her heart, before returning his hand to the wall.

It made her feel light-headed.

There was a hungry, possessive look in his eyes. "I hope I get the chance."

"Yes," she replied breathlessly, her body responding to his proximity. The aggressive male stance and the come-on were too divine.

"I was just about to call by and ask you out, tomorrow night." He continued to eye her up, all the while, as if he was about to eat her. "When I saw you drive off you looked upset. I had to be sure you're okay."

She wondered vaguely why he hadn't caught up with her when she was sitting on the side of the road, and how on earth he had found her, but she supposed he'd had to go off and get his car. How lucky that he had caught up with her at all. "Ask me out?"

He nodded. "There's a do, a dance of sorts, it's held once a month in the hall at the back of the Silver Birch. There's a mixture of disco and traditional Scottish dance…that's mostly for the tourists from the caravan site." He said the last with a wry smile. "It's a bit of a laugh, and the food and ale are good. Would you like to go with me?"

It sounded good, and it sounded like something normal. Why not? "I'd love to."

"Good. I'll look forward to it." He touched her then, one finger stroking slowly along the waistband of her jeans.

Minimal contact, but it seemed to connect with her libido, electrifying her.

"That place isn't getting to you, is it?" he added, but he didn't wait for her answer. "Some of the people hereabouts tell tall tales about Her Haven, about ghosts and all that. It's just a game for them, trying to scare off the tourists. If you hear any of that old rubbish, just ignore them."

His thoughtful words mellowed her. "Thank you."

"You're a very sexy lady," he whispered, his voice low. "Just standing here with you looking so good is giving me a hard-on."

Her eyes flashed shut, her head resting back against the wall for a moment. Clenching inside, she reached out and gripped at his sweater with one hand, her hips moving side to side, inches away from his.

"You don't mind me telling you that, do you?" He was whispering against her ear now, and she felt the firm pressure of his chest brushing against hers, making her nipples as hard as if he'd pulled on them.

"No," she responded, her hand resting against his hip to

steady herself. How hard was he? She wanted to put her hand on the front of his jeans to find out. Biting her lip and opening her eyes, she slid her hands around his hips and pulled him close, gripping his tight buttocks so that she could feel his cock pressed against her belly. There it was, the hard outline making itself felt right through their clothing. She was swamped in lust, her senses swimming.

His face was millimeters from hers, and she knew he was about to kiss her. Everything else melted away, the gloomy alleyway and the voices and sounds of the city streets beyond. Her head dropped back.

Hungry and forceful, he wasted no time in possessing her mouth, his tongue thrashing against hers. She felt him move his hand against her forehead, and he stoked his thumb over it, firmly. As he did, a series of images flashed into life in her mind. Him and her on a bed, naked bodies slicked with sweat and bucking wildly.

She tore her mouth from his, her hips nudging into his as desperation took hold. "Oh, God."

He shoved one hand down the front of her jeans. She heard the button pop, then the teeth on the zipper plucking apart as he roughly demanded entry. When he found his way inside her underwear he locked his long, strong fingers around the curve of her mons. Her clit burned, and she rocked against him, squirming for contact, needy for relief. As she did, one of his callused fingers slid firmly against her clit.

"Oh, oh, right there," she urged, her hips moving against him.

He grinned, nodding. Bracing herself with her hands on his shoulders, she smiled. With his free hand he plucked open the buttons on her shirt, then squeezed her breasts through her bra. Her head went back against the wall, her lips parting on a long moan. He pulled down the cups of her bra and tweaked her nipples between thumb and fore-finger.

"Oh, fuck," she said, when he pulled hard on her nipple and stroked her pussy at the same time.

"Turn around," he instructed, pulling his hand free.

Breathless, confused, she did as he instructed.

He pushed her up against the wall roughly, and shoved his hand back down the front of her jeans, rocking his groin against her bottom.

Through two layers of denim she could feel the rigidity of his cock. It pressed hard against the crease of her bottom. She pushed back against him, and he locked his free arm around her torso, holding her against him. Her back was melded to his chest, her hips spooned inside his. His long, deft, boat-builder's fingers stroked over her clit. Back and forth they went, in an almost lazy movement.

It wasn't a lazy response that she was experiencing. With her hands flat against the wall, she squirmed against him, crazy for it, crazy for it as if she could crawl up the wall on her hands and knees while she begged him to give her relief.

Again he brushed a finger over her forehead. She saw herself crawling on hands and knees, naked, hips swaying, with him kneeling down behind her.

"Am I convincing you to stay?" he whispered, against her ear. There was amusement in his voice and a certain smug self-assurance that might have ticked her off, if she hadn't been on the verge of orgasm.

She shoved her hips back, and he massaged her clit faster, flicking over it in the most tantalizing way, until she came in a sweet and sudden rush, a cry escaping her open mouth.

The rough surface of the brick wall grazed her cheek.

Shuddering with relief, her flesh both raw and sensitive, she lifted up and away from his finger. The climax blistered through her, and she slumped back against the wall.

"I wasn't ever going to leave," she said, when her breathing leveled off.

It was the truth. There was no question about it.

9

WHEN GRAYSON HEARD THE KNOCK AT HIS door his spirits lifted, because he hoped that it signaled Zoë's return. He was worried that he had unnerved her by pushing her too far too quickly. Sadly, he understood her denial far too well.

His father hadn't wanted him to dabble with the supernatural or magic. But it wasn't something Grayson had a choice about. It was part of him, handed down to him by his mother, a white witch from this area. Magic had, however, driven a wedge between his parents, and there was nothing his mother could do about that, even though her natural powers were immense. When he'd witnessed Zoë's dismay and denial that morning, it served to remind him about his own split heritage and all the grief it had brought to his family.

He darted for the door, wanting it to be her, but when he opened it he saw Elspeth McGraw on his doorstep, dressed in a low-cut top, tight black jeans and shin-high Dr. Martens with purple laces.

She was the last person he expected.

"Well, look who it isn't," he murmured under his breath, disappointment taking hold of him.

She stood at the bottom of the three old stone steps that led up to his door, examining her fingernails.

"Problem?" he asked.

"I snagged a fingernail on your door knocker," she said, somewhat suspiciously.

"I wonder why that would be." He rested one hand on the door frame, amused that she hadn't figured out that he had a boundary spell on the place. "What can I do for you?"

"I came to deliver a message from Cain. You were up on the grounds of the restaurant after hours last night—"

"My, my, news does travel fast around here," he interrupted. While he spoke he kept watch on a group of day-trippers walking by behind her, cameras in hand. When they saw that the lane ended just after his house they took a few photos of the sea view, and turned back. Just as well. There was liable to be a bit of a scene if Elspeth got any closer to the threshold of Cornerstone, and he didn't want to scare off any tourists.

"If Cain ever finds you poking your nose around again, he says he won't hesitate to call the police and get a restraining order slapped on you."

Grayson laughed softly. "The police? Cain? That would be interesting, given that he was pouring drugged brandy down a tourist's throat at the time."

The day-trippers were well out of view. Casually, he stepped back, bending to pick up some junk mail from the doormat before resting one hand up against the door frame.

As expected, she tried to follow, getting closer as she continued to warn him off. "It doesn't matter what you think, you're the interloper here. Cain is a highly respected member of this community."

"Yes, and all because he's brought a few badly needed jobs to the neighborhood. Very astute of him, that."

There was a smidgen of misgiving at the back of her eyes. She hadn't thought about it from that angle.

"Luckily for Cain the majority of them haven't latched on to his more nefarious interests as yet," he added.

"You just don't like him being in charge," she snapped, "but what it's got to do with you is beyond me."

Eyes narrowed, she assessed him with obvious annoyance.

He shrugged. "There's a lot you don't know. I'd put money on the fact he hasn't told you he's been called warlock on more than one occasion in his lifetime." Grayson had picked up that bit of information on the grapevine from the Abernathy coven along the coast. The derogatory label given to outcast witches may have been gossip and no more, but if Cain really had earned the title, it applied to his whole coven as well.

"That's not true." Even though she responded quickly she looked unsettled by the remark. If it were true it was bad news for her, and rightly so.

"What do you know of him, really?" he asked.

Even though Cain claimed to be from the area, Grayson could find no records of anyone by that name ever having lived there. Cain had convinced the locals he was one of their own, by means of magic, no doubt. It was the thing above all others that made Grayson mistrustful and afraid for the honest practitioners of the craft in the villages along the coast.

"I know enough," she said, defensively.

Momentarily, he felt pity for her. "I'm afraid it's true. Sorry, sweetheart, you're in with a bad crowd."

She didn't respond well to his sympathy. That would be his knack with women coming into play again, he mused, as her expression turned.

Her foot went onto the first step, closing on the threshold. Grayson watched with interest. Behind her, the waves lifted, crashing over the sea wall. She glanced back, her attention momentarily drawn by the noise, but she was so riled by what he said that she didn't think about it long enough to notice anything unusual and continued to rant at him as she took step two and three in quick succession. The second wave rose and crashed, quickly followed by the third, at over five feet high.

By the time she'd reached the actual threshold, she was drenched. The power of the water knocked her briefly forward into his arms, before sucking her back out of the house.

She screamed in outrage as she stumbled down the steps, her face flushing over her less than elegant retreat. Her clothes were wet through and stuck to her, her hair dripping.

She wiped her cheeks, and then peeled her hair back from her eyes. "A boundary spell? How dare you, you bastard!"

Grayson dropped the junk mail into the puddle on the hall carpet, watching as it soaked up the damp patch, before he re-engaged his attention with her.

It was such a shame that she was screwing her face up like that. She could so easily be an attractive woman—if she weren't hanging out with the wrong crowd—and she was a gifted young witch. But the venom oozing from her every pore right at that moment was tangible.

"I only returned the favor you and your master bestowed on me," he replied. "Except that my boundary spell actually works on you, whereas yours…"

He opened his hands to the sky and shrugged.

"A boundary spell, what…to protect this dump? When the sea comes to wipe it away?" She gestured at the sea, in between squeezing out her hair. "It will come, and this is the last house on the lane. It will soon be dropping into the sea, right where you deserve to be."

The last house in Carbrey, or the first of the villages along the coast? He didn't say it aloud, but he thought it.

The cornerstone cottage was here and his because he would not let the gentle and more caring practitioners of the craft that lived along this coast be infected by the rotten apple at Carbrey's heart.

Mistrust and anger burned in her eyes. "You are not one of ours, Grayson, and you are not welcome here. The sooner you realize that the better."

"I suggest you canvas all the villagers for their opinion before you speak on everyone's behalf. Besides, how long has Cain Davot truly been 'one of yours'?"

Mascara was smudged beneath her eyes, and her wet hair hung in black strings, making her look even more like a Goth diva than she usually did.

Her eyes flickered. "I hope the sea washes this place away and you with it."

"I'm sure you'll be the first to know, if it ever happens… seeing as you've got your finger on the pulse and all."

He was gratified to see the flash of doubt on her face, however brief, before she turned on her heel and flounced off.

He couldn't even begin to hope that the doubt he saw in her would take hold and result in a change of heart, not when Cain was in the background making promises. But he had a feeling things were coming to a head in Carbrey, and Elspeth would be one of many who finally saw Cain for what he truly was.

★ ★ ★

Zoë frowned as she parked her car outside Her Haven. She'd done something she never thought she would, with a man, down an alleyway. More to the point, she'd been sexually involved with two men—three if you counted the funny business with Cain—in less than twenty-four hours.

As she looked over at Grayson's house guilt tinged her mood. She hadn't meant to do anything with Crawford, but she hadn't been able to stop herself. What was happening to her? She'd never behaved quite so…wildly, before. Sea air. Had to be. She'd heard of it giving people an appetite. Maybe an "appetite" was actually a euphemism for "insatiable sex drive." As she'd returned to the village relief had welled inside her. Despite all the spooky talk and the appearance of the ghost, it felt good to be back. Climbing out of the car she stared at the beautiful sea vista, filling her senses with it, and then she turned and looked at the house. A great sigh escaped her.

Okay, so the place had a history, and Grayson was right— she had to respect that, and she had to respect other people's beliefs. And she *had* seen something, or somebody. Even before that had happened she'd felt something. It had been a presence, a sense of knowing who had been there in the house before her and what was important to them. That was an experience that she couldn't deny. She should be afraid.

Was she?

A small part of her wanted to pack her case and drive back to London. *I can't, not now.* Turning back to face the sea, she breathed in the air. She wasn't ready to go into the house yet. Instead, she locked the car and walked along the lane to where it forked and the sign directed hikers and ramblers onto the coastal path.

Stubbornly, she pursued her original goal of hill walks and fresh air, and took the path, leaning into the wind that caught the brow of the hill. This was what she came for, an experience that was different to living in London and dealing with irate commuters and the daily chaos management at the office. The thought made her smile. Different? Yes, she was surely getting that. Everything that had happened to her so far was way, *way* different than what she was used to.

Here in the lowlands of Scotland she was far away from all that was normal to her, and it was beautiful. The rough grass that grew either side of the cliff path was long, thick, and bunched in hardy tufts, like no grass in London. Out to sea, the small island off the coast seemed to gleam in the sunlight. The old lighthouse that stood there caught her attention more than it had from the harbor. From this viewpoint she could see it better, and she watched it as she walked, using it as her focal point. It was disused, had to be. There was a new, more modern lighthouse nearer the harbor and in direct line with the marina. She wondered vaguely about its history as she hiked up the path.

The only sound was the crash of distant waves against the cliff side and the occasional gull swooping overhead. She was close to the village, and it was a good place to think. Inside, she felt torn. Part of her did want to go home to London, because this was all too weird. The other part wanted to bang on Grayson's door and demand he make love to her and satisfy her again, the way he had the night before.

As the cliff path leveled out she could just about make out the next village along the coast. Abernathy, was it? She seemed to recall that Abernathy was the neighboring village, from the signposts and her maps. It was a fair walk, but it would be possible to get there and back on foot. As she thought about it, she felt that tug at her back again, the same as she had when she'd gone to Dundee.

Twenty-four hours she'd been there, and she'd been drawn into the village and the forces at play in the cottage. The sure and sensible knowledge that she could simply get in her car and drive off leveled her. Deep down, she didn't want to go. Go home to what? After last night's sexy escapade with the biker-prof—not to mention today's encounter with Crawford—the thought of walking away seemed ludicrous. She'd had more hot sex in two days than she'd had in the last twelve months. That was some major reason to stay, she had to admit. The men here might be delusional when it came to the subject of witches and magic, but they were damn good in the sex department. Perhaps she had yearned for this kind of an adventure, this little bit of sexy…magic, in her life.

She smiled as she thought about how much her mother would have loved this place. She'd be right there in the thick of it, with her crystals and her tarot cards. Zoë pictured her mother drinking cheap white wine while dancing barefoot by candlelight. She'd thought about her a lot since she'd got to Carbrey, and she knew that if her mother were here, she'd be communing with nature and trying to work out what was going on with the ghostly witch in the haunted house.

Ironically, that notion made Zoë feel closer to her mother than she had in a long, long time, and that realization took the stuffing right out of her. Slumping down onto the grass like a rag doll, she sat cross-legged and rested her head in her hands, her thoughts and instincts coming unraveled as long-buried emotions surfaced. Gina kept telling her she wasn't facing up to it, wasn't dealing with it, and she was right. It was hard. She resented the way their mother had died, crushed to death in her little Mini Cooper. No pagan hippie beliefs had helped her with that.

Absentmindedly plucking at tufts of grass, she let her mind wander back to happier times. Her mother had read every book on the subject of ghosts that she could get her hands on, and her life ambition had been to see a damn ghost. When Gina and Zoë were growing up, their mother used to book them into famous ghost haunts. Hotels, inns, B&Bs, all in the hope of seeing a ghost. Zoë recalled one particular trip to Cornwall when she was eleven years old. She'd lain awake half the night listening to the rustling sounds in the thatched roof above them, dreading the thought of the legendary ghost appearing, while Gina slept soundly and her mother snored the night away.

None of them had seen a ghost during their stay, but her mother had enjoyed the prospect of it. Their mother had always been ready to leap into the fray of some mystic cause. Whether it was helping out a Romany gypsy encampment, or volunteering to dig on some archeological site that had unearthed a medieval spoon—but couldn't get a grant to dig for more artifacts—she'd be the first to get involved. Her mother had loved that sort of thing, and she would have loved this.

Am I being too dismissive about this? Should I be enjoying it more, too? She sighed, because Grayson had touched on this very subject that morning, but he hadn't understood the real reason why his comments would get to her. She couldn't push this away because other people believed in it, even if she didn't. Knowing that her mom would have loved Carbrey and its curious inhabitants meant that she couldn't dismiss it. One way or the other, she was being inexorably drawn into the mystery, into the hotbed of village politics, rivalry and folklore.

She took a deep breath, feeling more together than she had all day. Standing up, she also felt empowered. Stretching, she glanced back along the path toward Carbrey. She could see the rooftops of the houses nestled in the place where the cliffs dropped down into the harbor. And there, walking toward her, was Grayson Murdoch.

He strode easily along the cliff path, his hair so distinctive and his posture easily self-assured. The leather biker jacket he wore only emphasized his stature. His eyes were fixed intently on her and every part of her body quickened in response to the sight of him. *I want him.*

Guilt roved over her again as she thought about what she'd done with Crawford. She pushed it away, wishing it away. Walking slowly at first, she set out to meet him halfway, her pulse racing ever faster as they closed on one another.

The wind had lifted and she realized her face was wet, from rain or sea spray she wasn't quite sure. She could taste salt on her lips and she smelt the sharp, fresh ozone in the atmosphere. She felt alive, truly alive, and the surroundings intoxicated her. Gulls soared in the sky overhead and her hair whipped up around her. They met where the cliff path was at its steepest, on the way back down into the village. They paused some three feet apart, cautiously greeting one another.

His expression was serious, and his gray-green eyes were searching her expression. "Are you okay? I've been worried about you."

"It's been a weird day, but I'm all right, thanks." Why did she feel like an awkward teenager? Because she had to back down from the stand she had taken that morning?

"I'm sorry I was so pushy," he said.

"I'm sorry I was so negative." She smiled. "I shouldn't have been that dismissive. After you left, I, um…I saw her."

He stared at her, and then his eyebrows lifted, imperceptibly. "You saw her, the ghost?"

"Yes, I did. Well, it was a reflection in a mirror, but I'm pretty sure it was what you'd call a ghost."

He nodded. It was understated. She was expecting him to be excited, eager to ask her for more details and get out his notebook and pen. He seemed unsurprised. Was he expecting that?

"I've been thinking," she went on, "I'm not quite sure why, so don't ask me to explain it, but I think I would like to help you with your research while I'm here." Pushing her hands into her pockets, she shrugged. "Maybe it's because I saw her," she added.

Maybe it's because I want to hang out with you, biker-prof.

There was a powerful physical attraction between them, and there was something else, something she couldn't quite put her finger on.

He was like no other man she had met. Is that what doing research into witchcraft did to you? Did it make you a bit alternative, a bit of a law unto yourself? More to the point, wouldn't it be fun to find out?

"Are you sure you want to commit to this?" He closed the space between them and put his hands on her shoulders, squeezing her gently.

A sense of security washed over her.

Then, moving closer still, until she was right up against him, she slipped one hand around the back of his neck. "Will it mean being involved, together, the way we were last night?"

His expression warmed. "It would probably be helpful."

Her body was throbbing with longing. She wanted to be against him, naked, to feel his hard body pressed against hers, to have him take her, over and over.

"Our ghostly friend did seem to respond to the mood," he added, and his eyes were growing dark as he considered her. With his hands moving in around her waist, he held her close against him.

Nodding, she smiled. She could feel his growing erection. The draw between them heightened with every passing moment. "I'd like to know more about Annabel," she said.

And—more to the point—I want to know more about you.

10

ZOË PEERED AT HER HAVEN DUBIOUSLY.

"Does it feel any different," Grayson asked, "now that you've seen her?"

"Let's just say that having seen…something, I am more willing to listen." He'd been watching her reaction as they approached, she was well aware of that.

"How about you listen while I cook you dinner, at my place."

That sounded good. "Do you cook dinner for all your research assistants?"

"Only if they look like you."

How many women had he seduced because they had a key to the house next door, she wondered. If it was the only way he could get inside, there might be a legion of notches on his bedpost. Luckily for her, he still hadn't found out whatever it was he wanted to know.

"Come in, please." He rested one arm up against the door as he ushered her in. The leather jacket he wore was open, and the planes of his chest and abdomen were visible under the T-shirt he wore beneath. Casual and relaxed, yet so rangy and hot, the very look of him lured her in, as if she were on a piece of elastic whenever he was around.

Curiosity split her attention as soon as she stepped inside. The space was arranged differently from next door. Here on the ground floor there was a tiny kitchen to the front, with minimal-fuss cupboards and a breakfast bar that looked as if it had been there since the 1960s. No fancy restoration work here. He led her into a second small room at the back of the house, which housed a desk and shelves crammed with books, and a large, rather dated-looking sofa. It was definitely a weekend retreat, rather than a proper home.

"You can put your bag and things there." He gestured at the sofa. She shrugged out of her cardigan, warming through fast when she saw the way he looked at her as she settled in.

"How did you get into this, ghost hunting?" she asked as she followed him into the kitchen area.

He pulled out a tall stool from under the breakfast bar for her, before walking around to face her over it. "The ghost hunting, as you call it, can prove valuable for the research. You're more likely to get the truth about what happened in the past from the dead than the living."

That was a pretty weird concept to get her head around. She climbed onto the stool, resting her forearms on the breakfast bar. "I really meant how did you get into this field of research?"

"Ah, right. I started out in psychology, and for various reasons I got drawn toward the history of belief and the supernatural." He reached under the breakfast bar and pulled out a bottle of wine.

The cat appeared from somewhere upstairs and sat close

by Zoë's feet, observing Grayson at work in the kitchen, purring loudly. She watched him uncorking the wine. There was something fluid about the way he moved that attracted her immensely. Despite his size, there was a subtle sense of physical ease and self-confidence about him that made her wonder. She sensed it would magnify, if need be. Like up there at the restaurant the night before. He was guarded, and yet he'd faced up to Cain Davot on his territory. "What do you know about her, the ghost?"

"Her name is Annabel McGraw. She lived here in Carbrey during the early 1700s."

It was kind of odd hearing him talk about the woman she'd seen. It was compelling, too. "Have you seen her?"

"Not as such." He went to a cupboard and lifted out two glasses. "I can tell you the facts I've gleaned so far. She wasn't originally from this area. I tracked her down in the Glasgow registry of birth. She was an illegitimate child, no siblings, and her mother was in service."

He poured out the wine and Zoë watched it turn the glass dark, thinking about how hard life must have been back then, so different to what they knew and took for granted these days. "Why did she come here?"

"I don't know. I'm not even sure when she came. There are various accounts of her in association with practicing witchcraft, and some quite lurid accounts of her death, but we have to treat that kind of information with a degree of caution. All I have in terms of official records is a note of her death in the council registry, where she was recorded as a beekeeper. That in turn led me to find her name on the candle maker's register."

"Beekeeping?"

"Yes. I imagine that's how she supported herself. Both the honey and the wax for candles were in great demand at that time, as you might imagine. People had to hold a license in order to be able to make candles, because of the value associated with them. You can still see the remains of the bole at the back of the house."

"What's that?"

"It's the place where the beehive is stored. In this case it's built into the wall out back. The keepers had to keep them close by for security. As far as I can discover, there wasn't a local supplier of honey until Annabel came and started her hive. Before that the villagers would probably have bought from neighboring towns where someone else kept a hive. Honey and beeswax were valuable commodities."

"You think maybe she came here and figured what the place needed, and set about supplying it?"

"Possibly. She could have learned the skill from a keeper in another town. From all accounts she was a canny woman." He smiled. "Of course, most of those accounts mention that in terms of being in league with the devil."

"There's that dark side thing raising its head again."

"The accounts I have to work with are mostly those kept by preachers and witch hunters. They don't paint a pretty picture, as you might imagine. They had to cover their backs after putting men and women to death."

Gritty stuff. "Um, so how did she die?"

"Do you like pasta?"

"I do, thank you. Are you avoiding my question?"

He went to a different cupboard, shuffled some things around, and brought out a bag of pasta. "She was ousted as a witch, strangled by rope, and then her corpse was burnt."

"Oh." Zoë felt a deep tug, like a well of pain being dredged inside her. She felt connected somehow, as if she was being told about a friend's demise. Grayson didn't seem altogether easy with that part of the story either, and went about his tasks silently for a while.

"It was the fate of many folk back then. Witchcraft was often used as a scapegoat in feuds. People were accused who weren't involved with the craft at all. Part of the job is trying to figure who was a member of the brethren and who wasn't." He lifted his wineglass, breathing in the aroma appreciatively.

"I take it that's a bit of a minefield?"

"Aye, that it is." He smiled at her, and the expression in his eyes was so warm and inviting, that she was immensely glad she hadn't left, and that she was here with him now.

With panache and ease, he set about cooking. While warming a pan on the stove, he crushed several cloves of garlic in his fist before chopping it finely, together with onions and peppers. Zoë watched, fascinated by him, as the vegetables sizzled in olive oil and he whisked up a quick sauce with passata and pepperoni. "I'm impressed by your skills in the kitchen. Do you live alone?"

"Yes I do, but I'm a typical bachelor, I can just about cope with the basic stuff." He winked. "You'll get no *cordon bleu* cookery from me, alas."

By the time the pasta was cooked, he'd flaked Parmesan cheese and torn a baguette into smaller hunks with his bare hands.

"My mother would have loved all this if she'd been alive," she commented, while he served the food, "all the talk of ghosts. She was much more into that kind of stuff than I am."

"She's not around?"

"No, she died in a car crash about three years ago. It's just Gina and me now. Gina is my sister, but she's married."

Gina would be proud of her, actually telling someone about their mother's death without being prompted into it.

His gaze was understanding. "It was just me and my dad for many years. He passed away when I was nineteen."

He fed the cat a tin of tuna before he served their food.

"Tuck in," he said, when he sat down on the stool alongside her. The steaming bowls of food on the breakfast bar in front of them smelled good, and she was hungry.

As they ate their meal, they talked. When their knees touched Zoë realized that they had turned to face each other. They were holding their dishes in their hands, just inches apart, as if magnetized. Along her thighs, the nerve endings tingled because of his proximity. She pressed her knees together when mischievous thoughts suggested she pull her legs apart and lean over to kiss him.

"You know what's bugged me most of all about this," he said, "is why Annabel is so close to the surface of the real world right now. She didn't haunt the place for years. But over the last year, year and a half, she's been increasingly visible. Sightings have been reported by several visitors. The psychic energy in the house is off the scale compared to six months ago."

This was all so new to her, but she was increasingly curious. "Any theories?"

"The only thing I can come up with is that it's to do with her physical anchor, the house. In a few more years the house will be uninhabitable, and then gone. Once she loses that anchor, she may not be able to surface so easily in our world."

"Oh, right, I see." The food was good, the wine was good, and the company was beyond good. Cat was back at their feet, purring and washing himself. As weird as the subject matter was to her, she wouldn't have changed it for the world. As she ate she glanced at the adjoining wall. "You said something about sensing the spirit, last night, or something."

"Yes."

"Can you sense it in here?"

"I'm aware of the activity, but it's not as easy to monitor on this side of the wall."

She was just about to ask how he measured the activity, when he continued on quickly.

"Are you worried about being in there alone?"

Immediately, she thought of sex, of having him with her. Her libido was on constant simmer since she had got here. Having him around would do that to a woman.

He paused and locked eyes with her. He knew what she was thinking, she was sure of it. Heat rose in her face and her gaze dropped. "Over the course of the day I realized I wasn't afraid of her as such, just…rather disturbed. I sensed no animosity in her. Really, it was kind of like she was curious about me, like she could really see me. Maybe she's like that with all the visitors."

He didn't respond.

"Why do some people become ghosts and others don't?"

"That's one of those eternal questions. It's open to interpretation, but the common belief is that if a person dies and is at peace with their lot, they pass on to their rightful resting place."

Did that mean her mother was at peace, Zoë wondered. It had to. She'd felt resentful about her death, the way it happened and the fact that she'd been too young, but now she felt somewhat reassured. If her mother was at peace, maybe she could be as well.

Grayson was still explaining. "It's a tormented soul who

lingers, someone who has an unresolved history, or an unjust end." He was looking at her intently. "The story goes that Annabel was ousted by a local woman who believed Annabel had put a curse on her family."

"I wonder if it was true."

"So do I." He wanted to know so badly.

"I felt something as soon as I arrived, actually. Funny, it never mentioned it in the brochure. But what would they say, 'cottage comes with own ghost'?"

He chuckled. "She likes you."

"Likes me?"

"Yes, the psychic atmosphere in there is up and bubbling, since you arrived."

"So what does being your research assistant involve?" She wanted to talk about the sex-in-the-atmosphere part again. "I've guessed that access to my holiday cottage is part of it."

"I knew you'd be a canny assistant."

"Hmm."

"A little bit of sleuth work." He shrugged lightly. "Annabel's spirit rises and lingers. If she's an unquiet soul, I'd love to know why, for the record. She's communicating with you, or at least she's trying to, so if you don't mind, I'd like to um, hang out with you."

"Do you use that line often?"

"What, I'd like to hang out with you because you're being haunted by a mischievous spirit?" His eyes twinkled. "No."

What was he going to say, that he shagged every woman who stayed here? Hardly. "I couldn't resist."

"I noticed."

"So what do we have to do? I mean, if we assume for the purposes of this discussion that I believe it."

"I'd like to give you a bit of background. I think it will help you understand her when she is around." There was something measured about the way he was talking to her that made her curious.

"Background?"

"About the craft, as Annabel and her people would have understood it."

"Okay, I can see why you teach the subject." She noticed that he was bemused, maybe even slightly embarrassed by that. He didn't have a huge ego, which was refreshing.

"The true essence of witchcraft is about being close to nature, about healing and wisdom, and about being in tune with the natural forces of the earth around us. It's a positive force, and pure in its intentions. But, much like any system in life, it is open to abuse. What tends to be reported more often is referred to as the occult, and that's where practitioners of the craft ally themselves with the dark forces in nature. They are drawn to what they see as more powerful sources, and that kind of magic is often driven by hunger for power." He paused. "You might have heard this referred to as the occult, or being in league with the devil."

"This is just background information, right. You're not trying to spook me right now, are you?"

He broke into a grin. It softened the bold angles of his face, making him more attractive than ever. "No, that's the last thing I want to do. Consider this—white witches are simply closer to nature than the average person. They continue practices that were widely accepted in the ancient pagan world—worshipping the seasons, the power and pull of the moon, the sun, and the cycle of birth, growth and death. They haven't lost that connection with the power and magic nature harbors. In the modern world we've become increasingly concerned with moving forward, technology, the synthetic and virtual worlds. Those things hold their own appeal, but they can pull us away from the forces of nature…if we let them."

"Is it like New Age beliefs?" Her mother had bandied about pagan theory and she had a heap of books on the subject, but most people called her a hippie, although it wasn't something her mother had particularly minded. Zoë always assumed she just wanted to be different.

"These kinds of practices are very close to each other. New generations need to reinvent things to make them theirs." He paused to smile. "The majority of witchcraft in Scotland is what today we would call Wicca, a pure creative and nurturing form of witchcraft that is very much in tune with the pagan way of life, but even Wicca is a fairly recent label for something very old. There's also a running pattern of belief about power and sexuality."

Sexuality. Just the way he said it made her body tighten with anticipation. "I take it this part ties in with what happened between us last night, about sensing the atmosphere?"

"Yes, it does." His response was steady, but he was looking at her as if he was savoring the memory of what had happened between them, as if he wanted to do it again.

She had to reposition herself on her seat, because her body responded so rapidly to the suggestion of having sex with him again. Casually crossing her legs, she wondered if she looked as keen as she felt. "Go on, you have my full attention."

He took a moment to respond, his gaze lingering on her. "Okay, we understand the part about the age-old, pagan belief that you can harness the power in the natural world?"

She nodded.

"That belief extends to the energy, the power, and the magic that is inherent in the act of sex."

She didn't doubt the power of it, that part was all too overwhelming last night. She'd never had sex quite like that before; she'd practically passed out afterward. His voice had gone low and soft when he said "sex," and she had no doubt that he was thinking about it as well. "So how does one get at this…power?"

"It's quite simple. It's the same as any natural power source, just like the power of the moon or the sun. Be open to it."

That easy, huh? She tried not to be skeptical.

"And when two or more people create it together," he continued, "it's an intense form of energy that is deeply connected to them."

Two or more? That made her think about the orgiastic dreams she'd had.

"It's a potent life force that can be harnessed in a psychic manner, if you know how."

She frowned. "Are you saying you're psychic, if you were able to sense that energy, last night?"

He took some time to respond to that one. "Let's just say I'm open to it."

Open to it, *as am I,* she thought. What was left of the food had been abandoned.

"Is it like tantric sex?" Someone in the office had recently been extolling the virtues of that one, she recalled.

"Tantric sex identifies the energy in a similar way, yes, but practitioners tend to focus on the sex act itself, or use the spiritual energy as part of a meditative cycle."

He lifted her hand in his and held it for a long moment. Her pulse raced. Then he bent and kissed her palm. "Tell me, what did you feel when I did that?"

It took a moment to put her brain back into gear, after the unexpected sensual offering. "The touch of your mouth, and then heat running over and under my skin, I guess."

"Like an energy force, yes?" He was looking up at her from where he was bent over her hand, and then he breathed along the inside of her wrist, offering her a whisper of sensation, powerfully erotic, nonetheless. "The more aware of the energy we are, the greater we can experience and adapt it."

Returning to her hand, he licked her palm. A shiver ran through her, right to her clit, and she exhaled loudly.

He looked at her with a question in his eyes.

She nodded. "I see what you're getting at." She swallowed, aware that her hips kept rocking backward and forward on the stool.

His gaze dropped. "What did your body do, when I licked your hand?"

Was talking about sex usually this sexy, she wondered? Had she ever even talked about it with a man, before? A man she was going to have sex with? "I got aroused, and my body gravitated to you, I suppose."

"Like a kind of magnetic energy, like so many natural forces—the tides, the phases of the sun and moon." He put both his hands on her stool and dragged it closer, positioning her knees inside his open thighs.

The bounce made her pussy want more of that kind of action. He rested his hands around her bottom, and leaned in for a kiss. Static seemed to cling to her face when he brushed his mouth ever so softly over hers, barely making contact. Every nerve ending in her body reacted, keyed up with anticipation, edgy and ready for the contact.

Moaning softly, she leaned into him, wanting it so much, needing it, until it was her that kissed him, and she put her hands around his head and drew him close, her back arched as she opened up to him.

He ran his hands up from her bottom and around her hips, to her waist, sensitizing her, making every part of her echo that electric connection of barely touching lips and the need that flared into life in its wake.

"See," he teased, when they drew apart, "now you're beginning to think about it, aren't you?"

Laughing breathily, she nodded, arching one eyebrow at him. "Pays to have a good teacher, I guess."

He was genuinely pleased. "Come on, let's go in to the back room and get more comfortable. I have more wine, and I can offer you ice cream."

Her libido wanted to play naughty. "You want to cool me down with ice cream?"

"Not in the least. I'd like to feed you the ice cream, though, if you are willing."

Naughty got naughty back, nice.

"And we can talk some more." He patted her on the bottom when she stood up. "Go ahead. I'll be right behind you."

The slow simmer made her feel warm all over, warm and happy. When she went into the sitting room she wandered over to the small desk that was stacked high with books. A laptop was perched on one end, a cold half cup of coffee next to it. She gravitated toward the leather-bound volumes teetering at the near end and lifted one. It had a faded blue-black cover. There was a raised pattern on the cover with traces of gold leaf, as if it had once been highly decorated and embossed, but had been worn away by the many hands opening the book. She could see no title.

A slim ruler bookmarked a page. She opened it. Dense black print covered the pages edge to edge. The pages were thick and yellowing compared to anything she might pick up to read herself, the edges of each sheet scalloped, as if the paper had been handmade. The language was old English and hard to follow.

Turning the pages carefully, she studied the illustrations. Several drawings seemed to depict tools, dubious looking they were, too. She flicked forward quickly, until she came to a rather badly drawn map of the area. The coastline wasn't quite accurate, but she could make out some familiar place names.

On the next page there was a line drawing of an old woman. A crone in rags, hunched and toothless. Only a few strands of long, straggly hair grew from her skull-like head, and her nose was hooked, her eyeballs loose in their sockets. The illustration bore Annabel McGraw's name.

Zoë's eyebrows lifted, and she couldn't hold back her amusement, laughing aloud. It didn't look a bit like her. Well, it didn't look a bit like the woman she'd seen in her mirror. Maybe that wasn't Annabel at all.

"Found something interesting?" Grayson was at her side, a glass of wine in each hand. He set them down on the desk and looked at the page she was examining. "Ah, our friend Annabel."

"Did she look like this? Do you know?"

"The historians who documented these stories at the time tended to be religious zealots who were convinced witches are evil and had to be burned out."

He spoke so calmly and rationally about things that should have been unnatural to her, and yet his bemused, seductive tone compelled her to believe.

"The tradition is to show the archetypal, ugly face of

evil, and it's meant to repel, to bring about fear in the reader. Whether it was true or not, we can only guess. Annabel died before she reached the age of thirty, however, so would she have looked like this?"

"Good point." Her curiosity was rising all the time. What was Annabel really like? So many stories, and yet there she was, in ghostly form, wandering around the house next door.

Grayson picked up Cat, who had followed him in. He carried him to the window at the back of the room, opened it and lifted the cat up to the windowsill so he could clamber through. Then he wandered off to the kitchen again, and Zoë stared back down at the drawing of the old crone. That wasn't what Annabel looked like. Although it was funny, it was kind of annoying that anyone would think she did look that way. Bit of a cheek, really.

Of course, being a gorgeous femme fatale didn't mean that she was a purehearted soul, and that was part of what was being portrayed here. What was she really like, Zoë wondered? As she did, her spine tingled. She ran a hand around the back of her neck, were she felt a rising sense of anxiety.

That's when she heard the voice.

Do you want to know me? Really know me?

The words whispered around her mind, low and enticing. Zoë tried to shake it off, but the question whispered around her mind again.

"She knows I'm curious," she said aloud, surprised, but fascinated, too. She couldn't deny it. She did want to know. Just as her mother had wanted to see and know a ghost, Zoë wanted to know more about the ghost that had shown itself to her. Even as she admitted that to herself, she felt dizzy, and reached for the edge of the desk. It didn't help. Her perception was shifting.

Look into my world, and know me.

Grayson would be back in a moment. She could hear him moving around next door. And yet she stared at the adjoining wall between this house and Her Haven, because the voice whispering around her mind compelled her to look, and learn.

She took a deep, steadying breath, and blinked. Right before her eyes, she could see it all, as if she were looking through the wall and into Her Haven—and into a different time altogether....

The preacher is here in Her Haven. Look and you will see him. Mean, lonely, and bitter with regret, he is here to tell me that his is the righteous path and I should be glad to follow it. And yet I do not see him holding the hand of the dying, or doing a good turn. He is too busy poking his beaky nose where it is not wanted.

He steps tentatively across my threshold, as if he might fall into hell if he treads wrongly, his wily eyes on me as he dares to enter into my kitchen. He doesn't have proof that I practice the craft, but he surely suspects it.

"I will have to continue with my chores while you visit with me, Reverend Slater," I state, annoyed. "I cannot leave the dough now." I busy myself again at the table. In truth I was expecting Ewan, and I want the dough on the baking stone in the fire before he arrives. But the preacher has called in order to do his duty and attempt to save my sorry soul from Satan's grasp.

It was the Reverend Slater who ousted a Carbrey witch before I came to the place, and I wager he relished the moment of her death, the rope that tightened around her neck and stole her last breath, and the smell of her burning corpse. I hate him for it. Every time I see him I want to curse him. I detest his beady eyes and his attempt to make me repent and be holy. Is it not enough that we have to sit in his cold, miserable church and appear pious, to avert attention from our secret craft? Every Sunday we do it, filing past the Rowan trees that he has had planted to ward us off. He watches, hoping to out us, and we smile and nod as we pass the trees by. I should laugh at his feeble efforts, yet it vexes me for I resent that sacrifice we make. Then Slater makes it worse still, for once a week he includes me in his visits.

I do not offer him a seat, but he takes one, warily holding his cassock in around him as though he will catch the pox if it were to touch anything. He even resents that he has to purchase candles for his church from me, and secretly travels along the coast for them.

"You would come to me freely if there was anything that you needed, Annabel, wouldn't you?"

What is it that he is getting at? "Of course, Reverend." I wonder if his eyesight is sharp enough to see the hazel and willow twigs I have hanging from the rafters, or the pouch of lodestones, ingredients for use in my enchantments. It does not worry me, for I could easily explain them away.

"I know you did not have such a good start in life, in Glasgee." He looks me up and down as if he can see the dirt from the gutter still clinging to the hem of my skirt. "You have a good chance here, you must make the most of it and keep yourself on the right path."

"I treasure my second chance, Reverend Slater. Never doubt that." I smile, probably a mite too smugly.

"You might consider dressing with more humility. Your attire is—" he pauses and mops his brow as he stares at my bosom "—wanton."

He wants me to wear a high collar and hide myself away, like a good spinster of his parish. 'Twill never happen.

"Shall I make you a dandelion brew," I say, "to aid your gout?"

His bald head jerks up, his beady eyes on me. "My gout? How do you know of it?"

"Women talk about such things," I say, lifting my shoulders. "Perhaps it was your housekeeper."

I see Ewan's tall figure pass the window and I brush my floury hands on my apron before I straighten my hair.

Ewan doesn't knock. The Reverend Slater looks at him suspiciously when he walks into the kitchen unannounced.

"Ah, greetings sire," I say to Ewan. "I expect you have come for your rent." I am Ewan's tenant, but it is not coins he is after.

Ewan is tall and dark, and today he wears his long coat open over a fine waistcoat. His hair is neatly tied with a ribbon at the nape of his neck. "Reverend," Ewan says, nodding in the preacher's direction. He stands by as if he has chores to undertake elsewhere, and the Reverend is keeping him from his rounds.

The Reverend climbs to his feet. "I'll be on my way. Thank you for the offer of the brew, Annabel. Another time, perhaps." He looks glad of the excuse to leave without imbibing any such brew, and he's rightly concerned, for if he had continued to preach at me I expect it might have given him a bad pain in his gut.

Ewan and I stare at each other as the minister slopes off, and when we hear the sound of door closing, Ewan smiles my way at last. "Keeping company with the minister now, Annabel? I can hardly leave you alone for a moment."

I put my hands on my hips, toss my hair back. "It was lucky for him that you arrived. I was sorely tempted to poison the ole' weasel for what he did to the woman they call Agnes."

Ewan's expression darkened. "That was long before you got here. You should not carry a grudge for her. We have our own people to watch over now. Besides, I have better things to do with my time than fret over the minister."

The look I see in his eyes tells me exactly what he has come for. Running my fingers along the top of my gown, over the bosom that the Reverend wanted me to hide, I watch Ewan as I reply. "What, even while the Reverend still walks along the lane?" I nod toward the shadow that is slowly passing by the window.

Ewan is beside me in a stride. Roughly he grabs my arms and

turns me to face the table where I have been kneading the dough. Bending me over it forcibly, he lifts my skirts and petticoats and his hand seeks my bare cunny.

"Even as he walks away, even as he might return, I will invade your body. I will think of his sermon about denying the flesh while I claim every part of your wicked body for my own, Annabel McGraw."

He runs his fingers up and down my slit. When his finger slips readily inside me he groans lustfully, and I feel his body stiffen at my back.

My face and hands are pressed against the table, my breasts squashed inside my tightly-laced gown. My hair is heavily coated with flour, but I am glad of it. "Take me Ewan, take me now, possess me."

I wriggle against his hand, eager to do as he suggests. He pushes another finger inside my entrance, testing me. I clutch at it, pushing back, inviting him in. A moment later he is there, squeezing his long, hard member into me, measure by measure. I swallow it up, wanting it all, wanting to ride it to slake my lust.

Latching my fingers over the edge of the table, I laugh when I hear it creak under the strain as Ewan rams his rod into me repeatedly, defying the pious old man who was here but a moment earlier. My feet lift from the floor and I squeal with delight.

Even while he rides me, he slaps my bottom until I yelp and leap at his touch, my bottom aflame. Then he explores me farther, inserting his thumb into my rear end and turning it.

"What if he were to see you now?" I cry out over my shoulder, laughing gleefully. "What would he think?"

He thrusts hard and then pulls out, directing his member instead to my rear end, pushing the slick head into my bottom, invading me in that tight, forbidden place.

I cry out. The skin on my back burns, my cunny clamping and reaching for his shaft, even though it is gone from there. My thighs *are wet and I peak when Ewan pushes his rod deeper still, claiming my forbidden place, filling it. I cry aloud, squeeze at my aching breasts with floured hands, my cunny awash with my juices.*

Ewan is about to spill. He ruts his member into me and holds me steady with his hands upon my hips, but still he baits me. "If he was here now, and he saw this, he would call you an evil whore for luring the town merchant with your sinful body and your insatiable lust."

"Yes, yes, he would," I cry, delighted by his words.

Ewan lets loose an animal sound and I feel him stiffen against me. Trapped, I wriggle and curse, for his rod is like a flaming hot poker and every part of me throbs and burns.

I cannot get enough of it, for this is what I am, a woman who wants to live and to feel and to ride the earth with fury and joy. This is what I am.

11

WHEN GRAYSON WALKED INTO THE BACK ROOM and caught sight of Zoë he put the ice cream down on the desk. Wisps of rose-hued light surrounded her. It seemed to swell and lift as if it were a living, breathing thing. The atmosphere around her was redolent with magic, as if someone had cast a spell over her. Was she in a trance? And, if so, who had done this to her?

She was breathing rapidly, her eyes focused in the distance. As he watched, her fingers clutched at the fabric of her shirt and her lips parted. He was reminded of the way she was last night, after they had made love on the staircase. He would have to waken her from the trance carefully because she was as vulnerable as a sleepwalker. Firstly, though, he wanted to see if he could locate the source of the magic.

He put his hand to the wall adjoining Her Haven. As soon as he did power shot through his arm from the house beyond. He looked back at Zoë. The light intensified. Curious. But he was glad it was associated with Annabel and the cottage next door, and not an external source. The night before, Annabel's presence was effervescent, nebulous, and brimming with excitement. A typical spirit unleashed from slumber. As such, it was difficult to get a grip on her intentions. It didn't seem as if she meant to harm Zoë. If he'd felt the least hint of that, he would advise her to leave the village and return to London immediately.

It wasn't a spell, ghosts couldn't cast spells from beyond the grave—well, not that he knew of. It had to be some kind of channel that Annabel had opened up to Zoë. Pretty determined she had to be about it, too, to traverse the space between Her Haven and the Cornerstone cottage. Why? Why was Annabel so powerful right now and what was it about Zoë that made her connect this way?

Closing his eyes, he felt his way around the images she was experiencing, in order to figure out their nature. A vivid cornucopia of sexual experience lay on the surface, but beneath that he sensed an uneasy layer of twisted intentions, jealousy and lies. He heard his name, and opened his eyes.

"Grayson?" Zoë's lips moved slowly, and it affected him strangely. Was it a dreaming whisper, or did she need help?

In his chest, a knot of concern grew. It was a risk, but he had to pull her out of the trance. Resting a kiss on her forehead, he held her gently around her shoulders, soothingly. "It's all right, I'm here."

Turning toward him, she gripped at the fabric of his T-shirt. She looked up, blinked, eyes focusing on him.

Whoa. Her mouth curved, her eyes darkening. The look she gave him hit him right in the solar plexus. Sexy lady.

"I think you were dreaming?"

She glanced quickly around the room, then her attention snapped back to him and she sidled up against him.

Her hands ran over his chest. She was aroused, deeply aroused. Her aura glowed with it, and her female scent called to him, keying into his desire for her so fast that his cock quickly grew hard in the confinement of his jeans.

Bending to kiss her lips, he couldn't help himself. Sexual desire had them both. He knew he should be checking on her, making sure she was all right, but for one crazy moment all he could think about was tasting and invading the sweet warmth of her mouth with his tongue, readying her for sex.

What had happened to her just then? Why was the psychic energy still palpable in the atmosphere? The questions forced him to pull back. "What happened, Zoë? Did you see Annabel?"

She moved against him, as if drugged by the attraction between them. Then her eyes flickered with recognition and she paused, pressing up against him, body to body.

"Yes, it was like a very vivid dream. I was standing over there." Gripping on to him with one hand, she pointed back at the desk. The book she had been holding had fallen on the floor. "I was looking at that picture of her, the one that we discussed. I was wondering what she was really like, and then I heard her voice." Unease flared in her. Her fingers went to her temples.

"Don't worry. I know it's strange, but you're not hearing things. Well, you are, but they really are happening. I know that it can be a really weird experience, but you're okay."

She gave a slow nod, listening to him as if cautious about her understanding. Her fingers gripped his T-shirt, and she was still provocatively aroused, but there was a sense of misgiving there that worried him.

"It was a dream, I suppose, but it was really vivid. She was in the kitchen in there." She nodded her head toward the adjoining wall. "There was a preacher, but after he had gone, there was another man. I saw him in a dream last night. He was wearing a cloak made of animal skin and his clothes were covered in blood."

A witch, a witch veering to the dark side?

She paused and stared directly at him, her voice faltering.

Grayson could see the pulse beating at the base of her throat. "There was sex?"

She nodded. "It was bloody hot stuff," she said, and gave a disbelieving laugh. "It was like an adult film rolling in my mind."

"How do you feel now?"

Her cheeks flushed. "A bit dizzy."

"Come on, you need to rest." As much as he wanted to do something entirely different, she was vulnerable. "You sleep in my bed tonight, I'll take the sofa."

"Oh."

The disappointment on her face almost made him change his mind, but he forced it back. This would have to wait until she was calmer. More importantly, it would have to wait until he was entirely sure that she was simply aroused by what she had seen and felt, and not acting under some other force.

Cain stood on the seafront outside the post office, breathing in the spiritual energy that was surfacing on the dark night air, his appetite for power growing. He'd returned to Carbrey to be where it had all begun, and in doing so he had given the village a project worthy of a strong coven, a goal. Until then they'd been mired in petty feuds and had no real focus. Not anymore. Not now that he was at the helm.

Necromancy and re-embodiment was no easy task, and his name and his coven would soon become synonymous with power amongst every practitioner of the craft. Then no one in this world would dare to call him "warlock" with spite and pity, for they would all be in his thrall.

The door to the post office opened and Crawford stood there, waiting. Cain stepped inside, nodding over at Elspeth. In the gloomy interior, he quizzed them about their progress over the course of the day.

"Zoë's turning, I'm sure of it," Crawford said. "She claimed she was doing tourist stuff, but I could sense the change. Something is surfacing in her. I didn't exactly feel Annabel's presence, but there was definitely a change there. It was fascinating to see."

Cain nodded. He'd found it irritating that he hadn't been able to see her today, but Crawford had reassured him. "And you say you will see her tomorrow?"

"Yes, I invited her to the dance at the pub and she seemed keen."

Cain looked at Elspeth. "And what about Murdoch?"

"She's spending far too much time with him." Folding her arms over her chest, she pouted. "We need to pull her away."

"We do need to bring her closer to our circle, yes." He pondered the situation. He'd done his best to shoo Murdoch back to Edinburgh, from whence he came, but Murdoch was a tenacious sort. No matter. He was a nuisance, no more. "Maybe it's not such a bad thing that Murdoch has her attention. As long as he doesn't pick up on what we are up to, he's keeping her entertained. She hasn't taken off. Perhaps we have him to thank for that." He smiled to himself. There was sweet justice in that.

"What if he does figure it out," Elspeth said, uneasily, "what if he figures it out and warns her off?"

"Can you put a stronger binding spell on her, tonight?" Cain asked. "I don't want her wandering off to Dundee again, or worse, heading back to London."

"Sure," Elspeth responded. "I'll need something of hers, something intimate, in order to make the spell stronger, but I can do that."

"Good. And unless Murdoch has the gift of second sight, which I don't believe he has, then he'll never find out what we're trying to achieve here. Our coven is sworn to secrecy. He'd be more likely to get the news from Annabel's lips than any of ours. By that time, it will be too late." He took a moment to savor that thought, imagining the look on Grayson Murdoch's face when Annabel was alive once more.

The clock struck the hour. Elspeth lifted the heavy velvet curtain at the back of the shop, led the way down the stairs and into the candlelit cellar. The space had been extended to run beneath the paved yard at the back of the building, and a skylight had been inserted there—a skylight that acted specifically as a moon-dial. When the moon hit a certain spot on the floor, it opened a portal into the world beyond.

They prepared quickly, donning their ritual cloaks and standing in place. Cain chanted the ancient language of black magic ritual. The requisite number of candles surrounded the circle, and when he nodded her way, indicating that he was ready, Elspeth wound a handle mounted on the wall. The blind that covered the skylight overhead folded back.

Moonlight flooded down onto the hallowed spot on the black marble floor, glinting off the silver pentangle painted there. Cain nodded at Elspeth again, indicating she should take her place. She moved to his left side. Crawford stood at his right, eyes glittering with anticipation within the shadow of his hood, and held out his offerings.

Cain flicked through the photographs. They'd been taken of the Londoner while she was in Dundee. "Nice work," he commented. He liked the expectant look in her eyes; that reflected what Crawford had said.

Crawford passed him something else, a silver earring.

"Perfect." Lifting his hands, Cain breathed deeply and began to speak in the ancient tongue, his voice ringing out across space, time and worlds. This was a crucial turning point. The three of them closed in, raised their hands until they were almost touching, and stared down at the pentangle. Then they waited, barely daring to breathe while the atmosphere shifted.

An icy chill flooded the room. The candles flickered.

Moonlight gathered within the pentangle, whirling in on itself. Cain thrust his hand into the passage of the moonlight. It condensed into the black jet ring he wore and then speared out from its center, creating a living symbol between them.

"The portal is open." He felt the power surge through his hand and into his body. His heart raced with the thrill of it. Elspeth lifted her head, her hood falling back, her hair spilling over her shoulders. Certainty bedded within them all.

Cain chanted the words from the forbidden book as he dropped the photographs one by one into the center of the pentangle, followed by the earring. The objects disappeared into the whirling portal at its center.

"For the soul of one Annabel McGraw," he stated, his eyes closing, power and redemption almost within his reach.

Annabel Annabel, my precious Annabel. How he longed to

have her in his arms again—to touch her, hold her, mate with her as they once did. *Soon, soon it would be so.*

The knowledge of that fact burned within him, and he felt as if the world was within his grasp. Uniting with a resurrected Annabel would not only return her to him, it would seal his destiny as the most powerful coven leader of all time. Together they would create unprecedented magic. Together they would live forever.

12

ZOË AWOKE IN THE EARLY HOURS AFTER A restless sleep spent tossing and turning and clutching at the pillows. Being in Grayson's bed, alone, was not a good situation. Drawing her knees up toward her chest, she squeezed her thighs together. Arousal had her in its grip and she wondered why on earth she had agreed to sleep alone. The pillow that she had clutched to her face held a breath of his cologne. Being in his bed, where he slept, naked and alone, was surely making this raging lust worse—then there were the dreams.

Once again they'd been torrid, filled with images of bacchanalian sex. Thankfully the dreams hadn't been as real as the vision she'd had earlier, that had amazed her. No, the dreams were about the forest. Again. In her dream, she'd weaved between the trees and come upon a dozen people, maybe more, gathered around a fire. Someone was playing a musical instrument and the group was divided into twos and threes. Images flashed through her mind. A man on another man's back, buggering him. A woman sitting astride one man while she sucked the cock of another who stood next to her, holding his rigid cock out for her attentions.

A shiver ran through her. If she went there, to the forest, she would know why she saw these things, she felt sure of it. Something was calling to her, and she wasn't afraid. Twenty-four hours had made a difference. She wanted to embrace this experience; it was her adventure. Smiling to herself, she contemplated the fact that she might have got a better night's sleep alone in her own cottage, ghost and all. Then she remembered the vision she'd had in the bathroom the day before, and thought that perhaps wasn't the case. That was Annabel's doing, she was sure of it. But—oh, boy—had it ever been good. She'd wanted Grayson from the moment she'd seen him, and as soon as she'd walked into the cottage and Annabel had keyed into that, she'd given her the most intimate erotic show she could possibly wish for. Spooky as hell at the time, but now it felt like a gift.

Zoë couldn't wipe the smile off her face. She rolled onto her back and thought about the way he'd looked as he took his cock in his hand and jerked off, nice and slow, totally male, totally hot. And it had been real, she knew that now. She hadn't imagined it at all.

What she really wanted was to be in that shower with him, stroking his cock for him. She imagined it in her hands as her fingers stole into the heated spot between her thighs. The thought of soaping his erect cock and milking it off, nice and slow, while she studied his face, made her clit throb, and she thrummed it until she reached climax.

Sighing wistfully, she rolled closer to his pillow again, breathing in his scent. It wasn't enough. She was still horny, and her sense of decorum had given up and checked out long ago. She sat up in the bed and watched the waning moonlight filter through the curtains. Was it simply because of the attraction she felt for Grayson, or was Annabel watching her now, egging her on?

Where do you end and I begin? she wondered, as she considered the ghost's influence on her. She was ready to admit that things wouldn't be this way if Annabel weren't involved. On the one hand she felt she should thank her. On the other…

It wasn't that she disliked the situation, in fact she welcomed it. It all just felt a bit strange. Rather like driving a car and yet having someone reach across occasionally and take the controls, forcing the speed up and dodging other vehicles.

It wasn't as if she'd done anything that she wouldn't have wanted to do anyway. It was more like her fantasies were attainable, because of Annabel's influence. It was exciting and scary, and it made her feel edgy and dangerous. It was also hellishly confusing. Even as she stepped out of bed and walked to the top of the stairs, she looked down and wondered if she was dreaming now. And yet deep down she knew that she'd be standing here under her own steam if the situation had been like this and Annabel hadn't been involved, because she wanted Grayson.

She was deeply attracted to him. He was down there and she knew he was interested in her. Okay, so his motivation for pursuing her was a bit muddy, because of the research angle. But she knew that if she went down there, they would have sex. There was no doubt in her, and that's where the difference lay. The Zoë Daniels who'd arrived from London might have had a doubt. Her confidence may not have been quite so buoyant, and she might not have been willing to risk going down these stairs with the intention of finding him, being with him. But the Zoë Daniels who had come into contact with the mischievous spirit next door was all too willing.

"I welcome you, Annabel," she whispered. As she did, a sense of female power rose steadily inside her, an erotic vapor that made her slink and purr and move her body like a harem dancer. Every bit of her thrummed with life and vitality. From her plump pussy to her womb and the heavy, peaked weight of her breasts, every inch of her felt opulent and feminine. She ran her hands over her body, reveling in its fluidity, its heat and energy.

I am woman.

She stepped down the narrow stairs and rounded the banister in the hallway. All was quiet. She tiptoed across to the sitting-room door and peeped inside.

Grayson was laid out at full stretch on the sofa, and he was asleep. His clothes were strewn on the floor nearby. Taking a slow, deep breath, she put one hand up against the door frame, and took in the sight. What a picture of male beauty it was, too.

He was naked, and Zoë's hand went to her throat, her pulse pacing up as she admired his physical form. The faux fur throw that had been across the back of the sofa earlier that evening was now laying over his hips and covered most of one leg. The other long muscular thigh was bare. The room was softly lit by lamplight and a book trailed from his hand to the floor, as if he'd been reading when he fell asleep. In repose, his features looked almost classical, much less rugged than when animated. The long, old-fashioned sofa seemed to frame him to perfection. If she hadn't already been in a state of arousal, looking at him lying there like that would have had her there in an instant. As it was, the nagging ache inside her had turned into a roaring inferno of expectation.

She stepped closer, close enough to see the dusting of dark blond hair that traced a symmetrical line from his chest down to his navel and beyond, where it disappeared under the throw. Her fingers itched to pull the cover back, so that she could see his cock and admire it while he slept. The bulk of it made a shape in the fur, and the thought of running her hand over that fur-covered outline sent a sensuous shiver deep within her core. On their first encounter, the night before, circumstances hadn't allowed her time to admire the view, and now her curiosity and desire were conspiring to get the better of her.

Leaning forward, she went to lift the throw.

His hand closed around her wrist, locking in her place. "Something I can do for you, Zoë?"

She gasped, startled, and yet secretly thrilled. His eyes were narrowed as he looked at her, and she saw concern there. After he'd studied her for a long moment, that concern morphed into humor, and passion. Had he even been asleep? Perhaps he'd heard her getting up and was waiting for her to appear.

As if to confirm that suspicion, he pulled her closer still. Her body tightened, the knowledge that she was going to get what she needed firing her up even more.

"Yes, there is something…" She was a mere two inches from his lips, and she closed the gap, kissing him, her hand closing over that fur-covered erection even while he held her wrist.

His cock grew and lifted under her hand, poking up from beneath the cover, as if eager to be held. Her hand moved, closing around the hot, velvety skin of his shaft.

Breaking the kiss, he inhaled a ragged breath, his hand tightening on her wrist.

Looking into his eyes and seeing the reciprocated desire

that shone there, Zoë knew that something had been let loose in her. It was as if every barrier had been stripped away and she was free to climb on and enjoy. He shifted, giving her room to kneel either side of his hips. She climbed over his thighs, one knee either side of him, and threw her head back, reveling in the sense of liberation she experienced as she stroked the upright cock in front of her.

His hands roved over the outline of her hips, and then reached up and ran his fingertips over her nipples. Although he barely touched them, her breasts burned from her nipples to her center.

He watched her as she explored his cock, and his mouth moved in a slow smile. "Do you think we can make it to the bed?"

She laughed breathily, her heart pounding, and then shook her head. "No."

The intimate connection he'd made with her felt special and it made her sure. "I hope you have a condom."

He reached out across the floor and snatched at his jeans, pulling them closer. With one hand, he held them up, the other rooted around in the pocket.

She lifted and lowered over him while she waited, showing him what she wanted. When she took a deep breath it came out shakily. Moving her fingers to her clit, she rubbed it, desperate for relief. Heat traversed her groin and her clit was pounding. Her mouth went dry.

His glance dipped to where she was masturbating. "I could watch you doing that all night long," he commented, and rolled the condom over the head of his cock.

Through her erotic haze, she experienced a vague sense of self-awareness. She'd never masturbated in front of a man before, and yet she hadn't even thought about what she was doing. Instinct had her in its grip. The last trace of self-awareness whispered away from her consciousness as she watched the way he rolled the rubber down the length of his cock, and when his fist was at the base, securing it, he used his thumb to direct it toward the place where she was rubbing herself.

All logical thought was gone.

Splaying her pussy lips with her fingers, she took his offering, rubbing her clit against the solid shape of his cock head. A sudden and almost serene climax hit her. Her head dropped forward and she reached out for him as she struggled for breath. He grabbed her hands, meshing his fingers with hers, holding her steady.

"Go slowly," he whispered, when she lifted up, eager to take him inside. She bit her lip, forcing herself to pause. He had a determined look in his eye.

"Any particular reason why?" she managed to ask.

He squeezed her hands where they were meshed with his, and the look in his eyes was commanding. "Because I want to watch you, and I want to savor every moment of this."

Pleasure burned in her. Hot liquid ran down her thigh. The need she felt was overwhelming. Moving forward, she let go his hands and eased the head of his cock inside. It pushed into her opening, stretching her, and how good that felt. Inch by inch, she lowered herself down, until he was thrust upright inside, filling her until her womb buoyed up and her entire groin was suffused with heat and pleasure.

"Don't move," he whispered, "stay right there." He touched her breastbone, gently running his nails down between her breasts, over her abdomen.

She moaned under the brusquely seductive contact. It sensitized the surface of her skin, making the heat from inside her leap to the surface and race over her entire body like a raging fever.

His fingertips moved on and down, until they came to rest over her mons. Touching her gently, tantalizingly, he squeezed the plump, sensitive cushion of her mound. Her tenderized clit went wild. She wanted to move, to lift and grind down on him, hard. Instead, she dropped her head back and opened her mouth, moaning aloud to allow some of the tension to escape her.

When he moved his hands, it only made it worse.

"Oh, Grayson. Please?"

"Hush," he responded, gruffly. "It's only because I want to learn my way around you." His gaze held hers.

His words made her feel treasured. And then his cock pulsed fiercely inside her, reminding her that he was holding back, too.

The soft stroke of his hands against the inside of her thighs made her desperate, and she tossed her hair from side to side. Leaning forward, she raked her fingers down his chest to where their hips met, awed when the muscles of his abdomen rippled beneath her fingers. The power contained there made her clutch the hard length inside her. Leaning forward like that, his cock arched inside her and pressed her sweet spot.

"Got to move." She rocked her hips back and forth, molding his cock inside her.

Grayson's head went back against the arm of the sofa, his eyes narrowed, his chin lifted, his chest rising and falling. "You feel so good," he breathed.

Hearing him say that made her reach out for his hands, and they meshed fingers again.

He nodded his encouragement, and she lifted up and sank down. He stretched the walls of her sex as she rode him, over and over again, the crown of his cock pressing deep against her cervix, making her womb feel heavy. Pure, undiluted pleasure washed over her, the rush making her high. She laughed, joyously, throwing her head back and riding his willing cock until her sex was on fire, and deep spasms of release ran through her core.

"Oh, yes, you look very beautiful when you come," he whispered, then let go one of her hands, and moved his fingers to the place where they joined, nudging her clit with one knuckle, until she came again, a succession of blissful peaks rolling together inside her.

She was lost to it, clutching and grinding on him until he groaned loudly and his body bowed up under her. His chest expanded and the muscles in his arms roped as he clutched her thighs and his cock exploded inside her.

Panting for breath, her body slick with sweat and her inner thighs damp with her juices, she buckled and fell forward into his waiting arms.

"Are you sure you don't want me to come with you?" Crawford asked.

Elspeth shook her head and glanced over at Her Haven. She didn't need any help. She was psyched, and she was dressed for a bit of stealth work in black leggings and a sweatshirt. "I'm the official key holder. If I get caught in the house I have a good reason."

He rested his arm around her shoulders. "Be careful, Elsie."

She smiled. He called her that when he teased her. They'd known each other since primary school, when she really had been Elsie, little Elsie McGraw.

"I'm not afraid of Grayson Murdoch."

"I know you're not, but maybe we should be a bit more cautious. Maybe we should be…content." He peered at her in the gloom.

"Content?" They'd had this discussion before. As far as she was concerned, Crawford had a lack of ambition. He was always the first to volunteer when it was about rituals and sex, but in other areas he could be lazy. "You'd be happy to potter along like the Abernathy coven, I suppose, with their craft shops and their nursing jobs, using their other powers for local do-gooding?"

"Who are we to criticize the way the neighboring covens function?" His eyebrows were drawn down.

She gave a derisive laugh.

"This is important, yes," he added, "it's a test of what we can achieve as a coven. But do you ever stop to think about the fact it's tantamount to murder?"

She folded her arms across her chest. "Zoë won't be dead, she'll just be…different."

"A hell of a lot different," he muttered.

"Most activities associated with witchcraft would be seen as illegal by normal folk."

"Yes, so would breaking an employee's arm."

"Isla deserved it. Besides, he healed her the next day."

"She was in agony all night. None of us had the power to do anything about it except him, and he ignored her."

"He was teaching her a lesson."

Crawford shook his head.

"Don't get all righteous on me now, Crawford, I need to be focused on my task."

He folded his arms across his chest, but didn't respond.

Clouds flitted across the night sky. When the moon was obscured, she took her opportunity to end the discussion, and kissed his cheek, waving him off as she darted along the street.

Outside the door, she paused and made sure he was gone, and then inserted the key into the door. She crept inside, shutting the door quietly behind her. The cottage was in darkness, and she had the annoying feeling that Ms. Zoë Daniels was not where she was supposed to be. That wasn't much good to her, when she was about to try to cast a binding spell on her while she slept. Crawford seemed convinced that she was going to stay around, but that would be his ego talking. By all accounts she'd been responsive to him, but Elspeth had caught sight of her stomping off across the cliff path that afternoon and wasn't so easily convinced. The only way to be sure was to bind her to the house, much as Annabel was.

Pausing in the hallway, she took note of the amount of psychic energy in the cottage. Putting her hand to the wall, she felt it racing across the surfaces. Her hands glowed, the energy throbbing in her veins. She shivered with delight but pressed on, eager to get her job done. She'd never seen the cottage quite so active, and it was a good sign.

She crept up the stairs, and drew to a sharp halt when she walked through an area of intense sexual energy on the staircase. It plumed inside her pussy, instantly making her want to bump and grind. Glancing around the spot she could see the phosphorus magic lingering in the atmosphere. Lust mounted inside her. She pressed on. If she didn't have something else on her mind, she'd have stopped to take advantage, but she could see to that later.

As suspected, there was no one in the bedroom. The bed was unmade and clothes were strewn across the floor from a suitcase. Where was Zoë? Had she seen the ghost and been spooked off? Elspeth already knew she hadn't moved to the B&B, nor she was staying at the Silver Birch. Her car was still outside. There was only one possibility—she was next door with that bastard, Murdoch.

She had to be sure, which was annoying. She didn't even

want to see Grayson Murdoch again so soon, let alone find out what he was up to with their guest. She was still smarting over the way he had humiliated her this morning. His attitude set her teeth on edge. How dare he come onto their patch and act that way? Luckily his boundary spell only covered the four walls, not the patch of garden at the back of his house. Or at least it hadn't done so the last time she'd climbed over the wall into his garden to get a peek through the window. Cain had sent her to find out what he was up to. Working on his laptop, mostly. There was also the fact that he looked so bloody hot strolling around stripped to the waist and barefoot. That alone kept her checking on him whenever he stayed here. If it weren't for the fact that he was the enemy, she'd have been interested for an entirely different reason.

Before she left, she picked up a bra that was lying near the suitcase and stuffed it into her pocket to use in a stronger binding spell. Then she tried to sense Annabel's spirit. The sexual energy on the stairs might be from one of her manifestations, or maybe their holidaymaker had a wild side. If that were the case, Zoë was even more appropriate a host for Annabel than they had originally thought.

Elspeth pursed her lips, wondering—as she often did—why it was that Annabel had never appeared to her. With them being bloodline and all, it seemed like it would be a given. That hadn't proved to be the case, which was disappointing—not to mention an embarrassment in front of the rest of the coven, several of whom sniggered at her behind her back about it. There had to be a good reason for it, and she certainly didn't want to probe into the subject too much in case Cain suggested that she herself become the vessel for Annabel's resurgence. There were a couple of times when she knew he'd been considering it—something about the way he looked at her gave it away—and she'd become wary. Dabbling in necromancy held its own thrill, and having Annabel around would liven things up no end, but she wasn't prepared to give up her own life for Annabel's. So, she'd proved herself indispensable in her own right and Cain had shifted his effort to acquiring someone with no connections. A blank slate, as he called it.

Retracing her path, she left the house and jogged back up Shore Lane until she came to a gap between the rows of houses. The alleyway that let down to the back gardens was dark and cobbled, but she knew it well. She passed by the walled gardens at the back of the houses, until she got to the creaking iron gate that led into the back of Her Haven. She skirted the garden furniture on the patio, peering over the wall at the house beyond. The lights at the back of Cornerstone were on. Using the ledges on the old bee bole as footrests she climbed up onto the wall between the two gardens, and then paused, squatting low, hands on the top of the wall for balance.

No boundary spell around the wall. Nettles grew tall against the other side of the wall, and they were even bigger than on her previous visits. Murdoch let them grow on purpose, she was sure of it. The rest of the garden was reasonably well tended, but the nettles were here to deter intruders. There was no other way into the garden, though. It was completely walled. She looked up at the bedroom. There was a dim light there, but there was also light on the ground floor, and that one was much more interesting to her because even from the garden she could see that it shifted and pulsated with energy.

Tensing, she levered off her perch and sprang out from the wall, aiming at the ground beyond the weeds. She made contact with the grass, but rolled backward on landing. Nettles brushed the back of her neck. Cursing Murdoch, she clambered to her feet. As she did, she heard a low growl and a hiss emerged from the border shrubs.

Light glinted off a pair of feral eyes.

"Shit." Ground level was covered by a new boundary spell. She wasn't willing to leave, but she had to get back up to wall level, and fast. Darting across the small lawn, she clambered onto the coalbunker that stood against the whitewashed wall of the cottage.

"Please, please," she chanted, willing the spot to be out of the boundary. Fuck knows what that bastard had lined up for intruders. What she could see of it looked like a very large version of that cat of his, and it was prowling around beneath the coalbunker, ears back, hissing. Her heart thundered in her chest and she watched as the thing prowled and then sat down, lazily washing itself right under the spot where she perched.

Okay, so it wasn't going to hurt her, but it wasn't being friendly either, and if it made any more noise it would alert Murdoch to her presence. She scratched at her neck, where the nettle stings were taking hold. Her shoulders slumped. Getting back was going to be interesting. She would have to cause some sort of distraction to gain enough time to get back across the lawn and vault over the wall.

When she straightened up she put her back against the wall and moved as close to the edge of the bunker as she could, so that the window was at her side. Making sure she stayed in the shadows, she turned her head and looked inside.

Zoë was in there all right, and from where Elspeth was observing she had a prime view of the Londoner's shapely arse as she rode up and down on the man she was straddling. She was completely naked, and Elspeth got a good look at the other woman's body for the first time. It was fuller and curvier than her own, soft and feminine. The globes of her arse just begged to be cupped and squeezed and what she could see of her breasts bobbing looked pretty good, too.

Each time Zoë lifted she leaned forward and Elspeth caught sight of the rather impressive erection that Zoë was riding. Elspeth's libido was still on standby after being next door, and getting an eyeful of the live sex show going on here made her hand dip between her legs, where she begged for relief. She moved her hand in time, her clitoris throbbing. If it had been anybody else she might have thought of an excuse to knock at the door and try to join in. The man she was riding meshed his hands with Zoë's, suggesting intimacy. They didn't look as if they needed company, which was a shame. She squeezed her pussy harder, until the sting in her tender clit surpassed the less pleasurable sting she felt on her neck. Craning her neck to see farther into the room, she scored confirmation that it was Grayson.

That familiar blond hair of his was just visible from her sidelong viewpoint. He was a beautiful man, and for one lonely moment she let regret well inside her. She'd flirted with him when he first arrived. She told herself it was a means to an end, but she did long for a man of her own, somebody who stood tall and proud like Grayson Murdoch.

He'd ignored her advances. In fact, he'd been wary around everyone. She hadn't known him to sleep with anyone here in Carbrey, not even a tourist. Until now.

The mystery surrounding him intrigued her. Why couldn't she have a man like that? Perhaps she was too close to Cain, because that certainly did put other men off. She couldn't blame them. And she was already growing weary of Cain's obsession with Annabel. They could have been good together, but deep down she recognized that she did not love Cain. If love even existed, she thought, sadly, as she peered into Grayson Murdoch's home, watching the way he looked at the woman who was now lying down over him, resting over his chest and shoulder in her post-coital bliss.

Turning her head away, Elspeth rested back against the wall and rubbed her pussy through her leggings, hard and quick, until she climaxed. Sometimes lust was a nuisance. Not very often, it had to be said. There were few things she loved more than sex, but right now a case of the burning hotties was an inconvenience.

When she looked back, Grayson's cock was no longer erect. It lay fat and large against his groin, rubber sheathed. He stroked Zoë's thick dark hair, holding her safely on top of him on the narrow sofa. Jealousy blurred her vision and she blinked, craning her neck to look farther into the room.

As she did she saw Grayson reach out with one hand to capture some of the phosphorus light that spangled around them.

Making magic, now? What was he up to?

Unwillingly, she became mesmerized by the way his hand moved through the atmosphere. He rested his closed fist against his mouth, and then lifted it into the air, his lips moving silently.

When he opened his hand the light shifted, hovering aloft in a gauzelike shape. He pointed at the window and then she realized what he was doing, too late. The square of light smacked up against the glass, white and reflective, blocking her view.

"Shit!"

Flattening against the wall, her cheeks flaming, she watched as the feral eyes below her lit up in anticipation.

He'd seen her, and she now had seconds to get across the lawn, if that. Bracing herself for nettle stings and fuck knows what else, she launched off the coalbunker as fast as she could.

13

THE DAY STARTED ODDLY FOR ZOË. EVEN though she awoke in Grayson's arms, it was with a vast sense of confusion—that feeling of not knowing where her dreams ended and reality began. Not only that, but she had a major niggle. It popped into her head as soon as she awoke—she'd forgotten to go back and pay her bill at the Tide Inn. That so wasn't like her—she was usually so organized and on the ball. She shot out of bed and pulled on her clothes, trying to ignore the great hunk of sex appeal unfolding in the bed behind her.

"I'll go up there for you," Grayson insisted, when she explained what she was doing.

He got up and hunted for his own clothes.

"No way. It'll only take me a few minutes and then I'll be back to do whatever research assistants do." Get into Her Haven, she assumed. Still, she'd be with him, she thought, admiring him again. And she could grab a shower and a change of clothes then. Right now she needed to pay that bill; it was weighing heavily on her all of a sudden and she simply had to get up there to the restaurant and sort it out. She reached up to give him a kiss and saw that his expression was tense. She didn't like the feeling that gave her.

When she headed to the door, he got very heavy-handed about the fact that he wanted to come along, asking her to wait and he would come with her.

"What's the problem?" she asked. "I don't need to be supervised. In London I keep a whole company of solicitors on their toes. This may be new territory, but, believe me, I can cope." She winked at him.

"I know." He ran his hand through his hair and she realized he was agitated. "I'm sorry." He forced a smile. "I just enjoy being with you. I'll tidy up and get us some breakfast." He paused. "If you're not back here inside a half hour, I'll be checking up on you." He cupped her face in his hands and kissed her.

Her hands went to his hips and she thought about the night before, how it had felt mounting his hard, strong body and sitting on his wonderful cock. What a rush. She sank into him for a moment, and then had to pull away, laughing. "I won't be long," she reassured him. "I just hate owing anybody money."

When she left he stood in the doorway of the cottage for a moment, but when she looked back he'd gone inside. Just as well, or she would be back there and clambering all over him. She wanted him, but she had to pay this bill. It was nagging the hell out of her for some reason.

The tide was out, and she crossed the road to the water, looking over the sea wall at the algae-covered rocks that were exposed. The heron that she'd spotted the day before was standing out on the last of the rocks, looking out to sea. He looked rather like a watchman. What was he waiting for, his mate?

When she reached the marina she glanced back at Her Haven and Cornerstone, then she stopped walking and stared back at the two cottages. They were so closely pressed side-by-side at the end of the Lane, upright and brave in the face of the elements. It struck her as poignant and fitting, and her mind flooded with images of what she'd done, how she'd pounced on Grayson in the middle of the night. Being here was making her more sexually expressive.

Are you really making me like you, Annabel?

Grayson had suggested Annabel's spirit affected people, and she welcomed that. Then there was that whole sex magic thing that he'd opened her mind to. Could it be true?

It was a curious notion, and she laughed softly. The sound of it lifted in the atmosphere and wrapped itself around her, lilting in the sea breeze. The dreams she'd had, the sensual images she'd seen, and that strange vision the night before, felt like a gift. Were they? Taking a deep breath, she reveled in the way she felt, sexually empowered. God knows, she had fantasies aplenty, but something about being here was enabling her to act on them.

Turning to face the sea, she rested up against the railing and looked over at the marina where the boats bobbed. The wind lifted and as it passed through the masts and tied-up mainsails it created a low and eerie sound, almost as if it were a lonely voice calling out amongst the boats. And yet all of a sudden Zoë didn't feel alone. She stared along the jetty, where the boats bobbed and gulls swooped low over the harbor. A curious feeling stole over her, and it ran alongside the contentment she had been nurturing, making her feel excited, edgy, and keenly aware of her surroundings.

Can you see him yet?

The question whispered around her mind, as if the breeze was carrying a misplaced sound. She took a quick, deep breath, snatching for the metal railing that ran along the marina to steady herself. Surely Annabel wasn't with her? She was too far away from the house, wasn't she? The wind whipped up around her, a sudden gust. The clouds moved faster across the sky. Her vision shifted and blurred, and she blinked, her fingers gripping onto the cold metal railing ever tighter. She shook her head, disbelieving. Annabel was here; she sensed her as if she were standing alongside her. She was with her even now, away from the house at the end of Shore Lane.

I want you to see him.

There it was again. Zoë swayed, her stomach tensing. Try as she might, she couldn't stop staring down at the marina.

Look harder. He is standing over there and he is looking this way.

Zoë felt excited, but a little afraid, too, and she wanted to turn away and close her eyes, but she couldn't, because she was compelled to watch, and as she did her perception of what was around her shifted dramatically.

The modern purpose-built marina that was usually crowded with swish boats was no longer there. Instead she saw a small clutch of simple boats pulled up onto a bank of pebbles and shale, and a crowd of people standing at the shore's edge as the boats were unloaded. And while Annabel's words whispered around her mind, Zoë could see exactly what Annabel wanted her to see; she could see it all….

He's tall, the man I desire, the tallest of the Carbrey fishermen. I can see him standing there amongst them, a good head above the other men while they work together bringing the mornin' catch ashore. They are laughing and jolly, for 'tis a good time of year for the herring. The lines are full and hopping, and they will fill their purses and their bellies.

Many of the villagers are gathered at the shore's edge, the fishermen's wives and their bairns. Ewan is there as well, his hat pulled low over his brow as he watches the men work. I notice how the buckles on his shoes gleam, as do the buttons on his frock coat. I wonder how I would feel if it was me who had polished them for him, as his wife. It cannot be, because of my beginnins' in this world. Instead, he has a servant to do such tasks, and I warm his bed only when he wants me to.

In his hand he holds a purse heavy with coins. He is ready to buy the best of the catch, to preserve and sell on. The wives watch eagerly, anticipating a good codling supper and some of Ewan's pennies for their purse.

I shouldn't go down there, there's no excuse, but I cannot help myself. I like to look at this one fisherman when he's celebrating the catch. I could watch from my window at the cottage, but I want to be close enough to see his smile and the sweat on his brow. So I am here, even though I know trouble could come of it. Ewan warns me often enough that I will be undone by my rebellious streak. I am contrary. It is the way I am, and I cannot help it.

I walk down the slippery stone steps, and then try to approach quietly, but the shale shifts under my shoes. Some of the children gathered by their mother's skirts turn to look at me. Ewan finishes counting out coins, taking the best of the herring for hanging and salting. He orders a young lad to carry his crate off, and then looks over. I nod his way, and he considers me for a moment before lifting his hat in my direction. In the pit of my belly, I cannot help savoring our secrets. I know what he's thinking—go home, Annabel—but I cannot help myself.

Then Irvine Maginty lifts his head and I forget Ewan for several long moments, because Irvine looks straight at me, and he *stares that hungry, silent stare that I have seen him give me before, the one that makes lust gather into a rolling, rollicking storm inside of me, for I want to take this man and make him my own.*

Irvine Maginty. Who would have thought that he would make me want him so? He fascinates me; I cannot deny it. He came here to Carbrey the previous autumn to make Hettie Shaw his bride. Hettie first met him when she visited her cousins along the coast. I hated her for marryin' him, and yet if she had not, he would not be here now.

With thick, red-brown hair, and eyes the color of chestnuts, he is a fine man. His skin is sun-kissed from his time out in the boat. He's strapping and healthy, and the sight of his strong arms makes me hanker for a taste of him. I want to be locked in his embrace, to wrap myself around him and to welcome his length inside me.

I could easily have him, and I do not want to resist. I want him, and I will have him.

Clutched in my hand is a pendant I crafted. It holds a lock of his hair that I snipped from his handsome head the evening before, while he was slumbering over a tankard of ale at the inn. With it I have cast my spell, and the pendant will act as my charm, drawing his attention to whatever it is I wish. When he stares at me across the crowd, I press my hand to my bosom. When I see that his gaze is drawn there and his lips part I'm quickly afire, delighted because my spell is clearly working on him. With effort I hold back the smile that rises inside me and move my hand lower, so that it presses on the front of my dress, over the spot where my womb simmers and my cunny is hot and needy for the thrust of his rod there.

He drops the heavy basket he holds. I cannot withhold a happy sigh. The man at his side punches Irvine's shoulder, laughs a hollow laugh. Irvine looks confused, and then bends to pick up the basket and the scattered fish. That's when I glance away, and I notice that Ewan's eyes are on me. He has not noticed the enchantment I am unfolding. In fact there is a look in his eye that makes me smile his way. Around him, the women huddle together and whisper, wondering why I have come. A dog howls, and the children are restless. Reverend Slater is there amongst them, too, and he peers at me with his beady eyes.

I want to laugh aloud. The air crackles, and it's as if a storm has landed upon us. Perhaps it has. My blood quickens at the thought. When I look his way, a wee lad gurns and weeps into his mother's skirt. The mother sends an angry glance in my direction. Still, I cannot stop. Is it the idle, lonely hours that drive me to do such things, to quicken my blood?

"What is it you want here, Annabel?" It is old Molly Shaw, Hettie's mother.

"To see the catch." The catch would be out on the marketplace later, but I didn't care about that. "I fancied some herring for my supper." Try as I might, I couldn't help looking Irvine's way when I said that. The other men have his attention now.

Hettie mumbles something under her breath and I see her scowl. I notice then that she has her hand on her belly. I see why, for she is with child. I try to study her, to learn more, but now Ewan is on his way up the pebbled beach, pushing through the crowd, directing the young lad carrying his boxes ahead of him.

I tuck my charm away in the pocket of my skirt, lest he senses it. I notice that Hettie lowers her head as if in shame as Ewan passes. He looks her way briefly, but I am his quarry.

He puts his hand under my arm, pausing. "I'll exchange two of my haul, if you would supply me with another pot of your delicious honey, Miss McGraw." Under his breath he says more, garnering my interest. "I have an ache that I am sure you can soothe." His handsome mouth lifts at the corner, and anticipation floods my private places.

The crowd of women and the old minister behind him watch on. "Now that seems like a fair trade," says I, for their benefit, and allow him to lead me off. It is hard, but I do not glance back at Irvine, lest Ewan notices.

We follow the young lad to the storage room at the back of Ewan's shop and our paces quicken as we close on it. Inside the storeroom, Ewan tosses the lad a coin, and when the lad scuttles off Ewan locks the door from the storeroom into the main shop. We are alone in the narrow room piled high with provisions, wooden boxes, and sacks of flour.

He takes off his hat, paces back and forth in front of me. "The way you flaunt yourself," he shakes his head, "it makes me want to possess you, out there, for them all to see."

"Now wouldn't that be a shocking sight for all to behold." I fold my arms beneath my bosom, and flash my eyes his way. "To see Master Ewan perform lewd, lascivious acts on a gutter slattern like me." I glance down at the front of his breeches. "I fear that the men of the village would feel quite ashamed of their ability to satisfy their wives, after seeing a sight like that."

Yes, I am not above flattering him, for I know what the result will be, something well worth having.

Fire rolls in his eyes and his mouth curves. "Lift your skirts, face the wall, and bend over those boxes," he instructs.

I do as he says, turning to the stack of wooden crates that are full with vegetables. I lift my skirt at the back, and bend over. It is cold and dark in here and my thighs tremble a little. I straighten my legs, determined not to show weakness. When I hear Ewan behind me I rest my elbows on top of the wooden boxes, my skirts captured in around my waist.

The first strike he lands on my bottom comes without warning and I jerk forward, my fingernails biting into the raw wood of the crate as the sting takes hold of me. He slaps the other cheek. I shift from one foot to the other, wriggling my hips, and then I place my feet a little wider, eager to manage this.

On he goes, punishing me for flaunting myself, for making him want me. I clench my teeth, savoring that moment where the pain turns to pleasure and my cunny seeps. He pauses, which only makes my skin burn more, and then he delivers several more slaps, fast, before sliding his finger up and down my nether lips. "You are ripe for this, aren't you?"

Unable to speak, I push my bottom out toward him. He pushes his finger into my hole, and I hear him utter an oath at my back. A moment later his rod replaces his finger and he pushes it quickly inside, his girth stretching me open. His actions are sudden and vigorous and they set loose a howl in my throat. My head jerks back.

Ewan claps his hand over my mouth so that the old man at the shop counter next door does not hear, but he likes that arrangement even more and he ruts me fast, his body pivoting against mine.

"You are a feral creature," he curses, "and you challenge me in ways that I cannot believe I have to bear." He grunts loudly, and I can tell his need to shed his seed is pressing. "If it were not for the fact you are so good for this, you would be more trouble than you are worth."

His words delight me, and I squeeze his rod hard, gripping the hard length of him inside my sheath each time he thrusts inside me. He curses again, his rod stiffens and bows within me, and it presses upon me in a way that makes me shudder and wriggle, needy for more there. I get more, because Ewan is locked into this and he moves faster still, his body bucking as he tries frantically to lose his seed. The rub of his rod in that place is too good, and I pitch forward, my face against his palm as I hit my peak. I bite at his fingers, delighting when it makes him wilder still, his hips bucking. I feel the buttons on his frock coat press against my stinging buttocks. The curious mix of pain and pleasure makes me dizzy, and I rove into delirium, my cunny on fire as I peak.

At the last moment, he pulls away, and clasps his hand over my cunny possessively even while he drenches the fabric of my petticoats with his copious seed.

"That is what you needed, isn't it?" He gives me one last slap on the rump, and chuckles to himself. "That's why you came down to the shore, because you wanted me and you needed me to slake your lust."

The nature of his comment has a curious effect on me, for it makes my mind wander back to that other man down at the edge of the sea, the one who makes me hanker for him so. These last few weeks it is Irvine Maginty that I think of when I am alone in my bed at night, but I cannot let Ewan know that. I have learnt my lessons in this life, and I am ready for Ewan.

My mask slides into place.

Straightening up, I shake my skirt free and look back over my shoulder at him. "Yes, Ewan," I lie, "that's exactly what I was looking for."

14

"IT'S A BEAUTIFUL MORNING."

Zoë gasped for breath and peeled her fingers away from the railing she was gripping on to, the voice at her side pulling her back from the vision fast.

Crawford was at her side, speaking to her. He looked out across the marina, where she'd been focused. "Enjoying the view?"

His eyes smoldered as he spoke and Zoë struggled to pull words together, her mind and her body swamped with the vivid imagery she had just experienced.

"Yes," she replied, breathlessly. Her sex was heavy with longing and right at that moment she would gladly have gone into a dark room with a man who would bend her over and give her a good seeing to. The vision had been so real, she could feel the heat between her thighs and her underwear was cloying to the groove of her pussy.

Crawford was standing close against her, looking at her with a half smile that assured her he was thinking about their encounter the day before. "I'll call over for you about seven o' clock, for the do up at the Silver Birch."

When she didn't reply, he nodded up the hill. "You hadn't forgotten, had you?"

"Of course not," she lied. It had slipped her mind completely and she realized that she hadn't mentioned it to Grayson. Unease crept up her back.

Movement caught her eye and she looked over at the post office. That was where they went, she realized, along there somewhere was the building where Annabel and Ewan had gone. Elspeth was standing outside the door to her shop, her hands wrapped around a large pottery mug. She smiled and nodded over.

Zoë smiled back, but all she really wanted to do was sit down and think about the vision she'd just had, to try to make sense of it, and to calm the raging lust that it had left her with. There seemed to be distractions at every turn, and it was only the nagging need to go up the hill and pay that damn bill that kept her from following Crawford back into his boat yard.

"I have to go. I have a bill to pay." She pointed up at the restaurant at the top of the hill.

Crawford followed her gaze. "I'll see you this evening."

She nodded and walked on. Elspeth lifted her fingers and waved as she passed by. Zoë returned the wave and pressed along, lust running her senses ragged. She put her head down and walked on to the top of the hill, her mind racing with thoughts and images. It was only as she closed on the restaurant that she wondered if it was even going to be open. Glancing at her watch, she saw it was after ten. As she rounded the corner to the entrance she was relieved to see that the large glass doors were standing wide open and a delivery van was parked outside. Two young men were carrying boxes into the building. She followed them in.

Cain was standing at the reception desk, leafing through a large reservations book. He was wearing casual clothes, an open-neck shirt loose over jeans. There was a slight stubble on his jaw which made him look more roguish than he had the other evening, and his hair was tousled, as if he hadn't been out of bed for long.

He looked up and broke into a smile when he saw her. "Zoë, what perfect timing," he said, as if he had been expecting her. He stepped out from behind the counter and put his arm around her shoulders. There was intimacy in his touch, as though they were old friends.

Her temperature rose. Her body was already wired, because of the nature of the images she'd seen back there by the marina, like her very own private adult movie show playing in her head. Now, Cain's touch was making her incredibly self-aware.

He led her into the restaurant. Two members of staff were busy polishing the large windows that led onto the terrace, and the deliverymen were disappearing away into the kitchens.

"I came to pay my bill. I'm sorry that I was remiss about it on Monday night. I completely forgot." She started to open her bag.

"Forget it." He waved his free hand over her bag and then pointed across the restaurant to a doorway marked with a sign that read Private. "Come upstairs with me, I have something to show you."

Zoë paused, resisting the pressure that he applied in the small of her back with his palm. "What is it?"

"You'll see." He looked at her intently. "It's not something I show to every visitor." His hand moved lower still, to rest on her bottom.

The pulse in her groin went wild, and she clutched her

purse and bit her lip, afraid that she was going to embarrass herself and beg him to spank her.

Grayson had said Annabel was a mischievous spirit, and he wasn't wrong there. If it was indeed Annabel doing these things to her, she had a mischievous streak a mile wide.

Cain looked at her with all-too-knowing eyes. Heat radiated from his hand where it rested on the curve of her bottom.

"Okay," she breathed, physically unable to turn away, put the money on the reception desk and leave, as planned.

He led her up a flight of stairs. At the top it opened into a sumptuous hallway. An ornate antique bureau stood on one side. The floor was highly polished marble, and heavy velvet curtains framed a window that looked out over the bay. The door into the space beyond was an artwork in itself, exquisitely carved black wood featuring a dragon. She was startled. "You live up here?"

He stood at the top of the steps until she was level with him. "Yes, my hideaway, where I keep my treasures, as you'll see."

He opened the carved door and led her into the room beyond. Zoë followed him into the large sitting room and gawped at the place, stunned. It looked like a museum, full of beautiful antique furniture. The walls were lined with bookcases, paintings and shelves displaying exotic-looking ornaments. Antique rugs covered the floors, and in the far corner a huge dining table and chairs looked like something from a stage set.

"There she is," Cain said.

Zoë turned to look at the painting he had led her to, her attention focusing rapidly. The portrait was of a woman, a proud beauty with long dark hair. She wore a silvery gray gown tightly cinched at the waist and full in the skirt.

Polished black shoes with large silver buckles peeped out from under the hem of her gown. On her open palm a small white bird lifted in f light, wings outstretched. Zoë's lips parted. She shook her head slightly in disbelief. "Annabel," she whispered.

"You've seen her before?" Cain's attention quickly shifted from the painting to Zoë.

"Yes, at least I think so. It was very brief, yesterday, but looking at this painting I now know for sure that it was her."

"Fascinating," Cain said, and his eyes gleamed. "How lucky you are to have seen her."

She was starting to feel very lucky, in numerous ways. She glanced at him. "Why have you got a painting of her?"

"I have paintings of many local historic figures," he replied, somewhat dismissively, and gestured with one hand, drawing her attention around the walls.

There were indeed several other portraits. Two were of men in uniform, one depicted a World War I hero, and the other was much older and looked like a seafaring man. On the far wall, a large, rugged man was depicted in Scottish dress, kilt, sporran and all. There were two other portraits of women in period clothing, but none of them were as interesting as the painting of Annabel.

She quickly returned her attention to it.

It was mesmerizing, but what struck her as odd was that there was a glamorous air about Annabel that didn't correspond with the vision she'd seen. The gown Annabel wore in the painting looked expensive, whereas the ghostly figure she'd seen wore a plain gown, as if she were impoverished. This woman had the healthy look and demeanor of a woman of wealth. This was a glamorized version of Annabel, more dream than reality. It made her wonder, what had really happened to Annabel in the end? Everyone wanted to know about Annabel. She was getting pretty damn curious herself.

Cain observed her while she stared at the painting, a smile playing around his lips.

"Do you know who the artist was?" Zoë asked.

He made a noncommittal gesture as he returned his attention to the painting. "I'm very pleased to have your confirmation that it's a good likeness."

The way he looked at it indicated how fascinated he was by her legend, as was everybody.

"She's quite the mystery," she commented.

Cain shrugged.

"All we need to know is this." He nodded at the painting and for a moment he looked as if he were in love with the image. Pathos and yearning seemed to surround him as he stared up at Annabel's likeness. Could you be in love with a ghost, she wondered? When she'd first met Cain she'd thought him arrogant and far too full of himself, and yet now he aroused pity in her.

"Does Grayson Murdoch know you have this painting?"

"No." His reply was quite curt, and he stiffened.

His eyes altered and the emotion she'd seen there was gone. Had she imagined it?

"He'd be interested to see it."

"I'm sure he would." Cain's mouth tightened into a thin, hard line.

Zoë remembered the tension between the two men that first night. "You don't approve of his research here, do you?"

"It's meaningless," he replied, rather obtusely.

"Perhaps, but he does seem keen to get into the cottage, Her Haven." She was fishing for information, because her curiosity was growing about the animosity between the two men.

Cain snapped. He turned to face her, gripping her around her upper arms with viselike hands, his eyes dark with warning. "Don't let him in."

His expression was so sinister that it made her think about the young woman who had died in London, the weird circumstances of her death and the police investigation. Whether there was any truth in his involvement or not, Zoë decided that she didn't like him, nor did she trust him.

With some effort, she pulled free.

"Why," she said, forcing herself to stand up to him, "why do you think I should keep him out of the house?"

His eyes grew shuttered. "If he gets enough information about sightings and so on he can write a bloody book about it, that's what it's about. Some of us don't want him writing a book about our village and our traditions."

His tone was so disparaging that Zoë decided there had to be more to it than that. His mood had changed in a flash when she brought up Grayson's name, and his control was gone. He was angry.

"I see," she responded.

Cain forced a smile, but she could tell it wasn't natural. He could turn on the charm, just like that. "Don't let him spoil your time here. He can be a very intrusive person and you mustn't let him get his way."

Was she letting Grayson spoil her time? She didn't think so, in fact quite the opposite. It was far from what she was planning to do, but she had grown rather curious about Annabel herself. However, she wasn't going to write a book about it at the end of her stay. Was that the only reason he'd latched on to her? The very thought made her heart sink, which was worrying in itself.

Yesterday she'd been able to face up to the fact that

Grayson was motivated by his research. She'd been able to get past that and have fun with it. But today—or rather, after last night, which had felt very special and intimate— it made her decidedly grumpy. Was all of that fake? Could Grayson muster up special attention for anyone—like Cain here—just to get the information he wanted? Was he back there at his house now, hammering away on his laptop, making notes about what she said after the vision the night before?

"Come, let me give you a guided tour of the portraits." Cain encouraged her to move to the next painting, and began to tell her about the person depicted.

But Zoë could barely focus on what he said, because her thoughts were with an entirely different man.

Grayson was striding up the hill to the Tide Inn when Zoë appeared and headed down the pavement toward him. He was glad of it, because he suspected that Cain would be up to his usual tricks and he was ready for a confrontation.

Relaxing somewhat, he took a moment to admire the way she looked as she approached. There was something about her sparky attitude that got to him, in a good way, and it made him wonder what it would be like to observe her on her own patch, organizing a bunch of busy city solicitors.

She gave him a terse smile. "So my time is up, huh?"

"Are you okay?" He turned to go back down the hill with her, when he realized she wasn't going to stop to talk.

"Yes, I am. I want to go back to Her Haven. I had another vision on the way up here." She shot him a curious look.

"Really?" How intriguing.

There was a determined look to her stride. She seemed rather tense and a little distant. What had Davot said to her? "Any trouble with Davot?"

"No. He has a very interesting portrait of your ghost pal that you should see."

That surprised him. "A portrait of Annabel?"

"Yes, I thought that would have your research radar up and running." Sarcasm rang in her tone.

He didn't comment, but he made a mental note that he had to find out about Cain's interest. "Why do you want to go to the house now? Was it something to do with what you saw?"

She took a deep breath. "I had a vision at the marina on the way up there. Ewan was there, the coven master, and another man that Annabel was interested in, a fisherman. He was married. She wanted him, although her lover was the coven master." She delivered the details in a perfunctory manner and continued to shoot sidelong glances at him as they walked.

"It seems as if she really likes you. She's keying in to you even more frequently."

"I suppose I should feel like the lucky one?" She looked at him with one raised eyebrow, and then shook her head. "Everybody seems to want a piece of her and right now she's all mine."

"Zoë, is this bothering you?" Her attitude was beginning to worry him. Davot had unsettled her, for sure.

"I really want to go back to the house. Before I was a bit, you know—well, scared. But now I want to see her, it's almost as if I want her to appear, to be sure it's her in that painting. Although I do know it is her, I can tell it is her by the way she talks to me."

Or it could be an enchantment, Grayson thought.

He didn't want to say too much on that point until he understood it himself. The fact that Davot had a portrait of Annabel alerted him to outside intervention.

They walked in silence for a moment. It was a warm day and the seafront was fast filling with day-trippers. He noticed that Zoë glanced left and right when they passed the post office and the boatyard. She had the hotspots off pat. Instinct or not, she was good.

"Do you want me to come with you?" he asked, as they approached Her Haven.

"Well, that's what *you* want to do, isn't it?" Her reply was sarcastic. Something was definitely amiss.

After the previous night he'd felt close to her, and that had been really good, but now there was a distance between them that he wanted rid of. The distance made him feel angry, an emotion he wasn't accustomed to. It made him want to snatch her against him and keep her locked there.

He never was good at communicating with women, but it seemed as if he was doing a worse job than ever with Zoë. It annoyed him. Protection was at the forefront of his mind, but he was also experiencing emotions that were new to him. It was unnerving. He had barely kept himself in check that morning, when he wanted to act selfishly and forbid her to go anywhere without him. He reasoned that it wasn't without cause. Cain had sent Elspeth to spy on them the night before. It had been a hard thing for him to let Zoë walk into the viper's nest without him.

He stopped walking and grabbed her arm, pulling her against him. He was about to demand to know what had been said up there at the Tide Inn, when her head dropped back and she looked up at him with her lips softly parted. All he wanted to do was kiss her, and that need surpassed all others.

There was resistance in her, at first. Her shoulders tensed but when he brushed his mouth over hers she gave a whimper and her lips parted for him, her hands rising against his chest. She nestled closer and when he tasted her mouth, her hips arched against his. His blood headed south and his cock grew hard inside a heartbeat.

She felt soft and eager in his arms. This is what he wanted, her desire. She clutched at him; she wanted him as much as he did her, and yet warning signals were sounding all around. He felt as if he wasn't up to speed with what was really happening here, and that didn't lie easily with him. Did he need to take a step back, or get even closer? His instincts were shot to hell, and the soft, luscious woman in his arms wasn't making that any easier.

The sound of kids laughing in the background brought them both back to their surroundings.

"Come with me," she whispered, smiling, when they drew apart, her eyes like melting chocolate as she looked up at him. "I need to take a shower, and I want you."

The invitation was right there, and there wasn't an ounce of him that could resist.

Zoë lathered his broad chest, and told herself to enjoy him and stop worrying. He was quiet, but the silence between them felt more comfortable than it had earlier. She noticed that he looked concerned, as if a small part of his mind was focused elsewhere. He did want her, though. The impressive erection that curved up to his belly proved that much.

You're not interested in research, she said to his beautiful, solid cock, silently, as she sluiced the flowing water over his chest with her hands, then moved down toward her target. *You just want to be inside me, getting your rocks off.*

His cock jerked upwards into her grasp, as if nodding in agreement. She smiled.

Sometimes simple was good.

Sometimes simple was magic.

Her head jerked up and she studied him. The shower-head was only just above him, and the water bounced off his head, radiating all around, making him look surreal. All this talk of ghosts and magic had her thinking crazy thoughts. A shiver ran down her back.

"What is it?"

"Nothing. Just got a bit cold, I guess."

He shifted their positions, putting her under the stream of warm water and pouring a generous amount of shower gel into the palm of his hand. "My turn," he said, with no small amount of relish.

The odd feeling that she had experienced was chased away when he started to lather her breasts and abdomen, his hands moving in a slow rhythm, covering her easily, his gaze constantly on her as his hands stroked farther down over her hips and between her legs.

She had to lift her arms and wrap her hands around the showerhead, to hold steady when he started moving his large hand back and forth over her pussy.

"Good job this is fixed to the wall so securely," she said, breathlessly, as he proceeded down her thighs. Between what he was doing, and what he looked like, her body was aching to be filled, to be taken roughly and pushed to climax.

Turning her round, he shampooed her hair with care and attention, and then soaped her back and her bottom, his fingers exploring all her intimate places.

Zoë could barely stand, by the time he was done with her and turned her to face him, and she had to cling to him. He kissed her while the water rinsed them both off.

Thrusting his tongue into her mouth, with his erection squashed against her belly, he felt as taut as a bow.

Damn you, she thought, damn you for being such a bloody good lover and for using it to get round me. Nevertheless, she wanted him and she wanted him so badly that she would have got down on hands and knees and begged him to fuck her right there and then.

"Please, Grayson," she whispered against his mouth, her hand closing over the swollen head of his cock. "You're driving me crazy. I'm so turned on."

"You're not the only one." His voice was low and gruff. Turning off the faucet, he reached out and grabbed a towel, quickly wrapping her in it as she stepped out of the shower.

She darted for the bedroom, unable to wait to get dry, and sat on the bed. Tall, naked, and gleaming wet he approached her, and the very look of him made her sex clench in anticipation.

Damn you, she thought again, her emotions clashing, and snatched at him. With her hands locked around the hard line of his hips, she pressed her fingers demandingly into the firm muscle of his gorgeous arse, and took his cock into her mouth.

He gave a ragged moan and his fingers moved into her hair, stroking her. His response showed her she could charm him, too, and she was glad of it. In that mood, in that moment, asserting herself over him was desperately important to her.

Stroking the underside of his cock head with her tongue she moved one hand to cup his balls, the other still applying pressure on his firm behind, keeping him close against her as she rode his cock in and out of her mouth.

"Need to be inside you," he said, and she realized he was close to coming.

She rested back, hands flat on the bed, catching her breath as she watched him cross the room to grab a condom and tear it open. The way he rolled it on, with his fist locked around it, looked so goddamn sexy.

"Ready?" A teasing smile passed over his expression and then he moved, fast, like a jungle cat descending on its prey.

So sure of yourself, she thought, feeling almost resentful of his sexual power over her. She moved fast, too, turning onto her hands and knees, and scurrying across the bed.

But he reacted just as quickly. One large hand closed around her ankle and he hauled her back, winding her. She grappled for something to hold on to, clutching uselessly at the bedcovers, but he had her. He dragged her back to the edge of the bed and locked his hands around the front of her hips. Before she could even try to resist, he had pulled her upright onto her hands and knees.

"Oh, dear God!" she cried out, when she felt his tongue in her groove.

He'd knelt down behind her and wrapped his hands around her thighs, to keep her from moving. Shuddering, she moaned uncontrollably when he licked, stroked, and sucked on her exposed pussy with slow deliberation, and then pushed his tongue inside, lapping at her sex.

"Delicious," he said, his breath on her sensitive folds infuriating her tender flesh.

She felt debauched, exposed and trapped all at once. The way his tongue explored her had her clit swollen and pounding. Her body was on the verge of release. Then, when he held her pussy lips apart with his fingers and sucked on her clit, her back arched, and she cried aloud, her sudden climax making her hot and restless from the top of her head to her toes.

With her head hanging, she panted for air, her skin burning up. She ached for more of him, and he was right there. He had her hips held tightly in his hands. Her bottom was in the air and he stood between her legs. Anticipation coiled deep in her core. Then she felt the head of his cock at her entrance. Her body swayed in his grip. Glancing back over her shoulder, she watched his face as he eased his way in, his jaw tight, his eyes focused, his damp chest rising and falling.

As the walls of her sex were stretched apart, her head dropped.

He pushed inexorably on.

She mewed aloud when the head of his cock wedged tight against her cervix. Her breathing was way out of whack, the sheer pressure of his erection there making her dizzy.

His grip on her hips was unforgiving, as if he had his own point to prove, and she couldn't have moved even if she wanted to. He stroked her back with one hand, soothing her tailbone while her cervix burned, then he drew back, and began to thrust. Zoë was gone on it, her entire nether region burning up as he gave it to her, riding her relentlessly, his hips churning into her over and over until she came, crying out as she did so.

Only then did he change his pace, moving in shallow, faster thrusts, until a moment later he joined her, whispering her name over and over as his cock jerked inside her.

15

AFTERWARD THEY LAY IN SILENCE—FACE-TO-
face, thigh-to-thigh—staring into one another's eyes. There
was something there, in both of them, she knew it. Un-
spoken questions?

Zoë was forthright by nature. She always asked questions
when she needed to. There was no shame in not knowing
everything there was to know. It was part of what made
her world function.

"Were there others?" Oh, dear, that had come out
wrong. "Were there others that Annabel communicated
with this way? The visions, I mean."

"Not that I know of. All I've heard about before now is
sightings, nothing like this."

Did you bed them to find out?

What if he had shagged them, all of them, to find out?
That was none of her business, she reasoned with herself.
Except it was, if ghost hunting was the only reason he was
shagging her. She wanted to believe that there was more

to it than that. For her, there was. She wanted him. It was more than a quick shag. She liked him. "Why me?"

He touched the side of her face, stroking one finger slowly down from the temple, around the edge of her cheekbone to the tip of her jaw. As she leaned into his touch, loving it, she wondered what he was thinking.

"I don't know."

"You're the professor. You're the one who should have all the answers."

One corner of his mouth lifted. "Why do you think I need a research assistant?"

Was he just teasing her, or was there more to it? Something about the way he looked, so thoughtful, made her wonder if he knew more than he was letting on. It was her that was being haunted; she deserved to know all that he did, surely? "If I'm going to help you with your research, it's all about sharing information, right?"

He seemed amused by her question. Resting one arm around her waist, he kept her close. "Yes, mostly."

Mostly?

He continued on. "I was doing research on folklore along this coast, but the mystery surrounding Annabel kept coming up over and again, this past year. Something is shifting in the atmosphere between the spirit world and the real world here in Carbrey, and it seemed necessary to question why she's become more active recently. If she's communicating through you, maybe we'll find out why this is happening."

He was very focused on that goal, and try as she might not to let it get to her, it did. She sat up, drawing her knees up. Wrapping one hand around her shins, she shook out her still-damp hair with her free hand.

He reached out and stroked her back. She closed her

eyes, savoring the way it felt as he moved his hand over her, gently, between her shoulder blades. He'd made her focus on every minutiae of their physical experience, which only made this more intense. Being touched by him was sheer bliss, and it made her body melt and mellow into a myriad of sensory experiences. It was hard not to just lie back and let him organize the rest of the week, just so she could have more of it. But she had come here to do her own thing and to have fun. Okay, she was having fun with him, but he was very bound up in his grand purpose, and he had his bloody book to think about.

That annoyed her, she couldn't help it. On an everyday basis she spent her time doing things for other people, being there for them, and organizing them. Just because she had the hots for him, she couldn't allow him to commandeer her whole week off.

Besides, she had other things to do. She had a trip to the pub to look forward to, a dance, a bit of fun. Immediately, she regretted not mentioning Crawford's suggestion before, but she tried not to let the guilt get to her. It wasn't a big deal.

"Oh, I meant to tell you. You know that guy, Crawford, the one who owns the boat builders," she stated, casually, "he told me about this event that's on at the village pub tonight, the dance. He suggested I check it out. It sounded like fun, so I'm going to go up there with him this evening."

The hand stroking her back stilled, and then moved away.

The atmosphere grew tense, and Zoë immediately felt even more awkward. Okay, she told herself, so things had got out of hand with Crawford the day before, and normally she wouldn't get involved with two men at the same time, but in the grand scheme of things she didn't feel as if she was dating either of them. The event at the pub was a social thing, not a one-to-one, so Grayson had no right to get in a huff about that. If he was in a huff, it had to be because she wasn't falling into line with his plans for his research.

Tension mounted.

"Are you going to the event?" she added, trying to force him to respond by taking the party line approach.

The dreadful silence looming at her back meant she was forced to turn around and look at him.

A heavy frown had taken up residence on his face, and when she looked at him he sat up, turning away so that he was sitting on the edge of the bed with his feet on the floor. After a moment he rested his head in his hands as if he had a huge weight on his shoulders.

Bloody hell. He was acting as if it was the end of the world. Why? It occurred to her then that she might have gone and wounded his male pride. That had not been her intention, but if that's what was happening here, maybe he did care about her? She reached out and rested her hand against his back. "Grayson?"

"You don't know what you're messing with," he said, sternly. "Stay away from Crawford—and Cain, for that matter."

Now she was officially confused, and perturbed. "There'd better be a good explanation for that remark."

He turned to face her, and she was shocked when she saw the warning in his expression. "I should have told you before now. I was just getting to it." Frustration flitted across his eyes. "Cain is dangerous."

She already knew that. "I've heard about the woman who committed suicide in London, if that's what you mean?"

"You know about that?"

"Yes, my sister told me, but it's Crawford I'm going to the pub with, not Cain."

He shook his head. "They are in league, and they are dangerous people."

"Dangerous? What do you mean dangerous?"

"They practice the craft, they are witches, but they are part of a coven without conscience."

What? A disbelieving laugh escaped her mouth. "I'm sorry, Grayson. I am just beginning to wrap my head around the persecuted witch ghost story and the fact that she can somehow influence me…but a coven, witches, here and now?" She shook her head. "This is way far-fetched. If you're angry about me agreeing to go to this event with Crawford, just say so."

He frowned, confusion in his eyes. "Only because he is part of a group that embraces forbidden occult practices."

"So now you're saying that half the village is practicing witchcraft?" She couldn't keep the sarcasm out of her voice. It was crazy talk, but one thing was pretty clear to her. His so-called work was his foremost concern, and he was so wrapped up in it that it was all he could think about. If he had been clever about it and said he wanted her to spend the evening with him instead, she probably would have succumbed to his charms. But now her pride was wounded, and she was not going to back down.

"Not half the village," he said, "but a few people, yes. Listen to me, understand me." He gave a frustrated sigh. "I'm not good at this, and I just didn't want to dump too much information on you all at once, but you must listen to me."

She put her hands up. "I've heard the rumors about Cain and the black magic business, and I don't like the man, but I don't believe a word of it."

"You ought to."

There was a threat in his voice, and she didn't take kindly to it. "Why? I was up there at the restaurant today and I didn't see him running around with a wand and a broomstick, all he bloody well did was shown me his art collection." She was really annoyed now. "This is ludicrous. First of all you try to take charge of me because you wanted to get in here, then you tell me that everybody else here is dangerous. Forgive me if it's beginning to sound a tad oppressive."

She was beginning to think he needed his head examined.

His eyes looked wild, desperate. "I am trying to protect you." He put his hands on her shoulders and rolled her back on the bed, leaning over her and pinning her down.

Zoë swallowed, hard, her emotions reeling. Fool, she had been a fool about him. The tension between them built ever higher.

"Zoë, they are up to something." His expression darkened, and then faltered. "I'm not sure what it is, not yet, but I don't want you to go."

He didn't have a good reason. It was about letting go his key to this house, the key to his research. She balked. "Let me go this instant. You've got no right to order me around or handle me like this."

"I'm not ordering you around." Even as he spoke he seemed to become aware of the way he was holding her down on the bed and lifted his hands free, shock in his eyes.

Fixing him with a determined stare, she spoke as firmly as she could. "I think you should leave."

He nodded and stood up, picking up his clothes quickly and dressing.

Her heart was thundering in her chest.

"I'm sorry," he said, when he was dressed. He didn't look at her as he spoke, and then went to leave the room. At the doorway, he stopped. "If you go to this thing tonight, please be careful," he added.

He just couldn't let it go, could he?

There was steely determination in his eyes. What was that about? Thankfully, he turned and left the room.

At first, she was relieved.

The man was crazy, getting all bossy on her like that. One minute he seemed like a perfectly logical and rational academic with a bit of a wild side, and the next he was talking a pile of nonsense. And then he went and got all heavy-handed with her, and she just wanted out of it.

Why then, when he left the room, did she feel an enormous pit of emptiness fast developing inside her? Bloody hell, she thought to herself, I really like the man. A lot. And he is a complete nutter.

She heard the front door close quietly downstairs. At least he hadn't slammed it on the way out, which she had expected. She pulled the sheet up to cover herself and then rested her hand over her eyes while she tried to get a grip on her emotions. Crazy, this was crazy.

Her mind kept working through it, trying to make sense of what had just happened. There had been tension all morning. Because of Cain? Then he'd flown off the handle. There had been conviction in his words, though. He believed what he was saying. And he apologized. But he was so bossy, and they barely knew each other. She sighed loudly, thumping the pillows, her heartbeat regulating.

After a while, the sound of crashing waves and the wind weaving through the boats calmed her down. Gulls swooped over the house, their calls adding their own rhythm. The room was warm and bathed in amber light where the sun shone through the ochre curtains, making it feel tranquil. She was tired, and her body wanted to rest.

Listen, for I must tell you my tale. Let me show you, and then you will understand all of this.

For a moment, Zoë thought the voice had spoken aloud, and she glanced around the room, peering into both mirrors. There was no one there. However, her curiosity had been baited.

Cautiously, she lay back on the bed and listened, giving herself up to it. The sound of the waves coming in grew more intense, completely filling her mind, as if the sea was right there in the room with her, and then it whispered away completely, and as it did, her eyelids lowered....

We will be alone at last, Irvine and I. I am determined. Desire draws me to him, even though I cannot explain why. I have never felt this way before. As I pass another evening alone, molding wax for candles and thinking about him, I decide it is too much. Too many nights spent here sitting by the glow of my peat fire, watching the flames dance and imagining the two of us together, until my desire for him is so desperate that it keeps me awake all night long. Oh, yes, you know how that ache of longing feels, don't you?

I cannot let another day go by without trying. I have to see him, to speak to him, alone, so I leave my half-made candle and fetch my shawl.

Out in the dark narrow street, I shelter and wait until I see him on his way home from the tavern.

"Who is there?" he asks, when he catches sight of me standing in the shadows.

I step across the cobblestones quietly, and reach out to touch his sleeve. "It is only me, Annabel." I marvel at the way I can feel his powerful arms even through the rough cloth of his coat.

"Annabel," he repeats and his voice softens on my name.

Ah, he is pleased that it is me, and not his wife. Would she scold him for spending money in the tavern? Or is there another reason that he is pleased? I cannot thank my magic, for I have not even brought the charm I crafted. I wanted to see whether he would spurn me if I did not have it with me. He does not. In fact, he steps closer to me, as if to take a better look.

I turn my face to the moonlight. "Would that you were on your way home to me, Irvine Maginty," I whisper, and I mean it. The words had risen unbidden inside me as I looked up at him, but it is the truth. Images of him fill my mind, and I toss and turn in my bed at night, my hands running feverishly over my body as I think what it would be like having him there with me.

"Aye," he agrees, as he nods his head. "You turn my head, Annabel McGraw, even though it should not be so." He reaches out to touch my hair and his touch is so gentle and curious that I lose my grip on the shawl I have around my shoulders and have to snatch at it lest it falls in the mud.

"It is the same for me. I wish that I could lie with you each night as Hettie does. When I am alone in my bed and I yearn for a man of my own, it is you that I am thinking of."

He sighs with longing, and the sound of it rumbles deep in his chest. He is there for the taking. Standing on tiptoe, I tip back my head and offer him my mouth.

He pauses but a moment before he grabs me into his arms. He is tender at first, then I push my fingers into his hair, tugging on it and drawing him closer, and he takes me roughly, landing kisses on my face and my throat, before returning to my mouth and plunging his tongue inside. He tastes of ale and tobacco and my hands are shaking as I spread them against the breadth of his chest. His hands are at my breasts, outlining them, and then they move quickly around my waist, easily spanning it and locking me to him.

When I hear voices nearby, I pull away and urge him into the shadows. "Be careful," I whisper. I press him in against the wall to be sure that he is concealed in a doorway, for my mind is sharper than his. I can be sure of that. His member is stiff in his breeches and presses insistently at my belly as I move close to him. Oh, how I want to feel it where I need it more. I rest my head against his shoulder, my blood racing. Again, he strokes my hair, and a sigh escapes him. There is no doubt in me. We must answer this call between us.

When the voices pass by I look on, up the hill, to where the cobbled street leads to the graveyard at the back of the kirk. He follows my glance, and I take his hand. "Come with me into the graveyard. I want you to kiss me again."

There was no hesitancy in him. He does want me, he wanted this is much as I! My heart beats fast, triumph bedding in me. We follow the street until we reach the grounds of the graveyard. The gate creaks open and we hurry inside, looking for a good spot to lie. The bushes and trees that run along the inside of the old stone wall seem a likely place, and Irvine nods when he sees me looking that way. He drops to the ground, pulling me down into his arms, his eager grasp just as powerful as I thought it would be, if not more so.

We roll back and forth, each as eager for this as the other, our mouths locked, our hands discovering each other, the flesh that we have thought about for too long, far too long. Yet now we are together and as sure as the tide cannot be held back from the shore, we were always destined to be entwined this way.

I have to have him mount me, and I can easily make it happen, but I want to be sure he will not be angry with me afterward. I could not suffer that. Arresting his progress for a moment, I press my fingers to his lips before he kisses me again. "Irvine, please, I want to part my legs for you, and if you continue to kiss me this way there will be no stopping it."

"I know," he says, and his voice is low and gruff. He runs his nose against the side of my face, tenderly, and then his hand is under my skirt and petticoats, stroking my knee through my wool stockings. "I have thought of nothing else, these past weeks. Whenever I saw you, I wished for this."

Could I be any happier? I move his hand a little higher, around my thigh. It feels so good, and I wriggle closer still. He grips me firmly, and then his thumb strokes the soft skin on the inside of my leg and my cunny is alight for him. I'm lost to the moment. "Touch me, please, I'm longing for you to touch me."

I open my legs wide. He plants his hand over my cunny, shakes his head. "I have to be in there."

He reaches for his belt, and the need I sense in him is so immense that my body tightens with anticipation. I feel my way to the spot where he has undone his breeches, and wrap my hand around his rod. It's hot, silky smooth, and arched skyward, and it makes me shiver because I think about how good it will feel, filling me. When I run my thumb over his tip and feel how large and honey-coated it is, his body shudders.

"Annabel," he pleads, "let me at you."

I pull my skirts higher and plant my feet wide, then grasp his collar, drawing him over me as I lay down. His large body looms as he positions himself between my open thighs, and then his member slides easily into my opening, and he stretches me open.

How good that feels! He pushes a little deeper and I think I might die from this. I arch back against the earth, for his member torments me, moving at my entrance.

"You're as luscious as a newfound pearl, I want to savor you but I fear I cannot. You make me want to rush."

I stroke his face and wish that I had a candle so that I could watch him. "I do not want you to hold back, I will gladly receive whatever you can give me."

He places his hands flat on the ground for purchase and gives me his length.

I'm full, my deepest parts penetrated and made alive by his member. With his rod buried in me to the hilt he looks down at me and shakes his head. I cannot see his face, but when he whispers my name and caresses my outline, I understand, for I know now that he has wanted this moment as much as I have. Bliss washes over me and yet I silently curse the world, for I want time and I want a bed where I can ride him over and again, eking out every last morsel of pleasure into the long night. When he begins to thrust, I grip his shoulders and I lift my hips to meet him, eager for all of him.

I hear a creature scurry in the bushes, voices in the street beyond. Fear that we will be discovered makes me desperate, and I run my hands over his back. The heels of my shoes are hard against his bottom as it bucks up and down with each thrust of his long rod inside me. It is so slippery there that he glides in and out with ease, and I feel him stroke every part of me. Overwrought, and overheated, we hurry, and we grind closer and closer still, until we barely move apart. Instead, we rock each other for the rub, gasping at each stroke, and when he spills I am folded beneath him and taking everything he has to give. There is a sob in my throat as I put my hand over the place where we are joined, relishing how that feels. I peak in his arms, even while he still jerks inside me. Clinging to him, my body arches and then seems to lift and peel away from this world, and I float, dazed, in the moment of my release.

Holding each other silently, I hate to feel him slip from inside me as we level, but I know he must. As he does, I turn my head away and I see lamplight pass on the far side of the graveyard, close to the kirk. As the lamp sways I see that it is the Reverend Slater out on some mission, and my breath catches in my chest at the sight of him. Nodding in that direction, I place my fingers against Irvine's lips, until the old preacher is gone.

"Hurry, go that way and be quick about it," I urge, pulling my skirts down.

He is hesitant. "I'll walk you back as far as Shore Lane—"

"No, no, it is not safe. We must go separately." I do not say what I really want to do—to take him home and lie with him all night long—because I want to protect him, and I know he'll be hounded out of the village if we are found out.

"Will you meet me again?" I ask, before he goes, my heart heavy with longing.

"Aye, gladly I will," he says, and kisses me one last time. A moment later he turns away, walks quickly out of the graveyard and is gone, and even though I'm alone now, I do not regret it.

I'm glad of what has happened between us.

Mighty glad.

16

ZOË'S EYES FLASHED OPEN AND SHE SAT UP IN the bed, clutching the covers to her chest, her heart pounding. Even as she did, her body jolted and her pussy dribbled hot juices between her thighs. She'd had another vision, and this one was even clearer than the last.

Annabel had addressed her directly and told her to pay attention so that she would understand. It was as if she had given her a window into a moment. Did she want her to know something, as Grayson had suggested? Would the mystery of Annabel McGraw be solved, after all these years, and could she truly be part of its unraveling? There was definitely an invitation there, something that gave her a choice to forge a connection with the dead woman. She lay back, wondering if she was ever going to get a solid couple of hours rest in this place.

"So much for sleeping alone," she said out loud as she slumped back onto the pillows. She took a moment to assess whether there was a presence in the room. There didn't seem to be. Her eyes closed but it wasn't sleep she wanted. Her thoughts were chaotic as she tried to recount every detail of the vision, to store it away. Physically, it had left her feeling aroused, and yet she was equally fascinated by what had been revealed. Annabel had had two lovers.

She ran her hands over her breasts and lower over her belly, to the juncture of her thighs. "I'm a woman, like Annabel."

That's when she remembered that she had a date with a man, a man who wasn't Grayson. Sitting bolt upright, she looked at the clock. She'd slept all afternoon. She only had twenty-five minutes before Crawford was due. Her stomach was growling. Pulling on a T-shirt, she darted down to the kitchen and crammed bread in the toaster.

After a quick snack, she checked the time. She had fifteen minutes. It was just about doable. She raced back up the stairs and into the bathroom, wondering if anyone had ever had such a chaotic, unusual holiday.

When Crawford knocked at the door, she was still in a daze, trying to find her fancy bra. Where the hell was it? She'd managed to lose an earring at some point as well, although she thought she'd probably dropped that while wandering in Dundee. Darting over to the window with her dress clutched to her chest, she stuck her head out and called down to Crawford. "I'll be down in a minute. Just getting dressed."

Great start to the evening. But after everything that had gone on, the visions and the weirdness with Grayson earlier on, was it any wonder? Regret welled inside her when she paused to think about him for a moment. It was him that had her in this mess, she thought, determined not to let Crawford know what state she was in. She was awake half the night because of him, and she'd slumbered after the latest vision, and now she couldn't even find the bra she wanted to wear.

All the same, she couldn't help wishing that it was him she was going out with, and that they hadn't argued. Snatching up the bra she'd abandoned earlier, she wondered if she'd even remembered to pack the pretty one at all, but she was sure she'd seen it lying around here earlier. That's what she got for not unpacking properly. No matter, the day bra would work with the summer dress she planned to wear.

Pulling on her outfit, she grabbed her strappy high-heeled sandals. After a quick application of lipstick and mascara, she combed her hair and was done. It was the fastest makeover job she'd ever done, but she looked reasonable, considering. The dress she'd put on was a clingy sheath. It outlined her figure, gave her a healthy glow, and when she wore it with heels it made her feel confident.

Jogging back downstairs, she paused. Despite the horrible disagreement earlier, she felt she ought to let Grayson know about the new information that had come to her during the vision. She'd agreed to be his research assistant and she hated to let people down. Scrabbling about in her bag for a pen and paper, she scribbled a message, crumpled the piece of paper in her hand and darted out the door.

Crawford was sitting on the sea wall, well back from both houses. He gave her a lazy smile.

"Sorry about that. I've just got to drop this note next door and then I'm ready." She thought he might come over and join her, but he stayed where he was. She walked to Grayson's door and slid the note through the letterbox. As she did, she wondered if she might have phrased it a bit better, but she was in a rush. At least she'd done the decent thing and filled him in on the latest information.

Crawford watched her with curiosity as she walked back to him.

"It's been a beautiful day," she commented, "was it good for work at the boatyard?"

"Aye, it draws the tourists and their cameras, too, which livens things up." He grinned.

She walked alongside him as they climbed the hill toward the Silver Birch. He chatted on about the boatyard, and she tried to maintain polite interest, even though her mind raced with an internal dialogue that soon had her on edge. Grayson had put ideas in her head about Crawford, and they all came rushing back at her now. She remembered that strange encounter they'd had in Dundee. How had he known where she was? If he'd been following her all the way from Carbrey, as he'd suggested, he would have found her sooner.

Okay, so Annabel could have been causing mischief, but did her influence really reach that far? Zoë didn't think so. Was Crawford—as Grayson had suggested—someone who practiced forbidden black magic? Was he in cahoots with Cain, who had left a murder investigation behind him in London?

Zoë was relieved to see the pub up ahead. The place was centuries old, and ivy grew up the side of the stone building. The painted sign overhanging the doorway showed a forest of trees, a silver birch at the foreground, its outline glowing. Cars were parked bumper to bumper along the street outside. At the far end of the building she saw a pub garden with activities for the kids, and beyond that, the forest.

Crawford led the way up the old stone steps and through the oak door. The steps dipped in the middle, worn from the many visitors who had walked up them over the years. She rested her hand on the door as she passed by. It was heavy with ironware, its hinges on the outside. Inside the pub was packed and noisy. The ceiling of the main bar was low, making it feel even more crowded. The sounds of bagpipes reached them as they moved through the crowd.

Stone slabs on the floor and simple, rough wood tables and benches added to the rustic charm. A fire burned in a large open fireplace, offering a welcome, even though it was warm. Half the village seemed to be there, along with the entire caravan site full of tourists. Excited children ran back and forth to the swings in the garden outside.

There was a small snug off to the left that seemed to be packed with locals, older men who looked rather grumpy about the festivities going on in their local. It was four deep at the bar.

"What can I get you?" Crawford asked.

"Whatever you suggest, something local?"

"You're on." He headed off into the scrum at the bar.

Zoë stood by waiting for him to return but soon found herself drawn toward the hall, a large extension tacked onto the back of the pub. Double doors were folded open and tartan streamers hung over the entrance. Tartan, for the tourists, she mused, smiling to herself.

A banner welcomed visitors to the monthly jig, and she stepped under it to look inside. Tables and chairs lined each side of the room, leaving the majority of the space in the middle for the dancing. The band was playing from a raised stage area. In the center of the room, on the worn parquet flooring, a man and woman in traditional kilts and buckled dance shoes were leading enthusiastic—if rather inept— tourists through the dance routine. The man wore a cute knitted hat—a tam-o'-shanter, she guessed—making him easy to spot in the crowd, and he carried a microphone, issuing instructions as he went. The atmosphere was filled with merriment and Zoë found herself tapping along as she tried to observe the steps.

"Here you go," Crawford said, arriving back with two large tumblers. Amber liquid glowed in them, a large amount, too.

"Scotch?"

He nodded and smiled.

Moving the glass around in her hand, she breathed in the rich, peaty aroma. Taking a sip, she held it in her mouth, savoring the distinctive, almost buttery taste, but when she swallowed it hit with a slow burn, flaring in her chest. "Oh, yes, that's good."

The man with the tam-o'-shanter deemed it time to give the dancers a rest, and announced a sword dance.

A lone dancer emerged onto the parquet dance floor, a tall muscular man in a kilt. He crossed two swords at his feet and when the piper began to play, he defied his size by dancing most nimbly. The crowd were mesmerized, and even the youngsters quieted to watch.

Crawford stood close by her, resting his hand up against the wall behind her. She was very aware of his presence as she watched the performance, her thoughts occasionally flitting back to that more intimate, private moment between them the day before. Once again it made her uncomfortable, because of Grayson, there was no denying it.

When the dance ended and the audience clapped, the man with the tam-o'-shanter was back on his feet, working the crowd. "Couples come forward, please, for a reel."

Crawford nodded at the dance floor and encouraged her to knock back the whiskey.

They joined the other couples, men down one side facing their partners across the dance floor. Zoë counted sixteen couples. The dance began, and she soon found out what hard work it was, trying to learn the movements and keep up at the same time. Giddy with laughter she grinned at Crawford when they met in the next circuit. "This is hard work."

"You'll soon get the hang of it," he replied, and slapped her on the arse when they parted, making her laugh. Happy that she'd come, she tried to push away those negative doubts that hovered nearby.

During the second dance, she found herself partnered with a different man, but she was having so much fun she didn't think about where Crawford had gone, not for a little while. Then she began to watch the crowd as she turned on the dance floor, looking for him with a growing feeling of unease.

Grayson picked up the piece of paper that was lying on his doormat and unfolded it.

Latest from Annabel—involved with another man. Not sure yet, but I think she likes this one better. Knows it's going to cause trouble. Zoë

The irony of the message did nothing to quell Grayson's bad mood. For a moment he wondered if it was a cruel jest. He hadn't known Zoë for very long, but he didn't think so. That type of barb was more like something his ex, Fenella the bitchy mathematician, would say.

"Idiot," he berated himself over again as he walked back down the hallway into the kitchen and put the kettle on the hob. He needed coffee. Badly. It was his intention to go up there and keep watch, whether she liked it or not. Coffee would steady him. He stared at the piece of paper in his hand again, teeth grinding. The last couple of hours had gone by in a flash while he nursed a furious mood. Then he'd sensed her leaving the house next door, and that didn't help one iota.

Despite the ironic slant to the contents of the note, it did bring him down to earth. It reminded him what he was supposed to be doing here. Namely, being a guardian. This was about the big picture. He'd become so wrapped up in his emotional reaction to the situation that he hadn't thought straight. *Fool.*

Was it normal to want to hold a woman in your arms so tightly that she couldn't go out with another man even if she wanted to? And why the hell did she want to go out with Crawford Logan, anyway? He couldn't figure it out, because he was so torn. As a result he'd reacted like the worst kind of aggressor, which meant he'd sounded garbled and idiotic when he tried to warn her off. She'd agreed to help him, have some fun along the way, maybe. He didn't own her and he had to accept that. Yet he'd felt that way for a moment there, as if she was his, his treasure. Loading his coffee with sugar, he downed it. Then he dressed carefully, readying himself.

He strode up the hill to the Silver Birch. The sun was getting low in the sky. Music and merriment poured out from the open doorway of the old inn. He stepped inside, and scanned the crowd.

"Come for a dance?" Crawford Logan was right there at his side, just inside the entrance. He must have been watching the doorway.

"I'm sure you're light on your feet, and it's kind of you to offer," Grayson replied, "but no, thank you."

Crawford shot him a warning look.

The drone of the bagpipes drew his attention to the room beyond the main bar. He edged through the crowd, but Crawford stayed close behind him. Suddenly Cain Davot stepped in front of him, blocking his path. Grayson frowned. They surely were doing their best to put a barrier between him and Zoë.

"Don't even try it, Murdoch." Cain's eyes glowed with restless energy. His smile was smug, his hands resting easily in the pockets of his expensive trousers.

"Try what? I came for a drink. It's still a free country, much as you would like Carbrey to be your little kingdom."

Grayson glanced at the bar and then away, all the time scanning for Zoë. He caught sight of her in the extension beyond, where the dancing was taking place.

Now that he knew where she was, he directed his whole attention to Cain. Another one of Cain's cronies had closed in at his right flank. Crawford was still at his left side. They had him nicely caged in.

Cain's eyes glittered. "You're not welcome here."

For some reason Cain thought he had the upper hand. Was it because Zoë had come here with Crawford? Grayson returned the smile. Did they really think he'd let it go that easily?

"Tell me," he asked Cain, "why the major insecurity about me being here? What is it that you're up to?"

Cain didn't like that. His smile disappeared, his eyes narrowing.

"Ah, a man with something to hide," Grayson added.

The tension between them mounted. His radar was up and on the alert for magic. Then Cain shoved him in the chest with his fist. His eyes had turned black.

Grayson stood his ground, but glanced around. "You'll have us thrown out. Is that what you want?" His blood pumped when he realized that might very well happen and then Cain would have achieved his goal.

Cain snorted derisively. "Thrown out, why no." He didn't like being second-guessed. His eyes illuminated, turning into incandescent discs. "Allow me to get you a drink," he muttered under his breath, and then clicked his fingers and pointed.

A passing woman teetered on her heels and her drink sloshed out of her glass and on to Grayson's clothes.

She stopped dead, hand over her mouth when she saw the huge wet patch on his shirt. "Oh, I'm so sorry."

Grayson flashed her a sympathetic smile, hard though that was given his current mood. "Not your fault, sweetheart."

"I must've tripped," she added, confusion on her face.

"Really, it wasn't your fault." The crowd was giving Cain cover. This was annoying.

The alcohol had soaked right through his shirt to his skin. There had been far more than a glassful. Apparently Cain had no discretion when it came to performing magic. As if to prove that very point, Cain nodded and the two men at his sides stepped away.

Cain lifted one hand in front of him, fingers splayed, energy radiating from his palm.

Grayson flew backward several feet.

He heard the crackle of flames. The fireplace was right behind him and he was soaked in alcohol. Cain's eyes continued to glitter, and his smug smile was back. Grayson didn't like this, not one bit. He was on the verge of losing what little cool he had left. Cain had put him in a position where he had to use magic to protect himself and others, in a crowded public place. Why? Just to find out if he could?

At his back, heat shot up to furnace level and the fire hissed and spat. Even as he lifted his hands and whispered an enchantment, somebody nearby shouted a warning about the log on the fire sizzling dangerously.

The doors and windows crashed open. Wind blew the fire back, dampening it down in the hearth. Inside a heartbeat, the atmosphere grew smoky.

"Happy now?" he snapped at Cain.

Cain's hands were back in his pockets, a nonchalant look on his face. People herded away from the fireplace, confusion reigning over what had happened. Tom Cadell, the landlord, was out and clearing up the charred logs from the hearth, fussing over the people who were nearby the incident, offering them a drink on the house.

"Grayson?"

It was Zoë's voice, and his heart sank when he turned and saw the expression on her face, the accusation and confusion was there in her eyes. She'd seen the whole thing. She knew that he was a witch, too.

"Oh, didn't she know?" Cain said mockingly, as he observed the pair of them.

Zoë looked from one of them to the other, her expression filled with wariness and betrayal.

That was the last straw.

"Get out of my way." Grayson pushed Cain as he approached, because all he wanted to do was get rid of him and talk to Zoë, to draw her back and wipe away the shock and disappointment he saw in her eyes.

Tom, the landlord, was on his feet and in between them in a flash, urging them toward the door. "Okay, fellas, if you're going to fight take it outside."

Grayson forced himself to take his eyes off his target, and that's when he saw Zoë turning away from him. Not before he registered the look on her face—a look that made him hate what he was, and what it made him do.

* * *

Zoë's stomach balled, her head spinning. Backing away, she turned and stumbled through the dance floor, then headed for the exit beyond.

She'd seen it with her own eyes—the way Cain had moved his hands like a conjuror, and the spilled drink, Grayson's expression when he was shoved by nothing at all. As they sparred, his eyes had changed color and shone silver, just as they had on their first night together.

Then the flames had shot high behind him. They framed him for an instant, and her heart had nigh on stopped, fearing for his life. His subsequent reaction had taken her breath away. Like a magician, he had countered Cain's move. The very same accusation he'd used against them—a supposed warning no less—and there he was practicing magic as well.

Her hands were shaking, her legs wobbly under her, but she managed to find her way into a lobby at the back of the hall. There was a door to the outside on the right, and it stood open. Lights illuminated a stone path that meandered into the forest. On her left was the ladies' cloakroom.

She stumbled through the door and stood at the sink—hands on the cool porcelain to ground her—and looked at her reflection in the mirror. Her skin was pale and her mouth was dry. Fear and betrayal shone in her eyes.

She turned on the tap and splashed her face with water, drinking from the cup of her hand. There was no denying it now, she'd been forced to believe by what had happened before her very eyes. When Grayson had said Cain and his lot were practicing witches, he meant it. And he knew that because he was one as well.

Lifting her head, she ran her damp fingers through her hair, forcing herself to breathe slower to regain her equilibrium. How could he? And yet it explained so much. As she stared at her own wild eyes, she also realized that she would never, ever forget how bloody sexy he'd looked, standing there with his arms lifted, eyes flashing silver and his hair blowing in the powerful wind he'd conjured. She couldn't deny that she'd been impressed—aroused, too— by his display of power. Guilt had shone in his eyes when he realized she was there, that was true, but he couldn't deny it. He should have told her, and she felt like a fool for not figuring it out earlier.

Magic exists, get used to it. She snorted at herself then grew thoughtful again. *Can I really accept it? Maybe.*

If she could, was it because of the invisible friend who walked alongside her or was it her involvement with Grayson? Or was it because she was good old Zoë Daniels, the reliable PA who could cope with anything you threw at her? Her boss always said she'd be the last one standing if war broke out in the office.

When she reached for a paper towel from the dispenser, the door opened and someone else entered the cloakroom. It was Elspeth. She was dressed entirely in black, her chestnut hair loose and glossy. The dress she wore was similar to her own, close-fit, but she wore it with knee-length leather boots.

Zoë dried her hands, tossed the paper towel into the wastebasket. Her thoughts untangled and then drifted back to that strange vision she'd had when she was with Cain, on her first night in Carbrey. Was Elspeth involved in this?

"Men, huh?" Elspeth said.

Zoë hadn't even realized she was in the pub, but she had obviously witnessed the whole thing as well.

Elspeth sidled over and stood right up beside her, hip to hip, looking at her reflection alongside Zoë's in the mirror.

"They're always fighting over territory like gnarly old tomcats." She chuckled to herself as if it was just a tasty piece of local gossip.

Was she one of them, a witch? Was the whole village riddled with supernatural secrets? "You knew about him when I came here, didn't you? When you introduced us in the post office you knew that he practiced witchcraft back then, that's why you were annoyed about him. It's not just about research and his book, is it?"

Elspeth shrugged casually. "I wasn't sure. I suspected it, but it's hard to get a handle on him when he's only around here occasionally." She spoke as if they were chatting about some inane topic, not the fact they were all stalking each other and casting spells at will.

"His guard has been down somewhat," Elspeth added, "since you've been around."

The comment made Zoë feel emotional and unsteady. Was it meant to? And why did her chest ache? *I care about him*. If only he'd explained all this. He'd had her trust. "What is it you want from me? To know about Annabel?"

Elspeth gave a slow, feline smile, and wrapped her hand around Zoë's waist, looking at her directly for the first time. "Wouldn't it be fun to have someone like Annabel around, for real?"

"What do you mean?"

"To bring her back to life."

For some unaccountable reason, Zoë felt annoyed and challenged by that. Was her spirit friend sidling alongside her again, egging her on, or was she getting a proper handle on the situation? "If Annabel wanted to do more than she already does, I'm sure she could. She's a powerful spirit."

Elspeth laughed softly. "It's not that simple."

"Have you seen her?" Zoë demanded.

Elspeth didn't reply, and that told Zoë what she wanted to know.

"If you had seen her and been inside her mind the way I have then you'd know how powerful she is, and what she can do. It's more than just appearing as a ghost, you know, she can make me see into her life as well."

"Oh, my, you two are getting close, that's good news."

Why the hell am I defending a dead witch? Zoë wondered. Was it because they all wanted a piece of Annabel, and she felt close to her and protective because of the visions she'd had, the moments of her life that Annabel had cared to share with her?

"Oh, hush, don't get upset, I'm just having fun with you," Elspeth added, and licked her lower lip, laughing softly. "Why not?"

Elspeth stroked her arm and hummed softly under her breath. Zoë forgot what she was going to say, because she became mesmerized by the way the other woman's lips looked, so soft and full and glossed red. Her perfume was exotic, something with musky undertones. Her breasts were lush under the sheath of a dress she wore. She certainly wasn't wearing a bra underneath it. Curious, Zoë found that she wanted to touch the other woman, to explore her, sexually. *I'm a mess.* Was this Annabel's doing? Her hands were shaking again and she clutched them to her sides to still them.

"You're looking very aroused, my dear." Elspeth looked rather pointedly at Zoë's chest. The direct stare almost seemed to touch her. "Is the cottage getting to you?"

Zoë couldn't respond to the question because Elspeth stood so close against her, and the mood had shifted. Elspeth lifted a stray hair from Zoë's neck, running the back of her fingers down her skin as she did so.

"They say it has a strange effect on people who stay there. You know, their sexuality thrives in the atmosphere." Elspeth's eyebrows lifted suggestively.

Heat surfaced in Zoë's face. Memories of the vision she'd had up at the Tide Inn filled her mind—Elspeth on her back, Cain behind her. Her breasts were chafing and she could tell by the way Elspeth looked at her that the other woman could see her nipples through her dress.

"Poor Zoë, you have got it bad." Elspeth cupped Zoë's breasts lightly through the fabric of her dress and bra, and then ran her thumbs over the surface of the material, tantalizing Zoë.

"Some women can come," Elspeth continued, almost idly, "just from having their breasts stimulated."

Zoë shook her head. That had never been the case for her. "I don't think that I—"

She couldn't finish the sentence, because Elspeth was already plucking at the slim straps on Zoë's dress, easing them off her shoulders and slipping her dress down so that it hung around her waist, exposing her bra. "Oh, please, you're so turned on, let me have a try. It's only a bit of fun."

The expression on Elspeth's face was so suggestive. Even though it seemed like an impossible idea, and the setup was so alien to her, she couldn't resist. "What if someone comes in?"

"So what," Elspeth replied, and reached around Zoë's back to undo the bra, her hair brushing against Zoë's face in a seductive curtain.

"There," Elspeth said, letting the bra drop down. "What gorgeous breasts you have." Her glossy red lips curved in a decadent smile, eager and unashamed.

Zoë staggered back against the sink, her bottom leaning up against it for support. She was giddy with arousal and when Elspeth cupped and squeezed her breasts, brusquely, and then rolled her nipples between her thumb and fingers, she thought she would keel over.

"Oh, oh!" Her hands clutched at the sink behind her as she tried to keep some measure of decorum. Elspeth had lifted one of her breasts high and was suckling on the nipple.

A dart of pleasure shot through Zoë, making her whole body thrill and pulse. Breathless, her pussy flooding, she had to grip on to the edge of the porcelain sink behind her and shut her eyes for a moment. The feeling was so intense, needles of pleasurable pain that made her squirm. Within moments she was gone on it and an intense climax hit her, an ecstatic release that looped from breasts to clit and back again.

"There," Elspeth said as she lifted her head. "You *are* a lusty lass." She moved straight in for a kiss on the mouth, taking Zoë unawares, and then pushed one of her knees between Zoë's legs.

Taken aback, Zoë's lips parted, and then she melted. Elspeth's mouth tasted of wine and sweetness, and Zoë clamored for more. Her hands found their way onto Elspeth's waist. Stroking higher, she felt her way until she was able to cup those breasts through her dress.

"Your breasts feel so good, so soft!"

Elspeth wasted no time. She pulled up the jersey sheath she wore so that Zoë could touch her bare skin. She had on a black G-string and she was maneuvering to straddle Zoë's thigh, pressing her pussy against it.

Zoë could smell her arousal in the midst of the musky scent she wore, and it sent her into overdrive. Shocked at her own behavior, she was scarcely able to believe she was doing this, making out with another woman, and yet she was unable to stop herself. *I'm lost to this, lost.* She cupped her own pussy in one hand, pressing hard for relief while she squeezed the soft flesh of Elspeth's breast.

"Oh, yes," Elspeth said, "I knew I liked you when you arrived, Zoë Daniels. You're perfect."

Panting in unison, they quickly found release.

"Come on, let's get out of here," Elspeth said hurriedly as she shrugged her dress down into position, before helping Zoë.

Awash with release and drugged on it, Zoë was unsure what to do, and took Elspeth's offered hand. Her body was still tingling wildly as they left the cloakroom.

The dance raged on in the hall, but Zoë didn't want to go back in there. Elspeth led her the other way, toward the open door and the path into the forest.

Zoë was glad of it. From the moment she'd arrived, she'd wanted to go there. Maybe now was the time. She hankered to go back and find Grayson, too, to have it out with him and tell him what she thought of his secrets and duplicity.

Elspeth was leading the way, gesturing for her to follow.

Just for a little while, Zoë thought, let him wait.

Yes, he could've told her the truth earlier if he really cared about her reaction, she told herself, as she darted out into the night, into the forest.

17

THEY COULD STILL HEAR THE MUSIC FROM THE pub as they wove through the trees, and the sounds of bagpipes seemed to dash and fly alongside them, like a wild Scottish sprite delighted to have them here in its lair.

Zoë's heart raced, liberation rushing in her veins as she and Elspeth moved through the tall trees and bushes. The sun had set and silvering moonlight spliced the dark shadows, eerily carving out shapes amongst the trees in the gloom. It was just as it had been in her dreams, mysterious and vibrant, filled with the secrets of all who had been here before.

Elspeth seemed to know the winding path well, and led the way quickly. The path soon got rougher underfoot, as if less frequented. Zoë stumbled and wobbled on her heels as she went, but didn't care.

Even though it hadn't rained in days there was a damp, earthy smell that intoxicated her, as if the humidity of the day had gathered under the foliage and in the rough ground. The creaking branches and scurrying noises in the undergrowth made the place come alive, and her senses responded, tripping somewhere between fear and elation.

Through the trees up ahead, she could see a fire flickering. Elspeth seemed to be leading her to it. The sight struck her oddly, because it looked like the place she'd seen in her first vision, the very night she'd arrived in Carbrey. As they closed on it she saw candles placed here and there on the rocks, lit and dripping wax, as if marking the path. As they approached the edge of the clearing she heard sounds, animalistic sounds.

The fire was built on a patch of ground strewn with sand and ashes. It stood in a circular clearing among the trees, and her breath caught as she stared at the scene. There, on the ground next to the fire was Crawford, and he was making love to a blonde woman on the forest floor.

"Stop, they'll see us if we get any nearer," Zoë whispered urgently, pulling on Elspeth's hand in an effort to halt her.

Elspeth smiled.

She knew, Zoë realized, and it didn't bother her. Elspeth already knew what they were doing when she'd headed up here.

"It's only Crawford and Isla, they won't mind." Elspeth urged her on, beyond the edge of the clearing.

Zoë stumbled after her and stared in disbelief, unable to drag her gaze away from the couple shagging in the firelight, right there in the open air. The woman was panting and grunting loudly, clearly loving it, her fingernails scratching at Crawford's back as he thrust into her. He had his jeans down around his thighs, and his arse looked fit and tight, flexing repeatedly as he thrust inside his lover. She had her knees drawn up, her heels digging into his buttocks, her skirt up around her waist. It was so lewd and debauched and it felt so odd to be standing there watching them, but Zoë couldn't turn away. It was just like it had been in her dreams.

Elspeth squeezed her hand, and nodded across the fire. Following her gaze, Zoë saw that there were others watching, too, their faces eerie in the firelight.

The couple on the forest floor had reached their crescendo, and Crawford then let out an almighty roar, lifting right up on his arms, his body arched and his hips pivoting at the woman's crotch.

His partner screamed with delight, her hips gyrating under him. She was milking him off, and Zoë's sex clenched, identifying with that most innate action. She felt hot and restless, anxious and aroused, even while her mind questioned what she was doing watching other people fucking on the forest floor.

Peering across the fire, she could see that the others were talking amongst themselves. One man swigged from a bottle of wine and then looked from the couple to her and Elspeth. Crawford stood up and turned to face them as he did up his zipper. "Who's next?" he said, with a lascivious, expectant grin on his face.

"Go easy," Elspeth said to him, her voice low, and then she closed on Zoë, wrapping her arms around her and kissing her cheek.

Zoë wavered, her ability to respond appropriately to Crawford vanishing in the haze of her arousal. "I shouldn't be here," she whispered.

She wanted sex, but her mind kept flitting back to Grayson. She scanned the faces of those present. Would he appear too, with all the other witches? Would he watch while Crawford fucked her, would he join in? The unbidden thoughts made her edgy and skittish. The urge to run crept up on her. Was this what people did, people who practiced witchcraft? The questions seem to wrap themselves around her, assailing her senses, making her feel light-headed.

She clung to Elspeth and Elspeth whispered soothingly in her ear, words that she couldn't understand, words that sounded deliriously intoxicating.

Her body seemed to lift and peel away in the moonlight, and she raised her arms above her head. Bathed in moon and firelight, she was filled with sensory seductions.

Then the others began to circle around her, chanting slowly. Zoë felt them touching her, stroking her. She felt kisses on her bare shoulders and arms. So many hands. Fingers whispered over her—soft feminine hands, and larger, rougher male hands that squeezed her flesh as if testing ripe fruit.

Grayson. Her body craved his. Was he here? She struggled to keep her eyes open, looking for him amongst the faces moving around her. Cain was there, and she was vaguely aware of him drawing a line around her with a stick, making a circle in the sand and ashes on the ground. When it was complete, the line flamed into life creating a circle of fire that enclosed her, separating her from the others.

I should be afraid, she thought, but she was too languid and aroused. The flames danced along the edge of the circle. Her hips rolled, her hands roving over her body, answering the call in her full breasts and the longing ache between her thighs, touching, rubbing.

Her eyes were closing, yet still she heard the voices chanting, and then she heard a word that she understood, a name: Annabel.

They were calling to Annabel.

Unease ratcheted inside her, her spirit torn between

earthly pleasures and fear of the unknown. Struggling to regain her consciousness, she found herself dreamlike and back on the path through the forest, running, racing through the trees.

But it was Annabel who was at her side and gesturing for her to follow, not Elspeth. Annabel in her long gown, with her hair trailing down as far as her waist.

A vision.

Annabel had been here, long ago. She'd been here in this forest, she'd had sex with a lover here, and she wanted Zoë to know that. Excitement lit Zoë's blood.

Stay with me, Annabel's voice urged within Zoë's mind. *Stay with me, and I'll lead you through this and out of here.*

But Zoë wasn't sure.

Ahead of Annabel it was dark, the darkest, blackest night she had ever seen. Would she ever truly find her way out if she followed? In the faint moonlight, Annabel's ghostly form wisped in and out of focus and Zoë yearned to follow her. She peered into the darkness. The voices chanted on around her, the heat from the fire swamping her.

You will understand, Zoë, you will.

"Wait for me, tell me what it is you want me to know," she whispered, unable to move forward, and yet desperate to keep up with Annabel.

It had to be done.

Drugged by the strange experience, Zoë reached again for Annabel, grasping at the lifeline she seemed to offer, her consciousness fading....

The master is leading me into the forest. He waylaid me as I was on my way to pick summer berries and ordered me to leave my basket and to follow him here instead. His mood is not good.

With one hand locked around my wrist he drags me alongside him, his handsome mouth tightly closed.

"Ewan, what is it? Whatever is the matter?"

He does not reply.

We follow the path to the place where the coven meet, but the brethren are not here with us now. It is just the two of us, and the master is like a stranger to me. His head is bare, his hat who knows where, and his necktie is askew. His hair is uncombed, and he looks as if he has barely slept.

Beneath the trees the scent is high for it rained heavily in the night, an early summer storm, and while it is fresh down by the harbor, up here in the trees the musky smell of damp undergrowth fills the air. The ground is muddy and the path is damp and slippery beneath my boots, sending me skittering on the path.

He does not look back, does not seem to notice. Why is he bringing me here now, and why does he not speak? My heart beats hard in my chest, for I have a dreadful bad feeling about this.

"Talk to me," I plead, "tell me what it is that you need. I promise I will do whatever you want, if only you would look my way and speak to me."

Still he does not answer. Instead, he drags me even faster across the ground, intent on some purpose known only to himself. I can barely keep up, my footsteps stumbling in his wake, my skirts snagging on branches. Then I see our own place up ahead, the clearing where our coven meets. The circles of rocks mark the five points where we have set our fires, and the earth is burnt from our rituals.

He stops walking and pulls me up short in front of him, strong hands wrapped round my wrists. I have to stand on my toes and stretch, for he seems determined that I look him directly in the eye.

"Feel my ire," he urges, "know it in your soul."

I do feel it, I see it and I feel it, a churning vat of pain that he wishes to share with me. Betrayal, there is betrayal there too, amid the rage in his expression.

"I see it, my beloved master, but I do not understand."

"I thought you had more sense, Annabel McGraw. You are fickle, as unruly as a bored child. I scorn you for wasting precious time, for inviting trouble upon the coven by dallying with villagers when you should be honing your skills." He kicks half-burnt logs out of his way before he pushes me down in the ashes.

My body hits the ground, my spirit fast feeling what he wants me to know—humility, shame. He is showing me how he could break me. That I could be as easily fated by him as a woodland creature or a captured bird that he would sacrifice for some greater purpose.

Clumsily I sprawl, charred wood and rocky earth rough beneath my back, my left leg twisted beneath me. As his chosen woman amongst the coven, I can think of no greater shame that he could bestow upon me.

I try to rise up on my hands, my emotions unsteady and my thoughts running this way and that as I try to understand his actions. I resent him for this. "Why do you try to shame me this way?"

He drops to his knees beside me and shoves me to the ground with his hand hard against my chest. I cry out when the rocks and stones dig into my back. His eyes blaze and his lips are drawn back from his teeth. His anger is overwhelming. I feel it pumping violently from the hand he has splayed at the base of my throat where the skin is bare. His palm is so hot it makes me squirm for fear of being branded by him, a demon's mark that I know he has the power to bestow. And yet it makes me lusty, too, for he is so handsome when his immense magical power burns in his eyes this way.

"You have been foolish, risking our secret, risking so much for a roll with an oaf of a fisherman."

Was that it? That he is jealous of Irvine? I cannot fathom it at first, for he takes lovers where he chooses and it has not bothered *him when I have done the same. But I am delighted, too, and I begin to see how I can turn this.*

"Why do you do this?" he demands. "Is it not enough that together we could own all of the magic in Scotland?" He closes his fist around the air in front of my face, and I see the immense light that glows from within it. I watch, secretly delighted by his actions. I am almost gleeful that his need for me has driven him to express himself in forbidden magical enchantments. He opens his fist and the light swirls out into the atmosphere, sparkling with colors, before darting away into the trees.

"Ewan, surely you cannot be jealous of Irvine Maginty?"

He snorts at me. "I am disgusted that you squander yourself, when you could be the most powerful she-witch in all of Scotland."

Oh, but his jealousy thrills me. "I amuse myself only when you are not there. It is nothing."

Oho, he does not take kindly to that, his lips tightening. But it makes him even more desirable to me. This man so wild and inscrutable has drawn women from far and wide, and here he is wrestling with a tide of emotion that I could ride upon the crest of.

"I know that you have bedded Hettie," I state, to rent asunder his attack on Irvine, but he's not surprised that I know. Women can find out these things, we know things men can only guess at, even the men who practice witchcraft. He's used to that. I clasp the hand he released the magic from, and hold it fast. "What will happen if the bairns Hettie Maginty carries are not Irvine's at all, but yours? Is that why she is so afraid? Is that why she dreads the day they will be born?"

He shrugs it off. "She was eager at first but she defied me, so I saddled her with two demon spawn." His mouth twists.

I feel a sense of pity for Hettie.

I am fascinated by the master's actions and I begin to see the truth of it. He knows that I like Irvine, that he is more than a passing fancy, and he is afraid of losing me. Me, the woman he has allied himself to in the coven. I sense it all too well. He'd break me in two rather than share me.

In that moment something turns inside me and his jealous rage begins to inspire me. Seizing my chance, I dare to challenge him.

"Your anger is a weakness." I flash my eyes at him.

Danger races fast within me, unleashing a rush akin to dancing with the dark Lord himself. His fury brings danger in its wake. Oh, but how very delicious that is. Brave or foolish, I cannot stop myself. I dare to take another step into the devil's stall. "A coven master must never show weakness."

He roars aloud, pushing my head back against the ground with his palm hard under my chin. My throat is closed and he could break me easily within moments, but I am herding my fear. Too many times it is that I have been in this place, when I had no home of my own and no one to call brethren, and I learnt how to think fast and how to survive.

His eyes are now dark with lust instead of anger, with the need for possession. I begin to gain the full measure of his mood. I gasp for breath. "I am your handmaiden, your bride in the coven," I whisper.

His hold loosens.

My body responds. The power that shifts between us baits my attention. I lift one booted foot alongside his knee, hooking him. He does not pull away, and the fire in his eyes shifts and burns in a different way.

I rub that foot up and down his flank, and then reach for the laces on my bodice, daring him with a glance, all the while.

He pauses, and I feel the rolling power at his back as he takes strength in the need I display for him. He wants to possess me. He needs me to prostate myself before him, to offer myself to him and him alone. This man who I look up to has weaknesses, and I am one of them. I could shape and twist and turn him as easy as if he were a broken doll in a child's hands. The knowledge burns within me and it makes me wilder still. I wriggle free of my bodice, exposing my breasts to him, pulling on the hardening nipples.

The air is cool on my knotted teats, but his gaze is hot. Oh, I all but have him now, and nary a spell in sight. How that delights me! He will ride me and he will ride me well, bucking like a young foal, fuelled as he is by this bout of jealousy. My anticipation mounts, my cunny fast growing damp and slippery as I see where this will go if I just push it in the right direction.

I grip my skirts in my hands, and as I lift them I let my legs fall open. My skirts and petticoats gather at my waist. Look at me, I silently urge him, look at me and take me.

Mercifully his glance lowers to my intimate parts and I know I will get what I want.

"I know what you need, master, I know what it is that tangles you so." I practically sing the words I speak them so beguilingly, and I'm pleased with myself when I see him at odds with his needs, his anger waylaid by a greater emotion.

"You need a ride of my cunny to soothe your temper. You need to spill your seed inside me to claim what is yours."

He does not answer me, but I see him clench his jaw.

"I'm wet between my legs now, wet because I want to please you." I shove my hand down there, spreading my nether lips so that he can see. That makes me buck against the ground, for the wanton in me loves to act this way. The cold air rushes over my bare flesh and I gasp aloud, my hips moving and lifting. I rub my fingers over the stiff bud of my womanhood, offering my lusty hole to him.

When I look down at his belt I see that he is large within the confines of his breeches, his shaft long and hard and poking through the material demandingly.

I run one finger in and out of my hole, nodding at his cock. "Spend your seed here, where it will be gratefully received, master of Carbrey."

He curses me even while he fumbles with his breeches and frees his member. It is stiff and large and dark with blood, and I lift my hips to receive it. He climbs between my legs, shoving my knees farther apart forcibly, muttering bitter words beneath his breath. While he rubs his fist back and forth over his manhood he stares down at me, and the head of his member grows darker still and juice oozes from its tip.

"Spread yourself wider, wench. Offer yourself to me again!"

A breathy laugh escapes my mouth as I lift my boots from the ground, my hands wrapped around the undersides of my thighs, and thrust my heels high in the air, opening myself wide, exposing everything to him, an invitation I know he cannot resist.

Climbing over me, he thrusts into me with all his might, claiming me. His manhood is so large I gasp when it stretches me to accommodate his fierce entry. He pins me down with his hands on my shoulders, throws his head back and roars aloud as he grinds into me, his hips working back and forth, back and forth, until I feel my own juices running down my bottom and onto the ground.

On my back, I have him.

From the ground where he threw me, I can make him do as I want. I cry out with joy, wild beneath him as he is riding me.

His sack bangs hard at my rear and I know he will not last long, but oh it is so good and my cunny squeezes every ounce of pleasure from him, until I wail with pleasure, my spending so thorough that I laugh aloud in my moment of release.

I want to test him, see how far I can control him, and I grasp his coat, tug on it. "You know that I only toy with other men to test my powers."

I swallow hard, denying the unbidden emotions that crowd in on me in that moment, the image of a strong young fisherman who plagues my thoughts and dreams, and I press on, denying it even to myself. "It is you and only you that I want plowing my furrow. It is you who makes me writhe with ecstasy."

As he ruts me vigorously, closing on his release, I cry aloud. A dark thrill has bedded inside me. I could roll away from him now, force him to spill his seed on the ground, and he would still want more of me.

I can control the coven master if I so wish.

Can you guess how good that feels?

Can you truly guess how good that feels, Zoë?

18

GRAYSON TRIED ONCE MORE TO CAJOLE THE landlord, who currently had him standing at the bottom of the steps outside the front of the pub, following Cain's complaint about his conduct. "Tom, it was a minor disagreement. You know me well enough by now, surely?"

"I do, and I'm sorry. I don't know what your grief with Cain is, but he is a big employer around these parts and he's brought a lot of business to this village. I'm grateful for that because we get the overflow when his place is full." As he spoke, Tom looked unsure, as if it didn't sit right with him.

Gray was desperate to get back inside but arguing wasn't the way to do it, so he held his hands up and backed off. "I understand. I don't want to cause you any trouble."

Tom nodded his thanks and then disappeared into the pub. Grayson managed to wait a whole two minutes before he edged back in, steering well clear of the bar, and headed through to the dance hall. Cain and Crawford and their other cronies were nowhere to be seen. He dodged through the crowd and scanned the room. Zoë was also nowhere to be found. She'd disappeared out the door at the back of the hall earlier and it didn't look as if she had returned.

Where was she? He walked straight across the dance floor, dodging several dancers who blocked his way. In the lobby, he pushed the door to the ladies' cloakroom open. It was empty. There was another door, and it was open to the outside.

The forest? Alone?

Unease ratcheted inside him, and he strode out the door and onto the path. It was dark, and he thanked the elements that the moon was almost full. He jogged along into the forest, senses on high alert. Zoë had definitely come this way—minutes before, if that—and she hadn't been alone. His jaw tightened. That was even worse than being alone, if she was with any of Cain's lot.

As the forest thickened, a wall of trees groaned and shifted and closed together in front of him. He slammed his hands up against the thick rough bark, just stopping himself before he ran smack dab into it. The surface was barbed, and he tore his hands away, pain needling under the skin.

A boundary spell.

Turning left, another wall of trees hammered him back.

The only way that wasn't closed off to him was the path back to the village. Not only that, the bark on the trees was dangerous. He shook his head. Normally a boundary spell would come with a warning—two would be fair and polite. Traditionally boundary spells were meant to warn people off a private zone, not go so far as to actually physically injure anyone. Of course, that was assuming the magic was being used by a coven with a conscience, which this one was bereft of.

They didn't want him in there, which meant Zoë was

in there. Cain had done his best to unravel what was between him and Zoë over the course of the day, and he'd now whisked Zoë away.

Grayson put his hands on his hips as he looked up at the trees. There was no moonlight shining through the boundary area, but neither could he see a full canopy of leaves overhead. It was rather like a stage set.

"Tacky," he commented, his hopes lifting. This boundary spell had been cast shoddily. No surprise there. Stepping back along the path he'd come along, he ducked down and picked up some stones. Aiming one at the top of the trees he threw it. It bounced back at him. He threw one a little higher and heard it plop down on the other side. There was no guarantee the trees wouldn't close in on him again if he managed to surmount the obstacle, but he had to give a try.

With apologies to the forest, he pointed up at a pine several feet behind him, and—whispering the ancient Celtic words—requested the tree aid him. The tree split at the base and, with a loud cracking sound, it fell, landing on top of the boundary. Testing the trunk, he clambered on to it. By the time he'd climbed up his arms were scratched and stinging, but he could see fire flickering on the clearing in the forest that lay ahead, and smoke rising into the night sky, shadow on shadow. It urged him on and pretty soon he was on top of the boundary wall.

Darkness yawned open below him on the other side. He couldn't be sure this was not a trap, but he could see the gathering up ahead and he had to find Zoë. Ready to scramble, he jumped down into the darkness. Mercifully, he hit rough ground.

Rolling free from the fall, he squatted, staying low and catching his breath. He heard voices up ahead. The moon shone through brighter here on this side of the boundary, and he could see that he was back on the path. Stealth was on his side now, but time might not be, and he hurried on.

The smell of woodsmoke filled the air and he could see the flames between the trees. They were performing a ritual up at the clearing, a spot that had been used for such practices for centuries gone by. Following the flickering flames he hunted them down, darting swiftly through the trees.

Figures moved in a circle around the fire. Cain Davot's coven. Craning his neck to see what was going on, he cursed low under his breath when he saw Zoë. The sight of her hit him like a fist to his gut.

Flames licked along the ground in a perfect circle some six feet across around where she stood. Davot's coven surrounded it, hands linked. Cain was chanting loudly.

Anger powered through him, the blood in his temples pounding. If anything happened to Zoë he would never forgive himself. If only he had explained the situation better, she wouldn't be here now. She seemed not to be afraid, as if unaware of the ring of fire, and he saw that her eyes were glazed and trancelike, her hands roving over her body in a slow, erotic dance of desire.

He recognized familiar faces amongst the coven. Along with Elspeth and Crawford, he saw Daphne and Isla, and two older women from the village. A couple of the waiters from the Tide Inn were also present. He'd never known exactly who it was that made up the full quorum until now.

The spell that was being chanted was unfamiliar, but he picked up words and meaning here and there. He suspected that it was magic from the forbidden book. They were beckoning to Zoë, keying into the deepest part of her as if trying to draw something out. What was it?

The slinky white dress she wore was torn, her bra strap down and one of her breasts was bared. Her beautiful body moved rhythmically through instinct, seduced by their spell and yet innately sensuous. In the firelight she looked like a captured goddess to him.

That's when he heard it, Annabel McGraw's name.

The information processed quickly.

Necromancy and possession? *Shit.*

Pure, undiluted rage powered through him as everything fell into place, his hands fisting at his sides. He had encouraged Zoë to stay here in Carbrey; this was his fault. He was furious with himself for not having seen this coming, for not realizing that Cain Davot was behind Annabel's increasing presence. He'd been blind, betrayed by his own instincts, and now he had to make that right. Taking a deep breath, he gathered his deepest energies and began to chant the ancient words, calling upon the elements.

Anger built inside him, threatening to trip him up. His enchantment remained incomplete. Leveling himself, he stretched his arms and looked up to the sky, and chanted again. Closing his eyes, he visualized the electricity in the atmosphere and turned it into something much larger, a storm so immense that it would crack the sky open.

Thunder rolled overhead and a massive strike of lightning lit up the treetops. One of the coven members screamed.

Grayson breathed deep into his lungs and harkened the unruliest winds from the north, the iciest sleet. As the storm built and unfolded, he hunkered closer to the earth, moving over the ground stealthily, watching as the circle broke and split into clusters.

Gale force winds crashed through the trees, making the

flames flicker wildly and sending the small crowd this way and that.

"What foreign spell is this?" Davot shouted.

The annoyance in his voice fuelled Grayson and he chanted again, wielding the elements at his command. Davot's hair was blowing across his face as he glared into the undergrowth, looking for his challenger, his body physically buffeted from side to side by the wind as he did so.

Lightning struck close by, right at the edge of the clearing. A hefty branch split, peeled away from its tree overhead and fell across the clearing. When the branch hit the ring of fire the leaves lit, flames shooting high and wild. Two members of the coven scattered into the trees. Grayson heard one of them scream, and knew that they had fallen.

"This isn't right, Cain," Daphne shouted out, her words lifted by the wind. "Something's gone wrong. This is too dangerous."

Davot yelled back at her, "Hold your tongue!"

Daphne shook her head and turned away from him. At the same time, the sky opened and torrents of icy cold rain lashed down on them. The circle of fire that locked Zoë to the spot was quickly extinguished. The flaming branch troubled a bit longer, before dampening down as well.

Zoë had reacted physically. The trance had been broken. Her arms were clutched against her chest for protection against the rain, and she was peering up at the sky. Fear filled her expression, making Grayson ever-more determined. He had to get her out, now.

The remainder of Davot's people clung together, hunched over—physically buffeted by storm force gales and drenched to the skin—awaiting his command. Grayson was close enough to see that there were only five of them left, and Davot. Even though he was behind Davot, Grayson could feel his rage building. It poured out of him in ugly, vindictive waves, his whole aura brittle and angry.

Grayson strode into the clearing.

Davot turned around as he approached. "Murdoch."

"You will live long enough to regret this," Grayson warned. "Go back to the village," he shouted across at the remaining members of the coven. "You were foolish to mess with this."

Davot moved to stand between Grayson and Zoë, blocking his way. Torrents of water ran down the hillside, turning the forest floor into mud. The rest of the group began to back away. Grayson saw Elspeth there amongst them, huddled against the elements, her expression resigned as she looked his way.

"Cain, I'm leaving," she called, and then encouraged the others to go. They headed in the direction of the village for safety, stumbling through the forest as they went.

Davot cursed them and then launched himself, aiming a static-filled fist at Grayson's gut. Grayson took the blow, but delivered one of his own. Davot cursed again, bitter Celtic words spewing from his lips.

"Grayson!" It was Zoë's voice calling to him, and it steeled him.

He studied Davot as he dodged another blow, sensing he was too angry to focus his magic effectively. Gathering his resources, he called upon the forest to exact revenge on the warped magic that had gone on here. Davot's feet went out from under him, and a boulder slid down the bank toward him as he tried to get to his feet. He scrabbled for purchase, knocked his head on a low-hanging tree branch, and fell.

"Come on, up the hill," Grayson shouted to Zoë, grabbing her by the hand and hugging her to him. "Away from the village."

"I can't," she said, pulling against him, her gaze flitting back down toward the village, denial and confusion resting heavy within her spirit. "I can't leave here. I have to stay near Annabel."

A binding spell? "Just as far as the main road. If we go back, we'll run into the rest of them."

Clutching at him, she looked up at him with a multitude of questions in her eyes. "What happened?" Her gaze went to the storm-filled night sky. "You did this, didn't you?"

He cupped her face, her confusion and pain a gnawing ache on his soul. "I'll explain as we go."

She looked over at Davot's slumped, mud-splattered body. "Is he…going to be okay?"

"He'll be awake soon enough. Let's get a head start." Leading her by the hand he struggled through the trees, encouraging her to keep up despite the driving rain. He headed up through the forest, inland, and away from the village. He knew a place where they could take shelter, somewhere off Cain's radar.

Zoë stumbled after him, one hand clutching her torn dress against her bared breast.

He paused, pulled the dress together and knotted the fabric on the shoulder. "Steady now. Follow in my steps."

"I'm okay, I think, just confused."

She didn't look okay. She was far from okay. He had to get her away and safe as soon as he could. He measured his steps, using the low-slung branches to haul them up by, lifting her over fallen debris, pausing frequently for her to rest. The slope was treacherous and the wind had not abated. If anything, the storm had more power.

"Why were they calling to Annabel?" she asked, and her words lifted on the wind. "Why did they have me in that circle?"

He paused by a large tree trunk for shelter and rest. "I think they're trying to bring her back to life." There was no point in beating around the bush, not anymore. She'd seen enough now, she had to be brought up to speed and made aware of exactly what it was they were dealing with.

"Elspeth said that." Light glinted off her eyes when they rounded. "Am I being pulled into some sort of reincarnation?"

"Well, re-embodiment would be a more appropriate term, but, yes."

"Shit!"

He nodded.

"Is that even possible?"

"Forbidden, occult magic." He shook his head, barely able to voice it to her. "Dangerous, evil, and totally against the laws of nature. Some people don't know when to stop."

"Shouldn't we call the police, or something?"

"And say what?"

"I see your point."

She looked so afraid, he hugged her to him. "Don't worry, precious, we'll sort this." He kissed her forehead. She was cold and afraid and he sensed that she was shocked to the core and closing up inside as the knowledge sank into her. He couldn't let that happen.

Taking her hand, he led her on and through the last of the trees. They had reached the low metal fence at the side of the main road, atop the cliff. They weren't far from the place where they had first met. If only he could have foreseen all this back then. He would have sent her on her way and things would have been different.

Zoë put her hands on her thighs and bent over, struggling to control her breathing. The rain was bouncing off the road. The lights at the crossroads up ahead made it look even more dramatic than it already was.

"I'm sorry I didn't listen, today," she said, straightening up. "I was upset."

"Hey now, I should have found a way to tell you, a better way." He pushed her wet hair back from her face. She was shivering violently. Part of it was shock, he was sure of that. "Not far now, there's a place we can go, over there on the other side of the road."

When she nodded, he clambered over the metal roadside fence, then gestured her closer and helped her to do the same. She stumbled over the barrier. With her hand in his, he listened for traffic. Nothing, except the crash of thunder and lightning in the forest behind them. It was going to run a while yet, and it would take its toll. There were huge stores of energy bound up in it, he could sense it. When he'd drawn on the natural forces he hadn't been totally in control. The destruction didn't lie easily with him, but nature would renew what was good. Nodding at her, he set off again and they darted across the road.

There was a cabin in the far woods on the other side of the east coast main road. He'd discovered it when he was tracing the ley lines in the area, a one-roomed wooden hut with a stone hearth, sturdily built, possibly an old shepherd's keep.

"My heel," Zoë said, limping to a halt beside him. The elegant heel was bent right off at the base. "I caught it back there. It's given way."

Lifting her in his arms, he kissed her forehead.

She clung to him, shivering, horribly wet and scared half to death. His resolve to undo the damage deepened as he covered the last few yards. When he set her on her feet next to the cabin door, he held her around her shoulders and squeezed her. "We can rest here."

Tugging the padlock, he whispered his command. At the very same time he was ruing the fact he'd had to use his magic so often this night. It tore him apart. He had no choice, because he'd rather lay his life on the line than risk Zoë's for another moment. Several bright, jagged sparks of fire leapt off the padlock and he tugged it free. The door creaked open.

Zoë pointed at the door frame. In the moonlight he could just make out what she was looking at. A spindly black spider disappeared off into the darkness. "Our friend came to see us again."

The comment made him smile. Things had changed since that first day, in so many ways. He lifted her and carried her inside. Although empty and disused, the cabin had retained much of the heat from earlier in the day and there was a slight fragrance of camphor wood in the air, making it more pleasant than it might have been. The floor was boarded and he would make it comfortable enough to shelter until dawn, when he would fetch transport.

He set Zoë down in the middle of the room. "Stand right here a moment. I need to secure this place."

She nodded, staring up at him for reassurance. It pained him to see the confusion in her eyes. It also gave his craft potency because it was him she was looking to, him that she had called for back there at the clearing, and that gave him the strength of a hundred men. It was a twisted reaction, to be sure, and he could only roll with what this situation was doing to him. He kissed her gently, reassuring her. A simmering arousal flamed in her, and he identified with it, responding, before he set about securing the small cabin.

There were no curtains on the two small windows to the

front of the property and he filled the windows with reflective light and then paced the edge of the interior walls, chanting a boundary spell. Pointing at one corner he led a line of fire around the edges of the floor. Lifting his arms over his head, he directed the seams of fire. They shot up the walls, spangling, and then closed into a central point on the beamed ceiling.

Zoë stared at the spectacle. "You scare me," she stated, simply. "This scares me."

That pained him deeply, but he understood it all too well, because of his parents. His mother's sacrifice on his behalf had been great. She'd given up the chance to be a proper mother to him, and he didn't want history to repeat itself. He didn't want his elemental magic to drive a wedge between him and Zoë, the way it had his parents. He strode back to her, taking her into his arms.

"No need for you to be scared of me, sweetheart. It's everybody else who needs to fear me, if they ever try to lay another finger on you." He kissed the top of her head, and was greatly relieved when he felt her hand curve around his waist. "You're safe now," he added.

She nodded, but he could tell she was still unsure as she watched the lines on the walls and ceiling fizz and settle into a warm glow.

He squatted at her feet and set about getting her out of her wet things. Lifting one foot, then the other, he took off her sandals. They were beyond a heel repair. She watched him as he undressed her, as if she were afraid he would disappear if she took her eyes off him. Rising to his feet he peeled her wet dress up from the hemline, encouraging her to lift her arms above her head.

After he'd helped her out of her underwear, she stood in front of him, entirely naked, shivering. He dropped the clothes to the floor, and rubbed her arms, drawing on some of the sexual energy between them to warm the room. Light from the spell he'd lodged in the walls shone on the side of her face, and his jaw tightened as he considered what might have happened if he hadn't got there in time. He bit back the rising tide of anger he felt when he considered how they meant to use Zoë.

"She's inside me, isn't she?" she whispered, staring up at him.

He shook his head.

If there was any possessing to be done around here, it was him that was going to do it. "Now that I know, I vow to stop it, to turn it back."

He wanted her so much, desire was driving him more than any other cause or ideal that he had ever held sacred before.

Kicking off his boots, he peeled his wet T-shirt off and opened his belt, shoving his jeans and jockey shorts down and off. Zoë watched, and the way she looked at him, with a haze of lust in her aura, sent his blood south. He pulled her back into his arms as soon as he was naked, and the heat between them grew and multiplied, warming the room, drying them both.

She reached around his neck, her hands on his hair as it dried under her fingers. Her eyes were wide and her lips were parted.

"I promise you, Zoë. I will find a way to stop this."

He stroked her, reveling in every soft curve. These past two days had set him spinning on the spot because of this, because of the way she felt and the way she responded to him. Her skin felt hot under his hands—was that good?— and her nipples were diamond hard against his chest. The smell of her arousal filled the place.

"I need you, Grayson." Her voice faltered, and she swallowed, color rising in her cheeks as she glanced down at his rising cock. With one hand, she reached down to cup his balls, rolling them in her hand. "I need you more than ever."

The touch of her hands made his back arch, her fingers handling him so boldly that it knocked the breath from his lungs.

"So turned on," she said, shifting from one foot to the other, she blurted the words out. "Need this."

"It's okay, I'm here. I'm here for you, right here." He'd barely responded, when her hand closed around his rigid cock.

Stroking up and down over the surface, watching it as she did so, she moaned softly.

Fuck. Too good.

The pressure she applied took away his ability to speak. Her hand was damp, and cooler than the rock-hard shaft of his erection. As she stroked the length of him, and then cupped his balls again, she whispered, "need this," over again.

He needed this too, needed this like he had never needed anything before. Ducking down, he found the condom in the pocket of his abandoned jeans and rolled it on quickly. Then he lifted her into his arms, and walked her back against the wall.

She clung to him readily, her shoulders resting back against the hard surface. With her hands locked around his neck, she pivoted against him, her breasts lifting toward his face. His cock bounced under her bottom, desperate to be inside her, desperate to claim her.

The smell of her arousal hit him like a drug he couldn't get enough of. He bent to kiss her nipple, pulling it into his mouth, sucking and licking it. She'd wrapped her legs around him and he was right where he wanted to be. He rested a kiss in her cleavage, and grazed her nipple with his teeth, sucking the soft, malleable flesh of her breasts into his mouth in hungry openmouthed kisses.

"Grayson, please."

There was such desperation in her voice, it wired him into her at the deepest level. "Yes, love, I'm right here."

Maneuvering her into position, he eased his cock between the swollen folds of her pussy.

An anxious cry escaped her open mouth when he made contact. The sound seemed to be wrenched from her. When he moved his cock, stroking it over the hard nub of her clit, she cried out again. Her eyelids lowered, her fingernails sinking into his back.

That was too much—he couldn't wait another second to be inside her. He eased inside her slippery opening. She clenched him in welcome, her head back against the wall, her beautiful neck arched, her eyes narrowed to slits as she watched him. Powerful, alluring, and all woman. She was like mother earth herself, aromatic and lush with fecundity, the welcome in her deepest embrace unmistakable. He struggled for breath before thrusting deeper into the tight, hot clasp of her cunt.

When he was deep inside her, her eyes flashed in the darkness, her head thrashed and she clung to him. His cock was curved inside her and made her crazy and that reeled his pleasure out into infinity. He rammed her up against the wall, staying deep inside the tight fist of her glorious cunt, holding her with his hands around her bottom, staying deep and riding her with shallow movements.

Writhing and lifting in his arms, she was total, pure female instinct. He sought her mouth, desperate to kiss her, and when he did she thrust her tongue between his lips and squeezed her cunt around his cock at the same time.

His spine was ramrod straight, his buttocks clenched, and the pulse at the base of his spine felt like a hammer. When his balls tightened, he knew he was going to come soon, and he wasn't going to come without her.

"Come to me, Zoë, come to me," he urged.

Panting, she nodded, breathing her response. "I wanted *you*. It was you I wanted, Grayson."

The way she said "you" triggered his climax and he pumped into her, the strength of the release blinding him for several long moments.

She clung to him, and he heard her sob. The sheath of her cunt tightened three times in quick succession and her body shuddered in release.

"Yes, yes," he urged, "I've got you, you're safe."

Clinging to him, her body vibrated in the aftermath.

He rested his forehead on the wall beside her head, grateful. This moment was theirs. His senses were honing all the while, his mind sharpening for what was to come. But this moment was entirely theirs, and he intended to hold her tight in his arms all night long.

19

ELSPETH STOOD, DRENCHED AND SHIVERING, in the apartment over the Tide Inn, looking to Cain for guidance, and yet wondering why she was even bothering. Apparently he'd lost it.

Prowling around his apartment, he looked positively insane. Where was the witch master they had welcomed as their leader, the powerful man she had put her faith in? He had drawn them together and given them strength and focus as a group, but he didn't know when to back off. She was growing increasingly concerned about his stability.

"You've got to go to the doctor," she pleaded.

"I haven't been to the doctor in my whole life. Not starting now." His hair was stuck to his head, his clothes covered in mud. His hand was cut. Blood dripped from the outside of the whiskey bottle he held onto the Persian rugs at his feet.

Crawford was there too, and he watched warily as Cain paced back and forth, swigging from the whiskey bottle, hurling things at the walls. He glared at them as if they were the source of his discontent. "Give me some peace and quiet and I will mend myself by magic."

But Elspeth couldn't let it go, because all around her it felt like everything was falling apart. She was angry, and they looked to him for guidance. "Why is Grayson Murdoch so strong? Why is it that we as a full coven can't stand up to him, a lone witch?"

Cain snatched at her, grabbing her around the back of her neck, his thumb digging into the soft skin of her throat. Her hair was caught up in his fingers and she cried out, her fingers plucking at his hand.

He ignored her plea. His eyes glowed fiercely. "The element of surprise was on his side tonight, that's all it was."

Her eyes were stinging with withheld tears. "You think more of raising a dead woman than you do about the people who are alive and closest to you."

"Don't you dare challenge me." He released his grip on her neck only to slap her with the back of his hand.

Elspeth jerked back, pain shooting from her chin to her forehead. His ring had caught her lip and she staggered away. "Fuck you," she shouted at him, and turned away.

She made it as far as the door.

Crawford caught her by the shoulder, swinging her around. "You sure about that?"

He gave a warning look, reminding her in a glance—as he so often did—that she couldn't afford to challenge Cain, because Cain could just as easily use her as the vessel for Annabel's soul.

She took a deep breath.

Only Crawford could make her listen. He was right, of course, and this time Elspeth didn't dare respond verbally. Instead, her hand went to her throbbing lip. There was blood on her fingers. She was dripping wet, her head was pounding and she had a cut lip. The skin on her hands was raw and she was desperate for a hot bath. She stared over at Cain, angry and hurt and wondering what the hell was going to happen if he didn't pull it together. Meanwhile Cain was standing in front of his portrait of Annabel, staring at her as if it would soothe him. Would it?

Keeping her voice low she whispered to Crawford, "He's losing it, he's obsessed with Annabel and he can't think straight."

Why? Why was he so bloody well obsessed with her? He had touted this to them as a worthy project, something that would bind them together and make them strong. Three members of the coven were now in the hospital in Dundee, having suffered injuries and shock. Daphne had sprained her wrist. All of them were injured in one way or another. This was tearing them apart, not making them stronger.

Crawford glanced over his shoulder at Cain, uneasy. "Hold it together, Elsie," he whispered. He only called her that when he wanted to remind her how long they had known each other. It touched her, as he knew it would. He spoke in a low voice, squeezing her shoulder for reassurance. "What has been done cannot be undone. In good time, Annabel will rise completely. Grayson Murdoch's interference shouldn't be this much of a problem. That is the only mystery here."

Elspeth nodded. Crawford wasn't sure of Cain either, not anymore, but he was right. Much as she was angry and hurting, she couldn't afford to be too much of a thorn in his side, not right now. Cain was capable of anything.

"I can hear the pair of you," Cain said, "whispering like a couple of old fishwives." He snorted derisively, but he didn't bother to spare them a glance. Instead he continued to stare at the portrait, reaching out with one hand to trace the edge of the frame, lovingly. "Nothing will go wrong. We just need to be sure that when Annabel surfaces, she doesn't bond with Murdoch. If the host is with him there's a chance that Murdoch could hold sway over Annabel's awakening form. That cannot happen. I want rid of him."

Elspeth took a deep breath. Cain looked close to insanity, and she didn't like it. But Crawford was right, the magic was done and would take its course soon enough. Elspeth wasn't sure she even wanted to be involved anymore, but what would she be, without her coven? Grayson didn't have a coven. Was that what made him strong?

That's when Cain turned and looked at them both.

His eyes glowed, fiercely luminous in the darkness, and they were alive with unruly fire, filling the atmosphere with menace. "Annabel is mine, and mine alone."

Grayson sat with his back against the wall, holding Zoë cocooned in his lap as she dozed through the night. He stroked her hair and kissed the top of her head, cherishing her.

As soon as dawn rose, he got up and pulled on his clothes. He put a small spell on her so that she would sleep on until he returned, so that she wouldn't wake alone and be afraid. Then he jogged through the forest and along the main road until he came to the turning down to Carbrey. Even though the sky was clear, streams of water still ran down either side of the road. The drains were struggling to cope.

As he closed on the harborfront, he found that several people were already up and working at the marina, securing their boats and examining the damage that the storm had brought. Guilt shot through him, but he'd done what had to be done at the time. He'd protected Zoë, and they finally knew what Cain Davot's intentions were. Now, he had to make sure it never happened.

He broke into Her Haven and found Zoë's handbag and car keys. He also picked up a change of clothes and her walking shoes. As he walked to her car, he looked out for Davot's crowd, but they weren't around. Probably up at the Tide Inn, plotting to steal Zoë away and attain their goal. His resolve strengthened all the while. Davot's magic had been put in motion, and now he had to set about undoing it as quickly as possible. He drove Zoë's car back up to the main road and parked in the layby where he had first met her, before returning to the cabin to wake her.

Standing in the doorway of the cabin, he stared over at her. Sunlight was pouring in the window, and she basked in it like a sleeping cat, curled up on her side, languorous. The soft, feminine arch of her hip and the dip of her waist drew his attention. She was exquisite, like a woodland nymph who'd taken shelter here in the cabin. It made him think about their first meeting, how she'd been looking so wistfully into the forest.

When he closed the cabin door, she rose up on her elbows and blinked at him, smiling. He put the bundle of clothes down by her side, and then drew her up to her feet, taking her in his arms.

"I didn't hear you go."

Soft and warm in his arms, she gazed up at him.

"I wasn't gone long." He kissed her, savoring it, before he continued. "Zoë, I'm going to stay in Carbrey and sort this out, but I want you to leave. You should go back to London, this morning."

"You want me to go?" Hurt flickered in her eyes.

"No, not at all. I want you to be safe. If you don't want to go home yet, you can spend the rest of your visit at my place in Edinburgh."

She placed her hands flat to his chest. "If you were there, that would be a tempting offer." She smiled briefly, and then it faded. "I can't leave. Now I've seen the magic it's got me thinking about something else. When I tried to leave, when I drove to Dundee, I had to fight the urge to come back the whole time. It was like this huge relief when I did get back."

Damn. He recalled her mentioning it the night before, as they made their escape. "Sounds like a binding spell."

She sighed deeply. "I can't get my head around this. I've seen it and I've been forced to believe it—all of it, even the visions Annabel puts in my head—but I still don't understand it, and I need to." She stared up at him. "Grayson, it was so weird when I was with them last night, I had so little control. And when I saw you…and what you did, the magic." She swallowed then shook her head. "I need to know why you're different from them."

He nodded. "The witchcraft that exists here is pagan in origin, pure and positive in intent. For centuries it's been practiced happily amongst normal folk who live normal lives and use their powers for good. Occasionally, however, a practitioner—a witch—will crave what they perceive to be the greater power that magic opens up to them—the darker path that it also affords."

"Cain?"

"Unfortunately, yes."

Her expression was unfathomable for a moment, and then she responded. "What are we going to do?"

If she wasn't able to leave, he wasn't going to let her stray from his side until she could. "First, we're going to move your stuff into Cornerstone. You'll be safe there. Then I'll begin to undo the magic that has been done."

"You can do that?"

"I need to get advice, but I promise you I will." Or die trying, he thought himself. "I'll take you to Abernathy, I can ask the coven there about undoing the binding spell that has been put on you."

"Will I be able to go there? I'm pulled back…even now I want to be in the village, and we're barely outside it."

"It's not far. As the crow flies, barely a few cliffs separate the two villages."

She nodded. She was quiet but thoughtful, and he sensed she was mending.

"Do you trust me?"

"I always trusted you. Even when I hadn't the first clue what you were on about." She reached for the clothes he'd brought for her. "Call it instinct."

He watched as she pulled on the clothes, each move she made washing over him like a wish coming true.

"Why didn't you tell me that you practiced magic, too?" she asked.

"What would you have done, had I mentioned it up front?"

She thought about it for a moment. "Hmm, difficult one. I guess I might have thrown you out?"

"That's why I didn't tell you."

She laughed softly, and rested her hand on his shoulder for a moment, looking up at him with affection in her eyes.

That made him strong.

When they got back to the car, he did a U-turn, driving slowly back toward the village. They passed the short journey in silence and when he pulled the car to a halt at the junction on the seafront, they both stared at the devastation. Signposts had been bent or ripped off their poles. A litter bin had strewn its contents across the road. The harbor was more crowded than it had been before, and the boatyard doors were open.

Crawford Logan was outside the boatyard, watching, waiting, as they drove back onto Shore Lane. He ran over to the car, shouting into Grayson's open window as he drove by with Zoë in the passenger seat. "It's only a matter of time, Murdoch. Wheels have been set in motion."

He had an insufferable grin on his face, and Grayson hit the accelerator, speeding past him.

Zoë's eyebrows shot up. "Blimey, they think they own me." She gave a disbelieving laugh.

"They don't, and won't ever own you." He hung on to that fact as he pulled the car off Shore Lane and drove up the narrow alleyway at the back of houses.

As he parked, Zoë's attention sharpened and when they got out of the car she peered over at the back of the house. "Is this where you said Annabel's bee bole is?"

Grayson nodded and walked around the car to take her hand and show her the way through the back gate. She stared across the patio at the old stone bee bole embedded in the wall, then walked quickly over to it and put her hand on the surface, as if intrigued.

"She worked here, she worked with this." Her voice ran on, excited. "This hasn't changed as much as the house. The house has been renovated many times."

She put her hands right inside, feeling all around.

A surge of energy rushed from the house into the old stone monument. It happened so quickly that it took Grayson by surprise, but he felt it pulsating rhythmically, flowing out from the physical anchor to this outpost, and Zoë.

"She came to me in a vision, last night, when they had

me…up there." She turned to him, her eyes bright. "It was as if she was leading me through the forest, and there was blackness all around, but she told me I'd travel safely if I stayed with her."

Oh, boy, he didn't like the sound of that.

"At first I was afraid, but then she showed me something that happened to her, something we didn't know. The coven master, the one who was her lover, she had ultimate control over him. She proved it to me."

Grayson frowned. These things weren't anything he'd ever heard mentioned during his research on Annabel. "Do you think it's significant?"

"Yes, because I think she wants us to solve the mystery of how she died, why she died. It's as if she needs someone to know, to understand it. I can't help wondering if she tried with other visitors but they were scared off by it. I almost was." She gazed over at the house. "Somehow, I don't feel afraid anymore, not of Annabel."

Grayson wasn't so sure. Maybe she was just being duped into feeling content about the attempted possession.

Zoë rested her hands against the bee bole again and Grayson watched, sensing the psychic energy pouring into her. Curious, he stepped behind her and put his hands on her shoulders before moving them down her arms.

"Yes, come feel it with me." She turned and smiled up at him, and then focused on the bee bole.

As she did, a rush of psychic energy came through the stones. It was so powerful that Grayson was surprised, and it pulsed powerfully all around them, like a mellow, tamed fire. "I had no idea it was this strong," he whispered, against her hair.

"Close your eyes," she said, "listen to the bees."

There was something so very seductive about her voice.

He closed his eyes, and as he did he heard the hum of the bees and smelled the heady, rich scent of the bole as it had been, alive and vital. The garden around them was waist high in blossoms. It was like full summer, and the heat had intensified. The sun beat down on them. He felt Zoë safe in his arms, but Annabel's presence was there, too, and he inhaled sharply when the sun dazzled him and then something moved, blocking the sun, and he saw her image for the first time. Her form was outlined in sunlight as she worked at the bole, a large hat trailing a veil over her face. She turned from the bee bole and lifted the veil when a man came up behind her and kissed her, grabbing her into his arms, braving the bees to get a taste of her.

Grayson pulled away, taking Zoë with him.

He was shocked at the strength of the vision, and scared for Zoë. How close to completion was Cain's handiwork?

Zoë rested back in his arms, unafraid as she continued to stare at the old stones. "She used to hate to come here, and then she grew to love it, the vibrancy of the bees, and the honey they made." Looking up at him, she smiled. "Did you see him?"

He shook his head.

"It was Irvine, the fisherman." She was fascinated by it.

Grayson remained wary. "Come on, let's go inside and get your things," he urged, eager to get her inside the safety of Cornerstone.

The hallway of Her Haven felt just that to Zoë, a haven. Why was she feeling that, she wondered, because it was Annabel's haven? She turned to look at him. "It feels weird, being back in here, now. Things fell into place overnight, and although I'm not afraid of Annabel, it makes me reconsider why she appeared to me, you know."

"It's bound to."

"Whenever I leave I'm drawn back here. Even in the cabin last night, I wanted to be here. It's so odd."

"I'm not sure that's a good thing." Concern emanated from him.

"Don't worry, neither am I. This isn't exactly like my everyday life, you know. It felt as if everyone was trying to seduce me when I got here, even Annabel." She chuckled softly then pushed her hair back over her shoulder, watching him for his reaction.

Grayson lifted her chin with his thumb to look into her eyes. "Even without the unusual circumstances, you'd have attracted a lot of attention. You're a beautiful woman."

Did he really mean that? Would he have been interested if she'd been staying elsewhere and none of this had happened? She stared at him for the longest moment. "I'm not normally as full-on and crazy as this."

"I guessed that you'd be a little bit more cautious about leaping into bed with a stranger."

She flashed him a look. "I don't mean that so much. If I wanted to have a relationship, I can go out and meet someone. It's more than that. It's as if Annabel planted a need to know inside me, a need to know that goes beyond the sex, though. Does that make sense?"

Grayson observed her, thoughtfully. "The visions?"

She nodded. "Yes, it's as if she really is sharing something with me. She wants me to know."

"Cain's hex could be made to work that way, but I can't imagine him being quite so subtle when it comes to his victim's experience of an enchantment."

She swallowed down the dread that statement filled her with, pushing it away. "No, it's not about Cain. I simply want to know what happened to her. I think I want to know as much as you do, and I think she wants me to know, as well. She wants the truth to come out."

"Why?"

"You're asking me?"

"Just playing devil's advocate." There was humor in his eyes. Even so, it sent a shiver down her spine.

"Don't say such things."

"I'm sorry. The question is why would she want you to know. It could be that she needs her story to be told, in order to move on and finally break with the real world. If so, Cain has wandered into that situation with his own project."

"It might explain why I don't feel as if she's the enemy in all of this." She sighed. "It would be good to get some distance. I wish I could get away, just for a little while. I'm so confused by all of this."

Especially you.

All she really wanted was to stay in his arms, to make love to him again, to chat over long dinner dates and get to know every little thing about him.

"I need to know which of the feelings that I'm feeling… are mine. If you see what I mean." She delivered the statement with more conviction than she felt. Saying that to him was hard, because mostly her concern was what she was feeling about him. Questions about Annabel echoed through her mind constantly, but for her it was increasingly bound up with Grayson as well. She gazed up at him, glad that they were together again.

Did Annabel really have such a powerful call on both those men? she wondered as she looked at him. It was an intriguing question. Even at her lowest, when her master could so easily have cast her aside, Annabel wove a spell over him that had nothing to do with magic. The inherent power of desire, of love? Zoë wondered if she could ever have that kind of power over a man, the way Annabel had.

Grayson meshed his fingers with hers when she touched his hand. "We'll go to Abernathy. I need to seek advice about the binding spell. We must try to understand the nature of your attachment to Annabel, so we can undo it. It's just along the coast," he continued. "It's the village you can see when you're on the cliff path."

Zoë remembered the sight of the other village on the horizon and how tempting it had looked. "I'll be pulled back, I know I will."

"If it upsets you, we'll turn back. The villages are separated only by the cliffs. My mother's side of my family hails from that part of the world."

He'd told her about his parents, but she hadn't realized they were this close to his mother's home. She began to make more sense of his presence here. "That sounds good. I'd like that."

"I'm sure it'll help you to see how a decent coven goes about things. Besides, I owe a visit."

Some small part of her wondered if meeting even more witches was going to help, but she trusted him. "I'll pack my stuff."

"I'll tidy the kitchen and we can be on our way."

"Deal."

When she got into the bedroom, she stared over at her half-unpacked suitcase with a smile. The fact that she hadn't unpacked properly was going to save her time, and that amused her no end. Drifting around the room, she picked up her bits and pieces, tossing them across the room in the direction of the suitcase. The bizarre part was that she was packing when she was only halfway into her stay, because she was moving next door. And that was because *that* house was protected by magic and this one was not. If it weren't for the fact that she'd seen it all with her own eyes, and other people had seen it, too, she'd think she was going insane.

After she grabbed her bathroom gear, she sat at the dresser and picked her jewelry and makeup, dropping bits and pieces into her makeup purse. The items were scattered all over the dresser, from her last hasty exit. Each time she sat at the dresser she seemed to have to race away.

The thought made her pause, and when she did, tension shot up her spine. Inside a heartbeat the atmosphere in the room changed. Was that because she had thought about it, or had it been like that when she walked in?

Lifting her head, she forced herself to look in the mirror. She thought about the other time she had sat here and the ghostly apparition that she had seen.

"Annabel?" she whispered, her voice faltering on the name. Still nothing in the mirror. But the atmosphere in the room had definitely changed, it was slightly warmer and she felt a presence, just as she had when she first arrived in the house, only this time it was much more obvious to her.

"Well, if you're not going to come out so I can see you…so that we can talk…" She swallowed hard, scarcely able to believe she was actually asking to see the bloody thing. "Then I'm just going to have to continue packing."

She threw the last of the makeup into the purse. All that was left was her hairbrush and her travel–sized perfume atomizer. She shoved the atomizer into the makeup purse, then picked up the brush and ran it through her hair.

As she did, she heard a sound behind her. A sound like she had never heard before, and it sent a chill down her spine. Her hand froze in midair, her stomach balling. Static clung in the atmosphere. The sound grew louder, and it whispered around the room like it came from far away, like an echo. A feeling somewhere between excitement and dread came over her. Someone was trying to say her name, and it sounded like a child who couldn't talk properly, barely audible.

Zoeeee?

Zoë lowered the hairbrush in her hand. As she did, a shadowy movement in the reflected mirror caught her eye.

It was her, Annabel, just as before, except this time she seemed much more solid. Zoë shut her eyes quickly and reopened them. Annabel was still there. In fact she seemed a little closer, as if she wasn't in the mirror at all. No. It couldn't be. But it was. Zoë could hear Grayson moving around downstairs, but she was unable to do anything, not call or cry out, as the ghostly figure moved closer and then drifted right across her.

She stared at the dresser mirror as the ghost walked right through her. Was it a trick of the light?

No, because as Annabel merged with her, she felt something like pinpricks all over her skin, and an intense of wave of heat washed over her. Her own image all but disappeared, and for one horrible moment everything that had happened the night before up in the forest flashed through her mind.

She's come for me. She's really inside me, now.

Her heart all but stopped.

Annabel paused, and then moved on, and the heat left Zoë in a rush.

Her heart thundered on.

Stopping close by, Annabel smiled back at her.

That was too weird. Zoë was relieved she'd moved on, but she couldn't bring herself to return the smile. She was well and truly spooked. Remembering that the vision had disappeared when she looked directly back, she turned around quickly.

Shit.

Annabel's ghost was standing right behind her, a mere three feet away. She was looking down at Zoë, as if intrigued. The feeling was mutual. Zoë could scarcely breathe, nor could she blink while she took in the sight before her. Never in all the visions or dreams had Annabel seemed as real as this.

Her eyes appeared like black coins and her face was so pale it was almost transparent. Her black hair hung messily around her face. The gown she wore was ripped and tattered and singed.

The skirt was singed.

Zoë put her hand over her mouth when she realized she could smell burning.

Annabel lifted one hand, gesturing in Zoë's direction, ghostly flames flickering along the underside of her arm.

Zoë could scarcely believe it was happening.

Annabel's lips moved, but she heard nothing.

"Can you speak?" Zoë swallowed. Bloody hell, she was trying to have a conversation with a ghost. It was one thing having steamy visions, sharing erotic memories and even feeling a presence, but this was something else.

Annabel put her fingers to her mouth and shook her head. Then she touched her forehead and pointed at Zoë's forehead.

"Right, you haven't got enough power to appear and talk, but you can speak within my mind, is that right?

Yes.

Zoë nearly jumped out of her skin.

"Okay. Right. Are you Annabel McGraw?" As she asked

the question she pressed back against the dresser, her clammy hands grasping at the stool she sat on.

The ghost nodded, her lips parting as she did so.

"What happened to you, Annabel? Why do you want to tell me your story?"

When the time is right, you will know why.

Annabel smiled and reached out her hand. The flicker of flames along the sleeve of her dress appeared and disappeared in the movement. She ran one pale finger down Zoë's cheek. Zoë felt a prickle, static, a gust of warm air, but no real touch.

Her skin crawled.

Her eyes shut.

When she forced herself to open them, Annabel was gone.

20

ZOË THREW GRAYSON HER CAR KEYS. SHE wasn't sure she was safe to be in charge of a moving vehicle. Besides, she liked the way he looked at the wheel.

"Right through me," she repeated, for what had to be the tenth time. "It was the weirdest feeling."

"You should have called me."

"I couldn't. Believe me, I wanted to." She gave a disbelieving laugh. "Don't worry, I'm okay. It was just so bloody strange!"

He didn't respond. A determined look had taken up residence on his face. He reached over and pulled her seat belt into place, locking it securely.

"She tried to speak, but she could barely say my name." Annabel could speak within her mind, but not aloud. Not very well, at least.

"Not enough power." He seemed pleased by that.

Did it indicate they had more time?

As he pulled the car onto the main road at the top of the town and drove away along the coast, Zoë tried to quell the curious mixture of emotions that assailed her—and that now-familiar insistent tug that she immediately felt to go back—focusing instead on the lowlands scenery between Carbrey and their destination. The rolling green fields and sturdy hedges were alternated with patches of sunny rapeseed and tides of wheat that moved lazily in the summer breeze.

Resting her head back, Zoë let the images blur into patches of color before her eyes, willing herself to get a bit of distance on this in order to make sense of it all. The man at her side had a call on her as much as the spell she was under, she was facing up to that now. Would she just walk away, if the spell were lifted?

That was a difficult question.

Staring out at the view, she let the question slip away un-answered, for now. The colors had captured her attention and the motion of the car was lulling her all the while. Grass to wheat to yellow to green, to wheat and back. Very soon she drifted toward the borderline between sleep and waking.

Annabel was still with her, she knew it.

Can you see him, Zoë? The question echoed in her thoughts, and, this time, Zoë didn't resist the vision that unfolded inside her mind….

Can you see him? He's over there on the far side of the wheat field, standing in the shade of the old oak tree, waiting for me. Before I mount the wooden stile, I look back over my shoulder. I want to be sure that no one has followed either of us here. Shading my eyes against the hot summer sun, I squint into the distance where the fields roll down the hillside toward the village and the sea glints in the sunlight beyond. I see no one. Sense no one.

Reassured, I lift my skirts and climb over the stile, dropping down into Farmer Erskine's top field. It is so much warmer up here on the mount, and the sound of insects hums all around. The scent of grain is high in the air. The tall wheat shifts in the breeze, a field of heavy stems ready for the cull. Harvest time will be upon us soon and young men from all over the countryside will come here in droves to work with their scythes. No longer will it be our secret meeting place and we will have to seek another.

I skirt the edge of the field, hastening all the while, until I'm within reach of the secluded spot beneath the oak. Irvine steps out as I approach, and the sight of him lets loose joy in my sorry soul. Resting one hand against the tree trunk, he smiles at me, as if he finds happiness in the very sight of me.

He is so tall and virile, it makes my body ever more eager for him. Lately, he has satisfied me like no other, and I have been increasingly drawn to him. There is a protective feeling that I have for him, too. Why is that? I wonder. Why, when I have a powerful coven master in the palm of my hand, do I come to this humble fisherman with such joy?

"I am mighty glad to see you," he says, "my jewel, my pearl." He regards me with an open, honest look in his eyes and my chest pains me.

Brusquely, I attempt to push that aside, and seek his embrace, cherishing the moment as he grabs me against him, all but crushing me in his powerful arms.

"And I you," I respond.

His work-callused hands are rough on my skin when he strokes my neck and my bare shoulders, and the touch of his fingers on me lets loose a desperate, animal craving.

Holding my face steady, he peers at me as if searching for some truth. "The sight of you makes me stiff."

His deep voice rumbles through me, his words teasing my overwrought body. I nod, take his hands in mine and let him know that it is the same for me.

He lifts me, handling me as easily as if he were reaching over the side of his boat and pulling in the baited lines heavy with the catch, and I cannot get enough of that feeling, for I am proud—proud to be wanted by him—and pride is an unfamiliar emotion to me. A bastard child, I was unwanted and spurned by a bitter mother then thrown onto the streets by her angry employer. There was little opportunity for me to do other than survive; selling everything I could steal, selling myself. I came to Carbrey to be somewhere no one knew me. It was only Ewan and his kind that welcomed me, at first. I bonded with them, for they drew on a side of me I had not discovered on my own, a side that flourished quickly. And then Hettie brought Irvine to Carbrey, and they married. Before long a shadow divided them. I believe that shadow is Ewan.

Hettie strayed first, and now Irvine comes to me, and he comes to me because he has to, because he cannot deny the desire he feels. I see it there in his expression and neither could I turn away from him, even if my life depended on it. Oh, but his hungry gaze makes me ache. It also makes me greedy and unruly in my soul, and dark, dangerous emotions rise in me.

I want him to be mine and mine alone, but we are entangled, us four, hopelessly entangled because of Ewan. The clawing need makes me despise his wife and the bairns she carries. It would be a simple task to make Irvine run away with me, and then I could surely take him for my own. The villagers would spurn us forever, but do I care? My coven would frown heavily on me. Ewan chastises me daily for the poor attention I bring upon myself. To lose them, to lose the circle that has taken me in, would deplete my power. But would that loss not be as nothing compared to the gain? I want him. I want him down there on the mossy ground where the massive oak roots plunge into the earth. In this hidden spot we have mated all summer, rutting and crying out like feral creatures in heat.

I kiss him fervently, my mouth against his neck, my hands moving inside his shirt for a touch of the coarse hair upon his chest and his solid, warm body. In his arms, I need to be stripped naked, to be pressed against him, bare skin to bare skin. I undo the lace at my breasts and pull my dress open so that my breasts can be against his chest.

He lifts me higher against him. "Wrap your legs around my hips," he says.

Clinging to my man, the scratch of the rough bark at my back is nothing to the thrust of his shaft through our clothing. "I must have you," I say.

But he breaks the kiss.

His eyes turn wild. "Tell me this, have you put a spell on me? I can take it, if you have, but I must know the answer, for the worry of it is pulling me close to madness."

His unhappiness over this question has arisen before, and it has made me unaccountably frustrated these past few days. It hangs between us and mars our long summer of secret passion. I cannot show him how angered that makes me. I do not want him to be afraid of me. I shake my head, desperate to reassure him. "It is not so."

Aside from the first wee charm I used to draw his attention to me, I hadn't practiced any more enchantments upon him. I hadn't needed to. The other men, they wanted me, but they were scared because of the rumors that I am a witch. Not Irvine. I soon learned that his lust for me was so strong that I had merely to beckon my finger and he came. Oh, how that knowledge burned in me. This glorious man, this virile, passionate man, wanted me. That made me feel more powerful than any magic ever could.

He nods, slowly, and I sense that he wants to trust me even though there is a frown upon his forehead. It breaks my heart to see it there.

"I need you, Irvine," I tell him, and we are locked into the

moment again. I nod at the ground and he lifts me against him as he drops to his knees. I'm so eager that I cannot undo the belt of his breeches fast enough. He teases me, but somehow I manage it. His member springs free; it's upright and reaches to his belly, and it is so thick and large that my cunny drips at the very sight of it.

I drop down and kiss the swollen head of his upright shaft, before taking it into my mouth. His massive body arches and he groans as I suckle on him, his ballocks lifted high against his body. The taste of him makes me feel as if I am drunk on him, his potency and his musk a lure that calls upon the very quick of me. I throw my head back, lift my skirts and prepare to mount him.

Even as he grips his mighty shaft at the base and offers it to me, he stares up at me, his gaze holding mine. I mount him and claim him into my body, looking directly into his eyes, wishing for something else, wanting something that I cannot ever grasp.

When I pause, he half sits, pushing his rod to my center.

With his arms around me he locks me against him, and then he kisses my mouth, stroking my hair in that way he does, as if he is afraid to hurt me in doing so. That tender gesture when I am so very full with him makes my heart feel as if it is breaking. I whisper words of love against his mouth and I grip his head in both hands, my cheeks damp with my tears.

Desire and frustration drive me and I ground down on his pole, taking it deep inside me. When it touches the deepest part of me I throw my head back, so close to ecstasy that I have to moan aloud as I rise and fall upon him. The sun is warm on my bared back and I am bathed in pleasure. Irvine reaches out, his large palms grasping my waist as I ride the length of his pole, and here in this field I am his woman and he is my man.

Then something changes.

Did a chill wind blow through the wheat just then? Or was it a sense of foreboding that came over me?

I shiver. I pause.

Even before the dark shadow falls over us, I know that we are no longer alone.

It was the car lurching to a halt in a layby that pulled Zoë back from the vision. She still had her head back against the headrest, but she knew where she was and kept her eyes closed, savoring the intensity and the emotion that had been conveyed to her. This time she'd been intrigued.

"What is it?" It was Grayson's voice.

She felt his breath warm on her face.

Slowly surfacing, she opened her eyes and looked his way. Concern filled his expression, and his beautiful gray-green eyes looked dark under drawn down brows. She wanted him. Her hips rocked against the seat, her pussy damp and aching to be filled the way Annabel had been in the vision, filled with potent male virility. But Annabel and her lover had been interrupted, and the overriding need Zoë felt in that moment was to finish what they had started. The goal burned within her. She would have completion, and she would have it with Grayson.

"Did you have another vision?"

She nodded, but she didn't want to talk about what she'd seen in the vision, not just yet. First, she craved his closeness and his passion—out there in the open fields with the sun on her bared breasts.

The corner of his mouth lifted, his expression softening. Shaking his head, he touched her shoulder, connecting with her deliberately. "You always look so sexy after you have these visions."

"Only then?"

His eyebrows lifted. "No. Hell, no. But you always look

as if you absolutely have to have sex—" his voice went low "—right there and then…and that does bad things to me."

Appraising him from under hooded eyes, she grabbed his T-shirt and pulled him to her for a hungry kiss. His hands roved over her breasts and in around her waist. Moving up against him within the confines of seat and seat belt, her back arched. She groped his shoulders, his back, needy and wanting.

"I want to get out of the car for a few minutes," she blurted, and she could hear the restrained need in her own voice. She wanted to be out there, in the wheat field.

She gave me a taste of intimacy, and I want more.

"I think it was near here, the place in the vision, and I want to try to find it." Pure, vibrant energy flowed in her veins, and she felt strong again, powerfully female and undaunted by all that had happened the night before.

She got out of the car, knowing that he would follow, and made her way along the grassy bank at the edge of the road until she came to a gap in the hedge. A public footpath sign pointed into the field beyond. The crop had already been harvested, and the ground was covered in stubby, shorn stalks. A path meandered through it, a simple earthen track worn into the crop by walkers. Grayson was close behind her. Quickly, she followed the trail across the field, looking left and right.

Turning on the spot, she scanned the landscape on the horizon. The sun dazzled her and she lifted her hand to shade her eyes. "It looks a lot different, I thought…I thought it was the same place, but now I'm not so sure."

Grayson followed, but he only looked at her, and he had a fiercely possessive look in his eyes, making her want him ever more badly.

"It may well be the place," he said, grabbing her into his arms and holding her tight against his hard, leanly muscled body. He stared down at her, longingly. "The landscape changes slowly over the years, it can be very subtle."

"Wait, the tree is the same." She pointed, broke away, and then headed toward the oak that stood at the brow of the hill. Her blood raced as she approached. Flanked by hedges on either side, the old oak looked different, but she was sure it was the same place. Something inside her knew it was. The roots were massive and lifted up from the earth around the base of the tree. The branches overhead gave shelter, offering a shady haven. Running her hands over the rough bark she embraced the tree, and then turned her back to lean up against it, looking at him as he ducked under the low-hanging branches and closed on her under the canopy of leaves.

He confronted her and narrowed his eyes, his expression fascinated as he observed her actions. "Are you going to tell me about the vision?"

He didn't look as if he was even thinking about that. They were stalking each other. "Yes, but not yet."

He was so handsome. All she wanted in that moment was to tell him what he wanted to hear and have him make love to her. But there was something deeper nagging her. She needed to know, did he only want her because of Annabel? He was observing her as much as he was doing research on the house. She was tied into this at a deep level now, and he wanted to examine her as if she were an artifact. It was getting to her, and she knew she mustn't let it. She wanted him badly.

Those intelligent eyes of his flickered with curiosity as he watched her. He knew how turned on she was, he always knew. And he was too, she could see it in him—barely re-strained lust. The bulge at his groin was large, the look in his eyes intense. The anticipation she'd felt was building, and the way he looked at her—as if he was undressing her by magic—stoked the fires that were already flickering wildly inside her.

"I want you, Grayson. I need you to make love to me." Cards on the table, but she wasn't done yet. Lifting one knee, she rested the flat of her foot against the tree trunk.

"I'll make love to you whenever you want me to." His tone was quietly amused, as if he knew. He touched her hair. As he ran his fingertips down its length and stroked the column of her neck he looked at the places he touched, as if to possess them more intimately.

Sensation fluttered wildly all over her, the mere touch of his fingertips sending her body wild.

"Grayson, I need to know that it's me you want." She rocked against the tree as she spoke. It was hard to do this, and not just go for the reward. Edgy, demanding need was creeping under her skin, and her body needed the promise of imminent contact.

His gaze dropped before lifting to meet her demanding stare. "All I want to do right now is show you. I want to undress you, to kiss every part of you before I make love to you. I promise that you will know exactly how much I want you, when we're done." He put his hand beside her head on the tree trunk, his tall frame engulfing her.

The look in his eyes left her in no doubt he meant to take action, and soon. Her senses were full of him, the pulse in her groin thudding wildly, but still she wanted him to say more. It was a hankering need to have a part of him for herself, something she would hold inside of her, and treasure, when they were apart. "Talk to me some more."

"It's hard." His voice was a low whisper. "I find it really hard to express myself about this sort of thing, verbally, but I can show you."

She saw it then, a hint of vulnerability in those gorgeous

eyes of his. That surprised her, deeply. Could it be that he was struggling with the task she'd set him? How strange that this man who was such a good lover could be shy about expressing his sexuality and desire in words.

He ran his thumb over her lips, connecting with her intimately through that softest of touches. It was a simple, tender request for closeness, and his eyes grew shadowed when she didn't respond. She wanted to reach out and comfort him, but her instincts told her it wouldn't be the right thing for either of them right then. For a few seconds she didn't know what to do, then the essential female in her responded to the situation and urged her on.

She opened the buttons on her shirt, exposing her bra to him. "Grayson, I need you." Her nipples were knotted and chafing. "Tell me, what do you see?"

He stared at her for the longest moment before he responded. "An incredibly attractive woman."

She brushed her fingers over her nipples, inhaling audibly when the touch lit a flare inside her.

His eyes focused. "A woman who is sexually aroused."

"Yes," she encouraged, "and I'm aroused because of you, Grayson. Because right now I want you so much I can't walk away from this situation."

The tension in his expression altered. Ah, yes, that got to him. Was he surprised? She swallowed, emotion building inside of her. His eyes seemed to burn into her, desire swamping them both.

She tweaked her nipples through the sheer fabric of her bra, gasping again. Then she moved one hand farther down, cupping her hand over her pussy through her jeans. "Are you aroused?"

The hand he had against the tree shifted. Tension emanated from him, his body taut as a bow. "Yes."

"Are you hard for me, for this?" Again she squeezed herself, and then she popped the button on her jeans open.

Staring down, he nodded. There was no doubting that she had his full attention now. Ghost or no ghost influencing proceedings, this time she knew for sure that his attention was all hers.

The knowledge burned in her. "Do you think I want a cock in here?" She stroked her hand up and down her zipper, noticing how liberating it felt saying that aloud. It was so blatant and sexual, so demanding.

I'm a woman. I'm powerful in my own right.

"Zoë…?" He had an increasingly desperate look about him.

She stared pointedly at his groin, where she could see that he was long and hard inside his jeans. "Do you think I'd like your cock in here?"

"Yes, I think you would."

She lowered her zip slowly, revealing the matching sheer black panties she wore.

"I'm going to need to be inside you very soon." His voice was low, and she saw a warning in his eyes.

Shoving her jeans down, she stepped out of them, kicking them to one side.

He swallowed. "Black underwear and hiking boots, you're my every wet dream come true."

"I am?"

"Zoë, you're bringing me to my knees here."

She liked the way that sounded, and she smiled in response.

"You really know how to make a man crazy."

"All I did was talk to you," she paused, "and take off my clothes for you."

"For me." Weaving his fingers in her hair until he had a

fistful of it, he pulled her head back with a gentle tug and looked down into her eyes, his free hand claiming her pussy. "Did you mean that, what you said about not being able to leave, because of me?"

"Despite everything else that's gone on over the last few days, yes. I meant that. That's how I feel."

A possessive look shone in his eyes, and the grip of his hand between her legs tightened, practically lifting her onto her toes.

She didn't want to say more, couldn't say more. Nothing was going to stop this now, not doubts or wishes or words. Her core had turned to molten liquid and her pussy was slick with her juices. She reached one hand around his neck and drew him down, opening her mouth to take his kiss. When their mouths met, they locked together.

Taking her hungrily, he pulled her bra straps down from her shoulders, unhooking it at the back and freeing her breasts. Turning in his grasp, she forced him to move with her even while he devoured her mouth like a starving man. She wanted to be in the sun, just as Annabel and her lover had been, and she moved out from under the canopy of leaves, pulling him down to the ground as she lay on her back on the rough ground.

Breaking free of her hold, he rested on one knee and hovered over her while he hauled her panties down her legs, murmuring incoherently under his breath as he did so. Then he pushed her thighs apart with a demanding knee, and lowered his head between her legs. "You, my dear, are delicious."

When his mouth closed over the mound of her pussy and he tugged on it, Zoë forgot how to breathe. His tongue pushed down and rubbed over her clit.

Oxygen sucked back into her lungs when she gasped with delight. The graze of his jaw on her tender folds made her cry out, but when he stroked and suckled her clit, it turned to a sigh. Her eyes closed, her hands trailing back against the rough stubble of wheat, her whole being and consciousness focused on that spot between her legs where he was stroking her with his tongue, up and down, exploring each sensitive, swollen fold.

She splayed her hands, thrusting her fingers into the loose earth on the stubbled ground. When she did, the heat of the earth seemed to rise beneath her and spread through her body, making her tingle all over before settling like a warm coal in her womb, increasing her pleasure tenfold. "Oh, oh, Grayson, I feel it."

"Open yourself to it, your mind, your heart." His breath was warm against her pussy. He kissed her softly, before he pushed his tongue inside her.

The earth itself seemed to rise through her, pushing her aloft. Her eyes closed, and when she opened them a haze of heat seemed to cling around them, so humid and bright she was bathed in it, her limbs languorous, and her entire body supine but for her sex. That part of her throbbed and swelled like a burning beacon. Grayson continued to devour her, sucking and stroking until she coiled beneath him and spasmed, liquid heat spilling between her buttocks.

When he kissed his way up her belly and between her breasts, she lifted her head to meet his mouth with hers. The haze around them hummed with energy. She kissed him deeply, clinging to his head. The taste of her pussy on his mouth made her want to wrap her legs around him. She pulled away, her emotions soaring.

"I want you so badly," she told him, then plucked his belt open. Taking his erect cock in her hand, she was reeling with the force of her desire for this man, high on the very nature of it.

"If you don't take your hand off my cock right now, I won't last long enough," he warned, and shoved his hand in his pocket for a condom.

A quiet laugh escaped her mouth and she watched longingly as he sat back on his haunches and sheathed his erection in rubber. When he climbed back between her legs, settling over her, the passion between them intensified and closed in, and the atmosphere shifted all round them.

She lifted her legs alongside his hips, opening to him, her fingers locked over his shoulders. When he thrust inside her, completely filling her, she almost passed out with the intense wave of sensation that it unleashed.

Lifting up on his arms, he rode her, thrusting his wonderful cock in and out, the muscles in his arms roped, his expression marked with concentration.

Once again she threw her arms wide and plunged her fingers into the earth. With the sun on her body, the earth warm under her back, the man between her thighs a flame that stoked the core of her body. She felt it all around, as if every atom of energy was vibrating into her, in tune with the deepest most essential part of her womanhood. She came in a series of startling spasms, her pussy drenched.

With his cock buried deep inside, he rutted fiercely, making her climax last and last. Rising up, he threw his head back; his arms went rigid, his hips working into her faster still. The muscles in his neck stood out and sweat glistened on his forehead. Then, as his climax approached, he began to chant words that she couldn't understand. Words like Cain had used the night before.

Despite everything they had shared, her pulse tripped and a shiver ran through her, fear gripping her. "Grayson?"

His eyes opened, but they were silvered disks that reflected the sunlight.

Her blood ran cold. This was his magic again, this thing that was so alien and made her want to pull away from him. Something in her chest hurt, a lot.

He didn't seem to hear her. His cock jerked deep inside her, and still he shouted strange, foreign words into the atmosphere above them. Then his head dropped forward, his hair hanging down over his face.

The strange chant had served to remind her how very different they were, and how little she really knew of his world.

21

THEY LAY TOGETHER ON THE ROUGH GROUND, silently looking into each other's eyes. After a while, she had to know. "What did you do? What was that you said, when you were about to come?"

"I harnessed the magic from our union and used the power to create a shield for you. No harm will come to you now." He traced a finger around her right nipple as he spoke, his gaze filled with a subtle sense of pride.

Could it true? She was still shook up, but if that were his motive? Her heart ached to understand, to overcome the last shreds of resistance to this world of magic and mystery.

"Do I have to believe it, for it to work?"

He laughed softly. "No."

"That's just as well." She took a deep breath. "I'm beginning to get my head around it, but I'm having the hardest time believing it."

"I know. Sometimes I don't even believe it, and I won't be relying on the shield." He paused. "But it's true and it works."

"What language was it that you spoke?"

"The most powerful enchantments I know are scribed in Scottish Gaelic and there are some Pictish phrases in there as well, an even older Scottish language."

"Are you better at magic than Cain, is that why you defeated him last night?"

Again he laughed softly. "Better, no. Different, yes." He rolled onto his back and looked up at the sky for a moment, then met her curious stare and continued to explain. "My feeling is that Cain Davot is an old and experienced witch."

"Old? I'd guessed he was in his forties."

"He may be older. He may be under an enchantment himself."

"Seriously?"

"It's possible. It's forbidden, because it messes with the natural order of the world, but we already know Cain doesn't like to play by the rules."

Zoë shuddered.

"I've tracked his history as far back as I could. He's lived in many places, attaching himself to covens, learning their ways and adding to his skills, often leaving a trail of devastation behind."

"The London scandal?"

He nodded. "There are similar stories before that, France most recently, Brazil before that."

"So why are you different?"

"I didn't properly learn or use my power until I was in my midtwenties, and I still do so reluctantly because my father was against it. This means that when I do use it, the magic is intense."

Zoë stared into his eyes for the longest moment, absorbing what he said. Minutes before he'd been radiant with power and then it had all converged on her, making her afraid. Now, he was tender and caring, explaining things to her patiently, and that other aspect of him was a secret hidden at the back of his eyes.

Emotion built inside her as she considered what had brought them together, and what might ultimately tear them apart. She touched him, weaving her fingers with his, not wanting them to be so very different. "Is all of this because of Annabel?"

"No, this is about you and me, and the earth and the sky and the sun and the magic of the moment."

He'd known exactly what she meant, and that made her ache for him. Wanting to believe him, but still unsure, she glanced away across the field. "Annabel was here, or in a place like this, with him."

"The fisherman, or her master?"

"Irvine, the fishermen. They had a secret meeting place on the far side of a wheat field by an old oak tree. She felt regret, because harvest time would steal the place away from them." She looked back at him. *Just as this thing between us will be over when this week of mine and this investigation of yours are done.*

She took a deep breath. "I felt it, as if I were right there. It was the most powerful vision yet. I think she really loved him."

He stroked her cheek. "You're not afraid anymore?"

She hadn't said that. "Do you think I should be, after what Cain did last night?"

"I've thought about it. Annabel wants you to know what happened to her, that's not Cain's doing. If it was part of his bidding, why would he bother to have you fill in the gaps?"

"You have a point." It seemed so odd, talking about some guy's manic intention to use her body as a vessel for a dead person, and yet here they were, and somehow they were able to talk about it. "So, if it's her doing, the visions, why do you think she wants me to know these things about her?"

"Good question." He gave a wry smile.

She couldn't help noticing the deep concern at the back of his eyes. "She and her lover had been here—or to a place very similar to this—many times before, but there was something strange about this one time. The man she was with, the fisherman, he was questioning her affection, and she was upset. Then someone else interrupted them. I didn't see more than a shadow, but there was someone else there."

Grayson's eyebrows lifted. "Interesting. If someone found them their secret affair may have been revealed." His beautiful gray-green eyes scrutinized her, his expression thoughtful. "Do you have any feeling about who it might have been?"

Zoë lifted one shoulder in a shrug. "Maybe the fisherman's wife, or the master of the coven. It could have been the minister, or one of the other women from the coven. Didn't you say it was a woman who ousted her?"

He nodded.

Annabel had to know who it was. Did she know, and, if so, would she eventually share that knowledge?

"If it was the man's wife," Grayson said, "that would explain why she ousted Annabel as a practicing witch, revenge." He shook his head. "It wouldn't have been anyone who was a part of her coven. They were clever and secretive, tight-knit. They usually are, but especially so in this case. I can find out so little about them other than that they resisted all attempts by the local preacher to break them down."

"What about the villagers?"

"The people who know about an active coven either accept it or live in fear, depending on where their bias falls."

She wished he wouldn't talk about the covens that way, reminding her that they were still about and how crazy Cain and his sidekicks had seemed the night before.

He had a faraway look in his eyes, and she could see how bound up with this mystery he was. "Did you only want me because of her?" There it was. It had forced its way to the surface and she'd blurted it out.

For a moment he looked confused by her question, and then he smiled. "I wanted you the moment I saw you daydreaming about the forest."

There was a knot in her chest and it wasn't going away. "But did you know then? Did you already know that I could help you with your research, when you saw me on the side of the road that first day?"

He frowned. "No, I didn't know. I never even suspected until I knew you were staying at the cottage and I saw how interested Elspeth was in you. She was like a terrier with a bone and she was prepared to defend it, that made me wonder."

Zoë recalled the strange vision she'd had while she was with Cain Davot. She'd chalked that up to Annabel's mischief. Not anymore, not after last night.

"After you'd been in the house," Grayson continued, "the atmosphere changed in the village, and I could feel the psychic activity through the wall." He leaned over her. Lifting a stray hair that was blowing across her face, he tucked it behind her ear. "Then Davot's citadel came to life. Your arrival caused quite a ruckus, my dear. But you'd already caught my attention."

Zoë wanted to believe him. Was she fooling herself? She

acknowledged that she was being seduced by an external force, and part of her welcomed that. Her own emotions were entangled, though. She wasn't fool enough to ignore the danger that pressed against her consciousness now that she knew the full extent of what was going on. And she was a gateway to knowledge for Grayson. If she continued to get visions like the one she'd just had, the chances were that they would solve the mystery surrounding Annabel's death and Grayson could write about it. He'd be able to complete his book.

He touched his thumb against her lower lip, which made her realize that she was pouting. How ridiculous was that? *I'm a grown woman. I should act like one.*

"Come on," he said, "let's get to Abernathy."

Abernathy. With everything that had happened since they'd left Carbrey, she'd forgotten all about it.

Grayson's mind was working overtime. "There's something I have to do," he said, when they got back to the car.

Zoë stopped walking.

"It's okay, you can get in." He waited until she was inside the car, and then he walked across the road and three paces back toward Carbrey.

He lifted his arms, reaching out for the long-nurtured power in nature all round, requesting assistance in the ancient tongue of the craft. As he chanted the words, he pointed across the road, slowly drawing a line of fire through the tarmac, marking the boundary. It burned like a seam of lava, bright yellow. After a moment it faded into red and darkened, until it disappeared completely into an invisible shield.

"What was all that about?" she asked, when he got into the car.

"It's a boundary spell, similar to the one in the cabin last night." As he spoke, he watched in the wing mirror as a car approached, passed over the boundary and shot on. There were two kids and a dog in the backseat. "It'll only affect those who seek to follow us. It won't stop them completely, but it will make things a little more difficult for them to find out where we have gone."

They had barely driven three hundred yards when there was a great cracking sound behind them. Grayson looked at the rearview mirror. A large branch from an old oak tree had split and come crashing down across the road. Zoë twisted around in her seat, exclaiming aloud as she did. She stared back at the tree blocking the road and then he felt her attention on him.

"I guess they were already on our trail." He flashed her a quick smile. They wouldn't be able to spend too long in Abernathy, not if Davot's lot were closing in. The boundary spell would hold them up, but not indefinitely. They would need to be out of there and on their way back soon.

Zoë looked shell-shocked, and she continued to stare at him in silence before sitting back in her seat. "Is there another road back?"

He noticed her voice was very quiet. Was she being drawn back to the village already? "Yes, inland. Do you feel yourself being drawn back to Carbrey?"

She nodded but stared straight ahead, and he knew she was fighting it. They sat in silence for the rest of the drive, although she responded when he put his hand on her thigh, placing her hand over his. He sensed she was working through everything in her mind. It had been a baptism by fire, for sure, especially for a skeptic.

He wondered what she'd make of it all when she met some of the Abernathy coven. Smiling to himself, he put his foot to the floor.

22

"GREAT, JUST GREAT," ELSPETH SAID WHEN THEY reached the fallen tree in the road.

Crawford drew his Land Rover slowly to a halt and climbed out.

Elspeth followed. "He's bloody good."

"Don't let Cain catch you saying stuff like that again, Elsie. You got very close to the line last night."

"Do you blame me? Our friends are being hurt, they're scared." There was a rising sense of rebellion inside her, and she folded her arms across her chest as she stared at the road ahead of the fallen tree. "What drives Grayson Murdoch? Why is he so strong, and why isn't Cain able to force him to leave?"

Crawford shook his head, clearly unsure of that himself.

"It's as if he has something to prove," she added, pondering the conundrum, "something that makes him tenacious and invincible."

"Do you think maybe he knew all along?" Crawford asked. "Do you think he wants to resurrect Annabel?"

Elspeth was surprised. Crawford only ever gave his opinion when he'd thought things through. Perhaps he had doubts, too. They'd all come into this with a very different picture of how it would evolve, after all.

"Could be. You think he might just be trying to jump Cain's bandwagon?" Oh, to have a master as good as him, she thought, half expecting to be struck down by a bolt of lightning for letting the thought cross her mind.

Crawford shrugged, but looked at her with a deadly serious expression. "All I know is that we have to see this through. It would be suicide to try and bail out on Cain now, and you should keep that in mind."

Elspeth lifted her eyebrows, and gave him a mocking smile. He was right, of course, but knowing that did not chase the rebellious urges away. Not completely.

Crawford shook his head. "I'll phone Dawson in the village." He reached into his pocket for his phone. "Get him to come up here and shift this."

Elspeth nodded, but by the time the tree was moved they would have lost the trail. Zoë couldn't go far. Did it even matter? She had visions of Annabel manifesting halfway up the coast. That would drive Cain completely loopy. For some reason, she couldn't help laughing at the idea of it.

Two more cars approached and Crawford walked out toward them, his hand held up to stop them getting any nearer. If much more traffic built up, it would be hard to loop back and try a different route. If necessary they would just have to wait for them to return from wherever they had gone. They would have to come back, because of the binding spells. Unless Grayson Murdoch was clever enough to undo that, as well. She wouldn't put anything past him.

What was driving him? she wondered again. Remembering how he'd been the night before, so powerful and so determined. He'd taken her breath away. It had to be Zoë. It wasn't just about Cain. It might have been to start with, but not anymore.

So, Grayson Murdoch wanted Zoë, and Cain wanted Annabel in Zoë's body. She wondered what would happen next. Moving closer to the boundary spell, she put her hands on the fallen tree. When she did, she felt Grayson's residual magic surging beneath the bark. He might not bandy his skills about much, but when he did, it sure as hell worked.

Cain had certainly met his match. Her instinct was to think about self-protection. She had cast her lot with Cain, bonding with him as their coven master, but if he went down she was determined not to go down with him.

When they reached their destination, Grayson slowed down and parked the car outside the cottage. His mother had lived here, and he stared at the house silently, trying to picture her, as he always did when he came here. Fourteen years he'd been coming here, and still he didn't feel part of it.

"What a pretty house. Is this where your family lives?"

Grayson nodded. "Yes, my aunt and my grandmother. They'll give me a chiding about not coming more often, but you'll like them." He smiled over it, and then reached over to take her hand in his. "I've told you a little about my parents, but I need to tell you a bit more before we go in."

She looked at him in that way of hers, the look that said "don't you try to pull the wool over my eyes, Mister," and he was willing to bet that nothing got past her, in her work. He could just picture her standing behind a desk in London, refusing to accept anyone's half-baked excuses for missing documents and tardy responses.

"You're a constant stream of information on topics I should know about," she teased.

"I'm sorry." He really was. It was now a constant wish that she hadn't been pulled into this.

She stared at him silently for a moment, her expression softening. "I don't regret coming here, don't think that." She locked eyes with him. "It could have been anybody, but I'm glad it was me because I met you." A moment later, she waved her hand expectantly. "Well, what is it that you have to tell me at this juncture in time? What new facts have you to reveal?"

"I can tell you work in the legal world."

"Yes, and doesn't it all seem so useless in the face of this magical world I have stepped into."

He took a deep breath. "Don't worry, this is about me."

He glanced back at the house. "My mother lived here. She was a white witch. My dad took me to Edinburgh when I was less than a year old, because of the craft. He was a regular bloke and he couldn't deal with it. To him, it wasn't right."

She didn't say anything, but she turned her hand inside his, and meshed her fingers with his.

"My dad was a teacher. He was a good man, but I never knew about my mother until after he died. I was almost twenty. I'd started studying psychology at university."

"I'm so sorry."

"I've had plenty of time to get used to it." It was still difficult, though. "He left a letter." He'd never spoken about this part of it before, not to anyone who didn't already know. That was because he was never in a position to tell a woman he was seeing that he was descended from a line of white witches. It was, however, important that Zoë understand that he was involved, but also an outsider.

"His references to the craft made sense of so much. It was always there in me. I was drawn to studying the subject, but never knew why. After Dad was gone, I finished my degree in psychology and moved into the supernatural field. It was the most natural thing for me to do."

"And you met your mother?"

It was a moment before he could reply. "She'd passed away the year before. I never got to meet her." He clenched his jaw.

Zoë lifted his hand to her mouth and kissed it. She didn't say anything. She didn't need to.

"I met my aunt and my grandmother, and their coven. The weird thing was, they knew all about me." He winked at her.

She nodded at the cottage. "Looks as if someone has spotted the car."

His aunt Maggie was at the door. She dried her hands on the flowered apron that she wore, smiling over and waving, her gray-streaked blond hair in a heavy plait over her shoulder.

"They will have known we were on our way before they saw the car." He went to get out. "Second sight runs in the females of the family."

"Second sight?" she queried, somewhat nervously, as she closed the car door.

"Yes, er, think crystal ball, but without the ball."

"Right, crystal ball." Her expression barely altered, but he could see amusement in her eyes. He had to smile. She was growing in acceptance, even if there was a certain set to her mouth that suggested she thought it was all madness.

"Don't be nervous, they'll love you." He said it to reassure her as they walked up the path toward the rose-draped doorway, but it was true. They would love her.

"Gray, it is good to see you." Maggie grabbed him around the waist, hugging him tightly, before she turned her attention to Zoë, kissing her on both cheeks in welcome.

"Come in, come in." She ushered them into the hallway, smiling at Zoë. "Well, isn't this lovely. You're very welcome, sweetheart. Ma will be delighted you're here at last."

Zoë shot him a querying look after the "at last."

He shrugged.

Maggie opened the door to the parlor and ushered Zoë in. Grayson was about to follow, when Maggie shut the door behind Zoë. "Let them get to know each other, you and I need to have words, in the kitchen."

Grayson stared at the shut door for a moment and then nodded his agreement. They always took charge this way, and "words" were what he'd come for, after all. He needed their advice and it was important to visit now, with so much spiritual activity going on along the coast. Zoë could take care of herself, he was sure of that, and her company would mean a lot to Fern.

He followed Maggie into the kitchen, ducking low to get through the doorway. The room was cluttered and small, stacked high with pots and pans and all manner of things hanging from the beamed ceiling. He always felt too large and unwieldy standing here in this house. It was a woman's house, and even though he was always made to feel welcome, he couldn't ever imagine growing up here.

There were lace curtains in the windows and potted plants and teapot stands and pretty things that he had no clue what they were supposed to be used for. Where there were ingredients for enchantments, pinned up to a rack over-hanging the hob, he felt a bit more in tune, but that was in the minority. It was as if being in their kitchen only echoed the fact that he hadn't the first clue to how a woman's mind worked.

Maggie gave him an affectionate, knowing once-over while she filled the kettle and put it on the range. "You and your lady friend are causing quite a stir. Everyone's talking about you—" she gestured with her hand "—all up and down the coast."

That wasn't good. "I'd hoped that I was being discreet about my investigations."

"It's not you. It's that damnable warlock, Davot, or whatever he calls himself these days." She rolled her eyes. "We haven't had any discord with the Carbrey coven in years until he turned up like a bad penny, stirring things up." She looked over at him affectionately. "Something about you has got his back up, that's for sure."

She chortled over it.

"You may think this is funny, but I was hoping to pass under his radar."

"Is that why you haven't called by these past few months? We know when you're in Carbrey."

"The less Davot knows about my connection to the area the better. I try to make good use of the fact that very few people know me well, nor understand my connection to you, and Ma, and the Abernathy witches."

Maggie patted him on the back as she walked by, which was a stretch, since she was barely over five feet tall. "You are a good lad, looking so positively on your lot."

It was Grayson who rolled his eyes this time. The way she stated the obvious on that point made him feel like a survivor clinging to a raft.

"So, I guess it would be some advice that you would be looking for?"

What with her innate foresight, Maggie didn't seem to

need to know much about anything. Unlike him. "Yes, Davot has been trying to re-embody Annabel McGraw.""

"And your lady friend would be the poor victim." The kettle whistled and Maggie filled the largest teapot in the house. There were two dozen teapots to choose from, and the largest didn't come out often. They were obviously in for a long chat.

"The deed is only half done, but I need to undo it, and fast."

"You'll have to use your powers." She fixed him with a direct stare.

"I've had to use them already," he pointed out, a mite too defensively. There was a part of him that still resisted, that part that didn't want to betray his father.

"A few boundary spells, harkening the weather," she said, "small fry in comparison to what you might need for this."

"You surely know how to boost a man's ego."

She chuckled. "You know what I mean."

"Yes, I do."

"If it's a re-embodiment he's meddling with, it'll be dangerous. First you'll have to undo each and every spell he's cast on her, and then be ready to pull Annabel out. I have a journal about this kind of forbidden magic. It's not comprehensive but you should be able to work out what Davot has done. I'll warn you now, it could take weeks to untangle it."

"We don't have that long. Zoë has her own life to get on with." As much as he wanted everything to be right for Zoë, he also didn't like the thought of her disappearing back to London.

Maggie studied him in a way that made him feel too easy to read, emotionally. Was there anything she didn't already know? "However you decide to tackle it," she said, "we're here to help. Just ask."

"Thank you. My biggest concern is that I care too much, that it will cloud my judgment." What if he got hotheaded and lost it at the wrong moment? What if he messed up, big time? He'd already made an arse of himself the previous day. He'd only just been able to pull that situation back from the brink.

Maggie's expression softened. "Don't deny the affection you feel." Her eyes shone. "Physical and spiritual love is the gateway to the most powerful magic we can ever know. You love her. You must have faith and you must use it, Gray. It will help you."

At first, when the door closed behind her, Zoë thought that she was alone in the room. It didn't faze her. So many strange things had gone on already that being alone in the pretty room was nothing.

"Come in, my dear."

The voice had issued from an armchair with its back to her, and Zoë had to crane her neck to even see the top of the head of the person sitting there.

"Hello," she responded, as she walked around the chair.

A tiny sparrowlike woman with pure white hair sat there, staring straight ahead but gesturing to the armchair to her left.

"Sit down, my dear. Maggie will bring us some lunch after she's spoken with Gray. It'll give us a chance to get to know each other."

"Thank you," Zoë responded, taking the chair somewhat awkwardly. They called him "Gray." She liked that. It suited him. She wanted to call him Gray, too.

Her hostess was still staring straight ahead, and after a moment it dawned on Zoë that she was blind.

"Please, call me Fern."

"I'm Zoë."

"What a pretty name. Would you mind if I familiarized myself with your features?" She leaned forward and put her fingers out.

"No, of course not." Zoë shuffled forward to the edge of the seat and leaned into Fern's touch.

"Dark hair?" Fern asked, as she touched Zoë's hair.

"Yes." Her style of dress reminded Zoë of an elderly teacher who she'd particularly liked—a box pleat skirt worn with a white blouse that had a ruffle at the neckline, thick, American tan shade stockings, and laced-up shoes. She lowered her eyelids as Fern's fingers gently touched her face, and she experienced a tingling sensation. Lifting her gaze, she saw what Grayson wanted her to see. The craft. She may be blind, but Fern was filled with magic.

They sat back in their chairs and Zoë reflected with no small sense of irony that this was what she might expect a witch's house to be like. The room was pretty and eccentric and somehow fairy-tale-like. The mantelpiece was heavy with pebbles and objects that looked as if they had been collected from the beach and the forest, bits of driftwood and curiously shaped stones. Heavy velvet curtains were tied back at the windows, and beyond that a beautiful garden was filled with tall stems, meadow flowers in an array of colors. Small, detailed paintings of birds and wildlife filled the walls. It was a lovely, magical, grandma's house—something she had never had as a child but had associated with the fairy tales she'd read.

Fern beamed. "Gray hasn't brought a young lady here before. This is a long-awaited treat for us."

"Well, we're friends." Zoë paused, not sure what to say. What were they? They were lovers, but it was an odd arrangement. She couldn't let Fern think they were an item, if they weren't. "I'm just visiting the area, from London."

Fern nodded, and Zoë realized that she had just told her something she already knew. That would be this second sight business, she supposed, somewhat amused. What else did Fern and Maggie know about her and Grayson? Everything? That might be embarrassing.

"It's been very generous of you, to help Gray."

"I didn't really have a choice. The ghost in the house seems to have formed an attachment to me."

Fern chuckled, as if absolutely delighted by that remark. "I doubt I shall be one for much of the haunting, but if I ever do, I'd like to think that I'll have Annabel McGraw's flair for the task."

Zoë didn't question the older woman's knowledge about what was going on in Carbrey. In fact it made her feel as if she could relax and chat about it. "I found it so shocking, what they did to her back then. I had no idea that people were persecuted for witchcraft here in Scotland."

"Oh, yes, barbaric acts. Often it was because it was tied up with religion, and that isn't what we are about. Thankfully, there are no such horrors these days. The worst the likes of us can expect is to be treated as if we're insane."

The way she laughed about it led Zoë to believe she'd been called insane many times, and was way beyond being upset by it.

"Tell me more about Annabel," Fern added.

"I sense sadness in her, sometimes." It wasn't something that she had told Grayson yet. Fern's sympathetic ear and the fact that she was a woman made her want to reveal that now. "She loved a man that she couldn't be with."

Fern cocked her head on one side. "It is for us to learn lessons from this…is that what you feel?"

Now there was a leading question, Zoë thought. Grayson's grandmother was indeed a canny sort. "I guess so. I want her to tell me what happened to her. It's like a hunger to know what happened to her and her lover."

"To love the man that you cannot be with is a terrible thing. It was that way for Gray's mother, poor child. She died of a broken heart."

Zoë was unable to find words to respond, for several long moments. "It was a dreadful thing that his father did."

"Well, yes and no. He meant well. He thought he was protecting their son when he turned his back on the supernatural. The moment he walked away she accepted that. It was never easy, of course, far from it. But the craft is an instinctive, elemental thing, passed from generation to generation, as sure as the color of your hair or the set of your nose. Gray was always going to discover it. His parents loved each other deeply, and they made the ultimate sacrifice for him. It's a burden to him and it is wrong in our eyes, yes, but they lived with their agreement for many years, so it must have been right for them."

"I see what you're saying, but it's awfully hard to imagine."

Fern seemed pleased by her response. "Tell me about yourself. You are from London, yes?"

Zoë talked about her job, and her sister, and Fern nodded, her head cocked on one side as she took it all in.

She was just about to ask Fern what she thought might happen in Carbrey, when the door sprang open and Maggie came in with Grayson behind her. Maggie carried a tray loaded with cups and saucers, and a humungous teapot, but it was the sight of Grayson that held her attention. In his hand he carried a three-tiered glass cake stand loaded with delicate sandwiches and butterfly buns. He looked as if he was afraid to hold the thing too tightly in case it shattered.

He lifted his eyebrows at her when she laughed.

It was the first time she had ever seen him looking helpless—she'd seen him in plenty of other moods, but never helpless—and so she stood up and helped him with his burden.

23

"YOU TOLD ME YOU WERE A LONER, GRAY,"
teased Zoë, as he drove them back to Carbrey on the inland
road. "You didn't look like a loner when you were in there
with your family."

She couldn't help asking, she was curious. Especially
curious about the odd-looking book that Maggie had given
him just as they left. It was thick and looked positively
ancient. The covers, if you could call them that, were two
pieces of silver bark cut to size, and it was tied like a package
with ribbons. Letters had been carved into the bark, but
they weren't in any language she knew.

He kept his attention on the road ahead, although a
smile played around his mouth when she called him Gray.
"Fourteen years I've known them, and yet I still don't feel
part of Abernathy. It's a hard habit to break, I guess." He
gave a sigh, and she had the feeling he didn't talk about this
much.

"After I came here, it was like all the mysteries of my
life started to fall into place, but where did I really belong?

When I was growing up, my mother respected my father's wishes about me not being in touch with witchcraft. But she couldn't live the way he wanted her to live, with no connection at all. Apparently she used to travel to Edinburgh to see me from afar. I always felt enormously secure, and yet I was oblivious that there was this whole network of women watching out for me and casting spells to keep me safe.

"I remember this one time I stepped out in traffic, when I was about nine years old. Someone hauled me back by my shirt collar. A car shot by, but when I looked around to see who'd got hold of me, she was walking away into the crowd." He shook his head. "I never saw her face," he added.

Zoë felt emotion pressing down on her like a weight on her chest. "That must have been so hard for her."

He nodded. "She didn't exactly break the rules my father had put in place, but she bent them slightly. There were books I wanted to read as a teenager and they would just appear in my school bag. Stuff that my dad didn't think was academic enough, like the psychology of dreams, things that were calling to me. I would find the books and assume that he'd had a change of heart. Once I learned about my mother it all fell into place."

He was silent for a moment, and she could see this was hard for him. She rested her hand over his thigh and he touched it briefly before returning his hand to the wheel.

"I was drawn to psychology because I thought it would help me understand why I felt so at-odds. There was something torn inside me, because the elemental nature of the craft was there but I didn't recognize or understand it. I was drawn to esoteric subjects, and that led me into research about beliefs and the supernatural and witchcraft. It was like it was my destiny, even though I didn't know about my heritage."

"So let me get this straight," she said, wanting to see him smile again, "your mother was an absentee witch, and mine was a ditzy single mother who was a wannabe witch."

He laughed, looking at her fondly. "You're right. What about your dad?"

She shrugged. "We have no clue, and Gina and I had different fathers. All we know is that neither of them wanted to stay around long to put up with her less-than-perfect hippie housekeeping habits." She winked, pleased to see the humor in his eyes. "Dysfunctional families are us, yes?"

"Yes, I suppose so. You know, I think that's the first time I ever laughed about it."

"Is that a bad thing? A good sense of humor gets you through life."

"You're not wrong there."

They passed a road sign. They were closing on Carbrey and that gnawing ache to return began to fade. She noticed that his attention was sharpening as they grew closer.

"With Maggie and Fern, my goal has been to reflect what they gave me in my younger years, just by helping to keep them safe now. In whatever way I can." He lifted his shoulders slightly, in a marginal shrug.

She squeezed his thigh, understanding at last. Guilt stole into her heart, because of what she had thought his motivation to be—a quick shag for access to the house and material for his research. There was so much more below the surface.

"Do you think they would be able to defend themselves against Cain Davot's magic?"

"Undoubtedly." He didn't hesitate a moment and he flashed her a proud grin. "That's not the point." He winked before returning his attention to the road.

"You were right. Meeting them has helped me feel more comfortable about it, the magic."

"Good."

He'd taken advice, he was focused. What could she hope to do to help him sort this out? Her life skills were in office work. No nonsense, straight down to business. She had an outstanding reputation as someone who could come in and straighten out the mess left by shoddy office staff. More than once she'd been headhunted, to no avail. Any desk mess, screwed-up filing system or urgent need, and she'd organize it. She could get to the bottom of any problem, you name it. What use would that be here in this strange place filled with the supernatural and the unknown?

Well, she supposed, she could just adopt the same attitude she did at work and try to unravel the mess. Annabel was the key, she was sure of it. If she were here and alive, she'd just ask her straight out what she wanted out of this chaos and get it sorted for her.

"It's weird, but I have this feeling about Annabel," she said, voicing something that had been rising within her since the night before.

"Go on," he encouraged.

"It was something I said unintentionally when Elspeth was winding me up about bringing Annabel back. The words came out of nowhere," she paused, wondering about the implications of that, and then pressed on. "I pointed out to her that if Annabel was such a powerful witch, she could probably come back any time she wanted. She didn't need Cain. In theory, at least, it made sense to me because of all that she is already able to do, the sightings, the visions, the way she tries to communicate with me."

"You think she has her own agenda?" His eyebrows

were slightly raised and she could see that he was considering her suggestion.

"Yes. I wondered about that when you said that her anchor in the real world would be gone, and shortly afterward I felt her presence and had a vision away from the house. Like in the forest, it was Annabel guiding me, until you got there. It was as if she wanted me to walk into the lion's den and look right into the enemy's mouth. I feel as if she wouldn't hurt me, when it came to it. I think that's what she was trying to show me this morning. She walked right through me, but then stepped away."

"How can you be sure?"

"She obviously can't materialize and tell me things at the same time, she either offers me a vision of her past, or she appears. I'm sure it's not just about…possession." She swallowed before she continued. "Not for her. Not unless she needs me to know all about her for it to work." She fell silent a moment, as she thought that through. Could it be the case? If so, she was being a fool. "Is there any way you can communicate with her, directly? Find out what it is she is trying to tell us?"

A frown gathered his eyebrows together. "Too dangerous" was all he finally replied.

"Why? Explain."

"It might be possible by means of hypnosis. It's not something I've tried myself, but I've read about it being done. The process is similar to drawing out a secondary personality in the split-personality mind. If I undertook the procedure, I would have no guarantee that she would leave. She's a clever spirit and if she does want to return to human form she might be duping us."

"But I don't think she does want to." A shiver ran up her spine when she remembered Cain and the weirdness of the night before. "I trust you to do it, and I trust her. Is it possible?"

"Zoë, I'm not going to take that risk." He spoke firmly and his mind seemed set on denying that avenue of exploration. Any residual doubt that he was only interested in the mystery surrounding Annabel was fast fading.

"What about magic? You are powerful enough to draw her out. That's what Cain tried to do last night, wasn't it? If he is powerful enough to do it, you are."

"It's too dangerous." His jaw was set.

"But she's connected to me, Gray, and I can't leave here. I can't let that go on. You heard what Crawford said this morning. It's a matter of time. Cain will draw her out through me by magic." She was afraid, but she had to know. "If he can, you can, too. I would much rather you did that, than him."

Grayson pulled the car up at the side of the road. They were at the top of the cliffs before the descent into the village. The sun was going down on the horizon and the sea gleamed like a mirror. The sky above raced with clouds as the light faded.

He turned to look at her, and he scrutinized her in such detail that she felt touched, touched everywhere—her eyelids, her lips, the skin on the side of her neck beneath her hair. His gaze devoured her, his expression serious but determined. "Cain is what we call a warlock, an outcast to most witches because he is practicing black magic and has allied himself to the dark Lord of the Hidden World. He is nothing to do with the craft as we know it. I have notes on the forbidden magic that he has been using." He glanced to the backseat at the bound pages that Maggie had given him. "I can undo the spells, but it will take time."

"What if we don't have time? Wouldn't it be better to get to the source, before he does?" It sounded like madness, but the other way would leave her even more deeply mired in doubt and she didn't want to be eaten away by fear of the unknown.

"I've tried to communicate with Annabel, many times, but she won't appear for anyone but you."

"I think she'll appear for you, if I want her to."

He watched the sun sinking, and she felt the mystery and the tension that slunk out during the dark hours rising in the atmosphere around Carbrey. He'd defeated them the night before, and she believed he could do it again and get them out of this. Even if his father had got his way and removed him entirely from his heritage, Grayson would be the sort of man who would stare down his enemy, who wouldn't acknowledge barriers.

When he looked back at her, he gave her a quizzical stare. "What is it?"

She couldn't help it. She moved closer. "I find I suddenly want to kiss you." It wasn't anything to do with Annabel. She was sure of that. Did he know that? Did he wonder, at times like this, like she did? The reasons they had originally been attracted to each other were far from cut and dried, but did he ever wonder, as she did, about their fundamental attraction? "It's me, I mean…what I am trying to say is that Annabel isn't with me right now. *I* want to kiss you." She shuffled closer. "Just in case you were wondering," she added, rather too quickly.

"I know." He gave a wry smile, a wise, almost-sad look in his eyes.

Of course he knew. He'd always known how much she wanted him. God, that made her want him even more. She kissed him hungrily, greedy for more of him, wanting it all. He held her close, his hand cupping the back of her head, his mouth owning hers.

"It has to be done," she whispered as they drew apart, "you know it and I know it."

He nodded, admitting it at last.

"We must strike some kind of deal with her, before Cain succeeds. I believe in you."

He was silent for an age, and then he pushed his hand through his hair. "If we do this, we need to be close enough to the cottage, to her anchor, but far away enough to be peripheral to Cain's jurisdiction. He has spells set all around here. Any psychic or supernatural activity, he knows about it immediately."

"Really?" That meant that every time she sighted Annabel, he knew. Then again, he was quite possibly the one who made it happen. She pushed back the doubts that kept niggling her. "Any ideas?"

As he looked away toward the horizon she saw his eyes gleam silver and for a moment she was adrift, because she felt as if she didn't know him. Then he blinked, and it was gone.

"Maybe." He lifted his hand from the steering wheel. She saw that he was pointing at the offshore island with the disused lighthouse. He put one finger against his lips.

She nodded, understanding.

24

THEY STAYED INSIDE CORNERSTONE UNTIL darkness fell. Once again Gray cooked, but this time she could barely get the food down. He paced up and down as he ate, skimming pages of the book that Maggie had given him, his eyes bright with concentration. Occasionally he would go to the windows and look out, and Zoë would see movement beyond. Members of the coven were watching, waiting.

At one point he picked up his loyal stray, Cat, and encouraged him to go out of the window at the back of the house. The cat climbed through the window eagerly and just before Gray shut the window, Zoë was sure she heard a roar from the garden beyond, followed by a high-pitched squeal.

Gray smiled to himself as he went about his business.

It didn't faze Zoë. She was beginning to take these things in her stride. Either that or she was just so numb that these strange goings-on barely touched her, things that would have freaked her out under normal circumstances. She'd walked into the twilight zone, but now she trusted Gray to guide her the rest of the way through it.

"Okay," he said. "It's dark enough. Are you ready?"

"Ready as I'll ever be." She pulled on the sweater he had given her, a long loose-knit in black. It went all the way down to her midthighs, which made her smile. He was dressed in dark colors as well, and he had a black backpack with him.

Before they stepped outside, he paused in the hallway and chanted again in that strange language, his eyelids low, and his expression trancelike. The nerve endings all over her body tingled, and she watched, wide-eyed, as his image shimmered and seemed to fade into the background before her. She could still feel his hands on her head, and when she glanced down she saw her own image was blurred and indistinct too.

He stroked her hair before he removed his hands. "It will be harder for people to spot us moving in the darkness now. Cain will be alerted that a spell has gone down, but he won't know what for a while. Hopefully, it'll be long enough."

She covered one of his hands with her own, and drew it to her mouth, resting a kiss on his palm.

They left the house and walked up Shore Lane hand-in-hand. Zoë stared out across the water as they went. The wind had settled and it was a clear night, although much cooler than it had been earlier in the week. The reflection of the moonlight on the water looked like white satin spilled across obsidian marble. When they neared the marina, Gray led her faster, his hand tightening on hers. Up ahead, outside the boatyard, she made out two figures. Watchmen. The young woman with the bleached hair from the forest the night before, Isla, was there with

Crawford. They were chatting quietly. Beyond them, she saw the older woman from the forest walking past the post office with a small dog on a lead. She had one arm in a sling.

As they closed on the main pathway of the marina, Crawford turned their way and looked straight at them. Zoë's footsteps faltered. She was sure Crawford had seen something, but Gray urged her on and Crawford returned to his discussion. They turned left and covered the length of the wooden jetty quickly.

He went almost to the end of the main jetty, and then branched off onto a smaller one that ran between the many boats that were moored there. At last he stopped. Taking one last glance around, he began to remove the tarpaulin that covered a small motorboat.

Zoë shoved her hands in her pockets until he was ready for her. Occasionally, a shiver ran down her spine when she registered what they were trying to do. She glanced back over her shoulder, toward the Tide Inn. Lights were off in the main part of the building, but there was an arc of light above it, which had to be coming from Cain's apartment. When she looked back at Gray, he smiled reassuringly. She took his outstretched hand and climbed in. The boat shifted underfoot, and she had to duck down quickly to grab the side of the boat and steady herself. When she was settled on the seat opposite him, Gray lifted the oars and began to row.

Nervous as she was, he made an awesome sight for her to look at in the moonlight. His chiseled features and unusual hair and eyes picked up the light when he turned to check their direction. Her emotions were hopelessly entangled here. What did that say about her judgment? Was she wrong to trust him? Doubts leapt on her back like hungry ghouls, reminding her how little she knew. What she did know didn't soothe her. There were three parties in this, Grayson, Cain's crowd, and Annabel. If Annabel came through in her, Grayson might be the only person who would want that situation to change. It was just as well she wasn't a gambling person because those odds weren't great.

Gray kept rowing until they were well away from the harbor, before firing up the engine. They puttered their way across the rest of the bay to the island. The smell of the fuel sharpened her senses, and she peered at the abandoned lighthouse as they closed on it.

Gray caught her attention and nodded inland. "Abernathy," he whispered.

They were yards away from the island, and when she followed his gesture she saw what he was drawing her attention to. The lighthouse was at a perfect midway point between the villages of Carbrey and Abernathy. Was that why he had chosen this place? Both villages nestled like gems in the cliffs, the lights from the houses twinkling.

The lighthouse loomed up ahead, somber and lonely, a stone tower some thirty feet high that belonged to a different age. "It's a lonely looking place."

"Don't think of it that way." He pointed along the shore. "This place is a sanctuary for puffins. Earlier in the summer the island was filled with new life and noise."

When he smiled over at her, she saw it. He was a guardian, in more ways than one. So many ways. His knowledge was sensitive and it ran deep—partly instinct, partly learned. There was no one else in the whole world that she'd rather trust. The fact that she was falling in love with him might be a mistake, but she didn't want to face up to that right now. Mr. Loner here probably had way too much to do in his life to take on a real relationship with her, even if he wanted to.

Moments later he moored the boat up at the stone jetty, tying it to the large metal ring embedded in the stone. When he stood and helped her onto the jetty, he lifted his backpack and a rope from the floor of the boat and took it with him. When he saw her stare at the rope, he said nothing, and she didn't want to ask. He made some sort of spell before they went any further, and then led her over to the entrance.

The door to the lighthouse finally creaked open after Gray put his shoulder to it several times. He fished a flashlight out of the backpack, switching it on once the door was closed behind them. Zoë looked at the old stone steps as the light fell over them. Dust and dirt and the remnants of time shadowed the place. Gray took her hand and led the way. Halfway up the tower there was a small living area. It was bare now, but for an iron-framed bed and an old table.

As they mounted the second set of stairs that wound around the interior of the tower it grew lighter, and he switched off his light when the moon from above increasingly lit the way.

"Quite a climb," Zoë said, catching her breath, when they emerged into the top of the tower. In the center of the space a huge rusty metal-and-glass beacon took up a large amount of the floor space. A metal table stood on the shore side and she rested her hands on it when she stepped over, looking at the lights twinkling along the bay in Carbrey. "It looks so pretty, so unassuming, from here."

Gray stepped behind her, holding her. "It does. Are you still sure about this?"

It felt so good, being held by him. She closed her eyes

and rested her head back against his chest. As soon as she did, she felt that mischievous nudge inside her. Her naughty friend was with them. Was she ever far away? Had she been with them every time? Yes, her instinct told her. All this sexmagic business, she'd likely been tapping into that, too. She felt jittery, and a sense of urgency over her. She wanted this sorted, now.

"Yes, it's time. Annabel needs to talk." She turned to face him, looping her arms around his neck. "Just promise me you won't get too distracted by her and forget me."

"Zoë, it's taken me this long to find you, I don't intend to lose you now." His voice was hoarse and his words made her heart brim. It was what she wanted to hear most in the world, but it only made what they had to do that much harder.

"I want you to kiss me and hold me, to make love to me, Gray, now."

Want to, in case I never come back.

He stared at her silently and she could see he was wrestling with all of this. Should she be worried that he was far from convinced by this procedure?

"You know that Annabel will respond to you, to your magic and your sex appeal." She poked him in the chest with one finger, teasingly, to take the edge off her fear. "Just so long as you are making love to me."

It took a long while before he answered. "The energy source would be helpful, but are you sure you would really want me to?"

The combination of fear and arousal was doing very strange things to her. "I do and I don't. I want you, I always want you." She paused and stroked his jaw. "But you would be making love to her if this works, wouldn't you? Maybe that's what she wants." It was a joke, but she wished she hadn't said it. "It'll help," she added, and she knew then that this was down to her. She had to put her life in his hands, and trust him, before he would take action.

Resting back on the old metal table, she sat back onto it, and lay down its length, her feet dangling to the floor.

"I'll compromise," he responded, his mouth set, and opened up the skein of rope that he had with him. "I'm going to tether you, because I'm not having her walk out of here in your body."

She swallowed, and gave him an uneasy smile. "Okay."

He drew her arms above her head and kissed both her palms tenderly before tying them together with the rope, securing it by tying it around a metal strut on the inside of the window frame. He shook his head as he looked down at her, his eyelids lowering. A wry laugh escaped him. "Having you tied up is a big distraction."

Arousal mounted alongside the mixed emotions she felt, and soon surpassed it, because of the way he was looking at her. When he put his hand under the loose sweater he had given her to wear and pushed it up and over her breasts, her arms lifted within their restraints and heat rose in her face. Being tied up was hellishly infuriating when she wanted to put her hands on him, but it was intoxicating, too, and it heightened the desire she felt.

Gray bent to kiss her throat. As he did, he began to chant softly. Butterflies wisped over her skin, one kiss setting them loose all over her body. Pleasure bubbled through her, frothy and all-consuming. The strange, foreign words sounded so much more seductive breathed close against her skin in between the kisses he rested on her skin.

With her hands bound and his hungry kisses on her throat, and then lower, between her breasts, she was set adrift on a wave of delirium. He pulled down her bra cups, exposing her breasts, pulling on the hard nipples. It was so blissfully painful and addictive that she arched on the table, offering her breasts to him again. He accepted her invitation, licking and sucking one nipple, then the other, before kissing his way down her belly.

Unzipping her fly, he pushed his hand inside her undies.

What a way to go, she thought, with no small sense of irony, when desire took over completely. Her hips moved instinctively, rocking into the hard cup of his fingers, darts of pleasure storming through her groin. The room had started to glow, an arc of rose-colored light rising above them that beat like pulse. He was making magic from her arousal.

He grazed her nipple with his teeth, the hand cupping her pussy teasing her until he was stroking her clit. She moaned aloud, close to coming after he made contact with the swollen nub of her clit.

Lifting his head he moved his free hand over her chest in a figure of eight, just as he had that first night on the staircase in Her Haven, but this time he was chanting that strange language under his breath.

Silver flashed from his eyes, as if his power reflected and intensified the moonlight. Static surged in the atmosphere around him and the rosy light rippled in waves where he had moved his hand.

A soft whisper of a sound drifted around her mind.

Annabel?

She looked at Gray. "She's coming, she heard your call."

He nodded, he knew. He could sense Annabel's spirit surfacing as much as she could.

This was it.

Because Zoë wanted him so badly, and because Gray was unsure about this, she resisted the transition for longer than she had the previous times. Then she felt Annabel rising within her, an erotic trance that took hold of her senses, rising on the cusp of flames and smoke, and she knew this had to be done.

"Fire, I feel her fire," she whispered, and lifted her eyelids one last time.

Gray looked down at her.

She studied his face and he studied hers as he brought her to climax, his fingers thrumming on her clit.

"Oh, oh, yes, oh Gray!" Her head rolled on the cold metal as her body tightened and her nerve endings ebbed and flowed with pleasure, heat rising in her core, swamping her in pleasure.

"Gray," she whispered, again.

The room had gone dark. She could no longer see him, and she lowered her eyelids as she relinquished control to the spirit who resided close by.

25

GRAYSON TOOK A DEEP, STEADYING BREATH. The fact that Zoë's aura was filled with sexual energy meant that his cock had been rock-hard and ready for action, right from the get-go. Never had it been so hard to hold back from making love to her. Never had he wanted to be inside her so badly. But observing her was a whole different kind of magic.

Denial had its rewards. Her sensuality almost overwhelmed him, and the way she responded left him with a sense of awe at the powerful desire between them. He'd almost lost touch with the vibrant psychic energy channeling through her, until he felt a needful, clamoring vibe pierce through and fracture the rose-hued atmosphere. It was begging for his attention, and it was a demanding spirit. Annabel.

Mercifully, Zoë was almost lost in her reverie, riding the moment while she looked up at him. But Grayson knew that time was against them and he had to act fast. He braced himself, ready for anything. Zoë's spirit faded, her breath coming out on a whisper of pleasure so sweet and poignant that his chest ached.

Moments passed. Long silent moments, and then she purred and growled in her throat and Annabel pulled free of the sleeping aspect of Zoë, her eyes opening.

Oh, yes, he could see her now, her eyes gleaming and catlike within her host. He rested his hand against her chest. "Annabel McGraw, I am warning you right now, you're not going to get the better of this situation!"

For several moments her spirit energy tussled with his, feral and playful. Then she chuckled and lifted one leg alongside his hip. "I can see why she likes you so much. You are a fine lover, worthy of the affection she feels for you."

Grayson drew back, thrown by her intimate comment and the knowledge it contained. Was she trying to derail his focus? "We have business to discuss, and you know that."

She watched him, and then yanked lazily on the rope holding her, laughing softly. "Why is it that you tether me, witch? It is not me that you need to fear."

"It's up to you to convince me."

"You think that I will try to keep her body, now that I am in possession of it?" A ghostly smile moved over her face.

It was so unutterably strange for him to see it there, knowing it was not Zoë's smile he saw on her lovely face. It made him want to bring her back, immediately. He had to get through this as fast as he could. "I'm not offering you a body, I merely want to talk. This was the only way."

"You have enticed me, witch. If it were not for the fact that I am bound to another lover, I might be tempted to stay."

Grayson shook his head. "Don't even start with me!"

She chuckled. Then she looked pointedly at the window, as if she was hankering for the shore.

"You're on the clock, Annabel, don't waste it. You know what this is about."

She lifted one shoulder within her restraints and sighed. "'Twas only a bit of fun. You know me better than that, scholar."

Mischief glowed in her aura.

Grayson fought back a growing sense of frustration. "I need to strike a deal with you."

"Strike a deal? Well now, strange words, but I think I understand your meaning."

"My wish is to protect Zoë, to protect the people of this village, and to undo the forbidden magic that is being done here."

"Fear not, scholar, for I do not want her body, I have no need for it. That's not what this is about. *He* might think so, but he doesn't know what he is doing."

The knot in his chest loosened a tad.

"I have tried to show her that." As if to prove a point, her aura glowed fierce all of a sudden and she slid her wrists free of the rope.

Grayson had her pinned down in a flash. "Don't even think about it. I've put a boundary spell around the lighthouse. You cannot leave here in her form."

"Aye, I know." She smiled softly. "You're worried that I might be a playin' with you and your lady love tonight. Mayhap I have been playin', but not tonight. Come now, it is my last turn in this world. Let me enjoy the weight of a body while we discuss our business, and then you will see that your fears are unfounded."

Doubt riddled him. He wanted her to be hateful and

angry so he could banish her back to the spirit world without further ado, but he couldn't get a handle on her. He also wanted to hold her down and restrain her again, in case she refused to leave Zoë's body. The rope was no use, but he would, if necessary, call upon the powers of all souls to harness her.

"Trust me, scholar." She reached out and touched him.

He fought back the emotion that hit him when she touched him with that hand, and rocked back on his heels.

"She is safe. Now, let me give you a word of advice."

Advice? Grayson's frustration only grew.

"Don't be like your father, he could have had family here and you are in danger of denying yourself the same."

"I don't want to talk about me," he responded, between gritted teeth.

She lifted her shoulders, as if amused by him. "Just an observation. Think on it."

Grayson wondered briefly if she'd always been this annoying. "You've come to the surface of our world because Cain has called to you, yes?"

She rose—and she did it slowly, as if hampered by the body she currently inhabited—then walked to the window and looked out across the bay toward Shore Lane.

"Cain? I have come because of him, but not because he called to me." She laughed to herself. "Besides, that is not his name, though he would dearly love to be the prodigal son who was welcomed home again." She smiled over her shoulder at him, a rush of colored light pouring from her eyes.

Grayson followed her. Now they were getting to the nitty-gritty.

"He has tried to draw a veil over their eyes, but at the end of it all he has only fooled himself, for his time is nigh.

You, scholar, you see his black soul and his vengeful spirit, no matter what he calls himself."

"Who is he?"

"An ancient witch. He lived about these parts when I did. We were lovers, but we have an old grief with one another. Time has made him forget the details. That, and a little magic." Again she glanced back at him and chuckled, the sound of her laughter echoing around the empty tower.

"Are you suggesting that you can perform magic from beyond the grave?" It was unheard of. A few haunting tricks, apparitions, mood alterations and so forth, but nothing real, and nothing that would rely on being away from the physical anchor, her home, or her grave if she had one.

"Well, not exactly, but I sacrificed a few hundred years of haunting rights for a little justice and retribution."

"Justice?"

"Cain Davot's real name is Ewan Findlay, and he was responsible for my death."

Grayson's eyebrows lifted.

"Ah, you see it now. Yes, and as you sow, so shall you reap." She rolled her eyes. "That was one sermon I did take notice of."

She grew more serious. "After I'd gone, he became even more selfish than he was before. He sought to ally himself with the dark Lord. Decadent in his tastes, he was greedy for wealth and power. He traded his soul for three hundred years more of it, and traveled the world wreaking havoc and bringing a bad name to our craft. Alas for him, that time is nigh.

"Because my life was wrongly ended at his behest, I earned the right to haunt for as many years as he was alive. I didn't want that, so I sacrificed my rights to haunt for a shorter amount of time, if I could be the one to guide him to his end."

What she was revealing was fascinating to him in so many ways. "Why didn't you appear to me, as I asked you to, and tell me this then?"

"The time wasn't right. You know how these things work, scholar. Besides, it was Zoë he wanted to use. She became receptive to me because of you and because of her grief about her mother, so Zoë had to be my bait."

Grayson narrowed his eyes. "You've had fun with us all."

"Well, now, you seemed to be enjoying it, for the most part." Again mischief sparkled in her expression. "You have done a good job of protecting your kind. You would have been here even if I hadn't, is that not the way of it?"

"I suppose so, but Zoë didn't ask for any of this."

"Scholar, I am surprised at you. Nothing worth having is ever easy, you should know that." She gave a sigh that sounded as if she was teasing him, but he wasn't sure. "Zoë had her own journey to travel. She was willing to take risks because of you. Otherwise I wouldn't have allowed her to be drawn into this by him. Desire garnered her interest and love made her stay, she told you as much herself."

Grayson stared at her. To hear it said aloud, that Zoë cared for him that deeply, made him strong. "I intend to undo the magic that he has done, to free her from his spell, but Zoë wanted me to speak with you first."

Annabel was looking at him as if she was amused. "Do you really think I would be so foolish as to let him build an enchantment so powerful over a blameless soul such as Zoë?"

Grayson was unable to fathom her meaning for one long moment. "What do you mean? Are you saying he hasn't cast a possession spell?"

"Oh, he has tried, but I arranged for each and every poisoned enchantment to be undone, as he cast them. Zoë is bound to me and Carbrey at the present time because I need her help, that is all. It will all be over this very night."

Davot had no power over Zoë, but a long-dead witch did. Grayson felt marginally better but no more, because he was far from sure that he wasn't being duped here.

"Right now, I will strike a deal with you," she said, folding her arms.

Grayson tensed. He half wished he hadn't asked her to strike a bloody deal.

"Let Zoë finish this, and I promise you she will be safe. But you must write a book about me, scholar, now that you know the full story. It would be nice to be remembered more kindly."

She winked at him, and Grayson saw that despite the fact he'd been put through the wringer over this, she was offering him a gift. Zoë's instinct about Annabel had been correct, but still he couldn't shirk the feeling that this was all an elaborate trick. Not until he had Zoë back and all suggestion of possession was a million lightyears away from them.

"This is nearly over," Annabel repeated. Her expression grew deadly serious. Then she drew his attention to the window. "They are coming for her. Time is short now."

"What do you mean this is nearly over? Explain, please."

She strolled to the table, and sat back down on it. "'Tis odd. I did not recall a body being so heavy as this." She ran her hands over the outline of her borrowed form, frowning, as if curiously dissatisfied. "Still, it makes no odds, for my place is not here." She shrugged. "It has been fun, but I'm longing to be back with Irvine."

Grayson was beside her, ready for any tricks she might

have. But she settled back down on the table in the very position she had arrived into the body.

With one hand, she reached up and squeezed his shoulder. "Thank you, scholar, for your work here. Now hurry, call her back. She will come to you and it is for her to help me finish this." A smile played around her mouth, and then it faltered. Her spirit was fading. "Call her. She will always come back to you, Grayson Murdoch of Abernathy."

Her words echoed around his mind as he leaned over her. Holding her around the shoulders, he shook her. "Annabel, tell me what it is we have to do!"

Her eyelids fluttered up. "Go back to the cottage." Her voice was faint, so faint he could barely hear her. "I can manifest there. Destiny's lass knows the way. She must lead him there, she must give me what I need to end this."

It was the last thing Annabel said to him, and then her body slumped back in his grasp.

Doubt swamped him. He could hear noise echoing out across the water, and when he glanced at the window he saw a flare launch into the night sky, lighting up the whole harbor.

Cain was on his way.

He had to pull Zoë out of this and fast. He couldn't trust Annabel's word that Zoë was not bound by Cain, and if Cain found her physical form in this state he would try to seize his chance to summon and keep Annabel. Who knew what that would bring about?

He pulled her close, chanted his call.

He kissed her face, her soft mouth and her lowered eyelids, willing her to return, begging all the souls of the hidden magical world to aid his quest as he chanted. It was Zoë's heart beating hard against his, had to be. "Zoë, come back, come back to me."

For an excruciating length of time he thought her face grew paler, and the horror of the possibility that he had lost her was immense.

Then her lips parted, and from a far, faraway place, she whispered his name.

26

FOR SEVERAL LONG MOMENTS ZOË DRIFTED alone in the darkness. Silence was all around. Her hands were still bound, but something shifted around her and she felt as if she were outside now, no longer in the safety of the lighthouse, no longer in the safety of Gray's embrace.

The wind blew cold around her, chilling her to the bone, and she shivered.

Do not weep for me, Zoë. Do not weep, sweet friend.

When the voice whispered around her, she struggled to see the vision that was opening up in her mind, and when she did, she was horror-struck....

Do not weep for me, Zoë. I need you to help me, and I knew that you would need to understand the reason why. You will. I have shown you everything as it happened.

This is the way it was at the end.

Do you see them? Do you hear how the crowd bay for my blood? Their jeers surround me. Can you feel their anger and their fear?

They've waited the day through for me to be brought from my cell, and as the sun drops low over the sea I am led out before them.

Somewhere a drum beats, slow, and I am forced to measure my steps by it, steps I am barely able to take. The executioner is at my back, and I can see the gibbet from which they will hang me, up ahead. Beside it, they ready the kindle. I do not fear death, do not think that. Not anymore. I welcome it. You will understand why soon enough.

Among the crowd I see brethren. Some of the women cry silently for me, huddled together for safety. The men turn away, lest they are called out if they show sorrow. Through the numbness in my heart and soul, I pause and look for my master amongst the crowd, but I cannot see him.

I am pushed forward.

The soldiers have to hold back the crowd. They would stone me and enjoy it, if they were allowed. They will warm their hands at the fire where my remains burn. All but a few condemn me now, but I know who my true persecutor was, and I know why.

The soldiers came to my home at dawn, two, maybe three days ago. I have lost track of time, for they would not let me sleep and I suffered greatly at their hands. Hard-faced soldiers they were, and they dragged me screaming from my beloved haven, my home. Reverend Slater had summoned two magistrates from Edinburgh and they questioned me about Hettie Maginty. She had lost the two bairns she was carrying. Her mother, Molly, accused me of cursing them. I had never used the craft in such a way, and never would. Aye, I made jests about it, but my error was no greater than that. The Reverend Slater beat me with his staff, and they threw me in stocks that crushed my legs. They brought me neither food nor water, and questioned me at intervals.

I did not deny their accusation of witchcraft, nor did I confirm it. Not until the news came of my dear heart, my Irvine. Even while the trial was underway, word came that he had been poisoned. The silent tears I spilled were not for myself. They were for Irvine. He had suffered a gruesome, painful death. I would gladly have given my own life to protect him. The pain was too much to bear.

They took my tears for guilt and contrition, fools that they are. Grief is a greater burden, and I have not spoke a word but to nod my acceptance of my fate, for the finger of blame was pointed my way once more, and I was condemned without further ado.

Do not weep for me, sweet friend.

I fear not the tightening of the rope nor the flames, for they will reunite me with Irvine, my one true love. If he will forgive me for the bad things I have brought his way, I will happily kneel at his feet for all of eternity. Now, as I near the end, I pray to any power that will listen to me to reunite us. I stare into the baying crowd and I feel pity for them in their ignorance. They thought I was jealous of Hettie and her place in his bed, but I could not honestly do her or her bairns harm, for it would hurt Irvine.

While the executioner turns the rope I take one last look at the crowd, seeking my true persecutor. I see him standing there, alone at the back of the crowd with a sullen look on his face: Ewan. I can see it in his eyes, the scorn and the jealousy. I have been ousted by one of my own, my master. How mistaken he was, when he took me into his coven. Who would have guessed that it would drive him to this? It was him that undertook those heinous acts and then whispered my name to Molly Shaw, who pointed the finger. The knife twists in my heart when I think of how Irvine and Hettie have suffered because of him. He has lashed out at us all, but our blood will stain his hands forever.

If Ewan had taken me as his wife, would any of this have happened? Sadly I fear I know the answer to that question, for love is stronger than any law. Irvine and I were drawn to each other as the bee to the pollen. Our fate was set the day he arrived in Carbrey.

The rope tightens around my neck.

They condemn me as an evil witch.
I know what I am.
I am a woman of the craft.
I open my arms to the sky and I dance with the wind.
I ride the earth with a lusty cry.
I love fiercely and I am proud to the end.
I close my eyes.
I think of Irvine and I reach for his hand.

When Zoë awoke it was with a sob in her throat.

"They killed her," she whispered. She took a deep, shaky breath, trying to get hold of her emotions. The oxygen only fuelled the sobs that racked her.

"Hey now," Gray said, and pulled her into his arms.

She clung to him, relieved to be back in that place and time, and yet filled with the pain of what she'd seen and felt. "They burned her body."

Stroking her back, he whispered to her. "It's hard, when you begin to feel close to the past and you see how cruel life can be."

She put her hand against his chest, calmed by the beat of his heart. "Someone betrayed her. It wasn't even about her witchcraft."

"Now we know for sure."

The sky lit up around them in a dazzling burst of light, as if a firework had gone off. "What was that?"

"A flare. We have to go, Cain is on his way. I'll explain more on the way."

She moved and felt dizzy. He put his arm around her as he drew her up to her feet, pulling her up with him. She was shaky and emotional. He rested a kiss against her forehead and she instantly felt stronger

"Come on, we can't afford to waste time." He grabbed

her hand and then snatched up the flashlight from where it lay on the floor. Moving quickly, he led the way down, the light bouncing off the steps.

"What happened while I was out?"

"Annabel surfaced. You were right. She doesn't want to come back to our world." He glanced back at her, but in the gloom she couldn't see his expression. "There was much more to it than we knew."

They'd reached the entrance.

Gray flicked off the flashlight and looked out across the bay. Peeping over his shoulder, Zoë saw two speedboats making their way from Carbrey. The relief that she'd felt about being back with Gray withered away into nothing. The speedboats would reach the shore within a couple of minutes. The sea looked horribly choppy, and heaven only knows what Cain had in store for them.

Gray nodded his head at the boat, squeezing her hand. "This isn't about Cain bringing her back," he continued to explain, as they clambered into the boat. "He thinks it is, because that's what Annabel wants him to think."

"What do you mean?" She clung to the sides of the boat as she sat down. The water was much rougher than before.

Gray undid the rope tying them to the shore and started the engine. "Annabel has…well, set him up." He had to shout across to her above the noise. He shook his head, as if he couldn't quite believe what he was saying. "He's not bringing her back to life. She's just luring him into a trap, and you're part of that. There is no possession spell. It's not about that."

It was almost beyond her to believe it, because if it were true it meant she was off the hook. "What is it about?"

Gray squatted low as he directed the boat, his gaze constantly behind her as he watched the approaching speedboats. "Cain is her old adversary."

Whoa, that shed some light. "Ewan? Cain is Ewan?"

It all began to fall into place, and as she thought about the images of Ewan that she'd had in the visions, she saw the similarity. Had Annabel wanted her to guess? It would never have occurred to her that he would still be alive. "Is it his magic that's keeping him…young, and alive?"

"Not exactly. He did a deal with the dark Lord of the Hidden World."

"Blimey, so how do we, er, get rid of him? I mean, he still thinks he can get what he wants, if he gets hold of me, right?" Those words made her feel queasy—that and the roll of the boat on the rough waters. She took a tentative glance over her shoulder. Spotlights on the speedboats scanned the water close by.

"Yes, but his time is up. Annabel needs our help to bring him in."

Zoë cursed under her breath, wondering if she was dreaming this. "How?"

"She was very helpful, up to a point." Sarcasm rang in his tone. "She said to go back to the cottage and he'll follow you, but I'm far from happy about you being used as bait."

"She didn't give you any more clues?" Another flare lit up the sky. It was as bright as day right above their heads. There was no hiding now. Zoë didn't even want to look back over her shoulder.

Grayson's expression was grim. "It must be something she can't do in spirit form. A ghost can move things around, cause apparitions and change moods, but a ghost cannot instigate things in the real world that are solid and factual. It's a natural law." In the bright light of the flare, his expression was intense. He looked at her with curiosity. "She also said that Destiny's lass would know the way to end this."

Oh, how that made her heart flip.

She stared at him in disbelief, a well of emotion dredging inside of her. "That's me. I am Destiny's lass. My mother's name was Destiny Daniels."

Could it be that Annabel had communicated with her mother? She shook her head, holding back the unshed tears. She was too vulnerable, too emotional, to think about that now. "What does it mean, Gray? What has my mother to do with this?"

"The spirit world has a network all its own, far beyond our understanding." Gray continued to peer across the bay, working the engine for maximum speed, weaving through the waves. "Get ready to get down, hunker inside the boat."

The noise grew louder. "I kept thinking about her," she called out. "I was angry that she'd never communicated with me the way Annabel had."

"If she hasn't it probably means she doesn't need to, she's a content soul."

"I understand that now," Zoë said, and it was to herself.

"Annabel has certainly used us for her purposes, but she put the pieces into place when you needed them. We're going to have to trust that she will continue to help, and we don't have a choice on that matter." He stopped talking, and pointed at the floor of the boat, his eyes bright as the spotlights hit them. "Get down *now,* take cover."

Zoë scrambled, glancing back as she did so. Waves washed over them as the large speedboat did a U-turn, sending water spraying up in the air before running parallel to their much-slower boat.

Above her she saw Cain, his hands on the side of his boat as he glared over at them. He shouted, but his words were swept up in the noise. Angry thunder roared across the sky.

The sky cracked open and lightning flashed, hitting the island behind Gray.

If Cain was using magic, they'd be lucky if they reached the shore alive, let alone work out how to get rid of him. Then a horrible noise sounded close by, a rasping sound. Zoë's skin crawled. This wasn't thunder or lightning, it sounded like something that was alive and hungry. A really bad feeling stole over her and her heart thundered in her chest. Something hit the side of the boat, making an ominous, hollow, knocking sound. On her knees and elbows, she scrambled along the floor of the boat until she touched against Gray. If she was going to die, she needed to feel him.

He put his hand against her head. "Don't look!"

She couldn't help it.

She looked, and then screamed. Along the edge of the boat nonhuman hands gripped the edge of the boat, hands that shimmered with blue scales. Sea monsters?

Okay, I shouldn't have looked.

Gray weaved the boat in the water but couldn't shake them free. They rose up in the water and attempted to clamber onto the boat, the awful stench of rotting fish filling the air as they did so. Zoë gulped down bile and fear as she stared at the spectacle. They had seal-like heads and black eyes, bodies shimmering with blue scales, spiked spines on the humped backs of their bloated bodies.

It's only Cain's magic.

"Not real, not real," she said aloud, trying to convince herself.

"I'm afraid they are real," Gray said, "but their place is at the bottom of the sea, not here. He's summoned them from the deep. Nice work, Cain!" He turned to her. "Take the rudder. Stay as low as you can, and I bloody well mean it this time!"

He glared at her. Lightning cracked again, right overhead, and rain lashed down on them. That hollow knocking sounded again. She stared in horror as one of the creatures bit into the side of the boat and water started to leak in. She clambered into Gray's place, hands shaking, mouth tightly closed. With the rudder at shoulder level she couldn't even see where they were headed, she just kept pointing their boat away from the white speedboat looming at their side. Cain leered over at her. She felt sick to her stomach knowing now that he was Ewan, knowing what he'd done to Annabel, to Hettie, and to Irvine, in the name of power and revenge.

She looked away, focusing on Gray instead.

With his feet spread wide to measure the sway of the boat, he opened his arms to the sky and shouted loud his magic. Zoë willed him on, watching as his hands filled with light and it shifted and changed into a huge silvery net which he cast wide over the creatures gathered at the side of the boat. He pointed down as if to the floor of the ocean. The creatures struggled against the net, but to no avail, because it dragged them back down to wherever they had come from.

Zoë felt dizzy with relief when the last of them disappeared beneath the water. Then the sound of a gunshot rang out.

Grayson ducked down beside her, shielding her with his body. Zoë stared, her eyes wide in disbelief as she looked beyond his shoulder at the sky. It was lighting up as if a huge torchlight had come on farther along the coast, a great band of light that swept their way. Unsure if this was more of Cain's magic, Zoë watched as the light sparkled, spinning and dancing like colored mists within the corridor of light. The waves it passed over settled.

Her hand went to her mouth when the mists shifted and formed briefly into images, images of people. She saw Maggie there, and Fern, and other women and men, their arms linked, their eyes closed as they created their own magic from the shore.

"Gray! Look."

He glanced back. As he did the corridor of light shifted and revolved around them. Zoë could no longer see their enemies beyond. The waters stilled within the corridor of light, and Grayson moved, quickly grabbing the rudder, directing the boat within the lane of safe passage they'd been granted. With his free hand, he took hers and she huddled closer to him, relief washing over her.

"A loner, huh?" she said, the reprieve making her slightly giddy.

His mouth lifted at one corner, but he didn't respond.

This wasn't over yet.

27

ELSPETH STARED AT THE SIGHT, OPENMOUTHED.

"What the hell is it?" Crawford asked from his place at the speedboat's wheel.

"The Abernathy coven," Cain replied angrily, gesturing with the gun in his hand.

Elspeth watched as the light pulsated with energy. It was mesmerizing, and within it she saw reflected images of women and men with their hands entwined. Envy and sadness filled her, because that was what she wanted—a coven like that, a united coven.

"How dare they get involved?" Cain said

Elspeth was amazed. "If you've got a problem with them, you should have told us." She didn't want to take on the Abernathy lot, no way. Territorial rivalry on their own patch was one thing, a full-on coven war was another. "You've kept us in the dark and put us all in danger."

"Elsie," Crawford hissed, snatching at her.

"No." She tore her hand free of Crawford's and launched herself at Cain, knocking the gun from his hand into the water. He delivered a blow to her right shoulder, flooring her. Pain shot through her arm and chest.

From where she landed she could hear Cain shouting instructions and she breathed deep before she tried to get to her feet.

"Sit down," Cain commanded. He shouted back to the boat beyond, "Can you get a good shot off at Murdoch from there?"

"You can't be serious," Elspeth said. "This is madness. Their powers are much greater than ours."

"Look there, take Murdoch out," Cain shouted, pointing into the dazzling light. Bound up within it Elspeth could make out the sight of the small motorboat carrying Grayson and Zoë back to the harbor. "Take him down," Cain shouted again to the other boat, where Warren Kirby had a rifle. "Mind you don't hurt the woman."

Two shots rang out.

Elspeth stared as the bullets exploded midair. Cain let loose a string of obscenities and then turned his attention to the wheel, pushing Crawford out of the way to take charge. Crawford tumbled backward down the boat as the front end lifted, and smacked his head on the side of the boat. He slumped to the floor, where his body lay still.

Elspeth swore aloud when she saw a dark patch of blood seeping from his head onto the floor of the boat. "Cain, Crawford is injured. Help me with this." He barely glanced her way, but when he did she saw the selfish smile on his face. He didn't care. "This is your fault! Use your magic to heal him! I am not powerful enough for this."

"I've got better things to do, and you know it."

He really didn't give a fuck. "Don't expect anymore help from me, in that case." She was furious. "You haven't the first clue how to keep a coven loyal, have you, Cain?"

Cain turned away.

She lowered her hand to Crawford's head, willing her old school friend to stay alive. She wasn't able to do much about the internal injury, but with her powers she could at least stop the bleeding. She chanted low under her breath, her entire will behind the process. Mercifully, the sticky puddle congealing at the side of his head ceased to grow larger. She shoved her hand into her pocket for her phone and entered the emergency number, requesting an ambulance at the Carbrey harbor. Then she lifted Crawford's hand in hers, squeezing life into it, talking to him and pleading with the powers that be to take mercy on him.

The boat bounced heavily.

"Take it easy," she begged Cain, when she realized he was in danger of running them aground, "you're going to crash the bloody boat and kill us all."

But Cain kept the speed at full throttle until the boat battered sidelong into the marina. Whatever internal injuries Crawford had were not going to be helped by that. "I hope you die a long and painful death," she shouted vehemently.

He afforded her a quick glance. "Undoubtedly I will, when my time comes." His smug expression faltered for just a moment, before he climbed out of the boat and headed off through the marina.

"You were a big, big mistake," she said to herself as she watched him go, hating him for the mess he'd pulled them all into. "I vow never to make a mistake like you ever again."

Annabel. My Annabel.

Cain's mind was full of her. Nothing else mattered anymore, nothing other than this reunion. Never in all his years had he met a woman like her. She had haunted his memory, her eyes reflected in those of every woman he had ever got close to, a constant reminder of a fractured affair. He'd wanted to turn back the clock. One day it came to him, he could. Why not? He worked hard for it, because he wanted to have what had been wrongfully stolen from him by another man, so many years before. It had been a long, lonely life without her, one filled with disappointment and regret. He'd lost count of how long he'd been alive but he knew the end of his borrowed time must be near. He wanted to reunite with her before then. She would make everything right again. Together they would be able to live forever. His heart flamed into life.

When he'd seen the Londoner in the boat with Murdoch, her aura had glowed fiercely and he knew what that meant. Annabel was with her. Annabel was inside her. The transformation was almost complete, had to be. She was here, and he would be reunited with her this very night. It made his heart rise within the cage of his chest, years of anticipation building to a cathartic release inside him.

He reached the promenade and turned right onto Shore Lane. That's where she was. As he approached the house he saw a figure moving quickly in the shadows ahead of him. Following, he strained to see. Was it the Londoner, Zoë? Or Annabel returning to her home? Could the transformation have taken place already?

His heart was thundering in his chest and he was finding it hard to breathe, but Her Haven was just ahead and all the windows were lit up. Then he saw the figure standing inside the window, and his heart stopped. Her hands were splayed on the glass and she stared straight at him, her eyes blazing passionately. She was as beautiful as he remembered, her long dark hair falling over her shoulders, her pale skin glowing.

"Annabel," he whispered.

Blind need had hold of him. He had to touch her, had to hold her. The door to the cottage was ajar and he pushed it open and staggered inside.

The door slammed shut behind him.

Instantly, he found himself shoved back against the wall. "Murdoch," he hissed, enraged.

With his forearm under Cain's chin, Grayson Murdoch had him pinned to the wall. "That's right, and I have a ringside seat for this particular show." His eyes flashed silver. "Don't even try to spill any more of your poison enchantments, they are futile."

Enraged and confused by that comment, Cain struggled to break free. He reached for his gun, to no avail.

"You can't stop this," he said, choking, and then faltered, when his attention was drawn beyond Murdoch to the place where Annabel stood. Her image shimmered, ghostlike, as she waited by the window, staring across at him, a smile on her beautiful face.

"Annabel," he whispered again. He struggled again to free himself from the ironlike grip of his adversary, then tried to issue a hex but faltered on the words. There were two women there, and he did not understand it.

Several feet away from Annabel stood the Londoner, Zoë. She looked like a drowned rat, her wet hair sticking to her skull, her eyes wide, a dripping wet sweater clinging to her body. Swallowing hard, he tried to reconcile it. With the two of them so close together, the transformation must be moments away. Yes, that was it.

The hex forgotten, all Cain could do was stare across the room at his proud beauty. He was longing to hold her, longing to bury himself between her thighs and pour himself into her. When she nodded and beckoned to him, her eyes aflame, he went limp in Murdoch's grasp, emotion unraveling him.

Murdoch's grip finally loosened, and his face swam in and out of focus.

Then the Londoner spoke. "Why do you want her to live again, Ewan?"

Ewan? The name unsettled him, coming as it did from his distant past. No one had called him Ewan for a long, long time. He wanted to question it, but he could scarcely draw his attention away from Annabel. "There has never been another woman like her, not in all the years I have lived."

He wanted Annabel to know that. He wanted to please her.

Annabel's lips moved, but he couldn't hear her speak, and then she looked toward the other woman as if communicating with her instead. Confusion hit him. Something was wrong here. This wasn't the way it was supposed to be. "You must die," he blurted, fixing her with a stare, "for this to be complete."

The Londoner lifted her chin, eyeballing him brazenly. "You're mistaken, Cain. Annabel does not want to live again, that isn't why she's here tonight."

"That's a lie, a lie from a desperate woman who doesn't want to die. She has called to me—"

"Yes, that's exactly it, isn't it?" Zoë interrupted, and stepped toward him, boldly. "She called to you. This is the result of her work, not yours."

He stared at her, incredulous. "Not possible."

"How much do you really want to be with her, Ewan? Why didn't you join her before, in the spirit world?"

Cain shook his head. He wasn't ready for that realm yet. He wasn't ready for judgment day. "I need her to be alive and with me, in this world. We can be powerful here, like we once were. As we should have been, for all time."

The room spun, and he realized they were all three staring at him, as if they all knew something he did not. Annabel smiled a ghostly smile, and then shook her head at him. A cold fist closed around his heart. "Annabel?"

He gripped at the back of a nearby chair as he staggered. His heart felt incredibly tight in his chest and he looked to Annabel, seeking reassurance.

Again she shook her head, but this time she also put out her hand to him. It lured him, lured him inexorably to her. How he had loved her, all these years. He swallowed, hard. This was wrong, it couldn't be. She was meant to come to him, not him to her. She would want to take the chance he had created for her in this world, the chance to live again, surely? And yet the thing he wanted most in the world beckoned to him again, her hand outstretched.

Oh, how he longed to touch her, to hold her.

Unable to resist, Cain took a step closer.

Zoë's heartbeat was so erratic that she could hear the sound of her own blood rushing in her ears. What the hell was it that she was supposed to know? Every time she looked at Gray, she felt his encouragement. He'd caged Cain from behind, urging him toward Annabel. He'd already told her that Cain wouldn't leave the house alive, but she didn't want that on his hands. She wanted to find the thing that Annabel needed.

All she had to do was figure out what was needed. She wasn't afraid. Gray had put a protection spell on her and she believed in him. Desperately playing for time, she spoke to him again. "Tell me, Ewan, are you not the one who is responsible for her death?"

That touched a deep chord. His face contorted and horror shone in his eyes. Was he remembering now? He shook his head in denial, never once taking his eyes off Annabel's ghost. "What do you know of what we had?"

"I know how much you loved her, and that you still do. But I also know how vindictive and angry that made you."

That touched more than a chord. He seemed to buckle in front of her eyes, his spirit visibly crushed, as if his soul was being taken from the inside.

Zoë swallowed hard. Annabel pushed her on. "It's your time, Ewan Findley," she said, wishing her voice didn't falter quite so much. "You sold your soul for three hundred years. Annabel has come to lead you because your time is up."

"You're lying! She's here to be with me again, because I want her back." He shook his head again, his eyes filled with confusion.

"Annabel doesn't want to be with you in the real world. It is Irvine she loves, it always was." Zoë could scarcely believe she was saying these words, and yet there was immense power in them. Cain was a broken man.

"Not supposed to be this way!" Cain cried as he staggered toward Annabel, one hand clutched to his chest, insanity in his eyes.

Annabel spoke within Zoë's mind. *Destiny showed you the way to end this.*

Zoë pressed her fingers to her temples.

"I have faith in you," Gray whispered across to her, his gorgeous eyes filled with love and encouragement.

She didn't want to let him down. She didn't want to let Annabel down, either, or her mother.

I never let anyone down and I'm not going to start now!

Think, think, she urged herself.

Destiny would know the way, but how, how? She thought of her mother as she always did. "Pass the crystal, spread the tarot," she used to say. The panpipes would be playing on the stereo and the white wine bottle would be there next to the candles that she surrounded herself with.

Her head shot up. The cleansing power of the flame! Yes, her mother had said it every time she lit a candle.

As if to confirm it, Annabel nodded and appeared as she had that morning, fire licking along the underside of her arms, ghostly smoke and flame all around her. Cain was right up against her, but he was so lost in his goal that he didn't notice the ghostly fire.

Zoë reached out to the old range that stood behind her, turned a knob and hit the automatic ignition. As a ring of flame danced into life, Annabel opened one hand to it and Zoë watched in astonishment as the flame bent in the air, drawn to her.

Can I really do this? she thought, unnerved.

"Bloody hell," she whispered. The house would go up, and Cain was so far in denial he might not even notice. But Cain had meant to kill her, to sacrifice her life for another, and this house was Annabel's anchor, an anchor she no longer needed. It was always Annabel's Haven, and this is what she wanted. Zoë faltered as she thought about all the passion, the pain, the pleasure and the heartbreak that love had brought about for these two souls and those around them, the ugly emotions that it had stimulated, and the forbidden deeds that had followed. Love demanded simple honesty and faith, and where there was none it could not grow or thrive.

"It's his time." It was Gray, and he was beside her in a heartbeat, drawing her away from the range. "You found the natural law," he whispered, and there was fierce pride in his voice. "There is destruction even in nature. It's the way of the world. Cain could walk away now, but Annabel has his heart. It was always the way of it."

They headed for the doorway, fast. The flames from the range had already licked along the work surface. Zoë's emotions welled as she saw Annabel as she would have been on the funeral pyre, ensconced in flames and smoke. But this time her eyes were open, there was no rope around her neck, and her arms were embracing the man responsible for her death.

Cain saw the flames, and wept aloud, grief and anger in his voice. "No, not like this," he bellowed, his scream of anger reverberating through the house.

"Hurry," Grayson said, hauling her away. They darted the length of the hall and out onto the lane. Lightning flashed overhead. Standing back from the house against the sea wall, they watched.

Through the window, they could see Cain. He tried to turn away from Annabel, and his howl of pain and outrage shattered the night sky above Carbrey, turning the skies to stormy rain.

Too late, his final hex.

Annabel had latched her fingers over his shoulders, clawlike. Daggers of fire shot into him. He struggled against her, and her fingers sank deeper, until the fire consumed them both and the room filled with smoke.

Zoë shuddered, grateful when Gray's arms enclosed her and she turned her face to his chest.

The sound of sirens in the distance was echoed by the rumble of thunder overhead.

It began to rain.

It was over.

28

GRAYSON WALKED BAREFOOT AROUND THE kitchen of the Georgian house that he had grown up in, and he finally felt content. It had been a long time coming. Retrieving the best sparkling vintage he owned from his wall-mounted wine rack, he kissed the bottle. It was a heady number with an aromatic bouquet, perfect for the evening. From the cupboard, he lifted out two glasses then paused, and smiled to himself.

Zoë was here in his home in Edinburgh, and he liked the way that felt. He liked it a lot.

That's what the house had needed: a woman's laughter, a woman's sensuality—the secret female knowledge of things that men didn't understand without them. Not just any woman, either, oh, no. The woman he loved.

Three months it had been and they hadn't missed one weekend. Either she would fly from London to Edinburgh, or he would travel down by train or motorcycle. It was only the days in between that were the problem. He picked up the bottle and the glasses and wandered back upstairs to the first floor where he'd left her in the library. His loyal stray cat followed him closely as he went. The cat had adapted well after his move to Edinburgh, and Grayson brought him fresh fish from Carbrey or Abernathy whenever he called by.

They'd be up there tomorrow for the demolition of Cornerstone. The fire had wiped out Her Haven and although Cornerstone was barely touched, it was no longer safe. It would be good to see the evidence gone. They'd heard from Tom—the landlord up at the Silver Birch—that the local council planned to build a proper lookout point on the spot where the two houses had been, so that tourists could enjoy the view of the cliffs beyond, as well as the puffin island, for as long as that patch of the coastline lasted. There would be a coin-operated telescope for when the puffins were nesting, as well. He liked that idea, and so did Zoë.

Cat leapt up onto a sill he favored, on the landing window. He'd taken to keeping guard at the windows and hunting in the garden, even though there was no real need, here at home. Because he liked the spot so much, Zoë had put a cushion there for him. He climbed onto it now, and purred. Gray rubbed him behind one ear, before he headed on.

When he walked into the library, Zoë was sitting on the top step of the sliding ladders, examining a book that she'd pulled from a shelf high up on the wall. She was balancing on one hip, her image radiant against the stack of books.

The close-fitting velvet dress she wore showed her figure to perfection. It ended midthigh, and that had been driving him crazy all evening because it made him want to put his hands over it, and under it. With her feet placed neatly on the steps below the one she was sitting on, high heels gleaming, he could only admire the view. Sheer stockings encased her legs, making him want to run his hands up to the top and pluck at the lacy stocking tops before having her wrap her legs around him, still wearing them.

He set the bottle and glasses on the old oak table in the center of the room, before joining her by the shelves.

"It says here," she said, gesturing with the book she was holding, "that sexmagic is one of the most powerful natural sources of energy a practitioner can harness, and that when a strong practitioner comes into contact with a receptive other, anything is possible." She waggled her eyebrows at him. "It also says, and I quote, 'patience with a female practitioner may prove valuable.'"

"You're in the section of books from the 1950s. Do I need to point that out?"

She winked at him, but carried on reading. "It states that, 'the female sexual appetite is such that the more sex a woman has, the more she wants.' Imagine that!" She rolled her eyes. "'The positive energy potential is exponential.'"

"You know, I think that Annabel McGraw has had a bad influence on you, you're getting very mischievous."

"You think?" Closing the book, she shifted on her perch, giving him a flash of lacy black lingerie as she shifted her position.

Grayson sighed. "I'm sure of it."

He rested a kiss against the top of her foot, where it arched from her shoe. Tension beaded up his spine. Moving a little higher, he brushed his forehead up the front of her shin and breathed deep the womanly scent that surrounded her.

He was already getting hard. It had become clear to him that he would never get enough of this woman.

She rose to her feet and made her way down the steps and into his waiting arms. "I'll tell you this much, there's one thing that Annabel introduced me to that I am particularly appreciating," she said, draping her arms around his neck.

"Just one?"

"Maybe two." She raised her knee against the side of his hip, and he clasped her leg against him with one hand wrapped around her thigh.

Arching one eyebrow provocatively, she continued. "She helped me find my sexual confidence, and she gave me the perfect victim to practice on."

"The victim, am I?" Now his cock was throbbing demandingly, eager to be inside her.

"Well, you did benefit, you can write another book." Her eyes twinkled. "After you've finished Annabel's book, I think you should write a proper guide to sexmagic."

"Oh, you do."

"Yes, as long as you dedicate this one to your research assistant, the one whose commitment to exploring the subject with you has revealed so much about the subject."

"You're getting very cheeky, madam."

"What are you going to do, spank me?"

"Annabel has definitely had a bad influence on you."

"You know, I think that next to Gina, Annabel is the best friend I ever had." Her expression had grown more serious.

"Well, I think you're using Annabel as an excuse." He ducked down to kiss her neck. The very touch of her soft skin against his mouth made him want to strip her and kiss every part of her, especially that part of her that made her writhe in ecstasy.

"Whatever do you mean?"

He lifted his head. "I don't think Annabel turned you into a rampant sex goddess, I think it was already there, simmering, just waiting for the chance to come out and play."

She looked startled, and there was a hint of blush of her cheeks. "You know, Gray, I think every woman deserves a man like you." She kissed his mouth, and his cock throbbed.

He wanted to come, but he also wanted this night to last forever.

"Notice that I said a man *like* you," she added, pulling back, "not you. You're mine."

He saw his window of opportunity. "How serious are you on that point?"

The atmosphere intensified. She'd been playing, and he'd made it serious. Was that wrong?

She gazed at him for the longest time, her eyes like melting chocolate, richly sensuous and filled with secret feminine fire. "Serious enough that my boss keeps telling me he can't afford to move his business to Edinburgh in order to keep me."

Grayson couldn't withhold his grin. He'd wanted to broach this subject, but he also worried that it was too soon. He had no clue on the finer points of making things permanent and he wanted it so badly. He'd just had to feel his way, like a blind man. "I've been looking at posts in London," he ventured, "and there might be an opportunity next year."

She smiled, pleased. "Maggie and Fern would never forgive me for taking you away from Scotland. Besides, Gina is begging for an excuse to have visiting rights up here."

"And you? How would you feel about a move like that?" He moved his hands over her bottom, squeezing the soft cushion of her delectable derrière in his hands, pulling her against him as they talked.

"Oh, Gray—" She gasped. "You know how much I

love it here." Her hands were on his hips, her statement double-edged as she moved up and down against his erect cock. "I can get work. My boss said he would be sorry to see me go, but he also said he would wish me well. He has colleagues up here who would take me in."

"I bet they would." He squeezed her bottom possessively, holding her still against him.

"Hey!"

"I'm glad, really. If it's possible, and you are willing to give it a try, you'd make me a very happy man."

A momentary doubt crossed her expression. "It's not always easy, relationships."

"I know."

"Of course you do, I'm sorry."

He cupped her face. "Don't be."

"It's not the magic. I think I can get used to that. Eventually. It's just that I don't believe it's all hearts and flowers all the time. We've both seen enough to know how hard it can be. Failed relationships for our parents, age-old vendettas over unrequited love."

"We've got something worth having, and we're both aware of how badly it can go wrong. I'm willing to work at this if you are."

Her soft, sensuous mouth curved. "Willing and able and reporting for duty."

He kissed her, probing the warm, receptive cave of her mouth with his tongue, anticipating probing every part of her until she screamed with pleasure.

"This calls for wine," she whispered when he finally freed her, "to mark the occasion."

"I agree, and I know just the way to enjoy it properly." He lifted her, carried her, and sat her down on the edge of the table. He opened her legs and stood between them, just inches from her pussy. She wanted him there, and that alone made him feel like a king. Easing the velvet dress up a couple of inches, he admired the look of her pussy through the sheer lace underwear she had on, and then reached for the bottle. Popping the cork, he poured one glass out and handed it to her.

Watching as she sipped from the glass, he plucked the velvet neckline on her dress, observing as her nipples hardened beneath the fabric. "Now that's settled, let's back up a bit, back to the part about you being a rampant sex goddess."

She gulped and spilt the wine from the corner of her mouth, her hand moving quickly to wipe it. He halted her hand and moved it away, then licked the corner of her mouth, slowly. She moaned softly, her eyes closing, her body leaning toward his.

"I was serious, it's in you and it always was." Drawing his fingers over the velvety dress where it covered her breasts, he teased her. He knew full well that she wasn't wearing a bra under the stretchy fabric.

She strained for more, her body exuding lush female power.

"Don't you think you might have been like this, even if you hadn't come into contact with her?"

She laughed softly, her body still arching under his touch. Her eyes challenged him. "Maybe. So long as I'd met you."

"What does that mean?"

Still she resisted him. He wanted to hear her say those precious words. He took the glass from her hand. Once he'd set it down, he tugged her dress up, pulling it out from under her bottom and off, over her head, before he eased her back so that she was lying down the length of the table. "Well, what does it mean?"

"I wanted you badly," she breathed. "I want you really badly now."

He loved the way that sounded, but there was more. He put his hand on her lace-covered pussy, and pressed.

"Oh, oh." She writhed, her arms rolling together above her head, her bare breasts cheeky and indolent. The white globes were firm and peaked, the tips dark and hard. He ran his fingernails over her torso from breast to pussy, scoring her body possessively.

She sat up, gasping. "I love you, Gray!"

Silence.

Neither of them moved, and then her eyes flickered. She was afraid. Even though they had committed to giving it a try, she wasn't sure of him. She soon would be.

"I know," he teased. "Annabel told me. I just wanted to hear you say it."

"You rotter! You and Annabel talking about me behind my…back. Er, front?" She laughed. "I love you, satisfied?" She put her hands flat to the table, her shoulders lifting. It made her breasts squish together in the most delicious way. Her eyes were downcast, her cheeks red.

"Yes, very satisfied. And I love you, Zoë. I think I always did, right from the moment I saw you staring into the forest, like the lost wood nymph who'd finally found home."

A tender smile lifted her mouth. "You're a hard man to please," she whispered, her voice tight with emotion. When she looked up at him, her eyes shone with withheld tears.

"Yes, but you do it, sweetheart, you do it every time." He put one finger under her chin, refusing to let her look away again. This was hard for both of them, because of all the very reasons she'd stated. Neither of them had been given much of an idea how to do the couple thing. "I love you so much that it hurts."

"Good!" She flashed her eyes at him, smiling.

"Now lie down. I haven't had any wine yet and I know exactly how I want it."

She did as he requested, watching with curiosity as he lifted the bottle and poured some of the frothy sparkling wine into her navel.

"Gray!"

He lowered his mouth and lapped up the wine. The soft curve of her abdomen shivered, and she whispered words of love to him. Pleased, he moved on. Holding one full breast in his hand, he poured some wine over her nipple and sucked it deeply.

A string of incoherent words spilled from her mouth and she bucked, and—much to his great surprise—came right there and then. Impressed, he repeated that trick on the other breast, stringing it out longer by licking around her nipple until she begged him to stop, then he sucked on the hard nub until she let loose that primal cry that made his balls tight.

Pacing himself, he poured some wine over the front of her sheer black G-string. He closed his mouth over it, sucking the wine off her and the net of fabric

She moaned loudly, her hips bucking under his mouth. He put the bottle down, and hauled the skimpy triangle of fabric down the length of her legs. Dipping between her legs, he nudged her clit with his tongue, and kissed it, adoring her, breathing over her most sensitive flesh and suckling her until she came again, her fist thumping against the table as she did. "Gray, please, have mercy! I need you."

He opened his fly, taking his cock in his hand. She watched and her expression was all he needed to know. He reached for the back pocket of his jeans, grappling for the condom. By the time he'd got the rubber on, she was undulating, her delicious pussy pink and swollen, glistening from his ministrations, an invitation he would never be able to refuse.

He moved into position. "So, are you ready to become my research assistant on the sexmagic front?"

"I thought I already was." She squirmed, edging against him, trying to force him on.

He gave her a chastising look, holding back from what they both wanted for one last moment. She bit her lower lip in that way of hers, and he knew she'd caught his drift. Her reaction was too adorable.

"We haven't even got started." He eased his cock inside her, watching as her expression changed, her eyes narrowing to dark slits, her mouth opening as he filled her. "And I want you to know a little about what you do to me, inside. Okay?"

Her eyes lit, and she nodded, her lips still parted.

He pushed deeper still, his breath stolen from him when he was buried to the hilt in her, his cock wedged deep inside her. The hot, wet sheath of her cunt held him so tightly and embraced him in such a visceral, explicit way, that he had to pause before he pulled back and gave it to her again.

"Too good, you feel too good," he whispered. It took a moment to find his rhythm, to control it. Then, riding her, he moved his hand above her face and above her heart, harnessing the essence of her desire. He kissed his palm and set the glow of her sexual desire free into the atmosphere. Then he reached right down inside of himself, and set some of what he felt for her free, into the room.

All of it would be too much.

She moaned and thrashed, her body arching, her cunt spasming. The room filled with colored light, and then the shelves shook, books dropping out of their niches here and there.

She laughed joyously, her eyes glinting as the light re-flected off them, and when she came her body gripped his so possessively that he couldn't resist a moment longer, his cock jerking as he let rip.

Falling across her, panting, he kissed her jaw.

"So, Gray," she said, as she tried to catch her breath, "do you think we can make it to the bed?"

"Definitely not," he responded, chuckling, and kissed her mouth. He was getting hard again already. "Maybe never. Is that a problem for you?"

She sighed, and then winked. "It's the kind of problem I guess I'll have to get used to, if I want to keep my position as your research assistant. And I have to say, this is a position I wouldn't give up for the world."

★ ★ ★ ★ ★

ACKNOWLEDGMENTS

I am indebted to the members of the Celtic Hearts Chapter of the Romance Writers of America, whose combined knowledge on Celtic matters is second to none.

In particular I wish to thank Cindy Vallar and Jody Allen, whose workshops on Scottish history and paranormal Scotland were not only educational, but inspirational.

I am also indebted to my writing sister, mentor and critique partner, Portia Da Costa. Thank you for your support, feedback and friendship.

naughty bits 2, the highly anticipated sequel to the successful debut volume from the editors of Spice Briefs, delivers nine new unapologetically raunchy and romantic tales that promise to spark the libido. In this collection of first-rate short erotic literature, lusty selections by such provocative authors as Megan Hart, Lillian Feisty, Saskia Walker and Portia Da Costa will pique, tease and satisfy any appetite, and prove that good things do come in small packages.

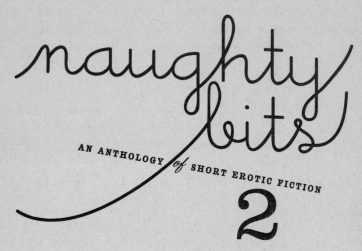

naughty bits

AN ANTHOLOGY *of* SHORT EROTIC FICTION

2

on sale now wherever books are sold!

Since launching in 2007, Spice Briefs has become the hot eBook destination for the sauciest erotic fiction on the Web. Want more of what we've got? Visit www.SpiceBriefs.com.

Spice

www.Spice-Books.com

SV60541TR

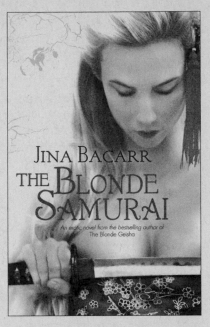

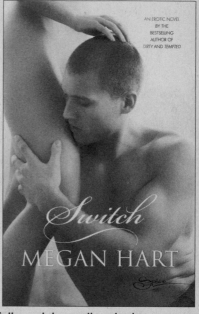

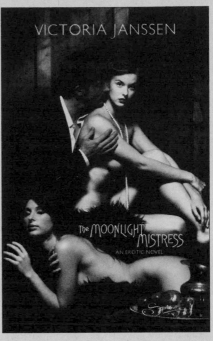

SARAH McCARTY

He is everything her body craves…and everything her faith denies.

Tucker McCade has known violence his whole life: orphaned in a massacre, abused as a "half-breed" child, trained as a ruthless Texas Ranger, he's learned the hard way that might makes right. So even he is shocked when he falls for Sallie Mae Reynolds, a Quaker nurse.

National Bestselling Author
SARAH McCARTY

A HELL'S EIGHT EROTIC ADVENTURE
Tucker's Claim

Spice

Every night they spend together exploring new heights of ecstasy binds them ever closer, slowly erasing their differences…until the day Tucker's past comes calling, precipitating an explosive show-down between her faith, his promise and the need for revenge….

Tucker's Claim

"Sarah McCarty's new series is an exciting blend of raw masculinity, spunky, feisty heroines and the wild living in the old west… with spicy hot love scenes."
—*Erotica Romance Writers*

Available now wherever books are sold!